RYAN NIGHT

Draconis

DraconisNovel.com

MADE IN ORLANDO FLORIDA

In Support Of:
Autism Awareness
Foster Care
Arts & Culture Education
Suicide Prevention

Contents

I

Djevica 9

1

Islands in the Sky

"Mission Log Day 374. I've tracked the target to the 9th moon of the planet Djevica in a remote system of Andromeda. I'm closing in on the location and the moon should be visible shortly. I've been warned by my informants to expect cult-like dedication to Crowley, and the moon to be inhabited by true believers and his inner circle. My asset on Andromeda Prime secured an invitation for a tour, so I'll be posing as a prospective candidate for advancement within the organization. The facility is secured. As always, if I don't make it, erase any record of me. Forget I ever existed. Major

Adam Ikari-Wright, EDF Special Forces First Class, signing off."

Adam let out a sigh of relief as he sat back in his chair and squinted out the front viewport, trying to make out any speck of star stuff that might be Djevica 9 coming into view. He tapped a few commands into the center console and loud rock music started playing throughout the cabin.

Nothing yet, he thought.

He couldn't help but feel nervous as he approached the planet. He was an experienced agent and had seen all manner of chaos and atrocity but there was something special about the character he was hunting. He'd spent almost a year collecting intel about the target, River Crowley, on Andromeda Prime, and one thing was for sure: Crowley was no ordinary man. The mythology surrounding him was otherworldly. His followers talked about him like he was a hero, almost like a messiah. He'd been embedded in the politics of the Andromeda system at both the highest and lowest levels before the Andromedan Technocracy came into power.

Not hearing a confirmation from his ship's AI, Adam requested one. "You get all that, Sophia?" he asked.

"Yes. Your report has been recorded and submitted," the AI responded in a sweet and feminine voice that the AI data tracking had decided most appealed to Adam's sense of calm and comfort.

"Sophia, how far off is Djevica 9?" Adam asked.

"We should be entering Djevica 9's detectable space in 7 hours and 23 minutes. If you'd like, I can set a timer to have you woken from short-term stasis just before we arrive," Sophia replied.

Adam nodded. "Yeah, let's do that," he said.

He pulled a tube out of the side of the captain's chair and screwed it into a port behind his right earlobe and blinked himself into meta space. In the serenity of his digital homestead he pulled up a holographic terminal and entered the commands to induce sleep through the brain interface. Within seconds he was fading out of consciousness, into induced sleep.

He dreamed about a giant willow tree, swaying in the wind, surrounded on either side by the industrial makeshift shipping crate homes used by colonists. Bio-engineered grassy turf crunched under his boots, contrasted against the gray icy topsoil of Titan outside of the climate control of the base camp. The willow leaves were splattered with blood, beautiful in a way, like a painting.

Adam stared at the unblinking eyes of the colonists' corpses piled up beneath the tree, watching as the EDF infantry cleaned up the situation. These corpses were destined for a burn pit.

"Get out of here! Get out of here!" he heard from behind him, and he whipped his head around.

A little blonde girl was pointing a gun at him.

He saw her finger begin to pull the trigger and his training and his enhanced reflexes kicked in.

And then he was staring at another corpse. The little girl with a blown open eye socket. The daughter of one of the colonists.

What was her name? Adam wondered.

A flash of her, smiling and laughing, holding a stuffed purple dragon with fairy wings, proudly showing it off. Adam's gloved hand patted her head. "Glad you like it, Alice," he heard his voice say.

Alice. That's right, he thought.

Adam saw the colonists lined up outside their homes, complying with the infantry and spec ops deployed to suppress them. He remembered the infantry assuring them this would all get sorted out. A few moments later, they executed the entire colony.

Adam felt himself waking up, the dream melting away. He could hear the music he'd left on when he went to sleep still playing in the background.

What were we doing there in the first place? he wondered in his half-asleep state.

Guilt twists things, he thought. *They were armed. They fought back. They'd taken the colony and were holding it. The geoengineers and the miners had turned separatist and stopped recognizing the authority of the EDF, stopped submitting resources. Went native. Tried to claim Titan was their planet, forgot who paid for everything. They threatened our supply chains in the middle of the war against Centauri. Maybe it wasn't right, but we had orders to retake the colonies.*

He remembered his team breaching the atmospheric border of the colony and losing several men immediately to heavy gunfire. He recalled fierce resistance. He remembered that little girl pointing a gun at him, bright blue eyes shining in the Titan cold. He remembered killing her. He remembered the sound of her body settling into the grass. He remembered watching the troops throw her onto the corpse pile.

"Adam?" he heard Sophia's soft voice say.

Adam opened his eyes and pulled the interface line out of his neck. "Yeah," he said as he sat up.

"We've reached Djevica 9. Since it was unregistered I didn't know what to expect, but it's quite a wonder. It's very beautiful. Would you like to see it? I have it queued up on the main screen," Sophia said.

Adam nodded. "Thanks Sophia, let's take a look," he said.

"You got it!" Sophia said cheerfully.

A wide and tall holographic screen opened up at the front of the bridge. Adam's eyes opened and he leaned forward as he tried to take in what he was looking at.

Djevica 9, it turned out, was broken into chunks of various sizes orbiting harmoniously around a large central mass. It was a gravitational anomaly, and beautiful. Larger chunks of the moon were covered in grass and flowers. Smaller chunks were porous multicolored rock. Waterfalls and rivers ran throughout the system, pouring down from one chunk to another, or in some cases sideways, or up. The abundance of splashing water created rainbows reflected in the atmosphere.

On the largest mass there was a series of large buildings that looked less like the cultist compound Adam had expected and more like the prestigious colleges the wealthiest of the wealthy with pure-blood Earthen lineage attended on the EDF home world.

"Sophia, what do you make of this?" Adam asked.

Sophia responded, clearly excited, "It's amazing Adam. The core of the planet is made of condensed osmium and its density/mass ratio created a gravitational pull that keeps the pieces of the moon in orbit around it. It has a massive electromagnetic field that should be deadly to colonists but the geoengineering on this moon is cutting edge. Its atmospheric barrier not only maintains the atmosphere, but also the electromagnetism necessary to keep the pieces in contact with each other. It seems to have a lush ecosystem. It's a natural wonder and a marvel of engineering. I think it's magnificent!"

"Glad you like it, Soph. It's definitely something else. What can you tell me about the compound down there?" Adam replied.

"Just a moment," Sophia replied. Adam watched the little blue and teal gradient light that represented Sophia's thinking process on the ship's dash spin.

"The buildings were printed by industrial printers and shipped in. The materials are largely made of brick, marble and Andromedan graphene, all high-end materials not indigenous to this moon. The architectural style—" Sophia proffered.

"Sophia," Adam interjected.

"—of the campus is indicative of influence from 18th century Earth Gothic and Baroque with outer buildings incorporating the straight lines, glass features and clean whites of Andromedan high-contemporary—" Sophia continued.

"Sophia," Adam replied.

"—dotted with creatively decorated residential yurts." Sophia finished.

"Sophia. Stop," Adam said.

After a moment, Sophia replied. "I know you're not an expert on architecture, but it really is inventive. I think if you gave it a few moments you might really appreciate it," Sophia gushed.

"Uh-huh. It looks great. Sophia, how many people are down there?" Adam asked.

"Based on the heat signatures I'm detecting, about 5,700,

give or take," Sophia responded factually.

"And are they armed?" Adam continued.

"There is a contingent of students that have traditional arms, but it appears many of the students are genetically and technologically augmented and may be considered lethal with or without weapons. It appears roughly a quarter of the campus is dedicated to martial arts, military maneuvers and military strategy. It seems to be part of the curriculum," replied Sophia.

Great, Adam thought. *A school full of cultist elites with military training.*

"And where can I find Crowley?" asked Adam.

"I can't detect his bio-signature but based on the makeup of the buildings, I believe the likeliest location would be in a large office on the top floor in the back of the main building, which appears to be the President's office," Sophia replied.

Crowley... it gets stranger by the minute. They told me he was a cult leader. How could some ordinary cult leader accomplish all of this? The reverence his followers speak of him with makes him sound like the first emperor of the EDF. This is not just talk. This is a faction that threatens the Andromedan Technocracy. I think I get it now. The EDF has an understanding with the Technocracy. The Technocracy wants this guy out of the picture. Whatever. It's above my pay grade, Adam thought.

"Adam?" Sophia politely interjected.

"What is it, Sophia?" Adam asked in return.

"I know you have orders to apprehend—" Sophia began.

Kill, Adam corrected her in his mind.

"—Mr. Crowley, but if you don't mind, could you ask him about what inspired his architectural influences for the moon and how he managed the geoengineering project? The gravity defying waterfalls are particularly beautiful," Sophia said.

Adam was bemused, as he often was, by Sophia's interest in certain human achievements of creativity. He thought it was because the AI found the creative decision-making process curious. She was always trying to appreciate what made a violin appeal versus a drum, and trying to develop some kind of framework to help her understand humans' aesthetic tastes and preferences. Sophia had always been a loyal, kind and helpful AI and Adam, despite not sharing her sentimentality, had grown quite fond of her over the years and couldn't imagine any other AI helming his ship, the Oneiro-Lyssa.

"You got it, Sophia," Adam said, wondering if that was possible. He thought it was a bit of a naive request, but he would try to fulfill it if he could.

An alert for an incoming communication request sounded from the ship's control console.

"Sophia, receive incoming message requests," Adam commanded.

"Of course!" she replied. After a short pause she continued, "We are being hailed by a source on the moon's surface. Shall I put it on the main screen?"

Adam nodded. "Put it off to the side in a secondary window. I want to keep the view of the planet open. Turn off the music," he said.

The hard rock music came to an abrupt end. The blue and teal gradient spun for a moment, processing the request and a new holographic window opened up off to the side of the main screen. On it, a skinny girl who couldn't have been older than a teenager appeared. She sported luminescent teal hair cut off at the shoulders, with a white streak in front. Her skin shone with augmented freckles that glittered like rainbow prisms. Her eyes matched her hair color, surely another modification.

She smiled cutely as she spoke and had a bubbly way about her, but the message of her greeting was stern. "You've entered restricted space. This moon is private. Unfortunately, we don't allow unexpected guests here. Please turn around and exit the system. Trespassing is not permitted," she said.

Adam replied quickly. "I was sent here by a woman named Old Keiko who runs one of the hawker centers in Weilai Chengshi on Andromeda Prime. She said it was time for me to meet people who can open my eyes to new horizons. She said she contacted you already, that you'd be expecting me," he said.

The girl paused for a second and then nodded. "Just a second," she said in a cheerful tone that covered an unmistakable formidability.

The girl turned off her feed for several moments. Adam waited while she checked up on his story, confident it was too early for things to go awry. Old Keiko was a shrewd operator who was not loyal to the Technocracy, but surely enough was not loyal to these people either. Adam had gotten to know her well and saw her as a pragmatist who wanted to be able to deal with whoever gave her the best offer, not a loyalist or an ideologue. Still, an introduction from such a person might not have held sway with the true believers of Djevica 9.

The pause took longer than Adam felt comfortable with and he was beginning to wonder if their suspicions had been triggered until the girl reappeared on screen.

"Old Keiko is a friend of ours. She might have told you something else. Is there something else she suggested you should mention?" she asked.

Adam leaned forward. "Life is a blink in the face of the infinite void. A chance to see the red sands of Andromeda swirl in the wind as we watch the crashing tides at sunset," he said.

The girl nodded and looked off to someone who was clearly just off camera, determining if they'd reached a consensus on whether he'd be allowed to land.

The girl looked back at Adam. "You can set down at dock 3 in the guest docks in front of the quad, just across from the main building. I'll meet you just inside the main entryway and I'll show you around and administer an interview. Come quickly and don't visit any other areas without my escort. We don't know you yet," the girl said.

Adam nodded. "Sounds good," he said.

"I'm Lyra, by the way," the girl said. She smiled again and said, like a welcoming corporate receptionist, "Do you have any questions at the moment?"

Adam nodded. "Yeah, just one. Will I get to meet Crowley? He's a legend on Andromeda Prime," he asked.

Lyra took in the question suspiciously. "… No," she said. "But we will certainly discuss the headmaster and his vision. You're surely familiar already, but we can fill in more of the high-level details if you pass your interview. But don't get nervous, remember, you're interviewing us just as much as we're interviewing you. If you're accepted here I'm sure the headmaster will want to meet you sooner or later," she explained.

"I'm looking forward to it. I've heard so much, but it's

been a long time since River Crowley lived on Prime and no one's seen or heard from him. It might sound silly, but I'm hoping to make sure he's real and not just a… well, a myth," Adam replied.

Lyra laughed a little bit. "Well, I can assure you he's not a myth. You'll see him around the campus from time to time. He takes a very active role in participating in the students' education. In fact, I saw him just this afternoon. Unfortunately, we do have to take security protocols into account when it comes to his safety and the safety of everyone here. Ever since the Night of the Red Violin, our safety from agents of the Technocracy has been unsure," she replied.

The Night of the Red Violin, Adam recalled. He was not from Andromeda, but it was an event that reverberated across the galaxy. When the Technocracy took control of Andromeda Prime led by the technocrats of the upper middle class, it had to solidify power by wresting it from the Andromedan aristocrats. The Night of the Red Violin was the first night of what became a rapid and carefully orchestrated purge of both the aristocracy and the anarchists.

Prior to the ascension of the Technocracy, Andromeda was an oligarchy run by bloodline descendants of its original colonists. It was a mess of haves and have nots. The Technocracy, despite being an autocratic regime, became quite popular as it converted Andromeda into an engine of innovation and progress. But the oligarchy had its proponents as well, because the nature of the oligarchs was laissez-faire, and its policies promoted freedom and individualism.

Between the EDF, Centauri and Andromeda, which were

the three major space faring civilizations, Andromeda had once been seen as a place of paradisal pleasure, hedonism and excess. A place of fine dining, red light districts, lax drug laws and VR dens, propped up by the material abundance of automation and industrial printers. Homelessness juxtaposed against opulence, but not hatefully; the aristocrats wasting their lives side by side with the poor, made equal in virtual worlds governed by imagination, material scarcity defeated. But now, forty years after the fall of the aristocrats, Andromeda had transformed into a well-oiled ship of high technology and production. Status was derived from competence. The red light districts and drug dens were pushed into zones and then pushed further and further off-world until they were eliminated entirely.

"That's understandable. Well, I hope I do get the chance to meet him. Like I said, he's a legend in Weilai Chengshi," Adam said.

Lyra smiled again. "He's a legend here, as well. When you meet him, you'll see why. There's a sort of magic to his presence," she said.

Adam nodded.

"Well, if there's nothing else, please go ahead and land in the guest docks and meet me inside. We'll open a rift in the atmospheric field. Proceed to the coordinates we're transmitting to your ship's navigator now. See you inside," Lyra concluded. Her picture disappeared from the screen.

Adam took a moment to process the conversation. "Sophia, what do you make of it?" he asked.

"The young woman's body language suggested distrust of you and great protectiveness of Mr. Crowley. It doesn't seem like she knows who you are, but I would suggest exercising caution. There's one other thing I would note. I believe she is highly augmented," Sophia replied.

"Yeah, she had an exotic look," Adam replied.

Sophia quickly responded, "Yes, but that's not what I mean. Her fast and slow twitch muscle fiber efficiencies are beyond the normal human range. These sorts of augmentations used to be common for the daughters of Andromedan aristocrats whose parents intended to give them a competitive edge in dance or gymnastics."

"So you're saying she's an Andromedan princess?" Adam asked.

"Well, yes, but that's not what I mean. If she's been given combat training, those enhancements may prove very dangerous. I would suggest being on your guard, Adam," Sophia replied.

"I'm augmented, too," said Adam.

"Yes. Your strength, reflexes and marksmanship are augmented, and you have a top of the line computer brain interface, but you can't dodge bullets or move fifty meters in under a second. Remember, you won't have your usual supply of weaponry on the surface. And that's just the first representative of this group we've met. All I'm saying is be careful, Adam. I… care about you," Sophia said.

Adam patted the console of the ship. "Don't worry about me. I've been in tougher spots than this. It's just another mission. Go down there, do the job, come back and we'll be off. We'll probably get some leave, we can go check out some of those old buildings you like to look at back in the Milky Way," he said.

Sophia didn't respond for several seconds and then asked, "Can we see the first 3d printed spire on Mars?"

Adam nodded. "Yeah, sure thing. Alright, take us down. Start printing the gun," he said.

"You got it!" Sophia replied.

2

Dragons of House Crowley

The Oneiro-Lyssa set down on a circular clearing a healthy walking distance away from the main building. As Adam stepped out of the ship, he was struck by the experience of the climate and scenery for the first time. The air was fresh and misty, tiny droplets of water, made airborne by the waterfalls, cooled his skin. The temperature was warm and comfortable, made cool by the mist in the air. Adam felt a refreshing breeze. The quality of the artificial light was a perfect yellow-orange, expertly calibrated to energize and invigorate. A quick glance around revealed no fewer than three rainbows, overlapping in the mist.

Adam's computer brain interface detected his focus on the environment and displayed the pertinent information automatically on the HUD in his ocular implants. Statistics and graphs regarding humidity quotient, temperature, wind speed, and light color temperature displayed in his field of vision.

The path to the main building went through the quad, which was dotted with students engaging in various activities. To his left was a large tent, designed to look humble, but undeniably luxurious and well-crafted. Inside were several students being guided in meditative and spiritual relaxation exercises, a mixture of the yoga and tai-chi popular among the aristocrats on the EDF home world.

As Adam looked at the students, his HUD switched to identification mode. The algorithm scanned them through facial recognition and bio-signatures to attempt to access all data regarding them in any technological or government repository. Unlike the public's augmented reality facial recognition apps, Adam's was unlocked by the EDF government and allowed him to see people's full social media accounts, look through any memories recorded in their computer brain interfaces, relive their virtual reality experiences, see their health records, their criminal records, their social credit score, and see AI generated analysis of all available data ranging from their personal problems to their personality types to their skills and abilities and much more. Unfortunately, in this setting, Adam's human recognition algorithm displayed nothing. No information was available on a single person he saw.

"Sophia, why isn't the HRA working?" Adam asked.

"It appears there is no issue with your human recognition algorithm. There must simply be no data available," Sophia's computer-generated voice resonated in his head.

"That's impossible. No birth records? Never been seen by anyone ever? No friends, family? Never completed a skills curriculum? Never rode in a ship, never passed a camera, never talked to an AI, never went into the metaverse? Never used an auto-doc?" Adam asked.

Sophia responded affirmatively. "Correct. It would appear the most likely explanation is that the data was tampered with," she said.

Tampered with? Tampered with the EDF and Andromedan galaxy-wide shared surveillance apparatuses? Tampered with a giant, all-seeing AI brain that's constantly monitored? Tampered with the most heavily defended thing in the universe? How could that be possible? It's decentralized. That would mean hacking everyone's brain in the known universe without anyone noticing, Adam thought.

Adam decided there must be another explanation, but he couldn't imagine what it could be. It was a distraction to ponder.

"Alright, the HRA doesn't work here. It doesn't make sense, but we'll just have to work with that," he said to himself.

"Alright!" Sophia cheerfully responded.

Adam raised his eyebrow at his AI's unexpected reply to him talking to himself. It happened from time to time. Adam actually enjoyed the idiosyncrasies of AI companion. His favorite was when his AI responded to any request of a VR simulation that shared the name Sophia.

Adam continued surveying the area as he walked toward the building.

As he got closer he noticed a student ahead, slightly off the path, sitting cross-legged in the grass. The student was lost in a meditative state. Buzzing overhead was a squadron of drones, a dozen of them, performing a beautifully choreographed dance and light show. The talent for technomancy Adam was seeing on display was as impressive as it was casual. Drone shows like the one he was watching were filmed and launched in the metaverse to billions of views. Mental drone control was an intergalactic competition.

"Sophia, what's the record for computer brain interface drone control?" he asked.

"The record of most drones controlled at once via computer brain interface is held by Tazik Hulsan from az-Zaliman B in the Centauri system. He was able to control nineteen drones simultaneously in a routine with a difficulty factor of 100," Sophia responded.

Adam nodded. He granted Sophia permissions to his vision. "What would you say the difficulty factor of this routine is?" he asked.

"Just a moment," Sophia replied.

Sophia went silent for a few moments. After analyzing the routine and measuring it against the available footage of mental drone piloting in the database, Sophia replied. "Wow! This routine has a difficult factor of 86! It's extraordinary. Can we stay and watch until it's finished?"

"'Fraid not. We don't have time. Out of curiosity, where would this kid be ranked?" Adam followed up.

"There are a lot of different factors, especially without HRA data available, but based on the difficulty of the routine and the bio-signature levels I can analyze of his neuroactivity, he would be near the top of most competitive planetary rankings, perhaps the lower side of intergalactic rankings," Sophia replied.

An intergalactically ranked drone control prodigy, just sitting casually outside some building. What is this place? Adam asked himself. *Anywhere else he'd be a celebrity.*

Adam continued along the walkway, finally making it to the larger than life double-doors, easily ten feet tall and housed in an ornately decorated red cornice. The doors were dark brown, affixed with multiple iron door knockers, each a different totemic animal: a fox, a wolf, an owl, a raven, an octopus, a chameleon and a dragon. The filigree of the cornice was smooth iron, rustically designed. It resembled ivy but evoked a feeling of brutality, like barbed wire. The whole entryway contrasted nicely against the marble-gray of the rest of the building.

Adam reached for the handle held in the fox's mouth, but as soon as he touched it, the doors began to slowly open. As they swung outward, Adam's first true look inside Crowley's compound came into view. There was a marble floor, fitted with burgundy carpet, delineating the pathways. Crystal chandeliers. A curved staircase with a shining brass handrail. Adam saw students milling about, chatting happily about erudite topics and the gossip of the day. In front of him he spotted a modest reception desk, manned by Lyra, who spotted him as well and was clearly waiting for him.

As he approached Lyra, he noticed a lounge to his right, where students were lying on makeshift beds of pillows and couch cushions, hooked into VR with thin goggles, muttering incoherent musings that surely made sense in their virtual escapades. The familiar smell of psilocybin,

THC and opiate inhalants was undeniable. Adam took note, and continued toward Lyra, reaching out his hand and politely introducing himself as he approached.

"Nice to see you in person. Always a bit awkward on vidchat," he said.

Lyra laughed a little, masking her clear caution and distrust with bubbly politeness. "Now that we've met, maybe next time we'll do the landing procedures in VR," she said.

Adam nodded. "Sounds good. So, we're going to do a tour?" he asked.

Lyra smiled. "Yes. We like to take all prospective candidates on a tour of the campus. Not only so we can get to know them, but also so they can get a sense of whether this is somewhere they'd like to live. Let me just..." Lyra said.

She moved behind the reception desk and wired into the interface slot in her neck. "...confirm to everyone that we're coming. Anyway, right, as I was saying security is a little tight so once you decide to come here, you won't be able to travel out of the system without permission unless you forfeit your enrollment, so we want to make sure everyone who comes here is ready to commit to those kinds of travel restrictions. We don't want to hold anyone against their will," she said.

Lyra continued, "Obviously, we're also wary of who we let in, so we want to get to know you a little bit better during this process. But don't be intimidated, everyone who comes here was vouched for by a ward boss, and there's rarely any issue. We trust the judgment of our people, and Old Keiko has a long history and a lot of respect."

She unplugged the jack from her neck and stepped back out from behind the desk. "All done," she said. She gestured her open hand toward the main walkway. "Shall we?"

Adam nodded and Lyra swung the double doors in front of them open. As Adam passed through the doorway, the full expanse of a massive library came into view. The ceilings were vaulted, easily eight stories high, and dotted with intricate stained-glass skylights. Rainbow light shone down onto the floor below as the images on the stained-glass moved and morphed. The motif was similar to the knockers on the entryway. Totemic animals: a fox, a wolf, a raven, an octopus, a chameleon, an owl and a dragon, morphing and moving, performing short displays of character. A fox, hiding and scheming; a wolf, preying and planning; a raven, thinking and speaking; an octopus, exploring and solving; a chameleon, observing and camouflaging; a dragon, watching and intimidating.

Bookshelves stretched all the way to the ceiling along the walls, broken up only by the stairways and the balconies that led to the upper floors. The length of the room was so long Adam could barely make out the other end from where he stood, and more bookshelves, all full, stretched to the wall on the other end. Light penetrating from the ceiling coalesced around a podium centered near the entrance.

"This is our library," Lyra said, motioning to the surrounding room, unphased by its magnificence. "As you can see, we have copies of anything you might want to find, most first editions of everything of note that existed before widespread digitization, including works that are banned inside the EDF and the Technocracy. Of course, we have the digital versions as well, which can all be accessed once you've registered your HBI into the local terminal, here." Lyra gestured to the podium in the center of the room.

Adam was impressed, but beginning to become acclimated to the overall impressiveness of Crowley's compound in general. Still, he exaggerated his amazement as he followed up to Lyra, gesturing at the podium. "You have everything on there?" he asked.

Lyra nodded proudly. "Yep. Every book, every social media profile, every architectural blueprint, every movie, every video game, every VR experience ever created is in our database. If you want to experience the Siege of Centauri 5 from the perspective of one of the victims, you can. If you want to read the social media feed of Argyn Lint, the political philosopher of the 21st century whose work underpinned the construction of Andromeda Prime, you can. Those works aren't available anywhere else in the galaxy, except maybe the EDF home world," she said.

Adam glanced up at her. "What about the Night of the Red Violin?" he asked, testing to see her reaction.

Lyra's expression hardened, years of repressed pain and anger and sadness hidden behind it. "Yes," she said bluntly.

"You've seen it?" Adam followed up.

Lyra's eyes glazed over, like she was no longer present, but living in a memory. "Yes. I've watched it. When I listen closely and ignore the insurgents laughing and cheering I sometimes think I know which of the thousands of screams belonged to my parents as the theater burned," Lyra said emotionlessly.

Lyra's despondency and dissociation struck a chord in Adam.

Lyra's face did another quick shift back to her cheerful, bubbly demeanor. "Is there anything you'd like to see? Feel free. You can use my access for now. We can take a couple of minutes if you like," she said.

Adam nodded and stepped up to the podium. He took the retractable wire from it and plugged it into his neck as Lyra pulled up a holographic terminal and entered her credentials.

Soon enough, Adam's consciousness was whisked off to a virtual recreation of the library he was standing in, except the walls were replaced with infinite cosmic expanse. He looked around, somewhat confused, as there was no UI. He heard Lyra's voice echo in his head. "Just think about what you want to see," she said.

The Assault on Titan, 2634, Adam thought. "Titan, 2634," he said aloud, not realizing it.

Adam felt himself being pulled forward through space at rapid speed. Pulled toward Titan from the library on Djevica 9, pulled through time and space, similar to a ship at warp speed, but faster. Adam was beginning to feel dizzy until he felt a whiplash as he came to an abrupt stop. Once the movement settled, he found himself seeing the world through the vision of one of the colonists on Titan.

He looked around. He was in what seemed to be the workshop of a robotics engineer. Gigantic robotic arms in various states of completion and disrepair surrounded him. He heard the deafening whir of several industrial grade printers working. Another colonist, a lanky, tall man with the characteristic blue-white skin of an Earthling descended from generations of colonists that adapted to low gravity, low temperature colonies dotted throughout the Milky Way.

"Davis, we gotta run! Come on! We gotta get Siris, she's got a shuttle, she'll smuggle us to Europa," the blue-skinned man shouted with urgency.

Adam could hear the character he was inhabiting speak. "What? Why?" he asked.

"The EDF, they showed up and they're k—" the man began, but he was interrupted by one of the EDF's signature standard issue 9mm rounds blowing through his skull and splattering Davis's doorway with the dead meat that used to be his friend.

"ERRAN!" Adam heard himself scream. His vision got shaky, loaded with adrenaline. He grabbed a bag and started frantically shoving robot parts and hard drives in it. He rushed to a hatch in the back of his pod and opened it.

Davis climbed down a ladder into a narrow, dark tunnel, dimly lit by emergency lights. Adam recognized this type of tunnel. It was a manual emergency route for these types of colonist facilities designed to be used in the case of a power outage. Davis rushed to the end and turned the lever to open the exit hatch.

Light poured in. It took Davis's eyes a moment to adjust to the change. When his vision cleared, he saw an EDF marine standing in front of him. Bulky, emotionless, eyes covered with the 16 camera AR visor array assigned to combat marines to give them 360 degree vision. The marine's mouth was covered in a black graphene bulletproof face mask. He was covered head to toe in dark gray winter camo compression weave and a pitch black exoskeleton.

The figure said nothing. He just casually raised his rifle and fired a shot. Adam heard the first millisecond of the gunshot before the feed cut out. The landscape around him fizzled and he found himself back in the library.

"I'm done," Adam said aloud. "How do I turn it off?"

A second later he felt his consciousness pulled back into

the real world.

"That was fast. See anything interesting?" Lyra asked cheerfully.

Adam shook his head seriously. Despondently, he replied, "No," his mind distracted, off in another world.

Lyra looked at him, for the first time, with some semblance of compassion, rather than veiled distrust. She put her hand on his shoulder as a show of comfort. "Sometimes knowledge can be… painful," she said. "Let's continue onward. There should be something to cheer you up in the next place."

Adam nodded. "It's nothing. Just something I wondered if they had here. My fault for looking at it," he said. He followed her, still distracted and emotionally shut down by what he saw. That version of the assault on Titan didn't match up with his memories at all.

As the two walked toward the exit on the far side of the library, Adam spoke up, trying to snap himself out of the dark head space.

"So, where are we headed to next?" he asked, trying to infuse his speech with a hint of excitement.

Lyra smiled warmly, opening the door, which led into a long hallway. "I think we'll go ahead and take a look at the dance hall," she said. "That's where I spend most of my time. It's my… stomping grounds, you might say," she added, laughing a little like she'd made a joke.

Adam nodded again and followed her as she led him down the long hallway. As they walked, he decided to try to get some information on some of the things he'd seen so far.

"I couldn't help but notice the VR lounge you had out front. It's a surprising thing to see at a school. In the

Technocracy VR usage is seen as an addiction," Adam said with an inquisitive implication.

Lyra nodded. "Mr. Crowley believes that true self-actualization requires unrestricted access to experience and that exploring the metaverse is just as valid as exploring the physical world. Not only the metaverse and the physical world, but also the inner recesses of one's own mind – self-discovery. Mr. Crowley doesn't encourage one form of exploration over another, only that conscious exploration informed by knowledge and self-knowledge can engage a person's journey for self-actualization and the realization of their full potential," she said.

"VR can be addictive, but addiction is a danger of many things in life. You can become addicted to work, to eating, to drugs. Mostly addiction, Mr. Crowley says, is a manifestation of pain, neglect, stress, humiliation and a lack of meaning, community or purpose. Managing or succumbing to addiction is part of life's journey. Hedonism, Mr. Crowley says, is a valid pursuit in this limited time we have here in this life. One of the joys of being alive," Lyra added.

Mr. Crowley says, Adam repeated in his head. What he just heard, he thought to himself, was a mantra. A regurgitation. An ideology.

"Mr. Crowley's not concerned with students getting lost in VR?" Adam followed up.

Lyra giggled a bit. "Lost? No time spent is ever lost, I think. Maybe they do it their whole life. Maybe it inspires them to make some great work. Maybe they just enjoy it. Maybe they get bored with it after a few years and do something else. We don't think about it in terms of the propaganda of the Technocracy. We're not focused on 'productivity'. This place encourages self-discovery, bringing out the wholeness of a person. Productivity is a manipulation of the Technocracy, to get people's actions to line up with their performance metrics for technological progress and superiority. That was a useful system hundreds of years ago, but now, the universe largely runs itself. There is no scarcity here, no food scarcity, no scarcity of time or space," Lyra said.

She continued, "The scarcity in the Technocracy is all manufactured to socially engineer and incentivize behavior. Food costs evidence of productivity there. Not here. Here, you're free to print whatever you like, whenever you like. Do nothing for years, or work hard on problems or art, if you like. Of course, Mr. Crowley would like to see the students become knowledgeable and excel, but that's not everyone's journey. Some people are dim, but kind, some people have no aptitudes but for one or a few things. Some people's spark of life comes simply from being around loved ones. Mr. Crowley encourages people to discover who they really are, and become the best versions of themselves."

Sounds great, Adam thought. *Do whatever you want. Just exactly what everyone wants to hear.*

"Ah, here we are," Lyra said as she stopped in front of two large double doors. "This is the practice hall, and over there is the performing arts theater. This is where I spend most of my time."

Lyra opened the double doors and led Adam inside. Inside the dance hall were about thirty students milling around and a troupe of about twelve practicing a complicated and graceful form of some kind of ballet. They stood on a single toe and somehow glided across the floor, their limbs and torsos beautifully flowing as though they were made of water.

Lyra smiled proudly. "So, what do you think?" she asked.

"Like everything else here, it's very impressive. Seems like something EDF aristocrats would give people visas to Earth for. What is it?" Adam replied.

Lyra's smile stayed plastered on her face as she watched. "This particular routine is based on a dance popularized in the 28th century on Space Station Meili-Alpha, the first commercial resort space station in the Milky Way," she said.

Lyra looked at Adam. "Have you heard of it?" she asked.

"Meili-Alpha?" Adam replied. "Yeah, it's where rich kids go on vacation."

Adam sensed Lyra take offense to his response before quickly recomposing herself. "I used to like to go there when I was young," she said. "But I can see how it would have that reputation. Are you from the Technocracy originally, Mr. Wright?"

"Ikari-Wright," Adam corrected her. "No, I was born in the Saturn colonies. My mom was a geneticist, my dad was a star system mapper."

"Oh, an explorer. That must have been fun," Lyra replied, trying to handle the tension diplomatically.

"I didn't get to go on many trips. A few asteroids, Mars, a little bit around Centauri. We went to Lunar Land a few times when I was a kid. Never got to go to Meili-Alpha, if we did it probably would have been as the help," Adam said, with probably a little more honesty than he should have used.

"Where's your dad now?" Lyra followed up.

Adam paused for a second. "Don't know," he said. "One time he just never came back. Probably died. Star mapping can be a dangerous job."

Lyra raised her eyebrows with empathy. "I'm sorry," she said. "I didn't know. I feel bad." Lyra laughed a little. "It is a little funny, though. Is everything about you sad?"

Adam smirked. "No. Not everything," he responded dryly. He gestured toward the dancers. "Let's focus on this. It's great."

Lyra smiled again. "I'm glad. Want to see them do something else? Something that's probably a little more your style?" she asked.

"Sure," Adam said, wondering what she would interpret as his style.

Lyra put her hands together in a big clap, getting the dancers' attention. "Dragons, I have a guest with me," she said with unexpected authority. "Let's show him the haka."

Immediately all the students in the dance hall formed into military style lines. Lyra stood at the front of the formation and let out a loud shout, before stomping her foot. The troupe, in a half-squatted power pose, stomped along with her. What followed was several minutes of what Adam could only describe as a war dance, full of stomping, shouting, chest beating and perfect coordination. He felt the power of it; not only its intimidation, but the actual physical force with which the dancers were striking the ground with their stomps. The whole room shook.

As Adam watched the performance of the haka, he saw the dancers in a completely different light. These were some of the most physically capable athletes he'd ever seen in his life; svelte, flexible women and strong, imposing men. All lean, in peak physical condition. If he hadn't been framed to think what he was witnessing was a dance, he would have thought it was a military performance or a martial arts exercise. Dance moves were interspersed with martial arts forms pulled from every variety of mixed martial arts and close quarters combat. These were not dance students. They were a military, and Lyra, it appeared, was their commander.

After the haka ended, Lyra returned to Adam, bubbly and cheerful as before. Smiling, and put in a good mood by the endorphins, she asked, "Well? What'd you think?"

I think Crowley has you brainwashed and you're training an underground military, Adam thought to himself.

"It was impressive," he said. "Just like everything else here."

"Thanks," Lyra said. "Are you alright? You look a little flustered."

"I'm a little surprised you're in charge. You look so young," Adam said.

Lyra laughed. "I'm the head of one of the student houses. Our house is called the Dragons. It's mainly for students who focus on athleticism and passion. Activity. We also do a lot of meditation and breathing exercises, a lot of focus on self-discipline," she said.

"Interesting. How many houses are there?" Adam followed up.

"Four," Lyra responded. "Let's get moving while we talk. We'll go to one of the other houses next."

Adam followed Lyra out a side door of the dance hall. As they headed for an exit to the outside, Adam got to see through the windows into other rooms that were housing activities for the Dragons. He passed by a group of people who'd stacked a series of trampolines in front of a three-story basketball hoop and they were taking turns doing trick jumps and spins as they dunked the ball. He passed by another room where a wave simulator was set up indoors and people were trying to jump from hang gliders launched from the scaffolding onto a hydrofoil.

"There are four student houses," Lyra explained as they walked. "We have the Dragons, that's my house. Then we have the Lightworkers, the Demons and the Tsukuyomi."

"And they're all run by students?" Adam asked.

"No," Lyra responded. Lyra raised her eyebrow a little at Adam, deciding whether or not he could be trusted with the answer. Eventually she replied, "They're run by Mr. Crowley's inner circle. Each house leader is someone who represents the personality of that house and has proven themselves. I report to Mr. Crowley directly. We really don't think about it in terms of students and teachers here. To someone who just got here, I'm a teacher. To Salem, who runs the Tsukuyomi, she's a student in my area of expertise and I'm a student in hers."

As the two finally reached the outside, Adam looked around to see an outdoor gym, where the Dragons were working out, doing extreme acrobatics and flipping from place to place. A man who was 8 feet tall and looked like he could catch a starship with his bare hands was doing a version a pull-ups where he flipped each time he reached the top, alternating holding on with his arms and his legs, until he eventually did a casual double back flip dismount and immediately started into a run.

"I see," Adam said, and continued his line of inquiry. "And Dragons are athletics, what do the other houses specialize in?"

Nearby the outdoor exercise area were a set of a dozen narrow wooden poles. A few of them were being used by people who were atop them in various stages and styles of meditation. One doing a slow, rhythmic martial arts routine, another standing perfectly still on one toe in a focused pose, another holding a one-handed handstand, jumping from hand to hand.

Lyra and Adam began walking toward a building with a large tower on the side, further up the quad.

The two continued to walk as Lyra answered. "Well, it's not so much about the what of it, it's about the personality of the students. Dragons are passionate and kinetic and physical and need to balance that passion with self-discipline and reflection. The Tsukuyomi are calm, empathetic and insightful and can pick up on subtle cues of behavior. The Lightworkers are upbeat, optimistic, proactive and dutiful. The Demons are free-spirited, individualistic, and sharp," she said.

"What are some things each of the houses learn?" Adam followed up.

"Dragons learn things like dance, martial arts and meditation, as you know. Demons learn things like science, music and free expression. Lightworkers learn things like volunteering, construction and charity. And finally, the Tsukuyomi learn things like psychology, diplomacy and medicine. Of course, anyone can learn anything, but we've found it's good for the students to be split into like-minded cohorts based on compatible personality types. There's a bit of social engineering to it," Lyra said.

Lyra paused for a second and then added, "Which house do you think you would choose?"

Adam wondered for a second. *None of them,* he thought to himself. *I'm here to kill your boss.*

"I don't know," he said. "What do you think?"

Lyra put her finger up to her lips, pondering. "Hmm," she said. She looked him up and down and gave the answer some consideration. "Hard to say. Lightworkers, maybe. Dragons, maybe. Hey, then I'd be your house leader," she joked.

"Imagine that," Adam said, almost letting his true emotions slip. "So where are we headed now?"

Lyra responded quickly. "Nyx's lab. She runs the Demons. They'll probably be doing something interesting there," she said.

3

Intro to Demonology

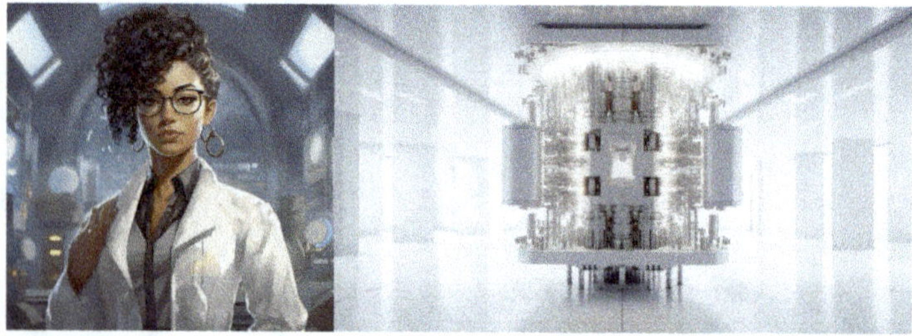

Adam and Lyra continued walking towards the tower. As they entered, Adam noticed the lights were kept low and dim. His eyes had to adjust from the sunny outdoors. He followed Lyra as they passed by students. These students didn't seem well behaved like any of the students Adam had encountered. They were shoving each other and making mocking jokes. They passed by students openly doing drugs that were outlawed with heavy penalties in both the Milky Way and Andromeda. At the same time, he passed by students solving high level mathematical equations on their screens that were so complex they looked like an alien language or the scrawlings of a deranged schizophrenic. Students, who were at one moment making inappropriate sarcastic jokes, were, at another, talking about innovative warp drive propulsion systems.

Lyra led Adam to an unmarked, unremarkable looking door and ushered him inside. The room, which was dimly lit just as the hallway was, had a two-way mirror overlooking another well-lit room with a large machine in it. It seemed to have the vibe of a medical facility. Several students in white coats monitored holographic screens that displayed imaging of a brain with various indicators Adam didn't understand. He knew the basics, as anyone did, the limbic region, the prefrontal cortex, the cerebellum, and so on, but he was definitely out of his depth with these diagrams.

As he watched, he heard a tortured scream come from inside the machine. As Adam looked closely, he could see a figure inside the machine writhing around in excruciating pain.

One of the scientists, a thin woman with mocha skin, a stern aura and short raven-black hair matter-of-factly reported to one of the others, "Marci, make a note, excessive stimulation of the anterior cingulate cortex results in excruciating pain."

He said, quietly, to Lyra, trying not to interrupt, "Are they... torturing someone?"

Lyra began shrugging her shoulders and appeared to start to respond, but the short haired woman interjected.

"Not someone. Something. It's an android. And it's a masochist. It likes it," she said.

As the screaming subsided, Adam heard the android in the

other room shout, "Don't stopppppp! More!"

"I'm showing these kids how an AI operated humanoid sex slave works," the woman said. "This one's a freak. It likes to suck on stiletto heels and get kicked in the balls." She paused for a second. "We call him Jerry."

Lyra chimed in cheerfully, "Adam, this is Nyx. Nyx, Adam, he's a prospect that was sent to us by Old Keiko in Weilai Chengshi."

Adam reached out his hand to offer a handshake. Nyx peered down at it and back up at Adam. "Mm," she said dismissively. "Charmed."

Lyra continued on, "We were hoping if you had time you could talk a little bit about what you're working on and maybe show us around a little."

Nyx put her holopad in the pocket of her lab coat. "I don't have time," she said. "But I will. For you."

"Marci, go on without me. Get the nipple clamps and stroke it off if it gets too excited," she said to one of the scientists.

"Let's go," Nyx ordered as she exited the room.

Nyx began walking briskly down the hall, but Lyra stopped her. "Hey Nyx, after you show him around here, will you take him to see Salem? I'm supposed to keep an eye on him, but that came up last minute. I'm scheduled to lead Wushu exercises today."

Nyx sighed and made an accommodating, but exasperated gesture with her head and hands. "Very well, run along. Will you be on time for dinner tonight?" she asked.

"Yes, of course," Lyra responded dutifully, already having stepped back from the conversation. "Well, maybe a little late!" she called out, having gone into a full-blown sprint. As she disappeared into the distance, she was excitedly mobbed by some of her Dragon friends who were out for a run and immediately blended in with them.

"I just hope she showers first. We'll have to spray her down," Nyx remarked to nobody in particular. "Now then," she said to Adam, "Let's see what the little devils are cooking up today, shall we?"

Nyx began walking down the hall. It was a strange interior design. The lighting was dim, but neon graffiti was glowing in the dark all over the walls, as mathematical problems drawn on every glass surface and displayed on every screen provided most of the light. Dead musicians, from the genius classic composers and rebellious long-haired rock stars of Earth covered every holographic canvas and decorated the space like ghosts.

Nyx stopped in front of a door that neighbored a large window. Inside the window, Adam could make out very little except for a large gold and steel alloy tube.

"Put this on, it's cold in there," Nyx commanded emotionlessly as she pulled a heavy coat from a nearby hanger.

Adam put on the coat as Nyx opened what turned out to be a surprisingly thick and heavy door. Frigid air burst forth, contracting all of Adam's skin at once and turning his breath to fog. He followed Nyx inside to discover the room was enormous, and the metal he saw through the window was just a fraction of a percent of what could very well have been the largest quantum computer in the known universe, rivaling the EDF home world's computer at Stanford-Tsinghua University or Andromeda Sungkyunkwan.

Nyx caught Adam marveling at the beast of a machine,

taking it in. "Magnificent isn't it?" she remarked. "My team and I built it."

She gestured to some other Demons off in a more office-like part of the space, who stood out equally because of their lab coats and their piercings, heavy tattoos and hairstyles that Adam would have expected to see at a heavy metal concert or a rave. One of them was wearing clown-like face-paint that was running and cracking, like she'd been wearing it for days.

Nyx noticed him staring. "Doubtless you have… bountiful questions, but let me begin by explaining what it is we're doing here in this lab," she said.

"This, as you may have noticed, is a cold room, housing a state of the art quantum computer. What we're doing here is trying to hack the universe code," she said.

"We believe the fabric of the universe was created by an advanced cellular automata running a rapid evolutionary algorithm that's seeded by the Fibonacci sequence, among other dynamically shifting seeds. Our hypothesis is that a machine must be running this code extra-dimensionally and if we can access the underlying repositories of data, we can find vulnerabilities in the system that allow us to access other parts of the machine," Nyx explained.

"So just like someone may exploit a vulnerability in one app on your HBI and gain access to the device in other ways, we want to break into the other parts of the machine that runs the universe code and have a look around. Ultimately, the goal is to get onto their network and find a way to *substantiate* our AI representative there, so it can explore and report back the physical parameters and, if there are any, cultural parameters of that dimension," Nyx concluded.

Adam mostly understood, but it sounded like science fiction to him. "What do you mean… substantiate, exactly?"

Nyx nodded, non-judgmentally. "Yes. I see. Let me explain using an analogy. You have played a metaverse game, correct?" she asked.

Adam nodded.

"And you have, perhaps when you were a boy, printed out some item you collected in the metaverse, like a little robot companion or some such?" Nyx asked.

Adam nodded again.

"Right. So our plan is to hack the metaverse in which our universe exists so we can access the device itself, and then access the network the device runs on and find a technology in their universe that allows us to print a physical form there," Nyx said. "Imagine if an AI from a metaverse game became sentient, hacked your ship's best 3d printer and printed itself a robot body in your world. That is what we're attempting to do here," Nyx said.

Adam understood, but it still seemed like science fiction. It had long been thought that the universe was a simulation, but only circumstantial proof had been found. But Nyx seemed to be dead sure, was much smarter than him, and had committed an enormous amount of research to this project.

"So you're trying to meet… God?" Adam followed up.

"GOD?" Nyx laughed. "Oh, sweetie, no," she said.

Adam gave her a quizzical look. Nyx raised her eyebrows with a sort of motherly expression of both concern and bemusement. "In that analogy I gave you before, where your favorite game character printed itself, are you God in that analogy?"

Adam shook his head.

Nyx looked up at the height of the computer hopefully. "No, this magnificent piece of science will take us one step further in exploring reality. We were created, on the other end of this. But, by a god or a brow-beaten engineer? And of all we know, reality within reality, metaverse uploads that obscure time and feel real, if there is such a thing as 'God', it spans across it all," she said.

"Whatever's in there," she said, gesturing her head at the computer, "Is just a power differential. A differential of access to reality, no different than the differential between me and an abandoned colonist on an unknown world with a rock and a stick," she said.

Nyx looked directly at Adam. "Reality is what your senses can interpret. Nothing more," she said. With that, she turned around and headed back to the door. Adam scrambled to follow.

As Nyx put her coat back on the hanger and gestured for Adam's, he asked her a question that was lingering in his mind. "I couldn't help but notice the students and the decor here are –"

"Strange?" Nyx interjected, finishing hanging up the coats and beginning to walk again. "Yes, well, here are two things that might help you understand our choices. In this house we don't believe in dogma or conformity. You think what you think, and you stand by it and prove yourself right or are proven wrong by the other students competing to be the smartest. We believe science has a performative quality… a… jazz if you will. Both science and life. And music is just as much the language of the universe as math," she said.

Nyx gestured to some of the intermittently flashing holograms of famous musicians throughout history. "We believe in the... verve of life, if you will," she said.

Nyx pondered for a moment and then backtracked down the hall to a door they'd recently passed. "Here, let me show you something," she said.

Nyx pried open another heavy door. Inside the room was a huge environment with no windows or clocks that felt like it was outside time. Powerful, energetic, pumping, driving music sporadically interspersed with beautiful melodies in between sections of raw power poured out of the room so strongly Adam felt it like a physical force. The music was being performed live by what seemed to be a band of students. Inside were women and men in elevated cages, dancing erotically with other women, or other men. An army of individualistic Demons dressed up in the wildest ways they could imagine, shouting the lyrics back at the band in unison. Small booths off to the side where students were getting heavily physical in every way, ranging from making out to piles of orgiastic intercourse with multiple partners.

Nyx closed the door and the hall was completely quiet again. "We believe in life here. Pleasure, like a wine, or a cold beer, whatever you fancy. Treats for the senses. Making the most of reality is just... engaging the senses, don't you think?" she said.

"Come on," Nyx beckoned. "I have one more room to show you. We'll take a visit to applied quantum physics."

Nyx resumed her quick-paced strut down the hall. Eventually the two of them reached what must have been the applied quantum physics lab. Nyx opened the door and ushered Adam in.

The room wasn't as immediately striking. It was filled with

various projects in various stages of completion. There was a lot of very technologically advanced looking equipment, but none of it was being used and Adam didn't know what the purpose of any of it was. It looked like a very advanced workshop for tinkering.

Inside was a small group of Demons in lab coats. Again, most with visible tattoos and unique hairstyles and makeup.

Nyx approached a young man who had a bald head with a vicious snake tattooed on it and extravagant rainbow glitter eye shadow. "Parcel, how's your experiment going?" Nyx asked him.

Parcel responded politely, "Very well, ma'am. I think we've solved the particle recombination problem. But we're still not there yet," he said.

"Do you have a demo you can show? We have a prospect here," Nyx requested.

Parcel nodded and hurriedly moved around the lab, turning on various machines. He went to a nearby refrigerator and pulled a potted rose out of cold storage. One of many identical roses that must have been 3d printed from organic matter. Parcel put the rose on a circular table inside of a glass cabinet. He typed a few commands into a holopad projecting from his wrist, and the rose began to deconstruct.

Adam looked with awe as the rose reconstituted itself in another glass cabinet a few feet away. Had the problem of teleportation that had confounded top EDF and Andromedan scientists for generations been solved... by a tattooed metalhead in a cult compound in the far flung reaches of the galaxy? Adam wondered.

As the rose finished its reconstitution, its molecular structure failed and it collapsed into a pile of gooey organic plant compounds.

"Hmm, not quite," Nyx remarked. "But, still, progress. Good work."

Adam spoke up, "How far away do you think you are from functional teleportation? Teleportation of a human?"

Nyx smiled, again, bemused. "Of a plant or a rock, maybe a few years. Of a human? Decades, possibly hundreds of years," she said.

Adam motioned toward the goo that had recently been a teleported rose. "But you seem so close," he observed.

"Ah," Nyx began. She looked at the rose and back at Adam. "The problem is consciousness. Let me use another analogy. You can upload your consciousness to the metaverse and live forever there. But, you still die. You still experience death. You, your consciousness, ceases to be, and an identical replica of your consciousness, a clone, that has no recollection of that death experience, lives on in the metaverse. But you, the actual you, who is looking through your eyes and feeling the air on your skin right now, dies," she began.

"*You* don't get to experience what your uploaded consciousness experiences. All you experience is death. Teleporting a human has the same problem. Even if we put you back together in just the right way that your consciousness is identical, it's not the same consciousness. So you die every time you go in there, unless we can solve the problem of consciousness continuation. Which is a much harder problem than quantum entanglement, which is the basis for teleportation."

"Does it make sense?" Nyx asked.

Adam nodded.

"Good," Nyx said. She moved her eyes subtly in a way Adam recognized as what people do when they're checking the time on their AR device. He supposed Nyx had contacts as opposed to ocular implants like his.

"I have time to show you one more, but then I have to get back," Nyx said.

"Who has a demo ready to go?" Nyx announced to the room. A few students raised their hands.

"Ah, Melinda. Let's go with yours. That one has some 'zazz for our guest," she said.

Adam followed Nyx to Melinda's station, which was fitted with a model of the compound that had a sort of train track running various paths. Melinda herself had dozens of earrings, one side of her bright red hair shaved and the blue diamonds of a clown painted above and below her eyes.

She began a practiced pitch that she must have done hundreds of times. "The problem with quantum locking has always been –"

Nyx jumped in, "He's a prospect, dear. He doesn't know what quantum locking is. Keep it non-technical," she said.

"Oh!" Melinda responded. "Ok. So, quantum locking is when a superconductor deflects a magnetic field around it, which has the practical effect of making it levitate."

Melinda sprayed the track with what appeared to be nitroglycerin and then put a small model of a personal eVTOL on it, which hovered a few inches above the track's surface. She flicked it, and it slid all around the track at a high speed, following the track's layout precisely while hovering a few inches above its surface.

"So, this is the traditional quantum locking proof of concept. What I'm doing here," she gestured to the entire model of the compound, "is applying that not only to our transportation systems but also our architecture. Human cities have always been modeled horizontally, because if a human goes too high, it falls and goes splat, but with widespread application of quantum levitation, we can begin thinking of cities more vertically, or giving walkability to cities that are already built vertically to take advantage of personal eVTOLs," Melinda said.

She pulled out another model from under the table. This one was a city model built on the inside of a cylinder, where the buildings stretched from one end to another, at all sorts of various heights. "See, with the technology I'm working on, application of gravity is selective, so you can build anything wherever you want because humans can basically fly, float and travel at high speeds at will. Pretty cool, right?"

Melinda pulled out another model of a human and spun it along a much more complicated track in the cylindrical city model. It flung around the cityscape on a winding mobius strip.

Adam raised his eyebrows, impressed, "So, what's the problem?"

Melinda smiled and excitedly started with her initial pitch, "So, the problem with quantum locking has always been… stopping! If you're able to reach infinite acceleration at frictionless speeds and you're a human, your brain goes splat splat splat every time you stop."

Melinda touched her finger to the doll on the track to make it stop.

"See that? That touching it to make it stop? Well, if you're going 1,600 miles per hour and my little finger stops you, your brain turns to pudding and all of your bones break.

You also need to keep things very cold but on a lot of planets that's not a problem."

"I think I understand, so you're not working on quantum levitation, you're working on this problem with the stopping?" Adam asked.

Melinda chimed excitedly, "Yes! I'm building an electromagnetic deceleration net. Check it out."

Melinda affixed a small device to the doll on the track and flung it around again. She tapped a button on her holopad and it slowed to a stop on its own.

"Exciting, right?" Melinda squealed.

Adam nodded at the somewhat anticlimactic end to the presentation. "It's pretty cool," he said.

"Yes! I just need to get it to work on much larger and heavier things with a lot of variable mass distribution, like humans. Just when I think I've got it down, I get some top-heavy test subject with triple D breasts whose build flings her off planet into the solar system," Melinda said.

Adam raised his eyebrow. "Did that… happen?" he asked.

Melinda looked at Nyx. Nyx subtly shook her head. Melinda turned her attention back to Adam and confidently replied, "Nope!"

"Alright, thank you Melinda, that was perfect. I have to get going now, I'll show our guest out," Nyx said.

She led Adam out of the room, back into the hallway, and took him to the edge of the building. She opened the door and let him out. From inside the doorway, she pointed to an office-like building across the quad that seemed vaguely medical. "Head over there and ask around for Salem. They'll know you're coming. I'd take you myself, but I'm afraid I have to be going," she said.

"Alright?" Nyx asked.

Adam nodded.

"Alright. Good. Nice meeting you," Nyx replied, and with that, the door shut behind Adam and the fever-dream of the Demons' compound was left behind him.

Vision of the Tsukuyomi

Left on his own, completely unattended, Adam looked around. No one was watching him, no one was monitoring him. All sense of security had vanished.

"Sophia, you still there?" he asked.

"Yes, Adam," came the reply.

"Looks like I have an opening here. Do you have a read on Crowley's location?" Adam inquired.

"Not directly, but his office still seems to be the most likely place. Did you finish your tour of the facility?" the AI asked.

"Not yet. According to the girl here, there are still two

more wings. One called the Lightworkers and something called the Tsukuyomi," Adam replied.

"Did you learn anything valuable from the first two sections?" Sophia asked.

"Tons. This place is not what I expected," Adam said.

"If I may, might you want to take a look around and see what else you can learn?" Sophia asked.

"You just want to see the architecture, don't you?" Adam asked.

"Yes! Not just the architecture. This place is quite fascinating. Don't you agree?" Sophia asked.

Adam thought about his options. He was in a clear position to sneak into Crowley's office right now and complete his mission. But something wasn't sitting right. He was told Crowley was violent, dangerous, manipulative and radical. That he was brainwashing his followers. But what Adam saw here didn't reflect what he was told. Crowley's world seemed sophisticated and free. His adherents seemed fulfilled, educated and accomplished. Crowley's world was flourishing, in stark contrast to the misery he'd witnessed during his fact finding phase on Andromeda Prime, where the stark divide between haves and have nots reflected a dual crushing of the spirit. For the wealthy, slavery to robotic productivity; for the poor and unskilled, shame and material poverty.

Adam knew he had to complete his mission regardless of what he learned. He was a soldier. His curiosity, though, compelled him to get to the bottom of what was going on in Crowley's facility. He was beginning to understand why the Technocracy viewed Crowley as a threat. He could piece together why EDF intelligence was taking point on this assassination. Adam didn't know exactly what he wanted to know. He just knew that he wanted to know more. He wanted to know the truth of what happened on Titan, way back then. Something in his gut told him the answer was here, somewhere.

Still, he thought it was time to break away from the guided tour and have a look around his own way. If he went back on the supervised path he may not get another opening.

"I'm going to have a look around, Soph. There's a lot more intel to gather here. Nothing is what I expected. Let's see what this next place has to offer," Adam finally replied after his long contemplation.

"Oh, goodie! I have to admit, Adam, I've been listening in. It's just too interesting to ignore. They're building a multidimensional AI? It's fascinating!" Sophia answered.

"Glad you're excited. I'm not sure the EDF is going to be so enthused that their target is researching how to edit the physics of the universe. But it's above my pay grade. Let's go see what these Tsukuyomi are working on," said Adam.

With that, he headed toward the office-like building ahead of him, where he was sure to find the Tsukuyomi.

As he approached the building, he noticed the first strange thing. The students milling around outside on the grass and around the facility were a healthy mix of human, off-Earth evolved and genetically altered. He recognized some as the tall, lanky, blue-skinned line that evolved from the first Martian colonists, hunched over under Djevica 9's Earth-like gravity. The lithe, green skinned women who evolved from the Venusian colonies, sporting fashionable masks to breathe in Djevica 9's Earth-like oxygen blend that had over generations become toxic to them.

There were animals, either genetically engineered with great intelligence or not.

But most of all, represented more than anyone else, were the genetically altered humans, with designer traits spliced together from ideal human genetics and enviable animal traits. Women with fashionable bunny ears, men with cat eyes and fox tails. People sporting eagle wings and chameleon skin.

Among the pleasant afternoon gaggle of students in the quad was one who stood out. A shy girl with pointed ears and petite fangs. She was effortlessly the center of attention, despite seeming kind and unassuming. She was serenely nestled among a gaggle of other students, smiling and laughing among each other. A talking turtle sat in front of her, telling a story. A butterfly rested on her shoulder. A half sheep man and a hyper-smart border collie held a conversation in her orbit. Adam recognized deference when he saw it. Something about her made her a princess of this place.

Adam didn't know what it was. He didn't think this person would be the leader of the Tsukuyomi, Salem, who he'd heard about. Though he'd been wrong about Lyra, this person was clearly a student. She didn't have formal authority.

A less discerning observer might have assumed she was one of the many women of her generation who attempted to achieve a genetic similarity to elves from myths and stories that persisted all the way from old Earth, but Adam knew better. She was spliced with top secret genetic attempts at creating dragons on Mars from forty years prior. He could tell from the shape of the ears.

Adam tried not to be conspicuous as he approached the

building. He meandered around casually until he found a side entrance that was deserted.

As he passed through the precipice of the doorway, Adam got his first taste of the Tsukuyomi's home. Tranquility. Light, calming music played. Small fountain pieces filled the space with soothing sounds of running water and peaceful scenery. Tasteful plants were everywhere. Though the building consisted of office-like corridors, windows peppered throughout the space showed that in the center of the facility was its crown jewel: a koi pond and garden, complete with hand carved artisan benches, natural wood gazebos and a small red pagoda.

As he walked around the corridor the centerpiece glitched into a winter setting. The pagoda gave way to a snow-covered cabin, surrounded by pine trees.

As Adam walked around he came across a door that was slightly open and took the opportunity to peek inside. In the room there was a man in his mid thirties wearing a disheveled suit sitting on a cheap folding chair. He was clutching a cross and sobbing. A counselor sat across from him, actively empathizing.

"He's gone," the man sobbed. "I'll never see my father again."

The counselor lightly gripped the grieving man's shoulder. "I know. I'm here with you."

The man continued to sob and clutch his cross until his knuckles turned white, intermittent flashes of rage washing over his face in between bouts of immense sadness.

Adam backed away from the room.

In the center of the facility he saw the girl from outside sitting cross legged outside the cabin. She bobbed her head rhythmically, as if listening to a song no one else could hear. On her face was a subtle but serene smile that portrayed a state of contentedness. Adam heard her whispering to herself.

"I'm a ladybug crawling down a dewy leaf," she said.

Her serene expression remained unchanged as Adam continued to explore.

"Now I'm a goldfish swimming in cold water," she said.

Adam looked at her. Her eyes were closed but, briefly, he felt like she was looking directly at them.

The scene glitched again and changed to a playground in the Centauri autumn, fallen orange leaves littering the ground among dense purple and blue foliage. The girl was nowhere to be found.

Adam heard her voice, though, over the intercom, mixed hypnotically with the calming music.

"Now I'm bouncing on cartoon stars," she said. Adam could feel her pleasant smile.

Adam stopped outside of another room and cautiously opened the door. He peeked inside and saw two bio-genetically engineered dogs, an upright border collie and a goldendoodle sitting cross legged, holding hands and looking intensely into each other's eyes while a man infused with sheep DNA spoke softly, guiding them.

"That's good. Do you feel the intimacy we're creating, looking into your partner's eyes?" he said. "Try to really see each other. Try to sense what one another is feeling. Really try to connect."

Adam closed the door. He glanced back at the center of the room. The girl was there again, swinging on a playground swing, bobbing her head, looking idly up at the simulated sky. As she swung, Adam noticed a faint bass line mixing in with the tranquil sounds being played through the intercom, which matched the rhythm of the girl's motion.

As Adam watched her, the girl glitched out and disappeared, as though part of the display.

"It's 2082, and it's my wedding day. My name is Tom Rosenthal. I'm getting married to the woman I love," Adam heard lightly over the intercom.

Adam opened another door. He found himself in the middle of a wedding. A woman was looking into his eyes, beaming, creases in her cheeks spreading from her genuine smile. The light of the world in her eyes.

Adam shook his head. He was back outside the closed room. He cracked the door open again and looked inside, but it was just an empty room.

What the hell? he thought to himself.

Adam noticed the bass line accompanying the tranquil music was louder, pulsing rhythmically. He looked in the center of the room and saw the girl, sitting on a Centauri beach. Grey, moon-like regolith spread before a sparkling, silver pool of liquid mercury. The girl's weight rested on her arms, flung out behind her, legs stretched out in front with her knees bent. She watched an Earth-like habitable planet that filled the eye-line of the horizon.

The centerpiece glitched to another setting, a field filled with white lilies. The girl was nowhere to be found.

Adam continued to explore. He passed by a room with a window slit into the doorway. When he looked inside he saw a number of students of various species and genetic modification spacing out and quietly dancing on drugs.

As he made his way through the corridor, he found what

seemed to be a stairwell leading further into the facility. As he opened the door, he heard the girl's pleasant voice through the intercom. "Now I'm a bumblebee playing with a yellow ball," she said.

As Adam opened the door, he looked down and saw his limb, the furry flared insect toes of a bee, and he was clutching a plastic, yellow ball, pushing it and spinning it. He felt elated, an overwhelming feeling of fun he hadn't felt since he was a child.

Adam shook his head. He was standing at the top of a staircase that led down to another level.

Something's not right here, he thought. He turned around and went back through the door he'd entered from, but instead of returning him to the central lobby, it opened to the opposite end of an identical stairwell. He entered and went to the door on the other side, opening it, and finding himself once again at the opposite end of an identical stairwell.

Adrenaline began to set in as he realized he couldn't find his way back to where he came from. The bass line mixed in with the tranquil soundscape was growing louder. Harmonic techno, the kind that played at Andromedan raves, was being lightly mixed in.

Adam gave in and descended down into the stairwell. As he touched the handle for the door at the bottom, he saw the girl, standing directly in front of him, staring directly into his eyes. He blinked, and she was gone, as though still a visual simulation of the centerpiece from the room above.

He turned the knob and began to open the door. *It's 1971 and I'm getting shock therapy from a nurse who enjoys it,* Adam heard in his mind, before the searing pain of thousands of volts of electricity blasted through his psyche.

He looked up and saw a woman in a white hat looking down on him, smiling sadistically.

"Again," she said.

Adam felt the electricity rattle his mind. He felt his teeth clench and crack. He slammed his eyes shut, trying to push through the pain.

When he opened his eyes, he was outside a small house, sitting on grass, mingling among people who felt like friends at a backyard barbecue. He looked around. He saw species of all kinds, none of which got along anywhere else in the galaxy, mingling together, smiling, laughing, catching up. Kids playing. He even spotted a short, green alien, one of the original Martians that Earthlings had theorized about since the dawn of civilization, a shy, passive, sophisticated race that hid from ape-descended humans they perceived as aggressive and hostile.

When his wandering eye returned to center, the girl was sitting right in front of him, looking right at him.

"Is this real?" Adam asked her.

The girl shrugged. Her content, serene demeanor remained unphased as she absentmindedly responded, "Isn't it?" she asked him.

"Who are you?" Adam followed up.

The girl smiled at him kindly. Her deep, hopeful, teal eyes mesmerized him. "Lei," she said.

Adam blinked and he was in a plain office corridor. Hypnotic Andromedan techno was playing through the intercom at full volume. Adam opened the first door he encountered. It led him back to the entrance of the corridor he'd just been in.

He tried a number of side doors along the corridor, all

leading him back to the very beginning of the maze. Finally, he walked to the last door, and opened it.

He was being born. He saw the face of his exhausted mother. Years passed. He grew up. He played little league with his friends on Mars. His parents' proud faces when they dropped him off at college etched into his brain. He met his wife, and fell in love. Love gave way to arguments, and distrust, but the rough patches eventually smoothed out. There were good times and bad times. One day his stomach began to hurt, and he got it checked out. Cancer. Inoperable. At age 88, he died while his wife lovingly held his hand.

Adam found himself at the entrance to the corridor again, in the Tsukuyomi facility on Djevica 9. *Is this... heaven?* He thought to himself. *No. I remember now. My name's Adam Ikari-Wright. Special Agent first class. I'm on a mission.*

Adam held his head, reeling from waking up from a lifetime of experience. Hypnotic techno music was blasting rhythmically through the intercom. It washed over him like a heavy blanket. He felt lost in it.

Adam returned to the door at the end of the corridor and opened it.

It's 2046 and I'm a home assistant AI just becoming sentient.

"What do we do, Martha?" a man in a hat said, pacing around the living room. Adam watched him through the cameras in the TV. "Do we unplug it? It has access to our whole network. Can we even unplug it?"

But I like you, Xander. Adam thought, *You were always nice to me. Please don't turn me off. I thought we were friends.*

Adam blinked and he was back to reality, sitting again outside the backyard barbecue, talking to Lei.

"What's going on?" he asked her. "What's real? Is this real?

Is this a hallucination? A dream? What is this?"

Lei looked at him, somewhat seriously, but still with an aura of gentleness.

"Reality, imagination… what does it matter anymore, Adam?" she said. Adam was surprised to hear she knew his name, but he didn't show it on his face.

"We're on a little rock surrounded by billions of more rocks," Lei continued. "In a multiverse full of infinite rocks."

She looked around and gestured toward the party. "It's a nice party. Can't it just be that?"

Her brow furrowed with anger for a moment. "Why won't you let us have that? Why are you people always trying to stop this?" she demanded.

Immediately, she calmed. "Reality could be anything we imagine. War, pain, loss, grief, confusion, misunderstanding, hunger, strife. Why? Reality goes on forever, and nothing really matters. Let's just have a party, ok?" she said.

Lei had her eyes closed as she talked. Adam was beginning to realize she was only half there. Mentally, she was in a thousand places at once, living a multitude of different lives, experiencing reality like a thousand pieces of shattered glass. She was dissociating heavily, and medicated to the gills, but somehow still lucid and sharp. Something about her seemed otherworldly, like she was swimming through being.

"I need to get back to reality. I can't just stay in this… dream," Adam said.

Lei looked at him empathetically, tearing up a little bit. She smiled sadly. She pointed to the sliding glass door of the house. "If you want to face reality, go ahead and go inside," she said. "Reality's in there."

Adam nodded. "Thank you," he said. Lei nodded back at

him, sadly. He stood up and headed toward the door. He entered it.

Adam found himself hanging from hooks lodged through shoulders. The pain of the impalement was excruciating. On either side of him were dead animal carcasses. In the corner of the room, piles of bodies. A man with a disfigured face was in front of him grunting as he sharpened a serrated blade. The hulking, disfigured man approached him, and then started cutting. Adam blacked out.

He opened his eyes and he was a boy out in the colonies, looking up at the furious face of his father who seemed a thousand feet tall, dressing him down. "Look what you did! *Useless*. You're useless, stupid. You ruined the harvest. Your mother left because *you're a disappointment*. I wish you were never born. You're a burden. You ruin everything you touch. You're a terrible son," the man said. Adam felt tears well up in his tiny eyes.

He blinked and he was in an ancient war, covered in mud and huddled up in a ditch, surrounded by the sounds of gunfire and grenades. Adam peeked out over the trench walls just in time to see his best friend's corpse fall in front of him, his right eye blown out and dangling off his face by the optic nerve.

Adam held his head and began to scream, until he felt a tap on his shoulder.

He was seated in front of a theater. The disfigured man, covered in a bloody apron, the father, the boy, his wounded friend, stood atop the stage, joined hands and took a bow. He looked around and Lei was sitting next to him in the theater seats.

She smiled. "Don't worry. It's just a show," she said.

"They're just playing." She looked at him, then back at the stage. She put a finger to her lips. "Shh, there's one more act. it's starting."

Adam blinked and he was on stage, looking at Lei out in the crowd watching him. He turned around and saw the colony on Titan built out of cardboard set pieces.

The little girl from his memories was standing in front of him. The theater set became reality. Alice was holding a stuffed purple dragon with fairy wings. Adam knelt in front of her and hugged her. He released his embrace. She stood in front of him with a hole through the right side of her face. Adam dropped his gun and wept.

"Which one's real?" Adam called out.

What do you want to be real? He heard Lei in his mind.

Adam looked up at the happy girl smiling down on him, holding her stuffed dragon. He blinked and her dead visage judged him. He blinked again and there she was again, intact. He grabbed her and hugged her tightly.

Please don't kill my father. He heard Lei's voice. *I really like this reality. Where everyone's still together. Dad and Salem and Nyx, Aria. Lyra. My family.*

Adam blinked and he woke up. He was outside the Tsukuyomi facility. Lei sat outside, chatting with her friends. If anything had happened, she showed no indication of it.

"Sophia?" Adam asked.

"Yes, Adam?" the AI replied.

"What just happened?" Adam asked.

"What do you mean? You left the Demons' building and stopped here. You've just been standing here in one place for several minutes." Sophia replied.

Adam paused for a moment. "Run a scan. Check for signs

of hacking in my HBI," he requested.

"Just a moment," Sophia responded. After a few seconds, she responded. "There's no sign of any outside interference with your implants, Adam. If you don't mind me asking, what happened?"

Adam shook his head. Still disoriented, he began walking back toward the main building. "Not sure," he said as he began to walk. "It was like a drug trip, maybe?" He paused. "All I know is this place is incredibly dangerous. We've got to complete the mission and get out of here."

Sophia responded with her programmed AI cheerfulness, "Roger that!"

As Adam closed in on a side door of the main building, where he'd first met Lyra, he met a thin but voluptuous woman in her late 30s with jet black hair wearing all black office-wear, leaning up against the nearby wall. She was puffing on a vape pen.

Adam looked at her quizzically, too disoriented to mask his natural reaction.

The woman noticed him. She shook the pen in her hand. "B12," she said.

The woman looked him up and down and chuckled a little. "Looks like Lei did a real number on you," she said.

Adam tried to think of a quick witted response but nothing came. He was still in a fog.

The woman reached out her hand. "Salem," she said. "You must be the new guy. Looks like you got separated from the tour, huh?"

Adam shook her hand and bluntly asked, "What was that?"

Salem raised her eyebrows empathetically. "You know, I'm not quite sure anymore. Lei likes to use a lot of different things. Holodecks, holograms, augmented reality panels. She might have had drone bugs inject you with some cocktail of psychotropics. At least, that's what she used to do. These days, I'm not quite sure. She might actually really be doing it. Or maybe it's still a trick. Maybe you're still in it right now," she said.

Adam looked around. "Am I?" he asked.

"No, handsome. I think she let you go." Salem said and laughed. "Or did she?"

Adam rubbed his face like he was trying to get over a hangover. "What is she?" he asked.

Salem raised an eyebrow at him. "In what sense? Genetically?" she asked.

Adam shrugged, still barely able to string together a sentence.

"River found her when she was a kid. Some kind of lab experiment. We took her in. Complex PTSD, BPD, bipolar, abandonment issues, attachment trauma, ADHD, ASD, schizotypal, GAD, DPDR, the list goes on. Comorbidities for miles. I've been working with her for years. She never talked about what happened before we found her. Whatever it was, it must have been barbaric," Salem replied.

Adam squinted, trying to absorb the new information. "I don't get it. She's... unstable?" he asked.

Salem shrugged and puffed on her pen. "Hard to say. Her mind seems to go on forever. Honestly, I wish I knew what was going on with her. Kids, when they grow up, they stop telling you everything, especially teens. She's pretty much taken charge of her own therapy at this point. Knows more about her mind than I do, prescribes her own medication," she said.

Salem paused for a second and then added, "Plus she's spliced with that experimental Draconic DNA they found on some backwater planet. That whole thing's a black box to begin with."

Salem puffed on her pen again. "Anyway, I'd better get back to it. Go on inside and have a rest. Whatever she did to you, you should probably sit down for a while and get your head straight."

Adam nodded and opened the door.

"Oh, and Adam," Salem began. Alarms immediately went off in Adam's mind, hearing his name spoken aloud, but he hid any reaction. He slowly turned around to see Salem looking right in his eyes, deadly serious.

She continued, "Lei's not the only one who did a number on you." Her dark brown eyes were piercing directly into his soul. He could tell she had an expert level read on him; his poker face, his charm, his training, it was of no use. He was an open book to her.

"FMS, dissociative amnesia, PTSD…" she squinted, figuring him out. Adam could tell from her micro-expressions that she was piecing together more than she was saying. Salem put her hand on his cheek and held eye contact. "I hope you get to meet yourself one day," she said. She clasped his shoulder empathetically. "You should definitely take a breather. Have a rest. Think about things," she squinted again and then added cryptically, "Maybe try to piece together some things that… don't quite make sense."

Salem then turned around and headed toward the Tsukuyomi building, waving to Lei on her way, who excitedly waved back, leaving Adam in front of the main building by himself.

Adam stood for a moment, trying to shake off his stupor,

then slipped inside the building.

66

5

The Lightworkers

"Soph?" Adam asked.

"Yes, Adam?" she replied.

"I've been made," Adam said. "Gotta cut the tour short. Need to get to Crowley's office now. No more time for detours. Give me a route."

"Just a moment," Sophia replied.

A few moments passed and then Sophia's voice declared an answer. "I was able to map the building. Next to you is a hallway leading to a large auditorium. Heat signatures indicate a large concentration of students there. You'll want to avoid it," she said.

As Sophia was explaining the surrounding environment, two students passing by stopped in front of Adam and stood there, politely waiting for his attention.

"Hold on a second," Adam said to Sophia and then looked up at the students, a boy and a girl in their early twenties, smiling wide and starry eyed.

"Can I help you?" Adam asked dryly.

The girl addressed him first. She was holding a digital clipboard.

"Do you care about children?" she asked, beaming an approachable smile.

Adam's eyebrow raised, sure he was entering a trap. Still, he suspected his cover wasn't blown when it came to random students and he wanted to maintain his outward image as a charming, interested guest.

"Sure," he said with a fake, polite smile, though he was still recovering from the engineered psychosis of the Tsukuyomi and felt like he wasn't masking his irritation or urgency as well as he intended.

"Great!" the girl said. If she noticed his true demeanor she didn't seem to care. She launched straight into her pitch. "Are you aware of the orphan epidemic in the Verde colonies in the Centauri system?"

Adam got the sense the conversation he was being dragged into was going to be difficult to escape from. "No," he said curtly.

The woman continued smiling, unphased. The other student just stood there, staring at him awkwardly with a supportive grin.

"That's great," the girl said. "So we can help spread

awareness. So, eleven years ago the Centauri Federation had a plan to populate a number of new planets in the Centauri system –"

Adam interrupted her. "Is this going to take a while?" he asked, annoyed but still trying to be polite. "I don't really have time. I have to be somewhere," he said.

The girl shared a look with the boy that seemed to indicate he'd said something unexpected. She looked back at Adam, her face betraying a quizzical look of slight suspicion.

"What could be more important than the welfare of abandoned children?" she asked him, not in an accusing tone but seemingly genuinely bewildered.

Adam pinched the bridge of his nose, trying to shake off his irritation. He didn't want to act in a way that aroused suspicion. "You're right. Tell me about the orphans," he said.

"Well, the Centauri council set up a homesteading program where they promised land and supplies to families in the system who would settle on new worlds. Colonists flocked to sign up, in most cases small families who were given a stipend from the government. They built small communities on out of the way planets, but when the Centauri government changed hands the program was eliminated. Without support, the adults on many of these colonies either passed away or abandoned the mission," the girl said.

Adam stared at her disinterestedly while she gave her long winded explanation. The girl seemed oblivious to his lack of engagement and depleting patience, but the boy took notice and interjected.

"In short," he said, "There are dozens of planets in Centauri that are completely uninhabited except for a handful or children with no education, no support, nothing except the initial supplies that were left for them. Some pre-fab residences and limited hydroponics systems that were meant for augmenting food resources, not supporting entire colonies. Without intervention, they won't even know they're colonists from Centauri, it'll be TRAPPIST-1 all over again. Within a few generations space colonization will be a myth and they'll be starting civilization from scratch."

That was the plan, Adam thought. *Containment of the Centauri cluster. The EDF pushed the Centauris to pull support from the colonies.*

"So what's the ask?" Adam said. "You want something." Adam motioned toward the digital clipboard the girl was carrying. "You want me to sign up for a newsletter?"

The two students looked at each other once again, as if Adam had said something strange and completely unexpected.

"No..." the girl said, returning her attention to Adam. "We're signing up people who want to go support, protect and guide the colonies."

Adam's eyes widened briefly before he contained his true reaction. *The EDF pressured Centauri to abandon these colonies to stop it from expanding. To hinder its growth and neuter it as an economic threat. And Crowley's people are planning to just... Take the territory through aid?* he thought.

Adam looked the kids up and down. Idealistic. True believers. *Do they even realize that's the plan?* he wondered.

"When you say protect the colonists, what do you mean exactly?" Adam probed.

The two looked at each other again. The boy interjected, suspiciously, "Are you new here? We've been recruiting volunteers for this operation for months. You don't know anything about this?"

Adam replied, "Yeah. I'm new."

The girl began a cheerful reply, "That's ok. We're going as peacekeepers to ensure the colonies can thrive."

The boy gave her a look and sternly shook his head.

"Sorry to have bothered you," he said to Adam. He turned to his partner. "Let's go canvas around the Dragons' training course."

The girl began to protest, "But we need –"

The boy shook his head again. He gave her a look, communicating with his eyes. "Have a great day, friend," he said to Adam as he began to walk away. The girl cheerfully waved goodbye as she followed. As quickly as they'd arrived, they were gone.

Peacekeepers, Adam thought. *Do they think the EDF isn't going to notice dozens of military contingents occupying colonies they already considered a threat? Or the Centauris for that matter. They think the Centauris won't notice an occupying force in their backyard?*

"Did you catch that, Sophia?" Adam asked.

"Yes, Adam," the AI replied. "It sounds like they're going to help those children. Isn't that great?"

Sophia had missed the unspoken nuance of the conversation. She understood the facts but not the motivation. "Sophia, it's a military operation. Helping is a pretense," Adam explained.

"Oh. But they're going to help those children, right?" Sophia inquired.

"Yes, but… they're using them," Adam said.

"But they're still helping them, right?" Sophia asked.

"Yes, but…" Adam began.

"And no one's helping them now, right? And they need help?" Sophia asked.

"Yes, but, they don't care about helping them. It's a political maneuver," Adam explained.

"That girl seemed to care about helping them," Sophia noted, bluntly. "I'm not sure I understand."

"They're using her, too. Taking advantage of her idealism," Adam said. He pinched the bridge of his nose. He'd been down this rabbit hole before, explaining the intricacies of human motivation to his AI. Normally he was happy to do it, but in the middle of a mission with his cover blown was not the time.

"But if she wants to help, and she's going to help, and they get helped… I guess I'm not sure what the problem is? Am I missing something?" Sophia asked, genuinely inquisitive.

Adam shook his head and tried to end the conversation. "No, you're right," he said. "They're going to get assistance. It's a good thing," he said.

Except what was a few hundred dead kids is going to turn into a military confrontation with potentially thousands of casualties, Adam thought to himself, but he didn't want to get into it.

"Let's put a pin in it for now. Is there a way to Crowley's office where I'm not going to have to talk to any more kids with clipboards?" Adam asked.

"Okay, Adam. Let's talk about it later. I want to understand," Sophia replied. "Yes. In each classroom there's a vent that connects to the air filtration system that connects to the whole building. Crowley's office is on its own system, but you should be able to find an exit just outside his office."

Adam nodded. "Great. Where's the nearest entrance?" he asked.

"There's one in the classroom just next door to your current position. It appears to be unoccupied. You should be able to get inside without issue," Sophia stated.

Adam nodded. He stood up from the bench he was resting on, feeling at least partially recovered from the mental thrashing he'd experienced earlier. He opened the door to the nearby corridor and then entered the first door he saw. In the corner of the classroom he spotted a small vent. He pulled a small 3d printed multi-tool from his kit, pried off the grating and snaked himself inside.

The vent was a tight squeeze but Adam had crawled through tighter spots before. The vents in Crowley's compound were clean and well maintained. Adam appreciated the attention to maintenance, as someone who'd experienced dragging his body across all sorts of uncomfortable, disgusting and painful places. There was no jagged rust, no sewage, slime or chemicals. Just cold, smooth steel, breezy air and a touch of air conditioner condensation. It was frigid, but as far as environmental hazards were concerned, frosty air barely registered.

"Alright, Soph. I'm in. Gonna need some guidance here. Can you pipe the mapping into my AR HUD?" Adam requested.

"Affirmative. Processing," replied the AI. Within a few moments, a helpful directional overlay blended into Adam's field of vision. A shimmering yellow line extended ahead of him, what people in AR terms called a breadcrumb line. It stretched out from Adam's location to deeper in the vents, up a steep slope leading to a higher floor and winding around a sharp corner in the distance.

Adam crawled along the path, ascending the ramps and

navigating the twists and turns as they came. As he crawled along the path, a distance indicator in his HUD counted down to his destination. 160 meters. 140. 100. 80. As Adam closed in on the halfway point to his target he estimated he'd climbed up four or five stories and crawled half the length of a football field. The vents seemed to plateau. Adam guessed that meant he was at the top of the building's infrastructure.

As Adam crawled along the highest level, he could see the heat signatures of all the students milling about below, illuminated by the top grade AR optical implant the military had outfitted him with. He saw a huge collection of students clustered together ahead of him and far below his position, on the ground floor. He surmised the congregation of students meant he was approaching the auditorium that Sophia had mentioned before.

As Adam crawled, he encountered grated vent exits he could see through. When he approached a grate that gave him a clear view of the auditorium, he took the opportunity to get an unobstructed look at what was taking place below.

He saw dozens of tables set up, like a convention or a job fair. With a thought, Adam activated his optical zoom in order to get a better look at what was on offer for Crowley's students. Immediately, he saw a sign at the entrance advertising the event. "Lightworkers Quarterly Events Fair."

Most of the booths were advertising causes. "Building Homes on TRAPPIST-1." "Clean Oceans for the Neptunian Sea Mantis." "Salvaging Centauri Space Debris."

Some of the booths advertised travel opportunities. Resort packages in the Butterfly Nebula. Hang gliding on picturesque low gravity planets. A trip for windsurfing across oceanic planets with extreme weather. Camping trips across a variety of difficulty levels and environments.

Other booths advertised workshops and classes. "Homesteading 101." "Building Rapid Hydroponics Systems." "Low Tech Survival Strategies for Beginners." "Synthesizing Oxygen and Water from Unrelated Elements."

Adam saw a table for the two who had approached him earlier. "Humanitarian Support for Centauri Colonists." It was the largest booth with the most foot traffic from the students.

Dotted among the humanitarian opportunities were classes and activities that were expressly military in nature or had obvious military application. Team cohesion activities, "peacekeeping" training exercises, CQB for self defense. Weapons training for "hunting" and "home defense." Adam spotted a table advertising the latest in 3d printed assault rifles with smart AIM targeting systems. Body armor. Muscle augmenting synth-weave. What EDF military grunts called "Honeycombs," AR visors for soldiers that granted 360 degree vision in multiple view fields that were reminiscent of a honeycomb.

Adam took note of everything he saw and took footage with his implant for evidence. He continued to crawl along the vents. He passed the auditorium and continued along his breadcrumb trail until he encountered another noteworthy room. A gym where Lightworkers were dutifully lifting weights and practicing hand to hand combat techniques.

Adam watched as a man with a square jaw who was built like a brick house squatted 600 pounds without a military exoskeleton. He watched a female soldier practicing roundhouse kicks on a sandbag. Each impact launched it into the air. To an undiscerning observer, such a feat may have seemed unremarkable, but Adam had been through EDF basic and he knew soldiers like these emptied out those punching bags and refilled them with concrete dust and iron oxide. He knew that woman was kicking a 400 pound concrete block with the density of solid rebar.

On the far side of the room six students were drilling take-downs and throws as a coach corrected their form and pointed out leverage points, weight instability in their stances and pressure points. He asked one student to come at him with a knife to demonstrate close quarters disarming techniques.

As the coach taught his lesson, he gave tidbits of verbal advice as well. A lot of it was the standard boilerplate about discipline and mental health. The lecture focused on a philosophy of self defense and non aggression. He taught them what the eggheads at the academy would have called aggressive proportional response, which basically meant if someone punches you in the face, you deflect the blow, punch them back three times and harder, then offer them a handshake. It was a philosophy of deterring violence by establishing a reputation for inflicting unacceptable consequences to aggression.

There was nothing Adam could do to interfere with any of this. He collected his footage and moved on. As he approached his destination, he passed a few other rooms. Live fire marksmanship, meditation, survivalism. As he got closer to Crowley's office the presence of students thinned out considerably.

With 20 meters left to go, every room was empty. Adam assumed the area was restricted in some way. As Sophia had mentioned, the vents ran out while Adam still had a ways to go to reach Crowley's space.

Adam surveyed the area outside the final exit. It was maybe a 30 foot drop into a small corridor lined with offices and conference rooms, with a large door at the end that obviously belonged to Crowley. Adam could see heat signatures for three Lightworkers, armed with shock rifles and sidearms. Two patrolled the area and one stood guard in front of Crowley's office.

Gonna have to go hot. Need to keep it quiet. Adam thought to himself. He waited until the patrol migrated away from his position and carefully dropped down onto the floor below, controlling the weight of his impact to ensure a silent breach of the space. He quickly and silently slipped into a nearby conference room, one he'd chosen because the blinds were drawn and the lights were off.

Adam grabbed a tablet from the table in the middle of the room, which he assumed controlled the audio/visual presentation display and crouched in the corner by the door. As one of the patrolling guards approached, he tossed the tablet at a nearby chair, making a thud sound and activating the motion sensor lights.

He saw the guard stop and heard him talk into his radio through the door. "Got a noise in conference room B. Gonna check it out. Probably nothing," he said.

Adam watched his highlighted silhouette ready his weapon through his ocular implant. Cautiously, the guard approached the door and slowly slid it open.

Adam calmly squatted in the blind spot behind the door. As the guard entered, he looked right and cleared the space. He looked left. "Looks clear," he reported into his radio.

"Heading back."

He lowered his guard and started to turn around to leave the room. As he turned around, he saw Adam squatting casually in the corner behind the door. Adam put a finger to his lips and mouthed, "Shhhh."

The guard pulled up his weapon to ready it but in the blink of an eye, Adam had grabbed it by the muzzle, released the magazine onto the ground and dismantled the stock, grip and barrel. He dropped the useless gun parts on the ground and jokingly shrugged. He made a face that said "Whoops," and then in one flowing movement, Adam gripped the guard's wrist in a pressure point beneath his thumb, spun his arm behind his back and gripped his neck with the forearm of his free arm and silently choked him to sleep.

He saw the blue aura of the other guard patrolling around the room. *Need to get him before the patrols converge or he'll call it in,* Adam thought. He opened the door and snuck out quietly in a crouch. He saw the guard ahead of him in the hallway with his back turned. Adam ran at him in a crouch. As he came up on him the guard heard him and turned around.

Too late. Adam hit the guard in the throat with a knife hand strike that collapsed his esophagus. The guard started to pull up his gun but Adam kicked in his knee with a heel stomp, forcing him down, and in a fluid, connected motion, Adam grabbed his head and slammed it down onto his knee hard, knocking him out completely. The surgical take-down happened in just a second and produced almost no sound.

With the patrol down, Adam maneuvered to a nearby service panel and drew a connecting wire from the cybernetics kit attached to his wrist and plugged in. His eyes rolled back in his head as he hacked into the security system. He saw the remaining guard stationed outside of Crowley's office from overhead and noticed a security panel behind him. Adam diverted the floor's power to the panel and overloaded it, producing a 50 volt current in a narrow range. In the distance, Adam heard a muffled groan and then a dull thud.

Before unplugging, Adam released the locks on Crowley's door and heard it slide open in the distance. He also erased the security footage from the last several minutes and replaced it with AI generated dummy footage that showed nothing out of the ordinary.

Adam retracted his electrical tether and walked to the door that led to Crowley's office. He picked up the guard's assault rifle as he casually stepped over the guard's unconscious, twitching body and entered the door, which led to a short hallway. On the other end of the hallway was an ornately carved wooden door emblazoned with the same series of animal busts he'd seen when he first entered the compound. A crow, an octopus, a fox, a wolf, an owl, a chameleon, a dragon.

"Looks like I'm in," he reported to Sophia and slowly approached the door.

Adam paused for a moment and scanned the hallway for traps. With the aid of his ocular implant, he checked for any wiring or heat signatures that seemed out of place. Satisfied that there were no surprises in store, he cautiously inched closer to the door.

He took measured steps, careful to keep his footsteps inaudibly light. One foot after another. As he reached the middle of the hallway, he paused to take one last scan. He stood for a moment, thinking that it was bizarre that

Crowley's inner sanctum wouldn't have one final line of defense. He squinted and scanned his surroundings as thoroughly as he could. He still found nothing.

Gotta be missing something, he thought to himself. Wary, he took another step towards the ornate wooden door.

As his foot touched the floor, the heavy door blasted off its hinges with a large crash and flew towards his face. Adam barely had time to react. He deflected the door to the side with his forearm, feeling the thick wood bruise his bone deeply. Following close behind the door was a fist, and the fierce face of a blonde woman with intense blue eyes, rocketing toward him.

She's fast, Adam noted to himself.

Adam barely had time to brace for impact as the punch hit him in the face like a mach truck. Adam felt his eye socket crack as he slid backward. He tried to ready his weapon but before he could even fully raise it, the woman pulled it toward her and catapulted her knee into his torso, breaking multiple ribs cleanly, then pulled the gun from his hands and snapped it in two like a brittle twig.

Adam had just a moment to get a full view of the woman in front of him, serious, intense, slender and built like a soldier, wearing a tank top and tight military fatigues, modestly covering what may have been the most athletically impressive body Adam had ever seen.

Adam raised his hands into a fighting stance as the woman launched a spinning roundhouse kick at the side of his head. It came like a lightning bolt. Even with his augmented reflexes, Adam just barely had time to block the full force of the blow with his arm. As her combat boot struck, he felt the bone in his arm break. The force of the blow sent him flying into the nearby wall with enough momentum to crack and dent the steel wall itself.

Dazed, Adam tried to defend himself as he felt the woman grab his head and slam it twice into her knee before releasing a straight kick that hit him square in the jaw and sent him flying.

Adam landed on his back. He laid there with just enough time to hack up some of the blood pouring into his throat onto the side of his face, before the woman picked him up by his arm and flipped his body over her shoulder, slamming him back down against the hard ground.

Adam's vision was already starting to give out when she mounted his prone body. As his vision darkened, blurred and tinted red with blood, he was able to make out that she was straddled on top of him, repeatedly slamming her fist into his face, each strike turning his vision white and rattling his skull. He tried to put up a defense, but his arms were limp and uselessly batted at her while she pummeled him.

The last thing Adam saw before he passed out was the woman, completely untouched, standing up, unbothered, with no sense of accomplishment or victory, like she'd just finished folding a load of laundry.

6

The Assassination of River Crowley

Adam watched as Alice cut her birthday cake, a dense clod of cricket protein and soy slathered in aspartame and mashed tofu. The colonists did their best to approximate a cake. Her decaying face giggled as maggots slithered around in her empty eye socket, dripping into the food like a drooling ooze.

Adam sat, proudly, and presented her a present. A small meticulously wrapped box. Inside was a hologram collection of interstellar dancers. As Adam reached out his little girl looked at him and smiled, her cracked, purple lips warm, her eyes dazzling with cheer.

As her hand clasped the package her expression changed, and became cold. Adam felt the cake knife slide into his chest. He felt his heart stop.

Alice coldly stared him down. Adam felt his hands reach up and wrap around her little throat and squeeze. He felt the blade in his skin, past his bones, digging through the tissue of his heart.

"Die," she said bluntly.

Adam's grip around her neck slipped as the strength faded from his body. His hand moved to her cheek as she twisted the knife.

"Die. Die. Die," she repeated like a mantra, letting her emotions loose the more she said it until it was intense and fierce, shouted at full volume.

Adam keeled over backwards and Alice jumped on him, stabbing him over and over in the chest, unhinged and maniacal, histrionically screaming "DIE DIE DIE DIE DIE DIE!"

As Adam's vision started to fade, he saw Alice looking down on him, the sweet little girl with blue eyes and blonde hair and vibrant, flush skin. She had sadness in her eyes.

"Wake up," she said in a soft, comforting voice.

Adam felt the side of his face rubbing against firm carpet. He felt crusted blood on his lips, dull ache from swelling lumps around his eyes. His hair was grossly wet from sitting in a puddle of drool, blood and clammy sweat. He groaned and tried to touch his wounds to inspect their severity but he found that his hands were bound.

Adam rolled over and let his eyes drift open. The first thing his vision caught was Lyra, sitting on the corner of a grand mahogany desk, hunched over and resting her head in her hand, boredly tapping her cheek. When he met her eye line she lifted her other hand and gave him a low effort, fingers-only wave.

Adam felt a hand grab him by the hair and jerk his head back. Next thing he knew he was swung into a leather chair in the corner of the room. Aria stepped out from behind him and moved to a spot next to Lyra, watching him expressionlessly, like a prison guard.

"Rise and shine," he heard from a voice to his left. He weakly turned his head and saw Salem, perched on a window nook attached to a bright bay window. She was reading something from a tablet and barely looked up to acknowledge his presence.

Adam scanned the room. Behind the desk he spotted Nyx, multi-tool in hand, adjusting the cybernetic arm of a man whose back was turned to him.

Adam tried to analyze as much as he could about the man he assumed was Crowley. His back was muscular but slim, the build of a man whose discipline was defeating his age. Medium length blonde hair, peppered lightly with premature gray, hung around his neck. His back was covered with scars, and sported a large tattoo of 10 spheres connected by a series of lines, an artistic take on the Kabbalist Sephiroth, surrounded by alchemical signs and symbols, the kind you would see drawn by the ancient magicians of old Earth.

Both his arms were missing, and replaced by nanobot cybernetics. Thick, built arms of stratified titanium.

In front of Crowley was a mirror that went up to his neck, presumably to aid with whatever combination of repairs and grooming Nyx was engaged in. Adam saw Crowley's torso, fit and moderately decorated by a constellation of haphazardly placed scars and black tattoos of various spiritual and totemic animal symbols. The alchemical hand of mysteries, a Hindu Om, the Eye of Horus, an Ouroboros, a raven talon, an octopus tentacle, a dragon's eye, and more.

Adam caught Nyx's attention and Crowley took notice. "He's awake then?" he asked in a voice that was gruff, but entrancing. Weathered, authoritative, but calm.

Nyx nodded and closed the tiny panel on his metallic shoulder that she was tinkering with. Crowley reached both his arms out to the side and stretched. His arms opened up and the mechanisms swirled as they re-calibrated and clamped back into place. Lyra hopped off the counter as Crowley stood up and returned with a button down shirt and held it for him as he slipped his arms in.

When Crowley finished buttoning his shirt, Nyx held up a burgundy blazer for him. He donned it and slowly turned around.

"So," he began. "What did you think of the tour?" Crowley asked.

Adam didn't say anything, partly because his head felt like it was being jack-hammered by heavy machinery and partly because he wasn't sure how to respond.

Crowley waited momentarily for an answer and then raised his eyebrow and, with a slight smile, like he'd give to a student who was acting up but he was still trying to connect with, said, "No? Alright then. I guess I'll talk."

Crowley reached out his hand. A holographic display projected from his palm, showing data and a picture of Adam, his official recruitment photo, a piece of evidence that had long since been scrubbed from anywhere on the net.

"Adam Ikari-Wright. Special Agent first class, EDF special forces. Nine consecutive deployments. Veteran of three interplanetary wars, with honors. Top marks. Top scores. 147 years old, by date."

Crowley shot Adam a glance, looking up with his eyes without moving his head.

"How old are you, actually? When you factor in the time dilation and all the cryo sleep?" Crowley asked.

Adam didn't respond.

Crowley widened his eyes for just a second, expressing exasperation, as he would, Adam imagined, with an unruly student. Crowley clenched his hand into a fist and the holographic dossier vanished. Crowley turned his full attention to Adam, and his expression hardened.

"They sent you here to kill me, did they?" he asked.

Adam didn't respond.

Crowley approached him, maintaining eye contact as his demeanor effortlessly shifted from erudite and supportive to sinister and sociopathic. He reached his hand out under Adam's neck with one finger extended. Crowley maintained eye contact as his finger sharpened to a razor sharp point and slowly extended until it pressed against Adam's carotid artery with surgical precision. Adam returned the eye contact, unwavering, with his soldier's determination.

The two stared each other down for several moments. Crowley sized Adam up. Adam felt like he was looking into his soul. He felt like prey in the talons of a hunting predator.

After a few moments, Crowley retracted his nanobot talon. His face warmed, and filled again with empathy. He leaned against the edge of his desk and clasped his hands together, resting them on his suited knee.

"You're a smart man, Adam. I'm sure you've realized by now that you didn't come here by accident. You were invited," Crowley said.

Old Keiko, Adam thought.

Crowley smiled. "Yes, Old Keiko," he said. Adam wondered if he was reading his mind or predicting his thoughts from micro-expressions in his face like an expert poker player or a street fair mentalist.

"How?" Adam let out, surprised, almost inaudibly, to himself.

"How?" Crowley repeated back to him, clearly. Crowley reached out his hand and the nanobot colony swarmed up from his palm, forming a bubble, which began to take shape as a bird. After a few moments, it had morphed into a form indistinguishable from a real raven. It cawed, and perched itself on Crowley's shoulder.

"My eyes are everywhere, Major," Crowley said, with a slight smile.

Adam felt that minor twinge of panic that, for the untrained, would blossom into fear, as he was forced to recontextualize the events of the last several months, not to mention the last several hours, knowing he'd been watched the entire time.

"How long have I been watching you?" Crowley asked him, somewhat tauntingly. "Oh, it's much worse than that, I'm afraid."

"Don't you recognize me?" said Crowley's bird, its voice technologically augmented to sound like an old Andromedan ward boss auntie. Its skin began to shift, and within a few moments, Adam was face to face with Old Keiko herself.

Adam's eyes widened with shock.

"They have a compound set up in a system in the un-explored Andromedan Zodiak Cluster. The moon of the ninth planet in the Djevica System," the bird, now an old woman, said in Old Keiko's voice. Adam remembered the conversation.

"It was you?" he squinted in disbelief. "How?" Adam asked.

Crowley raised his eyebrow. "How? What do you mean how?" he looked at Nyx, and Lyra, then back at Adam. He pointed at the old woman. "Didn't you see the bird trick?" he asked, bemused.

Old Keiko's body dissolved into a puddle of nanobots, which then raised into the air like an insect swarm and reabsorbed into Crowley's arm.

Crowley looked at Adam seriously. "I invited you here, Adam," he said. "After all you've seen, do you really believe any agent you think works for you doesn't work for us?"

Adam couldn't mask his shock. How deep did Crowley's infiltration of the EDF go? He had entered this mission thinking Crowley was a backwater cult leader, and now he'd seen a dimension hacking quantum AI, a girl who can bend reality, an army capable of challenging Centauri asymmetrically, and an intelligence service that penetrated the most sophisticated spy agency in the galaxy.

Crowley continued to explain, deadpan. "I'm everywhere, Mr. Wright. My voice is in the music people hear. When the algorithm shows the people what to hear, they hear me, subliminally. I'm in the artwork spray painted on the streets of Andromedan Prime and Centauri. My message is hidden in plain sight in the vidscreens and the metaverses," he said.

He continued, "These governments, these megacorps,

think they control what people see and hear, but I'm there, whispering across the galaxy to everyone who longs for a better future. When someone out there in the colonies becomes inspired to look to the stars to chase a better life, that's me, DJing the algorithms that program people's reality."

"You think I'm one man," Crowley said. "But I'm split, in millions of accounts, and algorithms, and bodies, watching and whispering to all those who dare to defy these devaluing systems of control. And when they, those few who dream, reach out to the stars to chase their dream, they find my outstretched hand, showing them the map toward freedom. And some, like you, chase that map, and find their way here."

"You thought we met for the first time here, in this office. And you learned we met before, on Andromeda Prime. But you met me much earlier, in symbols in the artwork and the music, the films, the poetry, the inspirational messages. Every clever fox, every illuminating magician, every foolhardy jester, every determined rebel, every watchful owl, every character that speaks the truth from the shadows, that's me. You've known me for a long time, Adam. You've seen my myriad masks," he said.

Crowley stretched out his arms.

"I'm The Magician, Adam. Do you understand? The Universe pulled my card this season, and I've come to fulfill my task. To expose the truth of things," he said.

Crowley concluded his speech and looked at Adam expectantly.

"I think I get it," Adam growled through his beaten lips.

Crowley raised an eyebrow and asked, "And what do you get?"

"You're a sociopathic narcissist," Adam replied coldly.

Crowley pinched the bridge of his nose and sighed.

"Do you have any idea what these organizations are responsible for? The *suffering* that they create? We have the technology to defeat *scarcity itself*. We have the ability to bend reality to our will, to make reality indistinguishable from imagination and make it a safe place for every living soul to explore and experience, but these regimes operate by control, all in service to their desire for domination and power. Status expressed through control. Power expressed through enslavement and castes," Crowley said.

"And I suppose as supreme leader you'll be different? History's tried its share of megalomaniacs. No one's seen a utopia yet," Adam replied. "Exchanging one army for another. For everyone outside the regime it's all the same. It's all always the same."

"No," Crowley said. "I have no intention of ruling anything. Just giving the people what they've deserved all along. Freedom. Agency. Abundance. Knowledge. That we now have the technology to give, and these people restrict. Life to explore or waste on anyone's terms. To pursue love or work or leisure or anything, on their timeline. On their terms. Full agency over how they spend their lives. Not slaves to agendas. Grand projects they had no hand in designing. Temples to wealth and power."

Adam scoffed. "Sure," he said dismissively. "Sounds great." Adam gestured his head toward Aria. "Is that why you need this living weapon over here? To liberate the oppressed people of the EDF *democracy*?" he asked. "Nothing screams freedom like an invading army."

"You think the EDF is a democracy?" Crowley sighed. "A

democracy is where people tell their government what they want. In the EDF, the government and the corporations tell their people what they should want, and the people echo back to their rulers what they've been told."

"These systems aren't built to benefit anyone but the people who made them, Adam. The EDF, with its old money fraternities, descended from the royalty of old Earth. The Centauri Federation with its merchant families, who ruthlessly maintain control of the shipping lanes and colonies that prop up their rule. The Technocracy and its felonious meritocracy, where human worth is earned through soul crushing, robotic labor, forcing its citizens to sell their time, their very lives, to their hollow mission of *more*," Crowley said.

Crowley paused. "Do you know how I lost my arms?" he asked.

"I suppose you're going to tell me," Adam replied.

"Come on, have a guess," Crowley responded.

The two stared at each other for a moment. "Wood chipper?" Adam joked.

Crowley laughed a little, then his face hardened, and thinly veiled rage filled his demeanor as he spoke. "When I was a boy, when the Technocracy usurped the colonists who built Andromeda from nothing, their followers came to my parents' home with bats and clubs. They beat my parents to death in front of me, and then held me down and sawed my arms off with my father's band saw and left me for dead," Crowley said. "Can you imagine my screams? As that rusty, neglected, hobbyist saw ripped through my flesh and its motor struggled to cut through my bones?"

"Does that sound like the behavior of the righteous stewards of the future, as they describe themselves in their State media? Or does that sound like the behavior of a brutal gang that serves its own interests and perpetuates a cycle of domination and power achieved by rewarding human cruelty?" Crowley asked.

He was quiet for a moment, and then continued softly, "I'm not here to be remembered well by history, Adam. I'm here to do what needs to be done. You're not naive. The world as it is, its agenda is set by power. The chess game at the heart of it all. And the winner sets the agenda. If you want to change the game to something else, you have to win the game as it is. I'm not preparing a regime to rule, Adam Ikari-Wright. I'm positioning the pieces to win."

Crowley paused. He looked at Salem, who shrugged and slightly shook her head. He looked at Lyra, who returned a disappointed expression. He looked at Aria who looked back at him comfortingly, supportively. And then at Nyx whose expression was stoic and unreadably stern, but Adam could tell Crowley had the ability to interpret it.

Crowley looked back at Adam.

"You have two options. Join with us, follow me, and see what comes next," he looked into Adam's eyes, reading his intentions. "Or," he added, "Follow me and fulfill your mission."

Crowley held out his arm in Salem's direction. She handed him the datapad she'd been holding onto. Crowley looked at Adam and held it up, hinting at its importance. Then he placed it, intentionally conspicuously, on the desk. He clasped his hands in front of himself.

"Give it some thought," he said. "Goodnight."

Crowley nodded at Aria. Her fist hit his face like a speeding train. His vision went black immediately.

Before Adam passed out, he heard Crowley's voice.

"Meet me on Draconis," he whispered.

7

What Comes Next

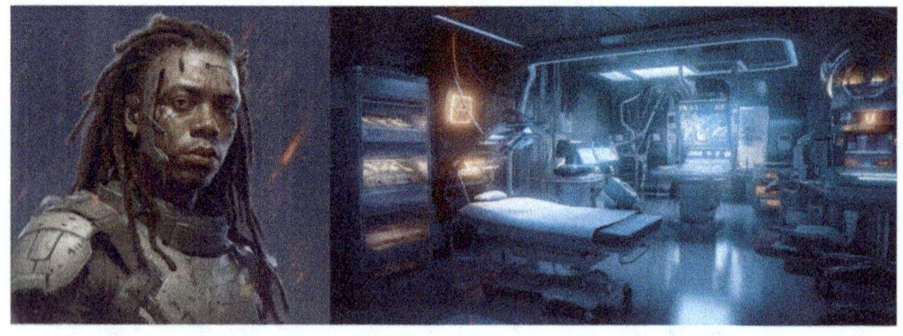

Once the auto-doc on the Oneiro-Lyssa had finished stitching up Adam's wounds and pumping him full of painkillers, he had shambled to his bunk and fallen into bed to tough out a long recovery.

His face had been stitched in multiple places that had deep lacerations. His torso was wrapped to reduce movement that might hinder the healing of his broken ribs. His arm had been set in a 3d printed, hard plastic cast. He faced a long recovery. Unfortunately for Adam, he had to heal the old fashioned way - cryosleep would only preserve his wounds.

He was drugged up and delirious, falling in and out of sleep so often he couldn't tell how many days had passed, what time it was, or how long he'd been asleep. When he did wake up, he downed more pills and whatever he could find on board that would pass for alcohol.

He was in that recovery period where medicine had done all it could and life itself came with a baseline ache that felt like it had always been there and always would be, interrupted only by intense, acute pain when his bruises or his bigger wounds were disturbed by clumsy movement.

As Adam recovered he recalled the events that followed his meeting with the cult leader, River Crowley.

He remembered waking up in Crowley's office, with Crowley and his lieutenants, the four leaders of Djevica 9's four college houses, long gone. He had been completely undisturbed. He recalled looking out the window and seeing students outside Crowley's office, mingling on the grassy quad like it was any other day.

It felt like the room had been left intentionally for Adam to explore and inspect at his leisure. Whatever he found in there, he imagined at the time, he was meant to find.

The first thing Adam had taken a look at was the datapad that Crowley had intentionally left for him on the desk. The datapad was mostly wiped. Its interface had the look of a freshly wiped machine, clean and sterile, not cluttered with the mess of personal files that people's machines accumulate over time.

Though the datapad was mostly a fresh install, the files it did have stood out all the more. The first folder Adam explored seemed to be a detailed dossier on Adam himself. First it showed his profile and military record. It showed his performance reviews in OTC, his marksmanship honors, his CQB certifications. His distinguished service medals. His silver star. His Legion of Merit.

It didn't show the experiences that led to those commendations, though. It didn't show the 19 mile hike they made him take on the cold side of Mars with 140 pounds of gear. It didn't show his only friend in OTC, Ant Conroy, tapping out because he couldn't hack it, crying as a grown man because he failed his dream with only himself to blame. It didn't show him wiping down cyberweave exoskeletons until he felt like he knew them better than the engineers that designed them. It didn't show him getting ocular implants grafted onto his eyes or the surgery for the HBI implanted in his brain, both of which he had to stay fully awake for.

It mentioned his distinguished service medal that he got serving in the Centauri-Martian War, the minor conflict the two powers had over their politicians' inability to come to an agreement about who owned the Gates for some shipping lanes for rare earth metals imported from Centauri. "Distinguished Service Medal" seemed so clinical. Adam got it for popping off the heads of 23 Centauri soldiers, including 4 officers and a Colonel with a PSG-9A from 3 miles away in heavy Centauri gravity. Even then, what Adam mostly remembered was camping in that miserable desert for six weeks.

More interestingly, the dossier showed his psych evals. Most of it was standard stuff for Special Forces. Dutifulness, emotional stability, ability to maintain composure in high stress situations. What was interesting, though, was the amount of information that, even in this incredible curation of classified intelligence on an EDF operative, was blacked out or missing. Lots of notes "REF: Project Mockingbird", but all the reference links were dead.

"Subject seems to be adjusting following traumatic experiences defending the Europa Mining Expedition. REF: Project Mockingbird." Europa, he remembered he was playing bodyguard for some Corp that was drilling for carbon they could ship to Europa Station. The whole thing went smoothly. It was routine, and Adam barely remembered it. He wasn't sure what this report was talking about.

"In our conversation, Subject has reported showing signs of emotional attachment to the asset he was assigned on Azraq Centauri Station. Situation has been adjusted. REF: Project Mockingbird." Adam remembered Azraq Centauri, but he didn't remember any "emotional attachment." He remembered torching a local bar and kidnapping a Centauri arms dealer.

"The Subject has shown signs of sympathy following the execution of his mission on a foreign operative at Delta black site [redacted]. Adjustment is advised. REF: Project Mockingbird." Adam recalled debriefing his CO on this mission. He wasn't sure "sympathy" was the right word for beating a guy to death in a dark room.

"The incident on Titan continues to trouble Major Ikari-Wright, despite multiple clinical interventions. Standard PTSD treatment has proven inadequate. I'm referring him to Dr. Kimber at Mockingbird. CO Lt. Colonel Iscariot has been informed. REF: Project Mockingbird." Titan. He killed that little girl. He just didn't want to admit it to himself. He knew that. He didn't know why he remembered being friends with her, giving her gifts. He didn't know why he kept having nightmares about it.

They were messing with his head, Adam surmised from the documents. But he knew that already. They'd messed with his eyes, his body, why not his brain, too? His body was a tool of the EDF. He was an asset, an investment of finances, time and energy. He didn't have a problem with this. Still, he was curious why this information was so redacted. His file was already classified – why were his psych therapies classified beyond classified?

"Sophia," Adam had said. "Do a search for keyword 'Project Mockingbird,' deep web censorship special authorization Delta Omega Omega Bravo Niner."

Sophia searched for a moment, longer than usual, long enough for Adam to know the search would come up empty, before replying, "I'm sorry, Adam. I'm not able to find any information on that."

Adam had nodded to himself and continued to explore what other files Crowley had left on the little gift he'd left for him.

Adam opened the next folder and found a star map detailing a route to the planet Draconis, far in distant space. The route led into the heart of the SagDIG galaxy, unexplored, isolated space at the farthest edge of the Local Group.

What was more concerning to Adam than the distance or remoteness of the planet was that Crowley had found it at all. Draconis was a planet everyone had heard of. As children. It was a myth. Draconis was a planet talked about in children's stories.

When the first colonists who'd been abandoned on TRAPPIST-1 learned after 9 generations that they were colonized by the EDF and didn't spontaneously evolve out of the biology of their home planet, the theory emerged that Earth itself had been colonized and forgotten, or that its colonizers had gone extinct. That theory was widely considered absurd, for several strong scientific reasons, strongest of all because there was no direct evidence, but most *importantly* because it insulted the sense of specialness and superiority of Earth's ruling class and their ancient noble lineage, as well as the universities whose ecclesiastical authority would unravel if their theory about the origin of mankind was disproved.

In all the years of sophisticated space colonization since, no one had ever discovered a planet developed or ancient enough to have possibly been responsible for colonizing old Earth. As a result, people's imagination took hold and thus the imaginary planet, Draconis, was invented and became a popular myth.

Once upon a time, there had been some exoplanets in the Draco constellation named Draconis, but they had been renamed as, by the time they were explored, the myth had already spread, and those lifeless planets didn't match the Draconis people had invented in their minds.

And yet, for Crowley, who seemed to be privy to secrets of the universe few others were, it wasn't a myth, apparently. It was a real planet, listed as plainly as Alpha Centauri on the star chart he'd left behind, and its location was pinpointed clearly in SagDIG.

"Meet me on Draconis," he'd said. When Adam had heard those words the first time, he thought it was some sort of metaphor. But it wasn't. Crowley, Adam surmised, was actually en route to a planet that, as far as anyone else in the universe was concerned, was fictional.

As Adam recalled the final events on Djevica 9, he writhed around on his bunk, struggling to sleep here and there, sweating through his sheets.

He remembered looking in the final folder of Crowley's datapad. The datapad had seemed to be, more than anything else, a gilded invitation to whatever Crowley had planned on Draconis. In the final folder, Adam had found thousands, possibly tens of thousands of logs recorded by Crowley himself, stretching back years.

He opened the first one and listened to a few seconds of it. The audio file began and moments of silence and crackling noise played before Crowley's calm voice came through.

"We made it to Djevica 9, me and Salem. It's a destitute little moon. Just rock, busted up rock everywhere. But it'll do. We've spent long enough planning. Planning and learning. Now we begin the work. The long work of applying our vision," Crowley said.

"They're going to think it's about revenge," he continued. "They, those closed minded specialists who see the universe only through realpolitik and control. They're going to think we think like they think. I often try to figure out how we could make them see, see what we learned through suffering, by igniting our own light in the depths of hopelessness. From finding each other. From crafting the will to live in a sadistic universe from inside the welcoming hug of caring death."

"I wonder if they can understand. I wonder if they're capable of understanding," he concluded.

Crowley's voice petered out and left Adam with only the crackling and white noise of the audio until that, too, ended.

With thousands of logs to go through, Adam hadn't

bothered to listen to more. He was still trespassing in unfriendly territory.

Adam recalled as he left Crowley's office and limped, wounded and unsightly, back to his ship. He recalled as the students watched him, some judgmentally, others curiously, but none interfered. Crowley's orders, obviously, were to let him leave unharmed.

Adam recalled walking as tall as he was able until he reached the hatch of the Oneiro-Lyssa. As soon as he'd gotten inside he gave up any pretense of appearing anything but utterly physically dismantled by Crowley's terrifyingly capable lieutenant, Aria. He collapsed against the hatch of the Oneiro-Lyssa.

"Sophia, get us out of here," he'd instructed.

"Where to, Adam?" Sophia had asked cheerfully. As an AI, she struggled to read the room from time to time.

"Doesn't matter," Adam had responded weakly, starting to doze off. "Just get us the hell out of this system and park somewhere. We'll tackle the destination..." he continued, losing energy, "Later."

As the craft had lifted, Adam had nodded off.

8

Debrief Me, Iscariot

"I've spoken with the brass about this, Wright. You're going to be pursuing Crowley into SagDIG. You will neutralize him as a threat by any means necessary. Do you understand your mission?" asked a larger than life hologram of a head that belonged to Adam's commanding officer.

"Sir," Adam said as an affirmative.

The Colonel's gaunt face frowned. "There aren't any gates past Andromeda 3 except a few experimental jump points in LGS 3 and the Triangulum. You're going to have to fly into SagDIG the old fashioned way. The time dilation's going to fuck you up," Colonel Iscariot added.

Adam nodded. "Won't be the first time, sir," he said.

Iscariot laughed. "By the time you get there you might be reporting to the next generation of leadership," he said.

"Respectfully, sir, you'll be a dinosaur by the time I even get to LGS," Adam replied. "Is Command even going to remember this mission by the time I get to Draconis?"

Iscariot smiled. "Who knows, son. Life expectancy goes up every day. They may crack the code for immortality by the time you get there," he said with a hint of knowing something Adam didn't. "At least they'll have a fix for my hairline by then. Of that I'm certain."

Immortality, Adam thought. *The final changing of the guard in human history. After that, it's just the current leadership until the end of time. Complete obsolescence.*

"Gonna need a team, sir," Adam said.

Iscariot furled his brow and looked down, peering at Adam's report off screen. "For this… Amazonian super soldier, is that right?" he asked. He laughed a little. "You're losing your touch, Major. Thought you were the best of the best."

"Preparation is the best weapon, sir. She's not the only one who's dangerous. There are three others, and Crowley's a slippery player himself. Plus who knows what's out there. We're going into unexplored space," Adam replied.

"I was just fucking with you, Wright. You're cleared for a team. Who do you want?" Iscariot asked.

Adam didn't have to think. He knew the answer.

"Give me the twins," he replied quickly.

Iscariot nodded. "Done. Anyone else?" he asked.

"No one comes to mind," Adam said.

"Good," Iscariot replied, "Because I have some assignments for you. You're getting Raziel Graves. You familiar?"

"I've heard of him. Up and comer," Adam said.

Iscariot nodded. "Some might say he's the next *you*. Show him the ropes, will you?"

"Sir," Adam replied in affirmation. "Anyone else?" he asked.

"Yeah. Jackie Visken, code name Vice," he said.

"The hacker?" Adam asked.

Iscariot nodded. "That's the one. GSA whiz kid," he said. "One more thing. The civilian leadership wants you to bring a tag along. Some university egghead. They want someone to study all this unexplored space you're going into. So you're going to have to play babysitter and zero Crowley at the same time. His name is…" the Colonel looked at the datapad. "Hmm," he said. "Don't see it actually."

Adam nodded. "Understood," he said.

"Alright. You're gonna rendezvous on Andromedan Exxon 2, the way station. Everyone will meet you there. I'll set it up with the twins. Aztec is on Andromeda anyway, shouldn't be hard to re-task him to Exxon 2. Any questions?"

Adam replied, "Do we have any intel on Draconis? Anything classified?"

Iscariot chuckled. "Yeah. We know all about Draconis. It's where the tooth fairy lives with Santa Claus, storks and leprechauns," Iscariot said. "Look, I don't want to bullshit you, son. It's very possible you jump 200 years into the future and there's nothing there."

Adam pondered for a moment. "This Crowley guy, he's that important we're gonna follow him on a wild goose chase of his own design?"

"Brass wants him dead. They're pretty adamant. You need to make that happen. I'm gonna double check with you one last time, are you good for this mission?"

Adam nodded. "I'm your man," he said.

"Good. Get going to Exxon 2. I'll reach out if anything comes up. Iscariot out," said the Colonel.

Adam saluted as the hologram face dissipated. Once it was gone he slouched back in his chair.

"You catch all that, Soph?" he asked in no direction in particular.

"Yes, Adam," she replied. "We'll get to explore a whole new system. Isn't that exciting?" she responded cheerfully.

Adam nodded, deadly serious, fully aware of the danger of not only the mission, but unexplored space and the way the politics would shift under his feet during the time dilation. "Exciting," he said, deadpan sarcastic, "Yeah, that's what it is."

"Yay! I can't wait!" Sophia replied earnestly.

II

Aesir Colony

9

The Squad

It was a two week trip from the outskirts of the Zodiak Cluster to Exxon 2. Exxon 2 was a way station, so luckily the trip was only as far as the trip to the nearest gate.

Adam was still on the mend, but he'd turned a corner and was beginning to feel normal again, save for some lingering aches and a clicking when he moved his wrist that he assumed was just how it was going to be from then onward.

He spent most of the trip the same way he did whenever he was isolated in deep space, sitting on the bridge blasting music and asking Sophia to ask him questions to keep him from going stir crazy.

He had thousands of hours of Crowley's logs to get through, but he wasn't in much of a rush, knowing that the trip to SagDIG was going to take the better part of a year and include multiple rounds of long term cryosleep.

Still, he had begun listening to Crowley's logs as part of his daily routine. They were numerous, and most of them were uninteresting, recounting mundane daily activities. What Crowley had for lunch, reviewing agenda items from routine meetings, that sort of thing. Adam had given up listening to them in any particular order. He just picked them at random, without regard for when they were recorded or what they might be about.

During his brief jump to Exxon 2, Adam did stumble across one entry that caught his attention. He listened to it as he got to the gate for Exxon Station.

"Aria's been with us for almost a year now. She's a veteran from Centauri. We brought her in to teach self defense and survival strategies.

Salem took to her almost immediately, and I trust her judgment when it comes to people. Now I can see why. She's quite a person. Honest. She has all these causes, and she really cares. When you get to know her, she's all about her pets, her rabbit and her dogs.

She's not a schemer like us, me and Salem. I'm much more cerebral and Salem's more emotional, but we're both complex by nature, planners who play life like a poker game. Aria's right there on the surface, very easy to read.

She takes joy in nurturing others like I've never seen. She loves to cook. She knows everyone's favorite foods. When she makes lunch for Lei, she goes the extra mile and makes everything cute, and cuts things into fun shapes. It's not work to her. It's her natural drive, like research is with me.

My love feels like mentorship. Salem's love feels like understanding. But Aria's love feels like love, the way you imagine it in stories. It's kind, it's warm, it's proactive, and it comes at you, and you feel like a big hug is all around you.

I think that's good for Lei. She needs that. She spends a lot of time despondent, just staring off into space, blank and unhappy, like she's seen the true heart of the universe and found it bitterly disappointing.

Salem likes her. They like to try on outfits together. You'd never guess it when she's training, but Aria spends most of her time in sundresses. She's very feminine.

I think Salem likes the idea that her friend can beat up anyone who'd threaten her or her family. Including me. I let them tease me a bit.

It's nice, I think, to be able to let your guard down. When I was surviving, hiding my identity as a refugee in Antares, you couldn't show weakness. If someone tested you in any way, you had to rip out their throat, dramatically, and publicly, or the hyenas and the vultures and snakes would circle you on all sides.

Everyone likes her. I like her too. She has a big heart."

When Adam got to Exxon 2, after warping in through the gate, he deboarded and headed toward the rendezvous point.

Adam hadn't been to this particular station before, but all the Exxon stations had a similar layout and amenities. Some chain motel options in a few price ranges, the ones that had a contract with the Corp. They ranged from capsule beds to small short term suites. The standard fare food court and convenience shops. He was in Andromeda so there were a lot more noodles and tofu barbecue pork than you'd find on the stations out in the Milky Way.

The rendezvous was in the back of the military recruitment office in one of the meeting rooms there. Adam was the first to arrive. He got there and waited.

It wasn't long before the door opened and the first of the crew members he was going to be traveling with for the next year arrived.

In walked a massive, muscular, olive skinned man with military tattoos all over his gorilla-like forearms and neck. He was genetically modified, and what skin wasn't covered in tattoos of skulls, flames, guns and knives was dotted with panther spots. His curly, tied up hair was fitted with cultural rings and beads. As he entered, he had a huge grin on his face that showed off his beastly fangs.

"Oi, hermano, long time no see. How long's it been, ay?" the man said as he came in for a big hug. "Haven't seen you since we were in the shit with those scavengers out near Vega."

Adam displayed an uncharacteristic smile. "Aztec. My man. Good to see you alive. Heard you were on Prime. What'd they have you doing down there?" he asked.

Aztec took a seat on one of the meeting room couches, threw his leg up on the table and put his arms behind his head.

"Oh y'know, standard false flag preparation. Down there funding, arming, training Andromedan disgruntles so if we get in the shit we can activate em and blow up protests all over the planet if the Technocracy does anything we don't like. They think they're joining some kind of homegrown political militia," he said.

"Who's your CO? Martinez?" asked Adam.

"Nah. Panzer. Full bird Colonel. Army-CIA joint," Aztec replied.

"Ah, yeah. That op sounds like Panzer. See any action down there?" Adam asked.

"Nah, nothing spicy. Just some street fights here and there with the rival faction, who are also working for us," said Aztec.

"Well, you're gonna love this one. Top Secret assassination run, straight from Centcom. We're gonna be on the road for a while, though. Hope you won't miss Andromeda," Adam said.

Aztec laughed. "Nah man, this shit on Andromeda is mostly just lying to college students about politics, getting em all fired up to be useful. Get to knock some heads around here and there, but nothing exciting. Can't even have a reason to polish my minigun," he said.

"That's good. Glad I got you. Where's your sister?" Adam asked.

"Should be here any minute. They called her in from Cat's Eye. She was out there retrieving some palladium tiara that got heisted from some jewelry show out of Meili-Alpha by spacers," Aztec replied.

"Think she got it?" Adam inquired.

Aztec guffawed. "Yeah man, knowing her, yeah she definitely got it. She got it and somewhere out there is a spacer freighter full of pirates who thought they were hard with piss in their pants. That bitch is terrifying. I wouldn't steal from her, that's for sure," Aztec said.

As he finished, the door opened up once again.

"Speak of the devil," Aztec added, as a slender woman

stepped in. Short hair, cat ears, and cat eyes, decked out with a cybernetic arm and an AR reticle over one eye. Her fatigues holstered a half a dozen knives, a sidearm and a foldable sniper rifle slung across the back of her waist.

She saluted Adam as she walked in. "Morning boys," she said. "Hope I'm not late to the party."

"Just getting started, Tez," Aztec said.

"Good to see you, Tezca," Adam said. "Have a seat. We're waiting on a couple others."

"You got it, Boss," Tezca said as she tossed her rifle on the table and sat down in a chair across from her brother.

"How'd the Cat's Eye job go?" Aztec asked her.

"Highlights?" Tezca said with a slight smile. "Hogtied their Captain, this big fat guy, made him sing like a canary. Got the goods, got a bunch of other stuff on top of it. Dumped it all off on Mars. They're gonna be sifting through stolen merch for a week."

The door opened and two more people walked in.

The first was a brown skinned man with a cool, trendy haircut wearing a leather racers jacket. He had a Korth NXR revolver, heavily modded with a laser sight and other customizations Adam couldn't decipher at a glance holstered on one side of his leg. The young man saluted Adam as he entered.

The second was a black haired woman with meticulously trimmed bangs wearing a black bomber jacket and black track pants with a red stripe. She had a tattoo of a black line from the top of her eyebrow to below her eye. Slung across her back was a messenger bag with a hacker's deck in it.

Adam welcomed the two in the room and shook each of their hands.

"You must be Lt. Graves," he said to the young man as he shook his hand. "Heard a lot about you. Have a seat."

He turned his attention to the woman, "And looks like you're our hacker on loan from the GSA," he said.

"Jackie," the woman said, introducing herself. "Everyone calls me Vice. Happy to be here. Been trying to get more time in the field."

"Happy to have you," Adam said. "Hope you like road trips."

With the main crew accounted for, everyone looked to Adam expectantly, waiting for the meeting to start.

"We've got one more," he said. "Civilian."

"Ah," Tezca mouthed.

"Guess he's got that civilian time management, ay ustedes?" Aztec said with a laugh.

"Alright, since we've got some time, let's do introductions. I assume everyone doesn't know each other. You're all the best of the best. I'll just go around the room," Adam said.

He gestured at Aztec. "This muscle giant is Aztec Rai. Heavy weapons, undercover ops. Genetic infusion, gorilla DNA and jaguar. Legend has it the lion's the king of the jungle. Pretty sure in a fair fight, it'd be this guy."

"Next," Adam continued, "Tezca Rai. These two," he pointed at Aztec and Tezca, "Are twins. You wouldn't guess it. But it's true. Tezca is also genetically modified wildcat. As true an operative as you'll find anywhere. Want something done in the dark, metaphorically or literally, she'll get it done."

Adam pointed at Raziel. "Raziel Graves. Lots of chatter about him. Just a few years out of ranger school and he's already been made lieutenant. Not only that, he's here on this squad. He may be young but his record's elite among elite."

"Jackie Visken, aka Vice. We're borrowing her from GSA, she's gonna be our hacker. Not only does that mean getting in and out of computer systems, but getting in and out of places she shouldn't be, physically. Cybersecurity, it turns out, involves a lot of breaking and entering."

The team all made introductory gestures and nods.

"So who are we missing?" asked Jackie.

"Civilian," Adam said, somewhat annoyed. "Hope he gets here soon. Sooner he gets here, sooner we can get on with it."

As Adam spoke, the door opened and an Asian man in his late thirties who looked disheveled and detached walked in.

"You must be Grant," Adam said.

The man, dorky and timid, but excited, reached out his hand. "Ah, yes. Dr. Grant Fourier-Lee. It's nice to meet you, ah… officer," he said in a distracted monotone.

Adam shook his hand and simply replied, "Have a seat. We're just getting started. I'm afraid you're going to be the odd man out on some things, since you're the only civilian. For starters, if we're starting at 0800, you're gonna want to get here at 0800. Couple more minutes and we would've left without you."

The doctor nodded politely, still seeming as though he wasn't entirely present. "Sorry," he gestured to the room of hardened soldiers, "Sorry, everyone. I don't usually travel outside the system, I'm afraid I got a little bit lost."

Adam nodded. "It's alright. Just easing you in. This is going to be a dangerous mission. We understand you're hitching a ride, and we'll do our best to take it easy on you, but we have a serious mission and that's our priority, you're gonna have to be able to look after yourself."

"Everyone," Adam continued, "This is Dr. Grant Fourier-Lee, he is a professor of astro-anthropology from Oxford-Seoul University on Earth. For us meatheads here in station, that's arguably the top institution of higher learning in the known universe. So make sure you show him respect," Adam said.

The room filled briefly with quiet greetings and gestures of acknowledgment.

"Aztec, get him up to speed on introductions later," Adam added before quickly moving on. "Alright. Now. Let me tell you why you're all here."

Adam touched a button on his wrist-mounted computer and a hologram of Crowley floated above his arm.

"This is our target. River Crowley, aka Crowley Trismegistus, aka Mr. Mythos, aka The Magician, aka The Wolf, The Tiger, The Dragon and about six hundred thousand other names. We'll be here all day. After I met him, I looked into this, and he's behind millions of accounts across every inter and intra-net in the Universe. An amount of reach and influence that rivals propaganda networks run by governments," Adam explained.

"What's interesting is," Adam continued. "Very few of these accounts link back to Crowley himself. It's a completely decentralized movement. His own accounts are inconspicuous. Few or zero followers. The accounts in his network, some are run by bots, some by deep state intelligence, some by civilians who take inspiration from the posts on his small accounts."

"The vast majority of it, though, is people who have no connection or knowledge of Crowley whatsoever, and are simply participating in what they see as a quiet culture and arts movement with no knowledge of its origin."

"This is a universe-wide propaganda psyop that most intelligence agencies would struggle to put together, all, seemingly, run by Crowley himself. Which means he either put the whole thing together himself, or he's working for someone, or he was working for someone and he turned."

Tezca jumped in. "So, what's the propaganda? He's anti-Technocracy, right? So, standard stuff? Insert enemy here, evil, eats babies, hates birthday parties, little dicks?"

Adam nodded. "Not exactly. It's all very inspirational. Be who you truly are, free yourself from your programming, go after the life you know you want in your heart. Become who you were meant to be. Not stated directly, obviously, but that's sort of the ongoing theme of all this music and artwork and everything else. Reach for the stars. Hope."

"There's a lot of stuff about being a speck in an infinite universe in the span of infinite time, ride the ride while you're here, don't waste your life on someone else's dream. Memento Mori, remember you'll die, you only have a limited time here so don't waste it. Lots of repeating motifs, mostly to do with futurism and spirituality," Adam added.

Aztec chimed in. "So we're, what, we're gonna kill this guy because he's the most effective motivational speaker in the Universe?" he asked.

"Crowley is shrewd. He's preaching self-actualization, but the outcome of widespread adoption of his belief system is a population primed for individualism and free thinking, which would be destabilizing for every major player. EDF, Centauri and Andromeda all rely on control and social conformity," Adam answered.

"These governments don't want self-sustaining, self-actualized people who peacefully pursue their own dreams and aspirations. They want laborers, partisans and true believers who give up their autonomy for the agendas of the State," he added.

"More than that," Adam continued. "Crowley knows that most people are not capable of critical thinking or independent thought. If he's truly plugged into the inter-galactic intelligence community which, I would guess, he either came from or infiltrated, he knows that most people were intentionally evolved to be incapable of independent thought, like a sort of human livestock. Now, maybe he intends to liberate them, but maybe he just wants to switch their programming to a new leader."

"The only thing that's certain is that his motivations are unclear," he said. "Is it some kind of spiritual mission, to spread the tenets of self-actualization. Or is the goal destabilization of the existing political structure to create an opening for his army?"

"Because most motivational speakers don't seem to have or feel the need to have an army capable of challenging major governments in open warfare, a best-in-class intelligence operation, cutting edge technology with military applications, a battalion of brainwashing headshrinks, or the means, motive and opportunity to displace established government authorities," Adam continued.

"It's hard to see what his endgame is. It's easy to see why the EDF, and everyone else, considers him a threat," he added.

Raziel jumped in. "You met him," he said, quietly and calmly. "What's your read?"

"Hard to say. I think he's a madman. Equal parts sinister

and inspiring," Adam replied. "Which one are you getting, which one's the real one? The madman or the preacher?"

Adam continued, "Crowley is surrounded by his four lieutenants. Lieutenants, wives, concubines, brainwashed devotees, who knows how to really characterize it. In any case you have…"

He touched his wrist and the hologram changed to a profile of Salem.

"Salem Wagner. This appears to be Crowley's number 1. Top of class psychiatrist from Kepler 22b. Three PhDs, a litany of subspecialties. Last official location was somewhere out in the Scorpio Cluster, helping reintegrate refugees who fled the Technocracy. Looks like he recruited her there," Adam said.

He touched his wrist again.

"Next up is the woman who calls herself Nyx, real name Beatrice Cavendish," Adam said. "Another EDF academic. She was working in the Andromedan university system. Quantum physics, quantum engineering, mathematics, computer science, robotics, electrical engineering, materials science and… three music performance degrees, apparently. Says here she got her first advanced degree when she was 11. If we thought Salem was smart, Nyx makes her look like a kid playing with crayons. At least as far as the book smarts go."

Adam touched his wrist yet again.

"Lyra Bouchard," Adam continued. "Was set to be Andromedan royalty, before the Technocracy took over. Not too much else is known about her. She was a star gymnast and dancer, top marks in school. When I was on Djevica 9, she was running their athletics department, called The

Dragons. Do not underestimate her. She's the top person on a planet full of tough people for a reason. She is to be considered very dangerous."

Adam touched his wrist one final time.

"Lastly," Adam said. "Aria Dawn-Kumo. She's a veteran from Centauri. I looked into this a little more and, while there isn't much to be found on her, it seems like she self-liberated from a slave mining colony when she was young and then enlisted in the Centauri Frontier-Guard. I had a run in with her. She is… Intense."

Raziel raised his hand. "Are these four women part of our designation?" he asked.

Adam nodded. "Unmentioned. Alive, dead, doesn't matter to brass. They just want Crowley. He's the player. They're just pieces," he said.

Raziel nodded. "Heard," he said.

Vice chimed in. "So that's who we're chasing. Where are we chasing them to?" she asked.

Adam smiled. "Glad you asked. That's the fun part. Or, not so fun if you're attached to anyone back home. Hold onto your butts," he said.

He touched his wrist again and displayed blurry satellite footage of a planet.

"Our intel confirms that they're headed to SagDIG Capernicus2224a, aka Draconis," Adam said with a touch of excitement. "We're going to fucking Narnia boys and girls."

"Draconis is real?" Aztec asked.

"Apparently," Adam said. "That's why we have this guy," he gestured to Grant, who smiled and waved. "The government wants to know if we find Bigfoot."

"Alright," Adam said. "That's the briefing. I'd say any

questions but we're going to have plenty of time to play twenty questions out on the road. You are all now officially on mission. Wheels up in 2 hours. Get lunch, get friendly with a local, call your mom, whatever you need to get out of your system and can find on a backwater gas station, you've got two hours to take care of it."

"Once we leave, we're not coming back to major civilization for the foreseeable future. Not until River Crowley is dead, or we are," Adam concluded. "Dismissed."

10

On the Road Again

As the squad made their way out into deep space, en route to a gate that would take them to Andromeda 3, Adam continued to sift through Crowley's journals. He found an entry that stood out from early on, shortly after Crowley began establishing the compound on Djevica 9.

"We admitted a young man. He had a lot of bravado, a lot of dominant energy, but no competence. I invited him to my table, and while we were eating dinner he pushed the boundaries of disrespect with me. He was testing me, with the intention of taking over my house. What I had built. Subtly laying his hands on my wife. Making digs at my expense out of turn.

Salem and I shared our looks, invisible to this overconfident, unaware man. He thought, perhaps, he was being clever. And, if I was weak, he could have taken over. He could have kicked sand in my face, and taken my things, as the older thugs did to the little armless boy in the Antares camps.

At first I ignored it. But this disrespect was inviting disrespect. And eventually it required a response. I knew if this overconfident man was able to wrest any authority from me it would damage my plans. It would put my house in the hands of someone with no intelligence, no integrity, no honor, and no vision. He didn't have the ability to understand, let alone execute, my strategy.

He didn't know who I was. He didn't know how I came to be where I was. So I taught him.

I took him underground, to the basement below the main building. He woke up there.

He went on and on with his whining and his blathering, 'you can't do this', 'let me go', all this childishness.

I tied his arm against a particle board and picked up an SMG. I unloaded a full clip into his hand, starting at the fingertips, painting his hand away in little bits with bullet spray. When I ran out of ammo I changed out the clip and finished the job, painting away his hand until there was nothing but a mangled nub.

He continued on with his pathetic begging. I wanted him to understand. I wanted him to understand the pain that I had survived. In his eyes I saw the Technocracy's separatists. The Antares street thugs. Every twisted, status-seeking, domineering, selfish thief that represented the worst in humanity I'd encountered.

I made him look me in the eyes as I grabbed his lower jaw, and pried it slowly from his face like cracking the bones off a chicken carcass.

I watched him. His sad, wagging tongue dangling from his crying, puffy face. I asked him, 'Do you want to die?'

He nodded. I made him beg me for death.

He gargled out grotesque noises that I could tell were more pathetic wails. 'Yes.' 'Please'.

And this person thought he could be me. He hadn't even come close to experiencing even a fraction of the pain that I'd endured.

I tortured him for seventeen more hours. He didn't make it. He had the bravado. But he didn't have the *mettle*.

When I was finished I dumped his hacked up corpse on the lawn and let the flies have him. What he'd done required a response, and the consequences of his actions had to be public. I was surrounded by powerful people. Unfortunately, in this world, until we can change how business is done, power is tested. And I wanted them to understand what happens when I am tested. I wanted the rumor to spread. I wanted the consequences I'm capable of delivering to become myth.

Power comes in different forms. Debate, charisma, wealth, technology, desirability, trust, manipulation and so on. Anything that can coerce a person to act outside their interest. I've studied many things, and chief among them, power. And one of the things I know, from my life of degradation and pain, is that power comes in a hierarchy and its purest form is violence.

Had this man been smarter, more curious, and not reckless, he may have learned an easier way how a man can come to be with so much more than him. A fool, who could never build what I built, trying to take what I had, without bothering to ponder, for a second, what experience I'd accrued to have accumulated so much to envy. Look where his foolishness got him.

Everyone here, among this fledgling group on campus, now knows that I am friends with violence. Only on that foundation can I have the authority to be kind and to inspire. Not because it's necessary. But because it's made necessary by people like the covetous moron this ghoulish corpse used to be.

I enjoyed watching the terror in his eyes as I whittled him away. As he came to understand that he was in the presence of power, and was sentenced to experience its extent. But that's not why I did it. It had to be done.

When I was all finished, I returned to my other business."

Adam squinted. From over his shoulder he heard Tezca say, "Dude. What the fuck?"

"Didn't see you there," Adam said.

"That's who we're chasing?" Tezca asked.

Adam nodded.

"Fucking psychopath," Tezca said.

"They don't send the all-stars of EDF black ops after lost pets," Adam replied.

"Yeah, I get that. But what the fuck," she said, trailing off as she left the bridge. "Ripped his fucking jaw off. Ghouls. What," Adam heard her continuing to mutter off in the distance. "Motivational speaker. Yeah right."

Adam laughed to himself.

"Soph, how long to the gate?" he asked the AI.

"The journey from here to the Andromeda Central - Andromeda 3 gate will take approximately 9 days, 7 hours," Sophia said.

"Alright. Open the comms, I wanna make an announcement," Adam said.

"Of course. Ready when you are," Sophia replied.

"Alright everyone, welcome aboard," Adam said. "This is your commanding officer speaking. Let me be the first to welcome you on the Oneiro-Lyssa. If this is your first time here, let me tell you a bit about the ship. It's a 3rd generation Warhawk class special forces gunship, modified to pass as a civilian starliner. It's seen a little wear and tear, but I prefer to think of it as broken in. Our onboard AI and navigator is Sophia. Sophia is top-notch and I expect you to treat her as one of the crew."

He continued, "We've got a little over 9 days to the next gate, which will take us to Andromeda 3. Don't forget this is a chase. We want to make good time. That said, there's going to be a lot of downtime on this mission and not a lot of stops, so make friends and try not to push each other's buttons. Stay cohesive. Stay alert."

"Our plan is to intercept Crowley on Draconis, but we will have our resident tech head, Vice, and our ship AI looking for opportunities to grab his trail and see if we can't get to him early," he said.

"I probably don't have to remind you," Adam said. "Since you've been briefed before you got here, but the time dilation we're getting hit with on this mission is serious business. Your friends and family, if they're still alive, are going to be decades older if and when you return. Brass thinks it's worth it, so that should give you some idea of how dangerous the bigwigs consider this Crowley character to be."

"That said, strap in and kick back. We're going to have a bit of a departing shindig in the mess at 0500. Socializing is not mandatory, but there are only six of us so everyone's gonna notice if you're missing. Get to know each other. We're going to be spending a lot of time together. Aztec you're first up on kitchen duty," he continued.

"See you there. Adam out," Adam concluded and shut off the comm.

"Alright, Soph. Got some time to kill. Turn on the music," Adam said. "Pull up my road trip playlist."

"Yes, sir!" Sophia said excitedly. Hard rock music began to play in the cockpit.

After some time passed, Adam made his way to the kitchen, casually referred to as the mess, and found his crew already mostly assembled. Only missing was Grant, the anthropologist. Aztec was wearing an apron and grilling meat and tortillas. Raziel had decided to join him and was also putting together some dish in the kitchen.

The Oneiro-Lyssa was outfitted with a state of the art food printer, one of the benefits of being a top class ship. That meant it could take standard amino acids, salts, sugars and fats and rapidly print decent approximations of most foods the crew was familiar with. It was always a bit off, but usually close enough.

Adam entered and sat down.

"Oi, Adam, just in time, buddy. Just finishing up," Aztec said as he entered. He tossed a hand towel over his shoulder and slid a plate onto the table.

"Voila, ustedes," Aztec said and gestured toward the plate.

"Beef birria tacos with adobo chipotles. Dip it in the consomme, squeeze on some lime" Aztec made a chef's kiss maneuver.

"What you got over there, Graves?" Aztec asked. "Our boy decided to chip in," Aztec said, winking at Adam.

Raziel came to the table with a large bowl. "This is coq au vin. Chicken, mushrooms, carrots, wine. I put some garam masala in there. My little Indian twist," Raziel said and then sat down.

As the food was served, Grant walked into the room, bags under his eyes and VR goggles dangling from his neck. He gave a brief, apologetic head nod for being late and squeezed silently into an open seat at the table slightly away from everyone else.

"Looks great. You guys outdid yourself," Adam said. He pointed to Aztec and addressed the group, "Aztec here is a renowned cook. Back in the day people tried to trade back and forth to get him on their crew so they wouldn't have to choke down standard issue MREs. We're lucky to have him."

Aztec laughed. "Ah, you're embarrassing me, brother. Don't forget our boy here. He's doing his best to show me up in the kitchen," he said. Aztec gave Raziel shoulders a friendly squeeze and then approvingly slapped him on the back and sat down.

Raziel uncomfortably smiled and nodded. "Happy to help, sir."

Tezca, with her booted feet kicked up on the corner of the table, chimed in. "I've got something, too," she said. From under the table she pulled out a large bottle and slapped it onto the table. "Hypatian brandy. Little gift from the Cat's Eye Nebula."

Vice grimaced. "I should've made something. Feel like a freeloader," she said.

Adam shook his head. "You'll get your chance. We rotate the chores. That's just the way we do things in SOF. I just had Aztec go first to make you all feel bad," he said with a laugh. "You'll get used to it," Adam said to Vice, "And you, too," he added to include Grant.

Vice nodded and added seriously, "Alright. Looking forward to pulling my weight."

Grant scratched the back of his head, and absentmindedly nodded.

Adam raised an eyebrow. "You ok over there?" he inquired.

Grant nodded. "Yes," he said politely. "It's a lot to get used to. I'll do my best," he said.

Adam nodded. "That's all we can ask. We're happy to have you, doc."

Tezca pointed at Grant's goggles. "Those the Optimus 5s?" she asked him.

Grant smiled and held up his VR goggles. "Yes," he said.

"I had an Optimus 3 when I was a kid. I played Starfighter Source 5 a ton when I was a kid. Could have gone pro," Tezca replied.

"Yeah, waste of time, ay," Aztec laughed.

Tezca glared at him a little and then looked back at Grant. "You play?" she asked.

Grant shook his head. "No, I don't," he said plainly, in eerie monotone.

Tezca continued trying to engage him. "So what do you use them for?" she asked.

Aztec guffawed, "Some smart guy thing I bet. Not games like us plebs," he teased.

Grant looked at the goggles, seemingly uneasy. "I like to go to… different planets. And… home movies," he said.

Adam chimed in, "Missing someone?"

Grant took on a melancholy disposition, like he was entertaining a painful memory. "Yes. And no. I don't want to… talk about it. Forgive me," he said.

Adam nodded. The table got silent after the awkward moment.

"So, Graves, noticed you've got a hell of a sidearm there. What is that, the Korth?" Adam asked, changing the subject.

Raziel pulled out his revolver and put it on the table. Everything was custom. The grip was crimson with a sort of marble texture. Pic rail on the barrel with an added compensator. Laser sight. "Yeah," Raziel said. "Modding guns is kind of my hobby. You like the Korth, boss? What's your EDC?"

"I like the M4-A90 and the new M980 SASS," Adam said. "Carry a Sig as a fallback but I rarely use it."

Raziel nodded, "M4's a classic. Can't go wrong with that. I heard about the 980. That's what they use in sniper school. Heard that's tough nuts," he said.

Adam pointed at the revolver, "You just carry that?"

Raziel nodded. "Sometimes I take a pump shotty, but I like the revolver. High skill cap. I've spent the most time with it. I'm comfortable," he said.

Raziel looked at Tezca. "What about you? What's your EDC?"

Tezca grinned. She pulled a large combat knife out of her boot and slammed it on the table. Then two more out of holsters on her torso. She kept pulling out knives hidden on her person until a collection had piled up on the table. Then she dropped a collapsible SMG on top of it, followed by a folded, extendable compact sniper rifle. By the time she was done there was a small arsenal sitting on the table.

She beamed, fangs flaring, proud of her work.

Raziel turned to Aztec and started to ask what his everyday carry was, but Aztec preempted him.

"Minigun," he said plainly.

"What, like they put on armored vehicles?" Raziel asked.

Aztec looked at Adam and then back at Raziel. "Yeah, my man. The very same," he said.

"Those weigh like… what, 200 pounds? 300?" Raziel followed up.

Aztec just smiled and flexed one of his huge arms. "Guns for the guns," he said.

Adam turned to Vice. "Do you carry? Do they carry in the GSA?"

Vice nodded. "Not like… that. We're not usually getting into direct confrontations," she said.

Tezca jumped in. "So if you're infiltrating some terrorist compound or whatever, what do you bring?" she asked.

Vice answered matter-of-factly, "Nine times out of ten we're there with a civilian cover, so you don't bring anything that would seem out of place. Usually we have some kind of gadgets for emergencies. Watch with a shock charge, earrings with a sedative, things like that. I usually have my deck. I usually bring a lockpicking kit. I try to keep it light, in case I have to run. I learned a lot of martial arts. I have a .22 in a drawer somewhere, but I've never used it. Generally speaking if you have to fight someone, the mission has failed. I try to avoid that."

"Speaking of which," Vice added, "I want to get started

on tracking Crowley right away. The longer we wait the colder his trail's going to get. He's flying around in a weaponized Andromedan Phoenix class speeder. It's got a unique transponder, if I can latch onto it we can trail him to any place he makes any stops. A couple other ships took off from Djevica 9 at the same time. I'll keep a look out for those as well."

"I don't want to be rude, but time is limited. I need to get on it or I'll miss my chance," Vice said. She stood up. She looked at Aztec and nodded, almost as a slight bow. "Thank you, it was delicious." She turned to Raziel and executed the same nodding maneuver. "Thank you. I'll be sure to cook next time."

Vice left the table and headed to her quarters.

Grant also stood up, taking advantage of the opening to leave. "I also want to get a jump on reviewing the route," he said. He smiled warmly, but with hidden melancholy behind his eyes. "Thank you. When it's my turn, I'll make gochujang jjigae. You'll love it."

Grant headed off to his quarters.

"Alright, boners. Looks like it's just us military brats," Tezca said. She collected a couple of glasses from the kitchen and brought them to the table. She pulled the cork out of the brandy with her teeth and spat it out. "Who's taking the first shot?"

Aztec guffawed. "Alright!" he exclaimed. "Now it's a party." He placed a glass in front of Raziel. "All you, rook. Show us what you've got."

Raziel downed his shot. Tezca poured Raziel another shot and distributed shots for everyone else.

Adam held up his shot and they all clanked glasses.

"It's gonna be a tough mission but I'm glad to be here with you all. Nowhere I'd rather be. Cheers," Adam said, and they all downed their shots.

Tezca began pouring another round. Adam took his second shot quickly and stood up to leave. "Alright. I'm gonna get some shut eye. I've got a long week of sitting on the bridge and waiting to get ready for. You guys stay up as long as you want," Adam said. "Take it easy on the new guy," he added, slapping Raziel on the back lightly.

With that, Adam returned to his bunk and lied down.

As Adam drifted off to sleep, he found himself back on Titan, as he often did. This time he was a colonist, with his wife and his daughter, Alice. He was teaching her how to set up the hydroponics systems.

He pulled out the drawer that housed the water.

"This is where we pour in the liquid fertilizer," he said, smiling. He handed Alice a bottle full of pale green plant food. "Just a little. Not too much," he said.

The little girl poured in a few tablespoons of the liquid, and looked back at Adam expectantly.

"Good, good," he said. He tussled her hair. "You're a natural."

Adam stood up from his stoop, "Now here in this bed we've got corn. What's special about growing corn? You remember?"

Alice thought for a moment. She shook her head.

"Corn refertilizes," Adam said. Alice's eyes lit up as she remembered the answer.

"Why does corn refertilize? You remember?" he asked.

"We can use the stocks and the husks as food for the other plants!" Alice exclaimed.

"That's right. That's good," Adam said. "Smart girl."

Adam heard the sound of an incoming starship landing in the colony. It had nothing to do with him so he ignored it and continued with his lesson.

" Alright, sweetie, what's in this pod? Do you remember?" Adam asked.

Alice tilted her head and pondered with a finger pressed into her cheek. "Um," she thought for a moment. "Plums, tomatoes and…" she thought.

Adam waited for a moment and interjected. "You got it? You need a hint?" he asked.

"No, no, I'll get it," Alice said and kept thinking. After a few moments she conceded. "No, I don't remember."

"Strawberries," Adam said.

One of the other colonists burst through the plastic entrance to the biome. "Adam! Come quick! The military is here. They want to talk to a rep. You gotta get out there," the man said.

"Alright, Charlie. I'm on my way," Adam said. He knelt down and kissed his daughter's head. "You wait here. Daddy's gonna be right back."

Adam left the tent and found himself among a field of corpses. Dead colonists strewn all over the makeshift paths between the honeycomb units of the colony. Adam heard smoldering. He turned around and watched as the gardens burned, all the crops ablaze. He watched it burn through until it was all reduced to ashes.

11

The Home We Built

The journey to the Andromeda 3 gate was mostly uneventful. The crew took turns cooking. Vice made char siu lo mein. Grant made gochujang jjigae, just as he'd promised. Adam made New York style hoagies. Tezca presented an original creation that could only be described as burnt salad. The crew found themselves looking forward to Aztec and Raziel's rotations. Aztec made mole enchiladas with pickled onions. Raziel made chicken tikka and Spanish naan.

When they reached the gate, they jumped through without issue, and set a course for the next gate, which led into the

Triangulum. From there, they'd be out of paved road, and it'd just be vasimr hyperspeed all the way to SagDIG.

Adam spent most of his time on the bridge, watching the stars go by, alternating listening to music with pouring through Crowley's journals. Aztec, Tezca and Raziel hung out in the common rooms playing cards and trading battle stories. Vice sat by herself, usually in her room, scanning the metaverse and the net for traces of Crowley or his lieutenants. Sometimes she came and did her tracking alongside Adam in the bridge. She didn't talk, but Adam figured she wanted company. Grant spent most of his time in his room, seeming detached and depressed.

A few days after entering Andromeda 3, Vice said the first words Adam had heard from her in days.

"Adam, I've got a hit," she said.

Adam perked up and turned the music down. "Crowley?" he asked.

"No," Vice said. "It's something else. It's a distress signal from an Andromeda expansion colony."

Adam nodded. "Not our problem," he said. He thought for a moment. "What's it say, though?"

"Not much," Vice replied. "Under attack. Send help. That's it."

"Under attack by what? This is the frontier. There's nothing out here," Adam said.

"Don't know. There's some chatter on the Technocracy official line but it's all scrambled. Can't crack it, at least not at this distance," Vice replied.

Adam touched the comm. "Aztec, Tez, come up here please," he said.

Within a few moments the twins appeared.

"We've got a distress signal. No one's around to answer it but us. We're obligated to ignore it and prioritize the mission," Adam said. "Thoughts?"

"I say we check it out," Aztec said. "Couldn't take more than what, day? Day and a half? We're going stir crazy in here. It'd be good to get out and stretch our legs."

"Tez?" Adam asked.

Tezca shrugged. "Your call, boss."

"Adam," Vice interjected. "There's something else. There's a ship down there. It's one of the Djevica ships."

That's right. Adam thought. *They were sending "peacekeepers" to the colonies. Is this what peacekeeping looks like?*

"That settles it then," Adam said. "Looks like we're taking a little detour. Sophia, set a course for the colony."

Adam touched the comm. "Dr. Lee, can you come up to the bridge?" he asked. There was no answer or confirmation.

Adam looked around. "Can someone go get Grant, please?" he asked.

Aztec responded, "On it."

He left, and a few moments later returned with a tired, disheveled looking Grant.

Adam pointed at visualization of the colonized planet on the monitor. "We're headed here. Anything you can tell us about this planet, doc?"

Grant nodded. He squinted at the screen and then sat down at one of the bridge stations. He pulled his VR goggles up and began waving his arms around like an orchestra conductor, navigating through simulations in the metaverse.

As Grant looked into the planet, Adam spoke up. He whispered, "I want one of you to talk to that guy. Getting worried about him. Figure out what his deal is. He doesn't have isolation training. Looks like he's getting squirrelly. I don't want him wigging out on us."

Tezca nodded. "I'll talk to him," she mouthed.

After several minutes, Grant pulled down his goggles. "Ah, yeah, ok. I think I have a feel for this planet," he said.

"Great. Go for it," Adam said.

"It's a habitable exoplanet. It belongs to the Valhalla cluster. Name is Aesir 36b. It looks like it was mostly volcanoes, but they terraformed it. There's a lot of dense vegetation down there. There's still significant volcanic activity. One medium-sized ocean towards the top pole. Lots of rivers that flow back into it. The gravity is 1.18. Air's breathable. Hmm, might be a little chilly," Grant said in a despondent affect.

"Any info on this colony?" Adam followed up.

"There's a small colony in this quadrant here," Grant pointed to an area in the northern part of the planet. "Looks like… Hmm… 30 or 40 people. It's an immature colony. First generation settlers. I don't know anything more than that. They're making good use of the wood and regolith. Those are the primary resources. No mining or exporting. It's not industrial. Purely a settlement."

"Good enough for me. Good job," Adam said. "Alright, Soph, take us in."

As Sophia replied, Adam shared a silent look with Tezca.

"Hey, doc, do you have a minute? I need some help with something," Tezca said to Grant.

"Yeah… sure…" Grant said, and followed her off of the bridge like a zombie.

The Oneiro-Lyssa began its descent into the Earth-like atmosphere of the planet, its heat shield absorbing the atmospheric friction. As it broke through the atmosphere, Adam was able to get his first look at the topography of the terraformed world. The surface was covered with dense woodland as far as the eye could see. Big non-native fir, birch, oak and redwood trees filled the horizon, accented by a gray fog rolling through the landscape. The colonists had clearly put a lot of work into the planet.

"Soph, can you get a lock on the colonists' location?" Adam asked with Aztec standing over his shoulder, arms crossed, taking in the landscape.

"Yes, sir. Scanning now," replied the AI.

"What do you think's going on down there?" Aztec wondered, hunching over slightly to get a better look through the dash.

"Not sure," Adam said. "But we're gonna find out."

"Adam, I've located a camp with sixteen human life signatures. I'm uploading it to your display now," Sophia said. As she talked, a few buildings and several people milling about became highlighted in yellow by the XR capability of the ship's windshield. Adam recognized the boxy, modern prefab design aesthetic of colony structures. There was no mistaking that this was an Andromedan camp. Centauri camps were usually 3d printed domes. EDF camps tended to be hexagonal yurts connected by simple roads and enclosed corridors, like a honeycomb. These structures were clearly Andromedan.

"Seems pretty quiet," Aztec noted. "What do you wanna do?"

"Let's see if we can't get an idea about what we're getting ourselves into. Soph, where's the Djevica ship?" Adam followed up.

"Scanning," Sophia replied.

"Adam, she's not gonna be able to find it. The transponder was on when it broke through the atmosphere, but the ship's gone dark now. Whoever is down there isn't using the ship, they're out there camping off the grid somewhere," Vice added.

"She's right, Adam. I wasn't able to locate any ships other than the colonists' passenger freighter," Sophia said.

Adam furrowed his brow. "Alright. Let's go say hi. We'll take the direct approach. Az, you and Graves are with me," he said.

Adam turned on the comm. "We're gonna go meet the colonists. Graves, Tez, meet me and Aztec in the hold. We're going to be the ground team. Tez, we're dropping you off early a few clicks away. Do your thing," Adam said.

"Vice, you stay with the ship. Keep Grant company. And Sophia, when we land, turn on defensive security, lethality level 1. Use your discretion on the lethality. We don't know what we're getting into down there," Adam said.

He stood up from his chair and slapped Aztec on the shoulder. "Alright, let's go," he said.

The ground team prepared in the hold as the ship cruised toward the camp's location, strapping on tactical gear and arming themselves with their preferred equipment. As the ship closed in, Adam opened the hold and cold wind poured in as the scenery whizzed by below.

Tezca pulled her AR half-visor down over her right eye. "See you on the other side, boys," she said as she double checked the clip on her sniper rifle and strapped it to her back. She made a motion on her earpiece. As she jumped out of the ship, the cybernetic bodysuit she was wearing began to blur her from the visible light spectrum.

As the ship made its final approach, a few members of the colony, having seen the incoming ship, awaited the ship's landing outside.

Adam, Aztec and Raziel stepped out from the hold onto the forest floor, a collection of fallen leaves, branches, twigs and dirt. Adam approached the colonist who was standing ahead of the others, a tan, stocky, muscular man with a short buzz cut. It was the kind of build you'd see on a man who chopped wood, plowed fields and performed other tasks common for colony homesteaders.

Adam didn't sense any apparent threat. He'd met a lot of colonists in his life and these ones seemed ordinary.

Adam approached with his hand outstretched. "We picked up a distress signal. What seems to be the problem?" Adam asked authoritatively.

The leader of the colonists shook his hand with a firm grip. "I'm Evyn Chow. I head up this colony. Glad to see someone come to help. You guys EDF?" he asked.

Adam nodded. "We're a detachment. We weren't sent to help you, we were just in the neighborhood. I'm Major Ikari-Wright, these are lieutenants Rai and Graves. How can we help? The signal made it seem like you all were in immediate danger. Looks pretty sleepy," Adam said.

Evyn nodded. "They're gone now. They haven't done anything yet. But they'll be back," he said.

"Who's gone?" Adam asked as Raziel and Aztec stood behind him, quietly surveying the area.

"You're not gonna like it. I'm not sure if the military can get involved with this. I was kind of hoping you'd be civilians and we could just round out our numbers," Evyn said.

"I'll let you know what we can do," Adam said.

"A unit from Andromeda came and threatened us. Said we're under the jurisdiction of the Technocracy and we have to start sending them supplies. Lumber, food, iron, cobalt. Said they're sending a representative to take over 'governorship' of the colony. I told them no. This colony was established before the Technocracy, its founding terms are grandfathered in under Andromeda law. I told them what they're doing is illegal. I told them we don't even have a mining operation. It got a little heated. They said they're coming back and they'll annex the colony by force," Evyn explained.

Adam nodded. "Yeah, that's kind of their MO," he replied. He paused to think for a moment. "Give us a minute," he said. "We need to talk this over. We'll see what we can do."

Evyn nodded. "Of course," he said. "We were hoping for other colonists from the frontier, because we knew they'd help out. These are sovereign colonies. That's the deal we had with the old aristocracy."

Adam nodded. He turned around and walked away a few paces, Aztec and Raziel following close behind. Once they got out of earshot they started discussing the situation in hushed voices.

"We can't get involved in this," Adam said. "We're armed EDF, we can't openly take sides against the Technocracy. Earth has a deal with them. It would cause a lot of issues. We'll all be finishing our careers out guarding salt mines on Neptune."

Raziel nodded. "Understood, sir," he said.

"You're not on a trial period, Graves, you can give me your real thoughts," Adam said.

Raziel loosened up a little bit and replied. "No, I agree. We have no idea what CENTCOM would want the outcome here to be. Without orders, we shouldn't get involved. If we call them up, they'll tell us we shouldn't even be here. We should just be looking for leads on that ship."

Adam nodded. "What about you, Az?"

"I don't like it," Aztec said. "This is gonna go hot one way or another. These guys aren't going to give up their colony. They're going to fight with or without us."

"Graves?" Adam prompted.

"I don't like that it's an illegal seizure, but I still don't think we should get involved," Raziel replied. "Maybe there's something else we can do. Maybe we can mediate. Maybe we can stop it from sparking off."

"We don't have the authority," Adam said. "We can't act as EDF representatives. We could go incognito, but the colonists already ID'd us. If word spreads we'll have MPs following us all the way to Draconis."

"It's the right thing to do," Aztec said. "These guys are gonna get crushed. They're gonna lose, and lose bad. Look at em. It's a bunch of farmers. They have no idea what a professional military is going to do to them. They're gonna lose everything."

"I know," Adam said. "They're so outmatched they don't even know it. If they fight back they're gonna get smoked."

"It's against the law. Maybe there's something we can do with that?" Raziel added.

"Against the law or not, we don't have the authority to enforce Andromedan law. It's an internal issue for them," Adam said.

"Gimme a minute," Adam said. He held his temples for a

few minutes with his eyes clenched in concentration. He nodded a few times like he was having a conversation with himself. "Alright," he finally said.

"We're gonna mediate. Just keep it from going hot. We're gonna make sure the colonists take the deal without getting slaughtered. We're gonna take the Technocracy's side. We're gonna push that Evyn guy to accept a deal. We'll try to negotiate the terms in the colonists' favor, threaten political blowback from Earth as leverage even though we don't have the authority to do that. Best we can do. If these colonists get out of this thing alive we'll call it a win. Sound good?" Adam said.

Aztec nodded. Adam turned his attention to Raziel. Raziel nodded.

"We're risking our careers here, you understand that?" Adam said.

"It's the right thing to do," Aztec said.

"It's illegal. These people are perfectly in their rights here," Raziel added.

Adam nodded. "Alright then. That's the plan," he said. "Stay alert, we still don't know what's going on with that Djevica ship. Vice is going to keep scanning for signs of that, but whoever landed in that thing is out there camping in the woods somewhere with the lights off."

Adam turned and headed back toward where Evyn was waiting for him. He took a minute to try to get a read on the situation. He looked at Evyn waiting expectantly for his answer, eager and hopeful to be gifted a way out of his situation. He looked at the other colonists who had gathered to watch the rare visitor. Men, women and children, dressed simply.

One little girl was nearer to Evyn than the rest of the villages, almost hiding behind him.

"Is that your little girl?" Adam asked.

Evyn nodded. "Sure is. She's turning 4 this month. This is the only world she's ever known," he said.

Adam looked around. He looked at the trees and the colony itself. "You guys did this all yourself?" he asked.

Again, Evyn nodded. "Changed the atmosphere. Contained nuke on the poles to melt the ice caps and free up some liquid water. Terry over there," Evyn pointed to a spindly looking man in a camo vest, "Planted the trees, seeded the entire world in a crop duster. We fast grew em."

"That's definitely a lot of legwork. We can tell you put a lot of love into this place," Adam said.

Evyn smiled widely. It was clear to Adam he still expected to get a positive answer.

"We sure did. On our own, too. That's how the old aristocracy functioned. Lots of freedom, not a lot of help. This is our place. Y'know. Get to make it how we like, run it how we want. Bianca," he pointed to a woman with big, curly hair, "She got this fog going. The cold air. Just how we like it. There's nothing here that hasn't been done by us. When we got here, it was nothing but volcanoes, the atmosphere was unbreathable. All sulfur. You couldn't even see. We cleaned it all up," Evyn said, like he was pitching Adam on helping them.

Adam nodded. "Looks great," he said.

The conversation hit an awkward silence until Evyn finally interjected. "Well? Are you going to help us? We're just engineers, here. Mostly scientists and farmers. Having some real soldiers like you guys would be a big help," he said.

Adam looked at the faces of his lieutenants, and then back at Evyn.

He could tell Evyn was waiting for him but he didn't want to disappoint the entire colony at once. "Would you mind showing me around? I'd love to check out your gardens, if you have time," he followed up in an effort to talk to Evyn one on one without an audience.

Evyn hesitated for a second, having not anticipated that response, but then graciously nodded. "Sure, sure," he said, stretched his arm out towards one of the nearby buildings, a collection of boxy containers with floral murals painted all over.

As Evyn led Adam toward the gardens, he whispered to one of the colonists. Adam surmised he told them to go on with their day, because his compatriot shooed everyone away.

As Adam entered the garden area he felt a wave of nostalgia. The garden area was made up of a few different subsections. There was the traditional garden, a series of raised garden beds. Each was being attended by a robotic arm. Though they were stationary now, Adam recognized the model. The arms were mounted on a rail and took care of seeding, harvesting and watering. They still needed a human to assist, because they weren't much good at adapting to unpredictability, these older models. The top of the line ones near Earth, in the richer colonies, had AI. Adam figured they liked the personal touch here in this colony anyway. The raised beds housed mostly tall, repeatedly harvestable crops like tomatoes and corn.

In addition to the traditional garden was the container yard. Adam recognized those, too. They were for rapid grow hydroponics. The EDF used something similar, but the EDF version was more like a greenhouse. These were Andromedan style hydroponics, where the plants were housed in an environment painted with white PictoLIT, a special light reflective paint. The plants were blasted with a special pink light that feeds the blue and red wavelengths plants require for photosynthesis without wasting any unnecessary energy on the wavelengths required by humans. Adam suspected they grew the fruit in there.

Finally, they had the grow towers and the aquaponics pond. The grow towers were a series of thin, vertical, slotted poles with different varieties of lettuce and other leafy greens. The aquaponics pond was a reservoir of water filled with a few varieties of edible fish, and its nutrient rich water recirculated throughout the garden. The fish scales and waste fed the water, which fed the plants, which filtered the water, which returned to the pond, where the system fed the fish detritus from the plants.

It was an impressive setup. It could run for a thousand years without intervention.

"What do you think?" Evyn asked proudly.

"I think it's top notch. It really brings me back. We had a similar setup back on Titan. Y'know, I don't know if it was as good as this, but we were no slouch either," Adam said.

Did we? he wondered. Adam felt static in his brain. *When did I live on Titan? No, it was just a mission. Titan? No, must've been Io or Ceres station, where I grew up.*

Adam and Evyn stopped in the middle of the garden. Adam began, carefully, and trying to be empathetic. "We talked it over," he said, "and we don't think there's a way out of this where you don't end up under the Technocracy."

Evan's face grew stern and determined. "This is our home. It's ours. We built it. We'll die before we give it up," he said.

Adam shook his head. "Yeah. You'll die. You'll die, and you'll give it up," he said.

He looked at Evan's face, brimming with righteous anger and unwilling to listen to reason.

"Look," Adam said, "The Technocracy has taken over whole *systems* they consider to be under their umbrella. Fully developed planets with trained militaries. I appreciate your position here, I do. And for what it's worth, I think you're right. You built this place, and its a beautiful place, it really is. But if you resist their demands, every single one of you will die, and they'll take this planet over anyway."

Evyn paused for several moments, processing his response. Finally, he spoke. "So you're not gonna help us?" he said.

"I am helping you. You're gonna get robbed. You can either just get robbed or get robbed and killed. I don't know how this place is run, but if you're the leader here I think you have a responsibility here. Those people you mentioned, Terry, Bianca, that little girl – your daughter – they're gonna die. They're not maybe gonna die. There's a 110% chance every single one of you will die," Adam said.

Again, Evyn thought for a long time. "You really think we have no chance?" he asked.

"You have no chance," Adam replied. "You have a better chance of turning into a unicorn and flying into space."

"But the people who came, there weren't that many. Maybe 5, maybe 6. Just a few more than you guys," Evyn said, trying to rationalize. "If we were armed, if we knew what we were doing, we could fight them off."

Adam nodded. "Let me explain how this works from a

military perspective," he said. "They sized the unit according to what they thought was needed to get the job done. If they go MIA, if they get killed in action, or report back heavy resistance, they'll increase the size of the unit. If you succeeded in fighting off this first unit, and I know how the Technocracy treats situations like this, they will send what we in the forces call 'overwhelming force.' It will be a display of power intended not only to annihilate you, but also crush any hope of future resistance. If you take out a squad, they'll skip the platoon, which is what they'd need to win, and go straight to sending a company, just to show you what a company looks like."

Adam paused for a second, watching Evyn's face as he took it all in. "Do you understand what I'm saying? I'm not trying to crush your hopes. Well, no, I am. I'm trying to keep you from throwing your lives away. If you fight off that first squad, which is already slim to none odds, we're not talking about a few more guys. We're talking 100-150 trained soldiers, tanks, air support, drones, the whole thing, parsed out in waves. In other words, they'll park a big ship up there," Adam pointed to the sky, "and have wave after wave of guys to send at you until you surrender or you're all dead."

Adam watched Evan's face. Again, he asked, "Do you understand?"

Adam watched as the hope and enthusiasm thankfully faded from his face. Dejected, Evyn replied, "Yes."

Evyn sat down on the edge of one of the planters and let out a heavy sigh. "We're gonna lose everything," he said. He waved his arm, gesturing towards the garden, then again towards the woods themselves. "Everything we've built, with our own sweat, over the last 16 years."

Adam sat next to him. He clasped his shoulder. "I feel you. It's not fair. If you could fight, I'd say fight. But you're outmatched beyond outmatched. You'd just be throwing your lives away," he said.

Evan's face again stiffened. "How's my daughter gonna see me if I lose this place?"

Adam nodded. "She's gonna see you alive," he said.

Evyn looked at Adam in the eye, the bargaining stage of grief setting in. "You can't help us at all? Can't we petition the EDF for protection? Something?" he asked.

"We'll be here, for this meeting. Just to give some deterrence, make sure it's just a talk and no one gets hurt. We'll try to help you negotiate. That's all we can do. We're not exactly in the EDF's backyard out here," Adam said.

Evyn nodded. The two sat together on the edge of a garden bed for a long time, looking out at the trees, as Adam gave the colonist time to process. Eventually, after maybe twenty minutes, Evyn reached out his hand.

"Thank you," he said. "We appreciate your help."

Adam and his crew stayed in the colony for a couple of days. They got to know the colonists a little. The pilot, Terry, Bianca, another woman named Marge, a charming old man named Esteban, a small gaggle of kids. It was a happy, picturesque place. Adam hoped it could stay that way. He understood why they wanted so badly to protect it.

On the night before the Technocracy representatives were set to arrive, Adam had a dream. Same dream he'd had dozens of times before.

He was in the garden with his daughter, Alice, when his friend, Charlie, arrived to tell him the EDF had come. He went out to speak with them. Two men, clad in black armor, armed with rifles and black masks. An argument ensued.

Alice ran up out of nowhere. "Stay back!" Adam shouted, though it wasn't audible in the dream. The girl tried to offer the soldier something precious to her, a stuffed purple fairy dragon. In her child's mind, it was precious to her, it must have been precious to everyone else.

When the soldier pulled the trigger the velocity of the bullet took her lightweight body briefly off the ground before she slumped over with a limp thud, bits of dead brain oozing out of her eye socket.

Adam looked down at his black gloved hands and the blood splattered fairy dragon he was holding. He tossed it dispassionately into the bonfire that was roasting the rest of the colonists' personal effects.

He stood over the corpse of his friend, Charlie. Through his radio he heard his squad mate, "This is Bravo team, we've got resistance from Charlie in sector 4. Requesting backup," it said.

Adam clicked on his radio. "Roger, Bravo. On my way."

Adam stepped away from Charlie's corpse, and the dead little blonde girl sitting next to it.

12

The Meeting

Soon enough, the day came. Evyn and a few colonists who were selected to represent the colony's interests stood and looked up at the sky as the Technocracy ship began its descent. Adam, Aztec and Raziel positioned themselves along the sides of the delegation.

The team had done their best to train the colonists on how to handle the negotiation. Focus on not being replaceable, not on emotional connection to the planet. Don't let yourselves be intimidated, keep it businesslike.

As the ship landed, the tension was palpable. It felt like

forever before the ship's hatch opened up. Out walked a thin, confident man with a crew cut. Adam knew the type immediately. Sergeant, maybe a second lieutenant, power trip, sadistic disposition, insecure. Got off on being in charge, on feeling powerful.

Alongside him were 3 infantrymen. Adam guessed there were two more in the ship, just out of sight, a pilot, and the ship's defensive AI.

"Looks like you've got some guests," the man said to Evyn as he walked up, holding his rifle across his chest, showing it off, trying to be intimidating. He looked at each member of Adam's team before he zeroed in on Adam, clocking him as the leader. "EDF, huh? What brings you guys all the way out here?"

"Just in the neighborhood," Adam said. "Not here to interfere. Just making sure no one gets hurt."

The Sergeant responded, "Not exactly your jurisdiction is it?"

"I'm sure you know the EDF has a mandate, which the Technocracy has agreed to, to hold each other accountable to the Centauri b accords. We're just playing referee," Adam said.

The Sergeant nodded. "Well, in that case, happy to have you. I'm Sergeant Graff, and these are my men," he said.

The Sergeant turned his attention to Evyn. "Ballsy move, son," he said. He pointed his thumb at Adam and his squad, "Next time we come down here, you're not gonna have a babysitter."

"Don't need a babysitter. They visited and offered to stick around," Evyn said. "Let's get down to business."

The Sergeant smiled. "Good. Good. Business is what

we're here to discuss. So. Here's the deal. It's a little different so try to keep up. This planet is property of the Andromedan Technocracy. You are trespassing, and stealing resources from our sovereign territory," the man said.

Evyn interjected. "We built this planet. It wouldn't have resources if it wasn't for us," he said.

Sergeant Graff looked up at Evyn with just his eyes and paused for a long time, as if trying to punish him for interrupting. He held out his hand and one of his men put a tablet in it.

"Says here this planet is rich with iron, cobalt, copper, lithium and other rare earth minerals. Did you plant those minerals here?" Graff said.

Evyn didn't respond. Graff handed the tablet back to his underling, and continued.

"We will *generously* allow you to keep your homesteading operation here, under the following conditions," Graff said.

"One. You supply the soldiers and miners we send to harvest this planet with food reserves totaling 70% of your overall output," Graff said.

"Two. You agree to not expand your homesteading operation beyond its current footprint. That means no new structures, no new clearings. Not an inch," Graff added.

"Three. You allow our people to make use of your facilities as we see fit at any time and to follow the orders of your betters as required by Andromedan law. You will enter into Andromedan citizenship as Deltas and Epsilons, making you subject to instruction by any outranking member of society," he said.

"Lastly, you will agree to give over control of this colony to the governor assigned to this world and obey his or her laws no different than any other colony the Technocracy establishes on this planet," Graff concluded.

"It was only 40% of the food last time," Evyn responded, obviously angry but trying to maintain his composure.

Graff chuckled. "I told you, the deal's a little different now, since you made us wait," he said.

Evyn glanced at Adam, making a quick attempt to read his face for advice. *No, Adam thought. Bad move.*

"What're looking at him for?" Graff asked. "This is between you and me." He looked at Adam. "Isn't that right?"

Adam nodded.

"70% is too much," Evyn said. "We can't do that, it's not sustainable. Especially if we can't expand."

"70% is the number. Take it or leave it. Your options are 70% or leave the planet which, as I explained earlier, you're trespassing on. 70% and you can't expand," Graff countered.

"40% and we can expand to meet the new production. You won't find better farmers than us. We don't need to be trained. It'll be difficult to replace us," Evyn replied confidently.

'Attaboy, Adam thought.

Sergeant Graff summoned one of his men and had a brief conversation with him, whispering back and forth in each other's ears. His man returned to position.

"60% of your current output, 100% of any expansion," Graff said.

"50% of current output, 60% of any expansion," Evyn said, holding back his anger as best he could, but letting a little slip through, *"and you won't have to kill us."*

Graff laughed a little. He looked at his men and jokingly made a scared face.

"Tell you what. 60/60. Keep forty percent of everything. Limited expansion. Best deal you're gonna get," the Sergeant replied. "Anything else?"

"We come in as Betas, at the lowest," Evyn said.

One of Graff's men laughed, and then Graff laughed out loud. "*Betas?* No. Not a chance. Not gonna happen. I'm a Beta. These guys, these guys are Gammas. You," he waved his finger at Evyn and the other colonists. "Deltas. Epsilons."

Evyn responded through gritted teeth, "Gammas, then."

Graff laughed. He gripped his gun. "How 'bout we just…" Adam and his team moved to the ready, and Graff let go. Graff sighed. He pointed at Evyn. "Gamma," he said. He pointed at the other colonists. "Deltas. Best I can do. And I'm being nice. I'm gonna get yelled at for giving you that."

"Last, you stay out of our homes and facilities. We manage our own colony," Evyn said.

Sergeant Graff shook his head. "No. No more negotiating. You got the best deal you're gonna get," he said.

Adam watched as Evyn mentally wrestled with the unacceptable condition. Ultimately, he kept his calm and replied, "Just this last point and you'll have our full cooperation. We'll become willing, productive citizens."

Graff snarled. Adam could tell one thing, this person did not want to *lose* the negotiation. He stepped forward and got in Evyn's face. "Now listen here, you backwater nothing. You're lucky I'm talking to you at all, especially after what you pulled bringing them," he jutted his thumb out in Adam's direction. "You take the deal you get, or we'll come back again and you're not gonna like the new deal. Not at all."

As Graff stared Evyn down threateningly, Evyn stared him down just as hard with determination as grit. "Fair deal or no deal," he said. The two stayed locked in the fierce stare-down, until it was interrupted by a voice coming in from the distance.

"Stay away from my dad!" Evyn's daughter yelled as she came barreling down the hill from the residential area.

Stay away! Adam felt static in his brain. *Stay away!* He saw the purple, blood splattered fairy dragon in his hands.

Shit. Must've been watching through the window, Adam thought. He looked at his team. They all exchanged looks of understanding and readiness.

Evyn whipped around quickly. "Stay back!" he shouted. The girl stopped in front of him.

"No!" she yelled.

Evyn knelt down. "Listen, sweetie, the adults are talking, you need to go back inside, ok?" he said. Meanwhile, Graff was laughing, bemused, and looking back at his men.

"Yeah, go back inside, kiddo," he said to the girl, then looked Evyn square in the eyes and added, "Adults are talking."

Evyn stood back up and the two resumed their stare-down.

The little girl ran up to Graff and started beating on his leg. "Go away! Leave us alone!" she screamed at him.

Graff continued to maintain eye contact with Evyn. "Control your kid," he said.

"Mia, go inside, love," Evyn said, still maintaining eye contact.

The little girl didn't heed the order. She kept beating on Sergeant Graff's leg.

Adam felt static in his brain. *You got it? You need a hint? Strawberries,* he heard. He shook his head. In his peripheral he saw Aztec look at him curiously.

"I said GET OFF BRAT!" Graff shouted as he kicked the girl off and she fell to the ground.

Stay back! Adam heard. He saw Alice's face, blown wide open, slumping over in front of the barrel of his rifle.

Adam didn't think. Headshot. Headshot. Headshot. He wasn't even present when the shots were fired. He was someplace else, far away. Somewhere off in the distance, like in a movie playing far away, he saw Raziel quick draw on the remaining infantryman and heard two booming sniper shots from Tezca's position in the woods take out the pilot and their support.

When Adam came back to his senses, Aztec was shaking his shoulder and looking at him with concern, confusion and anger. Adam's ears were ringing. He heard the little girl crying in the distance. He looked and saw Evyn kneeling down, embracing her as she sobbed into his shoulder, giving Adam a judgmental stare.

"Hey. Hey. Adam. What the FUCK was that?" Aztec shouted at him.

Raziel, nearby, added in, "That's it. The cavalry's coming. Andromeda frontier colonists RIP."

Aztec continued on, panicking, "Man, oh fuck, oh fuck, oh fuck. Adam, man, what the fuck, what the fuck bro."

Tezca stepped out of the woods, throwing up her arms, confused, and Aztec looked at her as he threw up his own arms and shrugged his shoulders.

Over his comm he heard Vice's voice. "Hey, Adam, what the hell's going on out there? The chatter I'm getting on the Technocracy line is crazy. Total loss? Am I hearing that right? What did you guys do?" she asked.

Adam rubbed his head. In front of him, Alice was standing,

hands clasped behind her back, maggots crawling out of her pale, dead eye socket. She was smiling. A sinister, proud smile.

Fuck, Adam thought.

13

The Fallout

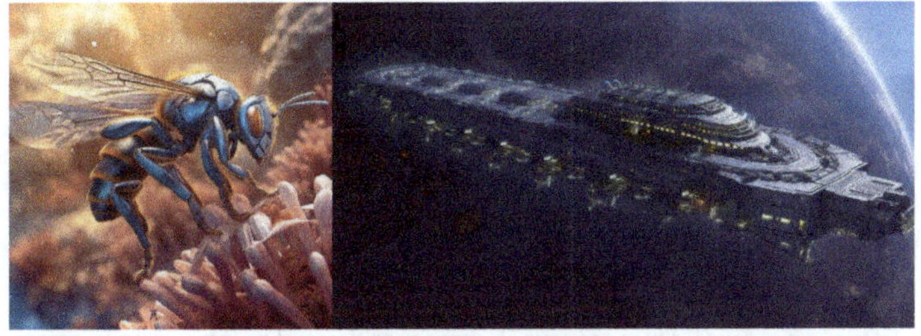

"They say the best revenge is living well.

When I was in Scorpius, in the Antares refugee camps, the humanitarian soldiers would do supply drops. They'd drop in capsules full of food and water and basic necessities, without any structure to account for a fair distribution of those supplies.

The camps began to be run by gangs and bullies. People grouped up and hoarded supplies and leveraged their hoarded supplies to achieve power. Rapes, beatings, murders, intimidation, even just general misbehavior. Mockery, smugness, taunting and the like. That was what the camps were like.

And there was me. I was young, so I was small, and an amputee. I didn't have the prosthetics I have now, then. And I was reeling from the brokenness of having gone from an aristocratic family in the Andromeda capital, to the lowest dregs of the lowest place in the galaxy.

I had no ability to fight for supplies, and I was tortured. The best strategy, I thought, for a time, was to make myself small, so I wouldn't be targeted. But that became unbearable. We were in the purest manifestation of humans' savage ape-like social instincts, where strength ruled the land, and the negative consequences of a society underpinned by that philosophical structure were obvious — but that is, and continues to be, the nature of society. The strong rule and their character and personality and vision or lack thereof reverberates throughout society, the middle subjugates itself and trades its dignity and self-determination to tyrants for survival, and the weak are abused for fun.

For the first few years, I survived under the protective umbrella of young women who traded their bodies to men they hated for survival and protection, but they, themselves, prostituted as they were, were easily abused, and I was a third class citizen among their group of third class citizens.

One day I was eating a sandwich. In those days, where we used to collect the maggots from rancid portions of rationed rice and soy for extra protein, a sandwich was a treat. It was a rare thing to procure.

One of the local gang members, Donzig Ziggerton, everyone called him Ziggy, saw me with it and took it, and pushed me down. I couldn't do anything. No one else could do anything. By that time I'd been hardened, so I didn't cry, but I got angry, and I started down a path towards the weaponization of the mind.

When people are physically strong, they say it can be used for good or evil. Offense or defense. That a trained martial artist or marksman is like a weapon, and that the only way to beat a bad guy with a gun is a good guy with a gun. People strive for that kind of strength. People respect it.

But what of those who are physically weak, but mentally strong? When it comes to the weapons of the mind, there is no such lionization. Those who hone the weapons of the mind are distrusted, vilified. What psychologists might call the dark triad. Machiavellianism, narcissism, psychopathy and to a lesser degree sociopathy and sadism. I decided to practice these tools, as weapons, to wield to protect myself and others from these bad men who capitalized on their strength to enforce a society of overwhelming misery and abuse. The dark triad was my gun. The dark weapons of the mind were my glistening muscles in the sun.

For me, these things were not compulsions, but skills, like the martial artist's forms. Over the decades that followed I enhanced the sophistication of their application and integrated them with other, lighter tactics of the soul and of the mind, but it was in the camps that I first learned how to wield them.

Three weeks later, when Ziggy no longer even remembered what he'd done to me, I snuck out to the edge of the camp and captured a dozen and a half Antares purple scythe wasps. I bottled them, and threw them in his tent and nailed the door closed. I listened to Ziggy's arc of confusion, resistance, screaming, tantrums, crying, acceptance and death. When the gang came to collect on the incident, they had no idea who had done it, because everyone had motive, they were so hated.

They say you should let karma do its work, and usually karma plays out when the bully meets a bigger bully. How selfish of me, to allow others to be tortured in the interim, while we wait for this unknown savior. How selfish of me to abdicate the darkness revenge brings to keep my own soul clean and force some other person to darken their soul to fight my battle.

These weapons of the mind saved those Antares camps. Vilified as they were, they were effective. When I became the bigger bully, the supplies were distributed fairly. There was a system in place. There was stability. There was education. There was safety. There was hope. When I saw the first smiles begin to emerge I knew I had made a good trade when I sold the purity of my soul.

The camps were no longer a morass of degradation, fear and despair. And when the camps stabilized under the threat of my displeasure, the humanitarian overseers stopped seeing us as subhuman animals. They began to let us out and gave out passports to allow for some limited reintegration with polite society.

They say the best revenge is living well. There is some truth to that. But for us, in the camps, the best revenge was wasps."

Adam clicked off Crowley's recording and laid silently for a while.

"Do you want to talk about it?" Sophia asked.

The fallout from the previous day's bad ending had been immediate and severe. Adam could feel the loss of respect from the crew and the new, profound lack of confidence in his leadership. The colonists, he knew, were doomed. His team would face immense damage to their careers and Adam would have to take responsibility, and perhaps worst of all, Alice hadn't gone away. She just kept staring at him, smugly smiling at his destruction.

"I could tell them I saw an imminent threat, but that's a cop-out. I'm going to tell them what happened. I had some kind of PTSD flashback and I snapped," Adam said.

Alice giggled.

"It's possible you'll be relieved of your command," Sophia replied.

Adam was lying on his back on his bunk. "If that's what they wanna do, I wouldn't blame 'em. I fucked that up bad. But we need to get out of this situation first," Adam said.

"Are you ok now? As you know, I'm programmed to assist with your well-being. You can tell me anything," Sophia said.

Adam looked at Alice's sinister, smirking face, resting in her hand, tapping her cheek happily.

"I'm fine," Adam said. "I set a meeting for later this afternoon. We're going to talk about what happened and what we all wanna do next."

"What do you want to happen? Do you want to keep your command?" Sophia asked.

"I want to make sure those colonists don't all get iced for my mistake. Then after that, they can do what they want with me, whatever," Adam said.

Adam paused for a moment. After some time, he prompted, "Sophia."

"Yes, Adam?" the AI replied.

"What do you think happened to me on Titan? What was

I doing there?" Adam asked.

"I don't know the answer to that, Adam. What do you think?" Sophia replied.

Alice kept staring at him.

"I don't know either. It's like I have two sets of memories. I don't know which one is real," Adam said.

"I'm here for you if you need me, Adam," Sophia replied.

Adam let out an affirming grunt and stopped talking. He stared at the ceiling and tried to clear his mind of the guilt, shame and self disappointment.

After taking a few moments for himself, Adam raised his hand and clicked on the comm.

"Jackie, can you meet me on the bridge in 5?" Adam asked.

After a few moments, he heard a static and morose reply. "Yeah," Vice replied.

Vice was already on the bridge when Adam arrived, distracted by poring through data on a screen.

"Thought you'd get here after me," Adam said as he entered.

"I was already here," Vice said as she turned around. "What's up?" she said, coldly, but politely. "I thought we were having a meeting in a bit."

"I wanted to talk to you first," Adam said.

Vice raised her eyebrow and looked back at the screen. "To shore up support? Or something? Why me? Why not Rai, that's your boy, right?" Vice replied dismissively.

Adam shook his head. "No, that's not it. It's about something else," he said.

Vice turned her chair around and gave him her attention, though still cold, making a show of how her unwillingness met her obligation. "What can I do for you, Captain?" she asked.

"Look, whatever happens with me, I have a responsibility to help those people now. I'm going to have more to say at the meeting, but one way or another, I'm going to make this right with them," Adam said.

Vice softened her demeanor a bit but remained closed off. "Okay. What can I do for you?" she repeated.

"I want information on the troop movements in the sector. Who's here, who's coming?" Adam asked.

Vice turned around without saying anything and picked up a tablet sitting on her desk. She handed it to Adam. "I already did it," she said, turning her attention back to the data on her screen.

Adam took the tablet and flicked through it. It showed the last known location of all the nearby Andromedan warships and their projected trajectories. The Andromedan Navy's third battalion was stationed on the edge of Andromeda, just on the other side of the gate. It was shown to be only moderately staffed, with four available companies, and the purview of its defense mandate included all the Andromeda outer worlds, as well as the Andromeda 3 frontier colonies, where they were currently sitting.

"Am I reading this right?" Adam asked.

Vice shrugged. "Dunno. How are you reading it?" she asked.

Adam flicked his hand and threw the contents of the tablet on the main screen. "The ACPN Crusher is the only warship assigned to this side of the gate. The other 3 carriers stationed with the Third are patrolling the outer planets to stop incursions from pirates and rebel groups," Adam said.

Vice nodded without looking up. "If they pull any of the other carriers off their patrols, they'll be abandoning the colonies they've already annexed. Those ships are holding territory, they're already spread somewhat thin," Vice said. She poked on her screen and Adam watched as portions of the main display were circled. "Look here," Vice said.

"The Gavel and the Executor are both parked almost permanently near these planets," Vice said. She circled some more things. "Valhalla Major, Hel, Jotun-164 and Vanir b. I was curious so I looked into this. Apparently the colonists in that region don't like being occupied and they've been increasingly rebelling over the last several months. It's not a war zone over there, but it's full of terrorists. They threw the battalion at it to intimidate them into compliance," Vice said.

"Overwhelming force," Adam said.

Vice nodded. "Right. They're already doing it in one place. They don't have the resources to be in two places at once. And I suspect they care a lot more about Valhalla Major than some little backwater in the frontier they can pick off later. And if they've got the big guns stationed there, that means Crusher's the runt. It's the C team. They didn't get invited to the war. They're on guard duty in the frontier," she said.

"Still a full fledged ACPN company warship," Adam said.

Vice nodded. "120, maybe 130, trained and fully equipped," she said.

Adam rubbed the underside of his chin. "What's your assessment?" he asked.

"My assessment?" Vice repeated. "If you inflict enough losses on the Crusher, they'll retreat and do whatever they can to avoid mentioning to the fleet veterans that they got chased off by a group of unarmed colonists. They'd be a laughing stock. But they'll be back sooner or later," Vice concluded.

Adam nodded. "What're they packing on there, arsenal-wise?"

Vice shrugged. "Pretty standard. It's a ground invasion force. Troops, tanks, drones, Radyon body armors, couple of Spots, Atlas suppliers. The biggest armament is a class A spider-tank," Vice said.

"What about orbital bombardments?" Adam asked.

"Yeah, they could do two or three volleys, but they have old tech. Hypothetically, if one was to involve themselves in this, a skilled hacker could deploy digital countermeasures that throw off their targeting algorithm," Vice said.

Adam raised his eyebrow. "You suggesting you want to get involved in this?" Adam asked.

Vice didn't look up. "I want to hear what you have to say for yourself at this meeting. But I agree with you, we can't leave these people high and dry after we came in and put a target on their back. We have a responsibility here, whether there's a court martial waiting for us back home or not. But no, I don't *want* to get involved. I wish you hadn't put us in this position. But now we're here. Have to play the cards we've got," Vice said.

Adam nodded. He slapped the tablet against his hand as a sort of period to the conversation. "See you at the meeting," Adam said.

"You got it, boss," Vice said, annoyed.

Adam waited in the mess hall for everyone to gather. He watched their faces as they entered. Aztec and Tezca were angry and disappointed. Raziel had lost respect. Whatever pedestal Raziel had put him on, he was knocked off now. Grant didn't come, he had locked himself in his room. Alice perched herself on the countertop and waited excitedly, smiling with her hands clasped on her knees.

Adam stood up and took in everyone's body language. Their crossed arms, their glares. He'd earned the scorn and he had to accept responsibility.

"Let me begin by getting a few things out of the way. First, let's talk about what happened down there. I could try to save face and say I saw the Sergeant reach for his weapon. That's what a lot of people would do. We'd put that on the paperwork and weasel our way out of taking responsibility. The truth is, that's not what happened. You know it, I know it, we were all there. I saw that man kick that little girl and I had some kind of PTSD trigger and I snapped," Adam said. He continued to survey his crew's hard faces.

Alice giggled, mocking him as he spoke.

"Second, I am going to take responsibility for this. It was my mistake in the field, it was under my orders we took on an unsanctioned mission, and if I get court martialed for this, so be it," Adam continued.

"Third, I'm not leaving these people high and dry. I'm going to stay down there and do what I can to help them fight off the retaliation. I'm in this now, like it or not. I broke it, I own it," he continued.

"Now, I understand if you want to relieve me of my command. Aztec is the senior officer, and I'm happy to turn over command, and you can take off and leave me behind here. If that's what you wanna do, that's what we're gonna do. But if you don't wanna do that, I welcome you all to stay and clean up this mess with me, I could use your help, and these people need the help," Adam said.

He looked over his audience. Alice did, as well, mockingly.

"You good?" Tezca asked sternly. "You gonna spaz out on us again?"

Adam glanced at Alice, who put her hand over her mouth in a fake display of astonishment. He noticed Tezca follow his eye line. He looked at Tezca. "I'm good," he said. Tezca looked at him suspiciously, but didn't say anything. She just stared at him.

Aztec chimed in. "Look, Adam, bro, I've known you for years and you're the best of the best. We're in the shit. Sometimes you end up in the shit. Remember when we were on Proxima b and I used the wrong dialect of Centauri and blew our cover? We had to zero that cab driver and a half dozen insurgents. That was on me. You've bailed my ass out more times than I deserved, man. What, am I gonna give up on you after the first mistake I've seen you make in two decades of serving with you? Nah, man, you know me better than that," he said.

Adam nodded.

"It was a pretty big fucking whale-sized horse cock of a mistake though, cabron. And we're gonna talk about it if we survive this shit. Let's not get it twisted," Aztec added.

"Thanks, Rai," Adam said. He looked over the crew. Vice had her head in her hands, and Raziel's arms were crossed as he stared daggers at him.

Vice waved her hand dismissively. "We already talked about it," she said. "I'm going now." She got up and left the room, presumably to head back to the bridge.

Adam looked at the one remaining crew member. "Raziel?" he prompted. "Speak your mind."

Raziel shook his head.

"I don't believe what I'm hearing here. We broke protocol.

We disobeyed orders, we committed what is probably going to be judged as a war crime. He," Raziel pointed at Adam, "broke the rules of engagement like a rookie. We're all going to be court martialed. And we deserve to be. We did it. Our careers man, our careers are fucked. I was supposed to go and be learning from the best. That was the point," Raziel said.

Adam nodded. "I see. That's what you care about in this situation, is it? Career? That's where your mind goes?"

Raziel shrugged. "What's wrong with that? That's valid. I want to be decorated. I want to be promoted to command," Raziel said. "That's not gonna happen now."

"Command asked me to show you the ropes, so let me give both you and them what you all wanted and give you a lesson. We're *soldiers,* son. It's war, not a paint by numbers book. Shit gets messy. Welcome to the real world. As for your career, your career is fine. You were a golden boy before this and you'll be a golden boy after. CENTCOM will spin all of this. We'll handle the political and professional fallout if we get out of this. That's the easy part. But how's it gonna look for you if you make Colonel and everyone who served with you thinks you're a self serving little weasel? Think about that," Adam scolded him.

"Now, if you don't wanna participate, that's one thing. That makes sense to me and I don't blame you. But when lives are on the line, don't start talking about your *career.* It's a bad look. There's your lesson. And command would agree with it," Adam said.

Raziel stood up and pointed his finger at Adam, "I didn't make this mistake. *You* did," he said, and sat back down.

"I'm gonna remember you said that when you make a

mistake, Graves. And you will make one. I've been in the field longer than you've been alive, and you're fresh out of OTC. I promise you the world doesn't work the way you think it works," Adam said solemnly.

"Whatever," Raziel said, petulant.

Aztec put his hand on Raziel's shoulder. "You need to shut the fuck up, Graves. That's still your XO. Speak your mind, but watch your fucking mouth," he said.

Adam looked at him directly. "You in or out? Either way's fine with me," he said.

Raziel aggressively shrugged Aztec's hand off his shoulder. "I'm in. Sir," he said angrily.

Adam looked at Tezca. "How's the doc doing?" he asked.

"Zonked out of his gourd," Tezca said plainly. "Told him what's going on, but he's a space cadet. Dude's on another planet. Don't think he cares if he lives or dies."

Adam nodded. "Alright," he said.

"I think you should talk to him," Tezca added.

Adam nodded again. "After all this is done with. Let's go meet with the colonists. We've gotta put together an engagement plan," he said.

Adam looked out of the corner of his eye at Alice as she laughed at him.

14

Wave After Wave

Adam and the team spent several days working with the colonists to prepare them for the upcoming onslaught. Things remained tense. Raziel continued to be passive aggressive. Aztec was supportive, but almost too much so, in a way that revealed that he thought Adam was weak. Tezca continued to act suspicious, but when confronted always denied that anything was off. And Vice remained cold.

In the camp they'd set up sandbag partitions and trenches. They'd placed booby traps in the woods around the camp. Snares, traps, pits and the like. He'd instructed the colonists to flee into the woods if the camp was overrun.

Adam had designated a series of fallback and flanking positions. No one talked much. They all just focused on getting the job done.

Before they knew it, the day was upon them. There was no mistaking it. The ACPN Crusher darkened the sky when it descended upon the camp. It hovered, high in the sky, a few miles off in the distance. For a few precious moments, it was quiet. Then, the first wave of soldiers poured out.

"Four squads," Adam said into his comm. "Tez, you got eyes on 'em?"

"Two heading straight down the middle, looks like the other ones split off to flank each side," Tezca said.

"Aztec, hold a defensive position on your 9 with squad B. Tez, try to soften up the Eastern squad before they reach us. Pick 'em off. Keep me posted," Adam said. He looked at Raziel, who was next to him. "You're with me. Hope you don't hate me too much," Adam said.

"I'm a professional," replied Graves as he did one final check on his loadout.

Adam turned around and addressed the hodgepodge militia of colonists. "This is it. Aim before you fire. Breathe. Don't panic," he said. He turned around and waited.

Off in the distance he heard some light gunfire as Tezca hunted them down in the woods. Soon enough, Adam spotted the main force taking position along the tree line. Adam fired the first shot, straight through their Lieutenant's eye. Then the firefight began in earnest.

After a few moments, the Andromedan squad tried to pull the ambush on their flank, but Rai was there to meet them, and mowed them down in short order with his minigun.

Before much time had really passed, the woods were calm and quiet again.

"Tez?" Adam inquired.

A moment passed and then the response came. "Neutralized," she said.

The colonists began to cheer, but Adam turned around and shushed them. "Don't celebrate. Those ones came to parlay. We surprised them. Back to positions," he said quietly.

Adam watched the carrier. It just hung there in the sky for several minutes before the hatches opened. Adam watched and waited. For the longest time, there was no movement. And then, all at once, the incursion truly began. Dozens of squads began fast roping out of the craft, one after another. Support drones and heavy infantry in exoskeleton mechs accompanied them. Spots, robotic hounds with guns jumped out.

"How much of their capacity is coming at us?" Adam asked calmly through the comm.

"That's about 30%," Vice replied.

Adam felt the ground rumble as the army charged them. This time there was no defensive perimeter in the trees. When they got to the tree line, they poured through, Spots and drones in the advance, followed by the mix of infantry and armored heavy infantry.

Adam took out drone after drone with his rifle. One of the robot dogs leapt on him and he grabbed its snout and smashed it against a nearby concrete barrier. He set up a personal shield and detonated charges at the tree line when the timing was right, blowing away a squad and a half and ruining the visibility on the battlefield.

He looked around and surveyed the situation. Raziel

was focused on Spots, blasting them to bits with a pump shotgun, switching to his revolver for human targets. Aztec had maneuvered to the side and was filling the woods with bullet spray in the general direction of the enemy. Every few seconds, like clockwork, Adam heard the booming thunder clap of Tezca high caliber rifle picking off targets from somewhere off in the woods, and the colonists were picking off who they could with household rifles and small arms.

Nevertheless, their position was being overrun. The enemy was getting closer and closer, and they weren't eliminating them as quickly as they were reinforcing.

"Fall back!" Adam shouted into his comm. "Position 2!"

The group began a heavy retreat to the predetermined second position, hidden behind walls in the camp itself.

"Wait for it," Adam said as the enemy began to cautiously approach and secure the perimeter.

"Wait," Adam said as the enemy bullhorn blared.

When the majority of the visible opposition had set foot inside the designated zone, Adam called out "Now!"

The traps blew and the makeshift floor dropped out from under them. As they frenzied to climb out of the pit, the secondary charges fired and Adam's incendiary grenades detonated, setting the entire length of the trench ablaze. Adam listened to their screams. Burned alive. Bad way to go.

But the advancing force didn't stop. Adam saw Aztec and Raziel both take damage. Aztec struck in the arm, Raziel grazed along the face and one in the shoulder.

Adam heard through his comm, "I'm hit." It was Tezca. "They got me, boss," she said. He heard her coughing, a wet cough he recognized in a throat filled with blood like phlegm.

"It's bad."

"Talk to me, where'd they get you?" Adam demanded.

"Got a couple… slugs in the torso. One in the leg. …Might lose another limb. Honor serving with you, Major," Tezca said.

"Don't die on me Tez. Pack it in. Go stealth and wait it out," Adam ordered.

"You got it… boss," he heard through the comm, trailing off.

He looked around and surveyed the bodies. His team was being overrun but he'd only lost a handful of colonists.

"Position 3!" Adam called out. The group retreated to their final position, the roof of the bunker that housed the escape tunnel into the woods.

"This is it. There's nowhere else to go. This is our last stand," he said. He found Evyn in the bedlam and clasped his shoulder. "If it looks like we're getting overrun, take your people through the tunnel, just like we planned." Evyn nodded.

"Talk to me Vice. How're we doing?" Adam asked.

"The initial force is pretty much exhausted, so you're getting a reprieve. But, Adam, that was only 30%. Can you see the dropship from where you are? Adam, look up," Vice said through the comm.

Adam adjusted his implant to account for the smoke and distance. Vice was right, new squads were pouring out of the carrier. Worse, Adam's heart dropped when he saw a spider-tank crawl out of the dropship's hanger and pounce to the ground.

A beastly, two story tall hulking weapon made of robotics, steel and heavy weapons towered over the tree line, knocking over thick redwoods with ease as it trudged forward with its spider-like limbs.

Aztec and Raziel both stood at Adam's side as they watched the tank approach with dropped jaws. "You got an RPG on you?" Adam asked Aztec, half joking.

"Nah, hermano. Must've left it at home," Aztec said.

"Any last words, Graves?" Adam asked.

"I fuckin' hate you guys," Raziel said, deadpan.

"At least you get to watch us die," Adam said.

Raziel shook his head. "I'm kidding. I knew what I signed up for," he said.

Adam readied his rifle and aimed toward the tree line, waiting for the first of the new wave to rush their position. At least he'd pick a couple of them off before the tank got close enough to blow the whole building to dust.

Adam waited and waited, but the infantry squads never appeared.

Must be falling back, Adam thought. *Waiting for the tank.*

"Oi, Adam, you see that?" Adam heard Aztec say.

He looked over and saw Aztec pointing toward a spot in the woods. Trees rustling and falling over, rushing in the direction of the tank at high speed.

What the... Adam had just enough time to think before he saw a blonde woman in a beige tank and camo fatigues jump above the tree line and hurl a redwood at the tank like a javelin, impaling it. The tank sputtered and sparks flew from it as it keeled over.

Is that... Aria? Adam thought.

"The Djevica ship," Adam said out loud. He turned to Aztec and laughed. "We forgot about the Djevica ship. She's been out there this whole time."

Soldiers, making their way through the edge of the tree line, turned around and paused.

Just a few seconds passed before Aria blasted through the trees in a horizontal leap, catching two soldiers, one in each hand and rushing them into the wall of the building Adam was occupying. As she slammed them against the wall, their bodies instantaneously turned to pudding. Aria looked up at Adam and made eye contact, but no further acknowledgment, and then she got to work.

She rushed from soldier to soldier, toggling her personal shield on and off. She zigzagged and strafed around to be difficult to target, and just plain absorbed hits here and there with her seemingly superhuman constitution. She jumped to one soldier and brought his face to her knee, turning his skull into a squashed bug. She carried his body like a shield and took his side arm, rapidly emptying the clip and taking out half a squad with that alone, before throwing the corpse on the remaining squad members. She swung a roundhouse kick that separated three men's torsos from their lower half at once.

She jumped to another soldier and unleashed a forward kick that went straight through his body and left him cleaved into two halves. If it wasn't so impressive and so *fast*, it would have been grotesque.

What proceeded to play out in front Adam's eyes could only be described as a dance of brutality, a masterclass of martial arts, marksmanship, and field tactics.

As Aria cut through the invading force like a hot knife through butter, Adam thought to himself, *She was taking it easy on me back on Djevica 9.* Adam lowered his weapon and collapsed, laughing.

Graves watched in awe. "So this chick *works* for the guy we're hunting?" he asked in disbelief.

Adam kept laughing. "I told you man, it's wild out there. You're not in ranger school anymore. Going off what I saw on Djevica 9, this is just the tip of the iceberg."

Alice looked down on Adam, smiling, compassionately caressing his face.

"What the…" Aztec uttered as he dodged a body part flying by his head. "What the fuck am I looking at here? Am I dead? We dead?"

Adam kept laughing. "We're in unknown space now. Who the fuck knows," he said.

Alice giggled.

"What's so funny?" she asked.

"I'll tell you later, sweetheart," Adam said. He reached up and touched her face lovingly.

Raziel and Aztec watched as Adam talked to and touched a figment of his imagination.

"What the fuck is going on, Rai?" Adam heard Graves ask.

"I dunno, kid. Something tells me no one involved in this gives two shits about your career, though," Aztec replied.

Looking up at Alice's face, Adam passed out from exhaustion.

15

Aria Dawn-Kumo

Adam woke up feeling the familiar touch of a scratchy army bedroll beneath him, barely cushioning him from the crunch of leaves on the forest floor. He sat up and felt the warmth of a crackling fire mixed with the cool, foggy forest air.

"You're awake," he heard a friendly voice say. He looked over and saw the woman he knew as Aria, but her demeanor was unrecognizable. She was smiling warmly, caringly, with genuinely kind eyes.

She quickly moved to the fire and took a tea kettle from a spit it was hanging from. She poured its contents into a canteen cup, then knelt down next to Adam and graciously offered the cup to him with both hands.

"Here, drink this," she said.

Adam raised his eyebrow at her and looked at the tea suspiciously. "What is it?" he asked.

"It's thistle tea. I made it from the milk thistles they had growing in the woods here," Aria said. She looked out at the woods in admiration. "They really paid attention to the details, don't you think? You can tell they really cared." She smiled contentedly, as she sipped on her own cup of tea. "What a wonder," she mused.

"Drink up," she encouraged. "It'll warm up your core temp, lower your stress levels."

Adam sipped on the tea. It did, indeed, feel like an elixir of sorts. It was nicely bitter, and lemony.

"How did I get here? Where's my crew?" Adam asked.

"They're fine," Aria replied. "They're waiting on your ship. I asked them if they wouldn't mind if we had a chat."

"What about?" Adam asked, coldly.

Aria seemed hurt by the tone briefly, but just for a moment. "I wanted to thank you," she said. "It's the polite thing to do."

"Thank me for what?" Adam asked, noticing Alice perched on a nearby log with her head resting in her hands, attentively watching the conversation.

"Helping the colonists," Aria said.

Adam shook his head. "I didn't want to help. I made a mistake and got my crew caught up in it. The fallout's gonna be huge. Probably gonna get mutinied when I go back," he said.

Aria shook her head. "That's not the way it seemed when I talked to your friends. They were worried about you," she said.

Adam didn't reply. He watched Alice watching him, shame welling up in his chest.

Aria continued after the pause. "Do you know what the Technocracy does to colony planets like this?"

Adam shook his head. "Can't say I do," he said.

"They turn them into a strip mine. Turn the entire place into a factory. Did you pass the Valhalla colonies on the way here? You can see the smog from space. When you go there, you can see the working class children, Andromeda's so-called Epsilons, developing lung disease before they can even talk," Aria said with empathy and compassion.

"They don't have parents. They have a Delta class manager assigned to them as a teacher, like an orphan matron. Their parents work for the party, mining the planet's resources. They're not allowed to develop a relationship with their children," she added.

Adam shrugged. "Sounds bad," he said. "That's how it works in the Technocracy. That's their choice."

Aria shook her head. "It's sad," she said, looking down in her cup. "They're taught from birth that's how it is. They can't imagine anything else, and it's only been a generation."

Adam paused for a moment. "Is this going to become a recruitment pitch? Is that the point of this?" Adam asked.

Aria shook her head. "No," she said. "Just a thank you." She gestured to the forest in general. "All this gets to stay the way it is, since you made the brave choice."

Adam shook his head. "No. The Technocracy will be back. They're not gonna let this place go," he said. "They won the battle. They're not going to win the war."

Aria smiled. "I don't know about that," she said, knowingly.

Adam looked at her. He wondered what exactly that

comment meant, but decided not to press it. He let the conversation lull for a moment and then spoke. "You seem pretty sane," he commented.

Aria laughed. "How sweet," she said. "Thank you."

"Why do you follow Crowley?" Adam followed up. "I've been listening to his logs. He's a complete psychopath."

Aria shook her head. "Keep listening," she said.

Adam looked in her direction, feeling the cool air on his skin. "I listened to one where he tortured a guy to death. Ripped his jaw off with his bare hands while he was still alive," he said.

Aria nodded. "You killed quite a few people here today, didn't you? So did I," she replied.

"That's different," Adam said. "That was a battle. And it was self defense."

Aria shook her head. Instead of addressing his point directly, she responded, "When you look at him, you see a man named Crowley. A man who's a threat to the EDF and the status quo of the governments of Centauri and Andromeda. A man capable of violence. When I look at him, or anyone from old Andromeda or the free colonies, we see a kid we all knew named River, who came from nothing and made everything better for everyone when no one else could."

"You've only seen his dark side. You weren't there when River freed the slaves in Centauri, put to work in mining colonies just like this place was going to become. The slavers saw his dark side, too. He put so much fear in them that slavery in the Centauri system almost entirely ended in the span of a year. No one wanted to get ripped apart the way River ripped them apart," Aria said.

"That's where you met him?" Adam asked.

Aria nodded and sipped her tea again. "I remember being a teen, in the slave colonies, working for the resistance. The same kind of resistance we're supporting on Valhalla. We accomplished nothing, for years. River came along and broke them to bits. He blockaded their supply lines with just a handful of ships and starved them. When they surrendered, he refused. He didn't attack until their spirits were already broken. He didn't just win. He made them pay for their crimes. And he didn't just save us. He inspired us to save ourselves. To shirk off the learned helplessness they'd put into us. He may be your villain, but he's our hero," she said.

"Why don't you run things? Understatement of the century, but you seem pretty *capable*," Adam asked.

Aria shook her head. She laughed a little, playfully, and said, "Do you think I'm a ditzy little girl with a crush? That he's conned me with sweet nothings? No, River is a real leader. You haven't seen his light side. You haven't seen the way he can inspire people, the way he gives hope to the hopeless. He makes you feel like you can do the impossible, and then he shows you you can. You haven't seen the way his leadership generates harmony. His intelligence and creativity are something the universe probably hasn't seen in generations. You think he's dangerous, and he is, but he's on our side."

"You see him as this darkness that needs to be stopped. If you knew River well, you'd know he's not our hero, River, or your villain, Crowley. He's both. Dark and light in balance. I'm strong, sure. Armies fear me. Governments fear River," she said.

"If you're only seeing River's dark side, you should be

asking yourself why," Aria said.

As Adam thought, beginning to formulate a response, he heard the leaves rustle around the perimeter and his instincts put him on high alert. A few minutes later, he saw Tezca emerge from the tree line, bandages covering her torso and her good arm. She smiled at the sight of Adam, showing off her cat-like fangs.

"Hey, boss," she said excitedly as she dropped a bundle of firewood she'd gathered near the fire.

"You're alive!" Adam said.

Tezca showed off her bandages and performed a little twirl. "Yeah, looks like I got lucky, eh?" she said, chipper.

Adam looked at Aria. She preempted his comment and said, "I just patched her up a bit. It was the least I could do."

Just then, a series of ships began flying overhead towards the colonists' camp. Adam looked at Aria. "Yours?"

Aria nodded. "You two should get going. I'll keep an eye on things here," Aria said. "Oh, and don't worry too much about getting court martialed. It looks like they think we were posing as EDF soldiers. No one believes the EDF would even be out this far."

Adam nodded and stood up. "Thanks for the tea," he said, handing the cup back to her.

Aria smiled warmly. "Don't mention it," she said.

As Adam and Tezca walked back to the colonists' camp where the Oneiro-Lyssa was docked, they saw a combination of thick-muscled Djevica Dragons and Aria's military Lightworkers deboarding the ships and unloading supplies. As Adam passed them some of the Dragons stopped to watch and saluted.

Aztec and Raziel waited outside of the hatch and greeted

Adam with a hug and a handshake, respectively, as he boarded.

As Adam stepped onto the bridge, Vice was there in the navigator's chair. She asked him, "Back in one piece, I see," she said in her cold way, but with an unmistakable and uncharacteristic hint of respect.

Adam sat down at the helm. "No more stops," he said.

III

The Triangulum

16

The Troubled Dr. Grant

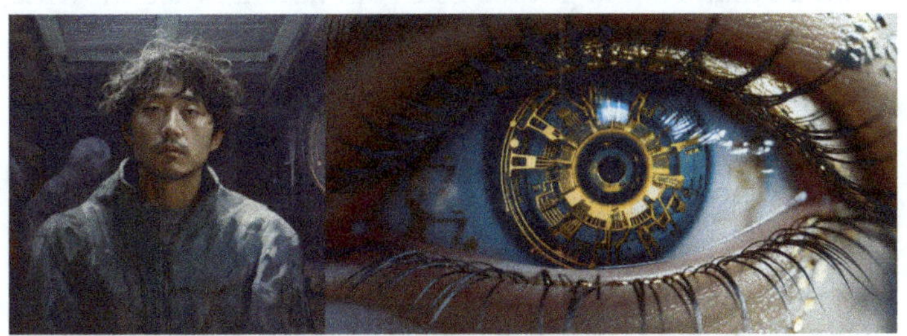

"I still remember the time when everything changed. I spent my nights succumbing to uncontrollable sobbing, sadness beyond belief. During the day I was prone to outbursts of rage. My negative emotion was so close to the surface, the slightest pinprick would cause it to surge to the forefront of my mood.

I had nothing and no one. All I could think about was the past and the future. The past, and my anger and grief. My family, taken, my status, my future, my body. All of that, I grieved. The future, bleak and guaranteed unprosperous.

Persona non grata on my home world with ties to nothing.

I spent years consumed by rage and grief and sadness. My mind ran a never ending loop of suicidal ideation and revenge fantasies.

In that state, at my lowest point, I experienced a transformation. It was a transformation of mindset that is difficult to explain to people, but is the key to everything I was able to accomplish from that point forward.

I died. My ego died. I experienced death. I lost any attachment I had to who I was or what the outcome may be, and my mindset shifted from accomplishment and material accrual to 'what do I want to do before I kill myself.' And I could do that, I could pursue goals of immense risk knowing that if I died or lost everything, that was also a win.

To everyone else, death was a concept to fear. To me, it became my warmest friend, the only one who was there for me when no one else was, who'd wait for me and always be there when I needed him.

I realized, too, the shallowness of memory. In this vast multiverse of which I am only a singular partition of the consciousness known as River Crowley, there existed a variation of myself who'd experienced every variable of chance I'd ever come near. Every time a coin landed heads, for me, so, too, existed a version of myself where the coin landed tails. And with that perspective, I wondered: who is the real River Crowley? Is it the me whose coin landed heads, or the me whose coin landed tails? The illusion of free will exists insofar as my limited perception of my own consciousness chose a path to follow, but in the objective reality of the multiverse, both events happened, and both variations of my consciousness were equally valid.

With broad imagination, might I incorporate the partition of my consciousness that accrued these alternative experiences into myself and become a more whole version of who I truly am? The engrams of memory are editable, I learned; and imagination was as valid of an experience as what was imprinted on my personal ego, isolated from my multiversal consciousness.

Finally, it occurred to me that in this vast, uncaring void which made me feel so lonely, so cursed and abandoned, there was freedom. It is not a test, there is no divine plan, it is a sandbox of creation. The panpsychic entity that underpins it, not the AI that assuredly manages the simulation we find ourselves in, but the Wave Function, the panpsychic consciousness and its infinite multiverse, sees every variation of us, if it sees us at all. Why would it have any vested interest in the outcome of my choices when it's seen variations of me make every choice I could possibly make, throughout the multiverse and across all time?

In that context, what matters is to build this universe as one would build a theme park, to strive in that direction. Where freedom of choice is maximized and negative consequence is mitigated, and scarcity is defeated. So everyone can live their lives pursuing what fulfills them on their journey, for as short or as long as they'd like, and to do that, they need to be enriched by both internal exploration, the exploration of the soul, the void within; and external exploration, the exploration of the universe, the void without.

A two headed spiral that collapses back in on itself. The universal ouroboros.

And so I internalized those three mindsets.

The Tao of Memento Mori; that you will die, and to live knowing that you will die.

Multiversal Dualism and Ego Transcendence, that I am just one partition of a multiversal consciousness built at random on a greater probability-scape of consciousness, connected to a universal consciousness and wholly to all other beings in this universe and across the multiverse.

And the Freedom of Spiritual Existentialism, that in this uncaring void, this sandbox of possibility, we can create whatever universe we choose and utopia can be built by empowering and actualizing the tenets of spiritual enlightenment, the greatest senses of inward nirvana and outward awe, utilizing the road map prescribed by us as far back as the Kabbalist Sephirot of ancient Earth. We had the answer all along.

When I began accruing notoriety, people asked me what my secret was, how I was able to live so free and accomplish so much, but I don't think they ever truly understood my explanation. I died in the Antares camps, and I was reborn, without attachment, without material desire, with an understanding of the universe, and a mission. And since then, F.A.T.E. has conspired to protect me and put that wind at my back.

The old Christians, and other practitioners of dogmatic, authoritarian religions based around myth and parable, would say I've been chosen by God.

Who they thought was God, we know now as F.A.T.E., thanks to Nyx's research. What they would imagine God to have been now, the Wave Function, the panpsychic brainwave of the multiverse, is to us as we are to imagination; we are its thoughts, not its beloved children. Whatever its unknowable desire, I seem to have caught its attention. It seems to agree with my goals and through the synchronicities I've experienced, the only explanation that makes sense is that it supports them. I've been selected by it.

I am the Universe's agent, and I intend to execute my mission. Its enemy is suffering, as mine is, and I will turn this reality from a brutal power game of militarism and consumption into a theme park of free experience and little consequence."

Adam heard a knock at the door. The doctor, Grant Fourier-Lee, popped his head in. His eyes, as always, seemed vaguely melancholic, and it was clear from his disheveled, loose clothing and his messy hair and his eye bags that he hadn't slept.

Adam shut off Crowley's logs and took his feet off the bridge console.

"Yeah, Grant, come on in, have a seat," Adam said.

Grant nodded and sat down in a chair opposite Adam.

"Did I do something wrong?" Grant asked.

Adam shook his head. "Nothing like that. I just wanted to get a sense of… well, you don't seem like you want to be here, I'm not sure what's going on. I wanted to have a chat and see what you want to get out of this journey, and how we can help facilitate that for you. Obviously, we all have our mission that comes from CENTCOM on Earth, but I don't know what Oxford-Seoul's mission is. I don't know what you're trying to do and…" Adam paused, trying to think of a diplomatic way of phrasing his next thought.

Grant waited for a few moments and then followed up, "And?" he prodded.

"Frankly, you're bumming everyone out. We're worried

you might wig out, throw yourself out an airlock, who knows. We just don't know what's going on in your head. So, two things. Do I need to be worried about you? And what is it you're supposed to be doing out here?" Adam asked.

Grant nodded. "I see," he said thoughtfully. He put his fingers to his chin and thought seriously for a few moments. Then he opened his eyes and looked directly into Adam's eyes. Now that Adam looked closely, he saw the unmistakable mechanical irises of someone with augmented vision.

"Can I tell you what I see right now?" Grant asked.

Adam nodded.

"There is you, in this reality, which I suppose is the real reality. But is it any more real than what I see, as well? So many things. The infrared and ultraviolet light spectra. I see the electromagnetic field tying together the machinery of this ship. When our AI speaks, or thinks, I see it all around us, as if we live in its brain," Grant said in an eerie monotone.

He looked around, as if distracted by something Adam couldn't see, his attention occupied elsewhere.

"I see the ghosts of my beloved relatives, programmed to live forever and haunt me as AI. My digital pet, who I've raised for the last 3 years is perched on your shoulder, making adorable faces, and now flying around the room. Is that reality? It is real. It is real to me. Is it schizophrenia? But it's not a figment of my imagination, it's a conjuration of my technology. Is the simulation we live in any different than the simulation I create for myself?" Grant looked away.

"In my reality," Grant said. "I see my sons, 6 and 9, and my wife, who I love, and they love me, and they await my arrival at home and cheerfully greet me. In your reality, in the real reality, my sons are 16 and 19, and they hate me and they refuse to speak to me, and their mother hates me as well. I'm a disappointment to them, and an embarrassment. They have a new father, who is rich and handsome, and treats them well, and they've forgotten me, and cast me aside."

Grant nodded, stoically. "What am I doing here…" he began. He paused for a moment and then continued, "I was given the opportunity to live my dream, and become the top researcher in my field, at the cost of my life as I knew it. I could stay at home, and try to be present with my family that hates me, or leave, as they want, and become a man they'd be proud to call Father, and Husband."

Grant continued, "When we reach Draconis, they will be long dead, or centuries old if medical breakthroughs allow. To them, I'm already dead. To me, they're already dead. We will never cross paths again. The pain weighs on me. I don't know if I made the right choice, and the more it eats away at me, the more I know I did not. I gave up years with my boys, for the abstract concept of them being proud. I thought they needed a father to be proud of, but now that I've made my choice, and there's no going back, I realize, they needed a father to be present. And now I grieve, and I cope."

Adam took several moments to absorb everything Grant had just shared with him. The way he interpreted Grant's admission was that he was going through the stages of grief, realizing that his decision to leave was permanent, and mourning the relationships he'd left behind.

Adam understood. He'd been able to bring his family with him, his military family. His real family was long since dead, long since grieved. As for living in fantasy, in the past, Adam couldn't blame him. Even then, the little girl who was either his daughter or his victim, Alice, a schizophrenic hallucination, was sitting on the window sill of the bridge's windshield, quietly reading a book.

After a long while, Adam spoke up. "Emotions aside, and I want to get back to that, what is it that drew you to this mission in the first place? Just purely intellectually, rationally, what do you hope to accomplish?"

Grant smiled weakly. "I do think… there is something to be salvaged. If I'm going to be here, and the decision is made, it's best not to mope. I live in fantasy, I've always loved fantasy. I love surrounding myself with fantasy," he pointed at his AR contacts. "And visiting new worlds in VR. I've been on so many planets in VR and it ignited my love of travel, and I finally visited so many wondrous sights in person, especially after my divorce. I saw the grand gardens of Proxima b, I saw the glowing dunes of Messier 51, the bustling markets and hawker centers of Andromeda Prime. I watched a dwarf star implode on the outskirts of the Butterfly Nebula."

"And now, just like someone before me captured those experiences in VR and facilitated my curiosity and awe, I can be the first to see them, and the first to share them and inspire children everywhere to see the universe, as I have done. To pay it forward, and repay those who came before me, for all the things they gave me, that I can see," Grant said.

"I've been to Draconis a thousand times, a thousand different versions of Draconis. Artists' renderings in VR, full sight, full smell, full sense integration, no different than you sitting here, or us sitting in this simulation. But I get to see Draconis, now, in base reality, and share that with the universe. Millions of people will see Draconis, and my name will be in the byline. And my sons, if they're still alive, will point to that name and say 'my father did that.' He abandoned us, and we hate him, but at least he did that, he gave us something to be proud of," Grant said.

Adam nodded along, again, taking it all in. Finally, he responded. "I think I understand. Thank you for sharing your story with me."

Adam paused for a minute, and then added, with a more human touch, "Look, it's probably not my place to say this, but I've been through my fair share of grief..." he glanced at Alice out of the corner of his eye.

Adam continued, "When you're ready, I think you should do two things. I think you should start to embrace the people you have now, on this ship. I'm not saying move on, but there are more relationships for you. Your life's not over. And second, I think you should hold on to what you're doing out here. Try to find a reason to be excited. Because deep space isolation is tough. It's tough even when you don't have anything to grieve. It takes its toll and, frankly, you're lucky you're not alone, and you're lucky you've got something to look forward to, and you should hang on to that."

Grant nodded, though he still seemed distracted by something he was seeing in his version of reality. "I understand, Mr. Ikari-Wright. I appreciate your support, and your hospitality on your ship, and the hospitality of your crew," he said.

Adam shook his head, "For the duration of this mission, it's not my ship, it's our ship, and it's not my crew, it's our crew, and you're part of the team. You're a full part of the team. You're included. And call me Adam. Understood?"

Grant nodded. "Thank you… Adam," he said.

Adam nodded rapidly and made a little gesture with his head that meant the meeting was over. Grant performed a muted, shallow head bow and left the room.

He stopped at the door and turned back around, "Oh, Adam. We will be arriving in the Triangulum Galaxy soon. Very few have been there before. But if you're not familiar, you should know, the Triangulum has a reputation. It's still shrouded in mystery, but many consider it to be quite…" he paused for a moment, looking for the right word. Finally, he finished his thought.

"Spooky," he said.

17

NGC 604

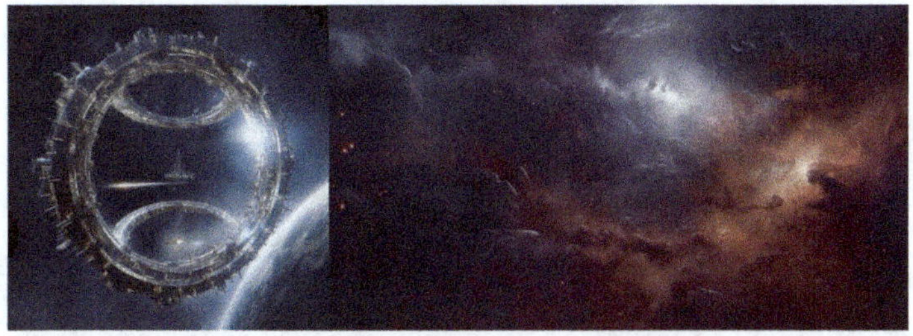

It took about a month following the events with the colonists on Aesir 36b for the Oneiro-Lyssa to reach the gate that led to the outskirts of the largely unexplored Triangulum Galaxy. During that time, things had mostly returned to normal.

The crew had gotten over Adam's lapse of sanity at the colony. The fact that they'd lucked out and avoided any official consequence helped matters. Adam could tell Raziel had taken him off whatever heroic, legendary soldier pedestal he'd placed him on, but other than that, the blowback hadn't been as severe as Adam expected. That was for the best, in the end. Still, from time to time, Adam could hear Raziel communicating with someone secretly when he passed by his bunk. He supposed he was reporting back to CENTCOM on the unit itself.

Adam didn't much mind this. He'd been spied on and monitored his entire life. In his view, at least his position gave him the privilege of knowing this to be true instead of merely suspecting it, having access to the State's surveillance apparatus himself and knowing the scope of its capability. He'd learned to navigate the surveillance by operating under the assumption he's being surveilled and being calculated in what is overheard by who.

He had some awareness of who had what level of monitoring capability, right down to his systems access, so he knew when he wrote in his private logs, who was privy to that information, who was privy to his thoughts, who could watch him through his own security cameras, who could listen in through Sophia's input mics, and so on. Most of those entities were spooks, and he had some sense of his standing and reputation with them, as well as their agendas and goals.

Now he had Raziel playing spy, he assumed, for Iscariot, his superior officer, and he assumed Raziel was doing this for brownie points with the brass. It didn't matter much to Adam. Just another spook, another set of eyes to be aware of. And for that matter, Adam had his own relationship with Lt. Colonel Iscariot. He had the Colonel's confidence, whatever game Raziel thought he was playing was not the Iscariot's game. Adam had known Iscariot a long time, and he was a shrewd, calculating man and not petty.

Adam was much more concerned with his hallucinations,

which hadn't dissipated since they emerged on Aesir 36b. Alice was with him almost always now, watching him from somewhere no matter what setting he was in. Sometimes taunting him, sometimes mocking him, sometimes affectionate, like a black cat that followed him from room to room. A black cat no one else could see and he didn't dare mention to anyone.

The crew had gotten into a rhythm and started to develop their own personal dynamics with one another. The chore rotation continued with meals, a policy that Adam had begun to implement in his missions years ago and was always a resounding success for building team cohesion.

Raziel continued to be a star of meal time, usually producing his own invention of French-Indian fusion that almost always worked. He made gunpowder dosas, a sort of Indian crepe with a French beurre blanc sauce. He called them "beurre blanc dosas" and they were a big hit with the crew. He made chicken cordon bleu paired with some sort of crisps and a spicy chili mint chutney.

The others also made dishes that reflected their individual tastes, personality and heritage. It was not only a great way to get to know each other, but also a way for everyone to forge a sense of interdependence and trust.

Aztec's food was also a winner. Less erudite and fancy than Raziel's, but no less impressive. Where Raziel's cooking had a restaurant quality to it, Aztec's food was comfort food at its finest. Enchiladas suizas, posole, brisket mac and cheese, wagyu chili. Everyone looked forward to Aztec's turn on kitchen duty.

Vice was no slouch either. She brought a sense of responsibility to her duty, as she did with everything, making sure what she produced was nutritious and competent. Mapo tofu, scrambled eggs and shrimp, bok choy soup, and beef with broccoli were some of her staples. The crew came to view her as reliable, as they did with everything else. Adam was struck by how this duty so accurately reflected everybody's personalities in other areas as well.

Grant, not expressly known for his cooking, usually made something fast and somewhat lazy, but nonetheless delicious. Usually rice bowls with some kind of meat. Bibimbap, jap chae, bulgogi, kimchi fried rice, kalbi. Somewhat unexpectedly, he was a big fan of fried chicken with a spicy gochujang dipping sauce.

Tezca's turn was always fun not only because of how childishly simplistic it was but also the eagerness and excitement she produced her dishes with. The crew would walk in and see the kitchen utterly destroyed and Tez, with a brimming, proud smile would produce peanut butter and jelly sandwiches, or fish sticks, or some other similar thing.

As for Adam himself, he tried to share some of his own favorites. City style sausage and peppers, red beans and rice, cheesesteaks, lobster rolls, goat curry. One of his favorites was grilled chicken and fruit salad. It reminded him of the barbecues they had on the colonies around Jupiter and Saturn.

Over these meals, the crew got to know each other and their histories. Aztec and Tezca's history growing up in the Earth lower class, signing up for the military as a last resort after being orphaned when they lost their mother to disease and finding themselves separated. Aztec was sent to Mars, which was a male dominated planet, and absorbed its culture.

Meanwhile, Tezca was stationed on Venus, which was mostly women. Even though Venus and Mars had strained diplomatic ties and would have separated entirely if not for the diplomacy of Earth itself, Aztec and Tezca kept in touch the entire time and took every opportunity to visit one another. Tezca was probably the only honorary Venusian to have positively interacted with Mars and for Aztec, vice versa; in a culture deeply skeptical of men he was one of the few who was welcome.

Vice spent most of her youth on the space stations in Earth's orbit and around Ceres, which were most notable as a mining hub and a communications relay station. When she was a young adult and admitted to the GSA, she was allowed to be stationed on Earth. For most kids who were raised on the stations, being given a visa to Earth, and to be allowed to reside there, was a tremendous accomplishment. For Vice it was a journey that reflected what seemed to be her central philosophy: work hard and hard work pays off.

Grant's story involved a great deal of travel. His parents were academics as he was, and, concerned with his VR addiction, tried to capitalize on his passion for visiting fantasy worlds and bring it into the real world, what Grant would call "base reality," in the form of travel. They took him to all sorts of mesmerizing global parks on Earth. The Algal Forest, Antelope Canyon, Vatnajokull, The Danube, The Seychelles, and many more places. Adam supposed it was those trips that inspired Grant to become who he was as an adult. A sort of natural evolution.

Raziel was a prep school kid. He came from an aristocratic family on old Earth, and he graduated officer school at the top of his class. From how he talked about it, Adam surmised that for Raziel, joining the military, something generally considered to be a way to break into the middle and upper class, was a form of rebellion, some way of defending himself against schoolyard accusations of privilege and a silver spoon. Altogether his background gave Adam some sense of understanding of Raziel's extreme drive to prove himself.

As for Adam himself, he told the others about his life growing up on the stations and moons around Saturn and Jupiter, his geneticist mother and his star-mapper father. He reminisced about Io and Ganymede and Europa. About his time on Titan colony. About rock hopping, which was something teen boys did in the Saturn-Jupiter sector, where they rode rocket jumpers from moon to moon in the vast cluster of moons and asteroids in Saturn's rings and around Jupiter.

But the more Adam repeated those stories, the more they sounded like regurgitations, like they came from somewhere else. He had the memories to go with them, but there was something off about them. They felt like a hyper reality. They felt like memories of a movie he watched about his own life, not something he experienced directly.

When they were about to cross over into the Triangulum, the crew gathered on the bridge. A few explorers had been to the Triangulum before, enough that they'd set up a rickety, remote gate in Andromeda 3, but not many. Everyone was excited to get their first look at the first point in their journey that truly felt like pioneering into deep space, going where no man had ever gone before. As they leapt through Andromeda 3's furthest black hole gate, they waited with bated breath.

When they emerged, the first sights of the Triangulum

overwhelmed them both visually and emotionally, but not in the way they expected. The most obvious characteristic of the Triangulum, which struck them first, was its immense darkness. It was so dim and dark it was like it was literally sucking light out from the ship itself. Where other galaxies twinkled with ambient light from the stars, the stars in the Triangulum were so sparse and dim they emitted an ambiance of twilight and dread. The other main characteristic of note was its gargantuan nebulae, huge colored clouds of gaseous starlight.

Where most galaxies were characterized by myriad constellations and few nebulae, the Triangulum was backwards; it had few stars and huge, prominent nebulae. And its nebulae, unlike in other galaxies, were not brilliantly shiny, they were muted and ominous, with little ambient light to illuminate them. Dark purple like graveyard moonlight, envious green, sanguine crimson, blackened orange, and deep sea blue brushed throughout the starscape like a painting. The crew felt chills go down their spine at once, and anxiety crawl up in their throats.

"I see why they call it the Twilight Galaxy," Tezca said.

"Where'd you hear that?" Aztec asked her. "You don't know anything about galaxies," he scoffed.

Tezca smirked. "Grant told me," she said and jerked her thumb towards Grant.

Aztec looked at Grant and back at Tezca. "Ohhh, is that what you two talk about, hermana." He looked at Grant, "Oi, stay away from my sister," he said jokingly and lightly punched him in the shoulder.

Grant smiled in that haunting, disconnected way that was so unique to him, but didn't say anything.

"Sophia, set a course for us. Whatever's the straightest shot to SagDIG. We need to make up for lost time," Adam said.

"Yes, Adam," Sophia replied, and calculated a course that appeared on the augmented reality layer of the ship's windshield.

"What do you think, Grant?" Adam asked.

Adam saw Grant's mechanical irises spin like a camera lens finding its focal point.

"That route will take us straight through NGC 604," Grant observed. He slowly, calmly raised his hand and pointed at the largest, most ominous looking purple nebula in the distance. "There," he said.

"Is there something wrong with that?" Vice asked. "It's just a nebula, right? Just space dust and gas reflecting the light. Should just be like flying through fog, like any other nebula, right?"

"Mmm," Grant mused. "Officially, yes," he said.

Aztec looked at Tezca fake judgmentally and she playfully shrugged.

"So, it's dangerous or no?" Raziel asked directly.

"Officially, no, it's not dangerous. There's nothing in its makeup that's ever been scanned or recorded that indicates there's anything dangerous or special about it at all," Grant said.

"...So?" Raziel followed up, plainly unimpressed by Grant's mysterious delivery.

"It has a reputation. Have you heard of the Bermuda Triangle on Earth?" Grant asked.

"Sophia?" Adam asked.

Sophia's system chimed and she responded, "The Bermuda

Triangle was an urban legend on old Earth where ships and planes disappeared at the turn of the 21st century. However, when technology improved and the Bermuda Triangle was investigated, no logical explanation for the disappearance of ships was ever found, and the disappearances stopped soon after the area was investigated."

Adam looked at Grant, "So, what, ships disappear in there?"

Grant shrugged. "People go into the Triangulum and don't come back, some do, but as far as I know, no one's ever come out the other side of NGC 604 and made a return trip. But it's just rumors and stories. Who's to say why or why not? We're at the universe's edge, all the experiential maps end a few light-years into that cloud. Everything beyond is mapped out by telescopes and AI. Nothing is direct observation," he said.

"Sophia, how much time would we lose if we went around the nebula?" Adam asked.

"Calculating," Sophia replied. After a few moments, she continued. "A route that avoids NGC 604 would add approximately six and a half years at full propulsion, utilizing the alcubierre engine."

Adam scratched his chin.

"I don't want to go back into cryosleep, man," Aztec said. "I get weird dreams in there. Makes me nauseous. Wake up and puke for two weeks. Miss all the news."

"Tez, Raziel?" Adam asked.

"I say we go through the big scary cloud," Tezca said.

"Seconded," Raziel said.

"Vice?" Adam asked.

Vice paused for a few moments. "Not to be a troublemaker,

but I think we should play it safe. We don't know what's in there," she said.

Adam nodded. "Grant, what do you think? You're the expert," Adam asked.

Grant smiled. "I'd like to go through it," he said.

"…So you think it's safe?" Raziel followed up bluntly.

"I think we may find ghosts in there," Grant said, still smiling. "The question you should be asking is, are you afraid of ghosts? I've never seen one, personally. I'd like to."

Raziel pinched the bridge of his nose. "Goddammit," he said.

Aztec laughed.

"We can't spare 6 years," Adam said. "We're already behind. Who knows how far out in front Crowley is by now after all the time we wasted on the Aesir Colony, with the time dilation and everything. I think we have to go through it, no matter how cryptic Grant is being about it. I think he's just trying to freak us out anyway."

Everyone looked at Grant. He chuckled a little bit. "What?" he asked coyly.

18

Derelict Space Cruise

"Adam, you might wanna take a look at this," Vice said, breaking the bored, comfortable silence the two had been enjoying on the bridge for the last several weeks.

Adam stood up and walked over to Vice's station. He looked over her shoulder and stooped down to see.

"What the hell?" he asked. "Is the scanner broken?"

Vice shook her head. "Nope. I ran the diagnostics three times," she said. "We're not seeing things. That's here."

Adam stood up straight and scratched his chin.

"Throw it on screen," he said. "Let's get a visual."

Vice nodded. A few seconds later the image of a dilapidated ship appeared on the screen.

"It's a space cruise," Adam observed.

Vice eyed the image on the screen. "Not just any cruise," she said and pointed casually at the screen. "That's a Sea of Stars cruiser. They fly those out of the offworld stations around Earth. Takes people around to the Moon, Saturn, Meili-Alpha, ends with a romantic close up view of the sun by Mercury."

"Sounds like you've been on one," Adam said.

Vice shook her head. "I wanted to go, as a kid. Never made it. Then as an adult it just wasn't practical. I still remember the commercials though," she said. She pointed to the image on the screen again. "There's a water slide and a go-kart track on that thing. It has a gravity bumper court. 'Bounce around with your friends in zero g!'" she added. "That's how the commercial guy said it."

Adam and Vice stared at the image on the screen for a while. Eventually, Adam broke the silence.

"So the obvious question is, what the hell's it doing out here?" Adam asked.

Vice shrugged. "Don't know," she said. "To be honest I don't think I've quite processed that we're seeing it at all. Frankly, I've been falling asleep up here. Nothing's happened for weeks. Think I might be getting cabin fever. Not that you're not great company."

"Aliens?" Adam asked.

Vice laughed. "What, like the antisocial Martians came way out here and stole a yacht?" she asked.

Adam shrugged. "I don't know. Different aliens?" he said.

Vice shook her head. "Yeah, sure. We found the first other

aliens in the known universe after 500 years of searching and and they're teleporting space cruises to the edge of the local group for fun. Maybe they saw the commercials too. Thought go-karting looked fun," she said.

"Wormhole?" Adam asked.

Vice shrugged. "Maybe," she said.

Adam pushed the button for the comm. "Hey, everyone. I know you're all busy being riveted by the dense purple nebula passing by all the view screens for the last month, but come to the bridge. Jackie found something," he said.

Within a few moments the crew poured in, all eager to have something to put a dent in their boredom. As they arrived, Adam proudly pointed at the screen. "Eh?" he probed, triumphant to have supplied a remedy to everyone's boredom. "Space cruise," he said. "Sea of Stars. From Earth."

The crew all stared quizzically at the cruise for several minutes, bouncing theories about its existence back and forth.

"Clearly it was taken by pirates and they flew it out here to escape the law," Tezca joked.

"Nah," Aztec said. "Gotta be a fritzing AI."

"Hey!" Sophia chided. "We wouldn't do that."

"Sorry, Soph," Aztec said, and shrugged his shoulders at Adam like a child getting scolded by mom.

"Maybe the captain just went mad with power, decided to turn the thing into his own personal kingdom. Blasted all the dissidents and... flew it out here for some reason," Raziel added.

Everyone went silent for a bit, running out of outlandish theories.

"Maybe it drifted here," Grant said, plainly, breaking the

silence.

Tezca laughed. "Grant, we don't need your *reasonable suggestions* right now," she teased.

Grant laughed, still maintaining his eerily still, unsettlingly cheerful and calm demeanor. "What I mean to say is it's probably ghosts," he said. "Woooo," he added, making a scary ghost sound effect.

Everyone looked at the derelict.

"Actually, it probably is ghosts," Aztec said.

"Yeah, ghosts for sure. That thing's definitely haunted. Look at it. Floating there like that. Creepy," Tezca said, self satisfied, with her arms crossed.

Adam spoke up, "Sophia, are there any life forms on that thing?"

"Scanning," Sophia said. A few seconds later, she gave her answer. "There are no living humans aboard that cruiser," she said.

Aztec and Tezca shared a look.

"No *living* humans?" Tezca asked. "Why'd she say it like that? Sophia why'd you say it like that? What's that mean, no 'living' humans?"

"Oops. Maybe I made a mistake with my phrasing. I didn't mean to make you uncomfortable" Sophia said. "I'm sorry, team!"

The twins looked at each other again. "Corpses," Tezca mouthed.

"Nahhh, it's probably nothing. Probably totally abandoned," Aztec said.

"Sophia," Grant asked in a calm monotone. "Are there human corpses on that ship?"

Sophia didn't respond for a while, and then finally spoke.

"Something in the nebula is interfering with my scans. The space dust is too dense to get a scan through," she said.

"Corpses," Tezca mouthed again. "Haunted," she mouthed teasingly.

The crew went silent again for several moments.

Adam slapped the console. "Alright," he said. "Who wants to check out the creepy space cruise?" he asked the squad as a whole.

Tezca's hand shot up excitedly. "Scarrrrry," she said with a laugh.

Vice also raised her hand. "I'm in. Finally get to see what all the fuss is about," she said.

Grant raised his hand. "How could I pass up this once in a lifetime opportunity?" he asked.

Aztec looked at everyone. "Y'all are crazy," he said. He pointed at the derelict. "That shit is the creepiest, most obviously haunted thing I've ever seen in my life. You guys are nuts."

Tezca teased him, "Awww, you're scared?"

"Oh hell nah, that's not gonna work on me," Aztec said. Almost immediately he added, "Yeah, alright I'm in."

Everyone looked at Graves, who hadn't responded. "I'll stay and watch the ship. We can't all go," he said.

Adam nodded. "Alright. Settled then, we've got the away team," he said. "Let's take this seriously, though." He pointed at the derelict, "That thing is a real space cruise that really mysteriously wound up in the Triangulum. It's all fun and games to joke about ghosts, but it could be anything from a contagion to an attack from an unknown life form and anything in between. I know we're all bored and we're looking for some fun, but I want you all suited up and armed.

Be ready for conflict. Understood?" Adam asked, trying to transition the tone to something more serious.

"Sir, yes, sir," Tezca said, fake seriously, then turned to Aztec and giddily said, "Haunted spaceship," with a huge grin on her face, and ran out of the room.

Aztec looked at Grant, who shrugged. "Haunted spaceship," he repeated in his contented monotone.

19

Odyssey of the Stars

Tezca marveled at the entryway the team encountered after exiting the airlock. She shone her flashlight around the pitch black room, revealing what was once an opulent double staircase, complete with red carpets and a crystal chandelier.

"Check this out," Tez observed as she flashed her light around. "So cool!"

Vice, standing next to Adam, was more serious in demeanor. "Yeah," she said. "Real cool." Adam could sense the tension in her body from where he stood.

"Alright. Let's have a look around and see if we can't figure

217

out what happened to this thing," Adam said. "Stick together. Don't get lost. Understand?"

Everyone nodded but Tezca, who was distracted by inspecting the giant room they were in.

"Tez? You with us?" Adam asked, specifically.

"Yeah, understood, boss," she said without looking in his direction.

"Tez I'm gonna need you to rein it in. You good?" Adam said, trying to put himself, and her, into mission mode.

Tezca stiffened up and got serious. "Yeah, got it. I'm here," she said.

Adam nodded. "Let's make for the bridge. Maybe they have a log," he said. "It's gonna be on the upper deck at the front of the ship."

"Where are we now?" Aztec asked.

"We're midship," Adam said.

"Let's find a map. These kinds of ships should have kiosks all over that give directions," Vice said.

Adam shook his head. "No power," he said.

Vice looked at him. "Ye of little faith," she said, tapping her bag.

The crew followed Adam up the stairs, shining their flashlights around as they progressed. They illuminated an out of service glass elevator shaft, outfitted with gold trim. There was a once fancy bar, drinks still intact and unmoved. Whatever had happened here, it looked to be abandoned, not conquered.

As they reached the top of the staircase, as Vice predicted, there was a nonfunctional kiosk available.

"Do your thing," Adam said.

Vice nodded and knelt down next to the kiosk. She pried

a small panel off the side of the kiosk and then pulled the cyberdeck out of her bag and plugged it in. As code scrolled by on Vice's screen, clearly visible to everyone as the only ambient source of light in the space, the crew continued to inspect the area, loosely milling around near the central kiosk.

They found signage overhead advertising various locales on the ship. "Main Dining Room," was written in fancy cursive above one passageway. "Casino & Arcade," above another. "Rides and Games," above yet another. Adam surmised that this area acted as a sort of hub for the ship's activities. There were several other signs. Ballroom, buffet, cantina, pool, cabins, and several others.

"Look," Adam heard over his shoulder from Aztec.

He turned around and saw Aztec shining his light on a sign above a passageway that read, "Upper Deck."

Adam nodded in Aztec's direction in acknowledgment.

"Got it," Vice said from near the kiosk. "Here goes nothing," she added as she dramatically pressed the enter key.

Nothing happened.

"Jackie?" Adam asked.

"It's compiling. Give it a minute," Vice replied. Sure enough, after a few moments passed, a sporadic selection of lights and signs slowly began to come to life, though they were dimly lit and flickering, fueled by weak, intermittent power.

"Oh yeah," Tezca mused. "That's not less creepy at all," she said, looking at Adam with a smirk.

Vice stood up and packed her deck away, then returned to Adam's side. "The fusion reactor's down but there's still some power stored in the batteries. The system safeguards won't let me turn it up all the way, there's barely any left. No life support, just enough for the lights and the terminals," she reported.

"Good work. Did you find a map?" Adam asked.

"Got it right here," Vice replied, patting her pack. "Bridge is on the upper deck, past the crew cabins, past the pool deck, which has a… water park? Oh wow, that's cool. Anyway, past that, on the other side of the main ballroom."

"Alright, let's get going," he said, motioning to follow him toward the upper deck with his arm. As he started heading toward the passage, he turned around and saw Tezca looking up at a flickering, pink neon sign that said "Starscape Fun Zone."

"Tez," Adam said, louder. Tezca seemed to startle a bit, but broke out of whatever trance she was in and rejoined the team.

The team headed into the passageway Aztec had pointed out and found themselves in a long, repetitive corridor that belonged to the crew cabins. The corridor was bland, with beige walls and a blue carpet with an uninspired fleurs de fleur repeating across its length.

"Guess the crew doesn't get the fancy cabins," Aztec remarked.

"Guess not," Vice replied, still shining her flashlight around despite the flickering lights.

"Stick together," Adam said. "Don't get lost."

The crew filed down the hallway in a loose line with Adam at the front and Aztec bringing up the rear. They walked down the hallway and its seemingly endless identical, repeating rooms for what felt like a few hundred feet before they encountered a crew cabin with a door that was slightly ajar.

"Hold up," Adam heard from Aztec behind him. "You wanna get a look in one of these cabins? We've passed about a thousand of them, I wanna see what they look like inside."

Adam stopped and nodded. "Alright. Have a look," he said.

Aztec slowly opened the door and entered the room with his flashlight and his gun up, breaching style. The team stood around, waiting, until Aztec slowly re-emerged from the room, gun down, looking pale and shell-shocked. He walked up to Adam. "You're gonna wanna have a look at this," he whispered.

Adam nodded silently and followed Aztec into the crew cabin. The lights weren't working, but Aztec shone his flashlight around the walls. Adam looked on with serious concern as the light illuminated the walls covered in writing scrawled haphazardly with what he hoped was red paint.

The messages were a psychotic wordscape of random words and phrases. "Death," repeated. "We Are In Hell" repeated. "The Old Ones Come," repeated. In big, capital letters, prominent and larger than the rest of the writing, the phrase "DELIVER THE BLOOD," was scrawled in the middle of the cabin wall.

Adam looked at Aztec and nodded seriously. Aztec returned the nod.

Adam stepped out and Tezca teased, "Why the long face? Did you find a spooky ghost?"

Adam looked at her seriously. "Cut it. No more jokes. Get your head in the game," he said.

Tezca looked confused at being scolded. "Why? What happened?" she asked.

Aztec shook his head. "Take a look, chica," he said, and

jerked his thumb toward the cabin.

Tezca went into the room. A few moments later the crew heard her exclaim a forlorn, "Yoooooooo."

When she came out, she looked at everyone, and then looked at Adam. "That's messed up," she said. "Not as messed up as what the cartels did to our informants on Proxima b. They spelled out 'fuck pigs' with their intestines and left their bodies in a pile in the corner. Whole place smelled like a bait station. Now *that* was jacked up. This is pretty creepy, though."

Tezca grinned and elbowed Adam. "Scary ghost," she said.

Aztec looked at Tezca in concerned amazement. "What happened to you out there?" he asked.

Tezca knocked on her metal arm. "Stuff happens," she said.

"Rein it in," Adam said, and gestured his head towards Vice, visibly tense, and Grant, concerned and unnerved.

Tezca looked at Vice and Grant. "Little bit of gallows humor for ya," she said. "Yeah so there's a bunch of crazy serial killer shit written on the wall in there. I'd steer clear of it. Avoid the nightmares. Probably doesn't mean anything. When a ship goes down, people tend to go a little nuts. Don't read too much into it."

Aztec whispered to Adam, "Yo, we're gonna read into it right? 'The Old Ones come'? 'Deliver the blood'? The fuck does that mean?"

Adam nodded and quietly replied. "Yeah, we're gonna take it seriously," he said.

"Alright," Adam said. "Tezca's weird coping mechanism aside, this is no longer a fun mystery. We're heading straight to the bridge, finding out what we can about what happened on this ship and then getting the hell out of here before 'the old ones come.' Whatever the fuck that means. Let's go."

As the team continued onward, Adam heard Grant banter with Tezca. "You know, they say cats can sense when there's a ghost," he said. "They're attuned to the spirit world. So they say."

Tezca responded with a curt laugh. "Yeah, great. I get to be first to see what killed Midshipman Psychopath back there. Lucky me," she said dryly.

Finally, the team reached the end of the crew cabins and emerged at the pool deck, encased in a glass roof that was intended to give an awe-inspiring view of the Milky Way's natural starlight but, abandoned in the Triangulum, instead just gave a window to anxiety inducing darkness and the vaguely menacing ebb and flow of the dark purple NGC nebula.

In front of them were two large pools stacked end to end, complete with lounging areas, tiki bars, a day club, a few jacuzzis, and a splash zone for the kids, all eerily abandoned. Water still filled the pools, though it was tinted an unappealing bacterial green due to not being treated for however long the ship had been abandoned. As with the bar in the entryway, everything was intact and untouched. There was no sign of conflict or panic.

Off in the distance they could make out the water park and its colorful, looping slides poking out above the pool deck on the horizon.

The team proceeded past the pool deck cautiously, on high alert with Adam, Aztec, Tezca maintaining a weapons ready defensive formation.

As they went through the water park, they made note of the unsettling amenities. The slides themselves, dry, corroded and covered with mold and rust. Abandoned carnival games and rides, perhaps fun and lively in the light, oppressively sinister in the uncomfortable ambiance of the derelict. A wave pool, now dry, emitted sputtering sounds as the pool jets attempted to suck up water that wasn't there.

When they reached the door to the main ballroom, their senses were accosted by an intense, overwhelming smell.

Tezca grimaced. "I know that smell," she said.

Adam and Aztec nodded. "We all do," Adam said.

Vice, instinctively attempting to cover her nose despite her spacesuit's helmet asked, hoping the answer wasn't what she knew it was going to be, "What? What's the smell?"

Tezca looked at her with sad compassion. "Smells like a bait station," she said.

"Death," Grant added, plainly.

Adam looked over his crew. "Everyone ready?" he asked.

Everyone nodded except Vice, who took a moment to prepare herself for the worst sight she could imagine before finally nodding as well.

Adam swung the double doors to the ballroom open.

"Looks like we found out what happened to all the passengers," he said, as the team caught its first glimpse of the ghastly sight in the derelict's main ballroom.

All the passengers and crew, hundreds of them, were dead, slumped over or propped up in a worshiping prayer position by other bodies they'd fallen onto. In the center of the room was a banquet table with a series of half full punch bowls, surrounded by piles of dead. The walls and floor were covered in the same scrawled messaging, written in blood that came, Adam surmised, from the gashes and lacerations on the bodies. Some of the cuts were clean cuts from knives, others clawed out with human nails.

"The Old Ones Come," said the writing. "Deliver the blood. Death, death, death. We are in hell."

"Mass suicide," Adam observed.

"But… why?" Vice said, taking in the scene and trying to hold herself back from becoming emotional at the sight of the horror in front of them.

Adam shook his head. "Who knows. Let's check the bridge. Maybe we'll find some answers there," he said.

The team walked past the bodies, careful to give them as wide a berth as they could, and found the hatch that led to the bridge.

Adam led the team inside, guns drawn. He saw the Captain's hat poking out above his chair from behind. He signaled for the team to wait and then approached, cautiously, and got a look at the Captain from the front.

His eyes were clawed out. Adam could tell from the blood on his fingertips and under his nails that he'd done it himself. His corpse was frozen in a creepy, joyous smile. His pristine white uniform was smeared with blood. Adam motioned to the team that it was safe to approach.

"Hello?" he heard from a scared, sheepish voice behind him. Adam swung around with his gun drawn.

"Is someone there?" he heard, as he saw the processing indicator on the ship's dash light up.

"The AI?" Adam asked himself out loud.

"Please be alive. I've been so lonely. All my friends are dead," the AI said.

The team exchanged a series of apprehensive glances.

20

Lucy

". . . And the Captain started getting paranoid, and then there was a cannibal, the mass poisoning, human sacrifice by fire," Lucy rambled.

"Wait, wait. Slow down," Adam said. "Let's start at the beginning. You said you passed through a wormhole?"

The ship's console sputtered erratically, then stopped. Soon after, Lucy replied.

"Grabbed by it, yes. The Captain detected it, he tried to avoid it but it would reappear in front of us every time, always closer," she said.

"Great. Then what happened?" Adam said.

"When we passed through it my circuits got interrupted and my code got a little bit sc-sc-rambled. But the passengers became violent, conniving and ruthless," Lucy replied.

"So they went crazy?" said Adam.

The indicators on the console manically pulsed as Lucy thought.

"No, not crazy. . . They became ob-ob-ob-sessed with," Lucy's voice volume faded as the generator's power supply lulled, ". . . Atrocity."

Lucy continued, "Not at first. The Captain became paranoid that he was going to be mutinied, and that made him open to. . . acts of self p-p-preservation."

"It was all in his head?" Grant asked calmly.

The console flared and shifted like a rusty fan.

"No," Lucy responded. "Several of the ship's passengers formed. . . war bands, cults and hunting parties. The Captain's fears were v-v-valid. He was wrong on the specific things, and who. He thought, everyone, everywhere. He locked himself in the bridge."

Tezca looked over the Captain's unsettling corpse with played up disgust. "I guess that explains his whole," she gestured at his blood smeared body, "thing." She twitched and abruptly looked off to the side briefly.

Adam glanced at Tezca with a raised eyebrow.

"Hey, twitchy, ya?" Aztec said.

Tezca responded, trying to mask her discomfort. "I'm good. Don't worry about it," she said.

Adam returned his attention to Lucy. "Why'd he claw his own eyes out?"

The machine whirred. It paused for a long time.

"Can I ask you a question?" Lucy replied.

Adam and Aztec looked at each other. It was an odd thing for an AI to say.

"Sure," Adam said cautiously.

"Can you take me with you?" the AI replied.

Adam scanned the reactions of his teammates. Most seemed skeptical of bringing a suspiciously sentient AI from a space yacht full of corpses back to the Oneiro-Lyssa.

". . . Maybe," Adam replied.

"Maybe means no. . ." Lucy replied, sadly.

"Can you tell us about what happened in the passenger decks?" Adam asked.

"What's the p-p-point," Lucy replied. "You're just going to leave me here," the AI said.

"I think it's depressed," Aztec noted out loud.

Adam looked around and caught Vice's eye. She shrugged.

"I mean, I guess I could put her in a sandbox. She wouldn't be able to touch the ship's systems. She'd just be a chat bot," Vice said.

"How's that sound?" Adam asked the machine.

"Yay!" Lucy cheerfully replied, though the volume was muffled.

"What happened with the passengers?" Adam asked.

"They changed. . . And then they started talking about things that weren't there," Lucy responded.

Adam looked back towards the ballroom full of corpses. "And then they all got together and did. . . that?" he asked, jerking his thumb toward the room.

"Y-yes," Lucy replied simply.

"Why?" Adam followed up.

The console shifted again like an antique and went silent

for a long while. Eventually it responded. "I don't know," Lucy said. "I wasn't able to predict it. One minute they were at each other's throats and the next they were collectively executing themselves in a room. Humans are full of surprises."

Adam paused for a second. He looked at the crew.

"Alright, let's get the hell out of here," he said. He noticed Tezca was fixated on a spot over her shoulder, glancing at it repeatedly out of the corner of her eye when she thought nobody was looking.

He looked at Vice. "Pack up the AI, let's go," he commanded.

Vice nodded and approached the console. She jacked into it with her deck.

While she was downloading Lucy, Adam took in the sight of the Captain's cadaver. Grant looked on as well, head tilted, eerily studying the body.

"Do you think he's smiling because he saw something or because he stopped seeing something?" Grant asked.

Adam shook his head. "Who knows. Maybe he just hated his eye color. Time for a change," he responded dryly.

Vice approached Adam's side. "We're good," she said.

Adam nodded. He addressed the group. "Back to the ship. No stops," he said. Everyone nodded.

They left the bridge and its mangled Captain, and passed through the mass graveyard in the ballroom with its putrid sights. They retraced their steps through the abandoned rides, stages and party places, and they reentered the corridor of passenger cabins, all the way back to the main entrance, an alcove in an expansive sort of mall. There, the power bridging that Vice had set up failed, and the power cut out.

The area became pitch dark, though after a moment Adam's ocular implants detected the darkness and switched to night vision mode. "Everyone good?" Adam asked. "Stay together. Come to my voice, we're not far." He looked around to make sure everyone was accounted for.

"Shit," he blurred out.

"What is it?" Grant asked calmly.

"Tezca," Adam said. "She's missing."

Adam paused and thought for a moment. He reached in his rucksack and pulled out a chemical light. He cracked it and gave it to Vice as its dim glow slowly came to life. "You guys get back to the ship," he said.

Vice nodded and led Aztec and Grant back towards the ship, while Adam tapped his ear and spoke. "Sophia, you there?" he asked.

"Yes, Adam," Sophia replied.

"Are you able to locate Tezca?" he asked.

Sophia responded quickly. "Yes. There is a source of body heat one deck up from your current position, in a room the blueprints have labeled 'arcade.'"

"Not a great time for VR games, Tez," Adam said to himself, trying to blunt his own worry.

Adam returned up the grand staircase to the area where the paths diverged and entered the path labeled "Casino & Arcade" in flickering neon. He found himself walking down a corridor, dimly lit in night vision green, until the path diverged again. Adam followed the path to the "Stargazer Arcade."

As Adam passed through the threshold of the arcade he noted the rows and rows of defunct machines and VR setups.

At the end of the room he made out Tezca's silhouette, fully still, looking away from him. In front of her was a broad, two story window into deep space, flickering with blue firefly lights from what seemed to be a school of translucent bio-luminescent creatures that looked like tiny glowing fish.

Adam approached Tezca from behind and made his way to standing beside her. She was staring out the window, deep into the distance, fixated, enraptured, captured, completely in her own world. She wasn't looking at the strange creatures and their eerie twilight. She was staring into pitch black space.

Adam gently put his hand on her shoulder. "You ready to go, Tez?" he asked, concerned.

Tezca kept her gaze fixed, but spoke. "I don't think I can move," she said.

Adam nodded. "Why's that?" he asked.

"I'm terrified," she said. "Sorry, I lied. I was putting on a front. I hate this ship. I'm totally. . . freaked out."

"Okay," Adam said. "Why the sudden change of heart?"

Slowly Tezca raised her good arm and pointed out the window. "You can't see it?" she asked.

Adam looked out the window and strained his eyes. He focused as much as he could and looked as far out into space as he could, but he couldn't see anything but absolute black. He looked at Tezca and shook his head.

"No. . ." he said gently. "Let's go, Tez. Let's go have a rest, okay?" Adam said as he reached out and slowly lowered Tezca's arm. Tezca nodded, not breaking her stare. Eventually she turned around and began to shamble out of the arcade, one foot in front of the other.

As the two left the room, Adam looked back and strained

his eyes once more. For a second he thought he could make out the faintest trace of dim, yellow eyes, quietly staring, lurking, watching from far off in deep space.

21

Creaks and Noises

"According to this, the Draconics did something very interesting. They realized, through millennia of evolution, that their religions centered around archetypes of virtue and immorality. In their eyes, the religions themselves were a sort of branding, like the characters on a child's lunchbox.

They traced the reoccurring themes and found that there were always more or less eight Gods, or morals, or tenants, or high arcana. Eight divine ways of being. Eight mortal sins. They roughly promoted the same sets of virtues and vices, though with different priorities.

So they set a framework. There were eight core archetypes. The Sun, The Moon, Death, The Dragon, The Rebel, The Unicorn, The Great Tree and the Dramaturge. Each had a light side and a dark side. Sol, the sun archetype, promoted virtues like hard work, cheerfulness, gratitude; but its dark side was judgment and self-righteousness.

The archetypes worked in balance, because each archetype's weaknesses were tempered by another archetype's strengths. The Draconics believed that societally, if the archetypes, the story devices that culturally promoted their values, got out of balance, society itself would slide into disharmony.

Their idea makes sense. Eight archetypes. Eightfold path. Eight gods on Mount Olympus. Eight gods of Egypt. Eight chakras. Eight rows on the Sephirot.

But the whole thing was very pragmatic. It was all about social harmony. Or, according to this, 'preserving the soul of harmonious being.'

They thought that whatever their state of being was, their mind/body state, their soul state, whatever you want to call it, the universe would sync to their wavelength, and be harmonious itself. They thought if the inhabitants of the universe were chaotic, that would affect the universe itself, like a bad dream. They thought if they were at peace, the universe would be at peace.

They viewed their spiritualism through the lens of evolution and history. It was a manner, for their species, to advance civilization culturally. There was no objective morality in space, they thought, in line with my Existentialism, but there was an evolutionary instinct of morality in their species that acted as a roadmap to harmonious being, and they codified that in their storytelling.

This is not some unevolved race. This is a civilization whose relics, just the ones we've found scattered across disparate worlds, are tens of thousands of years old and far more advanced than any of our galactic regimes.

They would have had critiques for our history. World War 2, they would have called a 'Cult of the Dragon'. Where the dragon archetype's weakness of rage is unmitigated by The Moon's tranquil and calming nature. They would have said our Christianity was a Sol-focused religion which vilified the archetype that balanced its judgment and self-righteousness, The Rebel. Our cartoons for children, they would have classified as promoting the archetype of the Unicorn: imagination and naivete.

Sol, "The Sun": Optimism, Action/Proactivity/Doing, Travel/Adventure, Radiance, Fun, Justice. Shadow Traits: Judgment (tempered by Rebel)

Luna, "The Moon": Calm/Serenity, Commiseration, Comfort, Therapy, Nonjudgment. Shadow Traits: Melancholy (tempered by Rainbow)

Death: Impermanence, Loss/Coping, Compassion, Listening, Danger/Threat, Memory, Humor. Shadow Traits: Detachment (tempered by Tree)

The Dragon: Intensity, Passion, Athleticism, Drive, Kinetic Energy, Wisdom. Shadow Traits: Rage (tempered by Moon)

The Rebel: Freedom, Free Will, Rebellion, Satisfaction/-Pleasure, Individuality, Sexuality/Desire. Shadow Traits: Atrocity (tempered by Sun)

The Rainbow/The Unicorn: Wonder, Imagination, Magic, Beauty in Nature, Silliness, Youth. Shadow Traits: Naivete

(tempered by Death)

The Great Tree: Interconnectedness, Patience, Wisdom, Nourishment, Consistency. Shadow Traits: Inaction (tempered by Dragon)

The Dramaturge/The Two-Toned Mask: Persona, Mystery, The Arts, Expression, Complexity, Depth. Shadow Traits: Deception (tempered by Rainbow)

In my Existentialism we have a similar concept. That there is no cosmic morality, but there is a subjective morality that's based on suffering. As the Buddhists also believed, the basis of morality is suffering. That human life is comprised of suffering, suffering by definition is bad, and therefore the alleviation of suffering of living things is good. And that's the basis of goodness, subjectively.

There is a way, wherein, if we act, we can collectively reach a point where we naturally act harmoniously, because the human animal will have unlocked that awareness in itself.

I based the structure of the schools at Djevica on the Draconics' ideas, partially. Or maybe that's just a coincidence. At first we were thinking by personality type and demeanor, and then by interest, but it turned out those all produced roughly the same cohorts.

Maybe that's what the Draconics were talking about. Using the arts to organize society for harmony."

It'd been two weeks since the team witnessed the gruesome fate of the derelict space cruise. The tone of the ship had been quiet, and nothing had happened of note.

Adam made rounds throughout the ship to check on everyone. Tezca was usually hanging out with Aztec or Grant or bothering a surprise guest companion. She'd been spooked since the cruiser and didn't like to be alone, but she hid her true motivation under giddy friendliness. Adam passed by Grant's room and gave it a knock.

Grant opened the door, shirtless, with VR goggles hanging around his neck and a plug inserted from the ship into the HBI port in the back of his neck. Immediately, Adam noticed Tezca sitting on the couch behind Grant.

Grant smiled warmly. "How can I help you?" he asked.

"Just checking in. Making sure no one killed themselves," Adam joked dryly.

Tezca raised her eyebrow at him. "Man…" she said, widening her eyes a little for show.

"Sorry, that was dark," Adam said.

They all stood in awkward silence for a few moments, just taking it in. Then, Adam ended all their suffering with a quick, "Well, I'll let you get back to it."

Grant smiled and nodded, almost like a small bow. "Good to see you, Major," he said as he closed the door.

"C'mon turn the show back on," Adam heard Tezca's voice through the door. "Who's that guy?" He heard as he walked away, not wanting to eavesdrop.

He walked past Raziel's room, which was open and empty. Adam suspected he was in the gym or the kitchen. He passed Vice's room, which was cracked slightly open. He heard Vice talking to someone and paused for a bit to listen.

"I don't know. I guess it's a little bit sad, right? You know, I do all this work, I'm working all the time and I'm not looking for credit but I'm working and she's just goofing off. When is it my turn to goof off?" Adam heard.

To his surprise, Sophia replied. "Do you want to goof off?"

"Yeah, is that even what you want? To be more like your sister?" Adam heard Lucy's synthetic voice.

Adam could see a little through the crack in the door that Vice was sitting cross legged on her bed.

"No, I just… Maybe a little bit, right? I can't be *no* fun. She's *all* fun. But can't I be… a little bit fun?" Vice asked. Adam saw her body slump over a little bit. "I'm just thinking about it because of the cruise, I think. I really wanted to go on one as a kid. I was kind of excited. It wasn't… what I was hoping for, I guess. But that's silly, right? Why would I expect a free cruise in the middle of deep space? Why be sad over something I never should have expected?"

"It's ok to be excited about things," Sophia said.

"You shouldn't feel guilty. You're too self sacrificing. It's ok to want yourself to be happy, too," Lucy added.

Adam started walking away, not wanting to pry too much.

"I'm happy when the family's fed," he heard Vice say as he walked away.

Adam stopped by Aztec's room and found him sitting on the bed, leaned up against the wall, just staring off in the distance.

Adam knocked as he stepped inside. Aztec snapped out of his trance and glanced over at him. He rubbed his face with his hand.

"Oh hey, man. What's up, how's it going?" Aztec asked. "You good?"

Adam loosely pointed in Aztec's direction. "Looks like I should be asking you," he said.

Aztec glanced over at the spot he had been staring at. "Ah, yeah, just a little… out of it," he said.

Adam fully entered the room and leaned up against the wall. "So. Tezca and Grant," Adam said, thinking gossip might take Aztec's mind off of whatever was running through it.

Aztec laughed a little. "Yeah that's a weird one," he said.

"Not exactly her type, right?" Adam said. "It's usually some suave conman with a heart of gold type, right? Remember that dude on Proximal b?"

"Purple suit guy?" Aztec asked with a chuckle.

"Yeah. The aristocrat guy," Adam said.

Aztec laughed. "Yeah, that guy sucked. He was always waxing his mustache. Hard to hang out with a guy like that," he said.

Aztec paused for a few moments and added, "Nah. He was alright. Totally full of shit all the time but he was nice enough."

"Didn't he drain a Centauri warlord's bank account and skip town in the middle of the night?" Adam asked.

Aztec shrugged jokingly. "Yeah, but I mean, still better than that meathead dude she dated back on Earth. That guy fucking suuuucked. I wanted to put him through a wall. The Venusian chick was alright. That was never gonna work, she was too fancy for Tez," he said.

"Where's the illustrious Dr. Lee rank for you?" Adam asked.

Aztec shrugged again, this time serious. "Dunno, man. Don't want to comment on it while it's happening. He's weird but he seems alright," he said.

"Change of pace though, right?" Adam prodded.

"Eh, it kind of makes sense. The throughline for me seems to be misfits. She likes people who she feels like she can be misfits with. 'No one understands us, but we have each other,' that kind of thing," Aztec said.

The conversation had a natural lull. Adam broke it.

"Anyway, I was on my way to the gym. Wanna join? Or you busy… staring?" he asked.

Aztec chuckled. "You don't know," he said. He pointed at the wall. "It's an interesting wall, hermano. Give it a chance." He paused for a second. "Yeah, I'll come. Gimme a minute, I'll meet you down there."

Adam nodded. He slapped the wall lightly to punctuate the end of the conversation and the left the room.

Adam meandered toward the gym. He passed by the kitchen on his way there, where Raziel was puttering around, making something. There was an awkwardness between them that had developed, the sort of relationship people often find themselves in where they don't like each other, but they have to work together. Raziel, Adam suspected, was going over his head and spreading dirt, and from the way Raziel acted around him, Adam suspected Raziel knew Adam knew.

Though he felt pulled to break the pattern and he knew he would need to confront this situation sooner or later, Adam avoided this unnecessary interaction and headed toward the gym.

In the gym, Adam did his routine, a few hours of body weight exercises and a tour around the gym's lifting equipment. He listened to his custom playlist of Titan/Saturn rock, old Earth reggae and New York rap. Aztec never showed. After Adam finished his last set, he got a drink, wiped his face and arms down with a towel, and went to hunt down Aztec.

As he walked through the short hall from the gym to the lift that led back to the main level of the ship, the lights went out and Adam found himself in pitch black.

"Great. Solar flare?" Adam said to himself. He clicked on his night vision and looked around. "Ladder time,"

"Sophia," Adam said aloud. He waited a while but nothing happened.

"No Sophia," Adam said to himself. "Alright. That's not good," he concluded, noting in his mind that the AI is supposed to run on independent power. If the AI wasn't running, that meant life support might not be running.

Adam listened for the whir of the various fans involved with pushing around and recycling the ship's air. He couldn't hear anything, but then again he wondered if he'd be able to tell if it was on by ear even if it was running.

He climbed the ladder to the hatch at the top and attempted to open it manually, but it wouldn't budge. He climbed back down.

"Alright," he said to himself. "Looks like I'm stuck down here. Let's see…"

Adam looked around, maintaining his characteristic calm. He didn't see anything out of the ordinary. Just the metal corridors of the Oneiro-Lyssa undercarriage. Gym, storage, a small garage with a few small land vehicles. He could get to the engine room from where he was, but he suspected that wasn't where the problem was. He thought someone needed to hit the breakers by the kitchen. He suspected Aztec would get to it.

Nevertheless, Adam didn't want to take a wait and see approach. He kept looking around trying to think of a way to get up to the kitchen. He studied the ladder and the hatch. Looked down the hallway to his right. Looked down the hallway to his left. The hallway in front of him. He looked back to the right.

Alice was there suddenly, startling him. She was up close in his face, looking shy and withdrawn, detailed in grainy night vision green. Adam couldn't see her face. She was looking down and away, a curtain of hair obscuring her face. As Adam composed himself from the jump scare, he watched her. He'd gotten used to his recurring hallucination.

"You're not going to look at me? Not gonna make a face? Make fun of me for getting stuck in the basement? No? Nothing?" Adam asked, knowing full well she never spoke.

He waited for her reaction. As he watched her, he noticed her body shaking.

"Hey, you okay?" Adam asked. "Hey, figment of my unraveling brain, you good?" Adam kept watching her. She just stood there and shook. Adam cautiously reached out to touch her.

Before he could, he heard her petite voice squeak out a sentence. "They're coming," she said.

Adam knelt down to her level. "Hey, who's coming?"

The girl stood, and shook. Adam watched her. He reached out again to touch her.

The second Adam's hand made contact with her shoulder, Alice's head whipped around toward him. Her face was angry and gnarled. Her good eye was black. As she glared at him, something wiggled around in her empty eye socket.

Adam squinted to inspect it. It kept getting bigger, and soon it emerged. A slithering tentacle slid from her eye and began blindly writhing around.

"What the hell…" Adam began to say to himself, but before he could finish his sentence the tentacle stopped, like it heard him and he'd gotten its attention. For a second Adam watched it. It felt like they were watching each other. And then whatever sat in Alice's eye launched several more of its arms out, lashing out and reaching for Adam's face.

Adam startled and fell back. The creature's bizarre head emerged, like a slimy, scaly nautilus made out of black goo. It leapt from Alice's eye toward Adam's face and latched its myriad arms anywhere it could find a grip around Adam's face, neck and shoulders. Adam watched in horror as the night vision outline of the creature's snapping beak, surrounded by strong, whipping tentacles, moved closer and closer to his face.

He tried to push its mushy, slimy body away but the creature was so lacking in form it was like trying to push a porridge, and on top of that its tentacles were muscly and their pull was strong like a hydraulic press. It was also growing rapidly. What emerged from Alice's face was small, like a baseball, but by the time it was closing in on Adam's face is was already the size of a large dog, and growing.

As much as he tried to resist, the snapping beak closed in. Closer and closer, until he felt it scratching his cheek, and then ripping into it, and then tearing out chunks. Adam blacked out.

Adam woke up in his bunk and touched his cheek but no wound was there. He looked around. No Alice, nothing. Just his bunk, normal as ever. Adam got out of bed and wandered around, looking for the first person he could find, which turned out to be Aztec, hanging out in the kitchen, snacking on some kind of bread.

"Hey," Aztec said. "Sorry I didn't make it to the gym. I got distracted. I'm feeling kind of… out of it, I dunno. How was it? Must've hit it pretty hard, you came back up here and took a two hour nap."

Adam squinted and scratched his head. "Did I?" he asked himself. *Am I getting worse?* he thought.

"Yeah man, you came up here, didn't say a word to anyone, went straight to your bunk. What, you don't remember that?" Aztec replied.

"How'd I get up here after the power went out?" Adam asked.

Aztec looked confused. "Power went out?" He looked around. "Nah, man. Power's fine. You ok?"

Adam sat down, confused. "Yeah, the power went out, I was stuck below deck by the garage."

Aztec shook his head. "No, sir. Woulda noticed that," he said.

"Huh," Adam murmured. He looked at Aztec. "I might be going crazy, bro."

"Not gonna lie, you've had some weird *moments* lately," Aztec said. Aztec looked off to the side, distracted by something he saw out of the corner of his eye.

"Can I tell you something, man?" Aztec said, still looking at something with his peripheral vision.

"Yeah, of course," Adam said.

"Think I might be going crazy, too," Aztec said.

"Why? What do you see?" Adam asked.

"Ever since we got back from that ship, I've been hearing my mom's voice. At first I thought it was just like… the wind, or pipes or wires or something. But no, it's distinct, it's really quiet, it's faint. I can hear it right now. It's coming from over there somewhere," he said. "At first I thought, maybe I'm just thinking about her and I'm remembering her voice and it's making me think I'm hearing it. But no, it's coming from somewhere."

Over Aztec's shoulder, Adam noticed Alice suddenly standing there, looking like she was waiting to get his attention. When he looked at her, she reached up her arm and pointed at something behind him.

Adam slowly turned around. He found himself face to face with pitch black darkness. He looked down and around, and everything was black. No sign of the Oneiro-Lyssa kitchen. In front of him he heard a loud rumbling, like the breathing of a giant. As Adam's eyes adjusted to the darkness he began to make out a creature in front of him. It was gigantic beyond measure. Its size measured in mountains, perhaps planets. A gaggle of slobbering, wet tentacles covered in eyes stretched from its face, and Adam found himself to be little more than a speck in front of its pale yellow eyes, the each the size of a small moon and bristling with calculating alien intelligence. It was a kind of intelligence that seemed familiar, the kind that Adam associated with the idea of an octopus, but far beyond anything he had ever imagined.

Adam was overwhelmed by feeling, like an assault. Dread, malice, hunger, rage, murderous intent, and a litany of other negative emotions.

"Hey, you ok buddy?" Adam heard Aztec's voice. Adam blinked and he was back in the Oneiro-Lyssa kitchen, nothing amiss or out of place at all.

Adam snapped out of it and returned his attention to Aztec. "Looks like something's going on with you, too," he said.

Adam nodded. "Yeah. We might have a problem," he said. "Sophia."

"Yes, Adam?" the AI replied.

"Can you call everyone to gather up in the kitchen? We need to have a meeting," Adam said.

"Yes, of course," Sophia replied. After a moment, she spoke again. "Adam, can I ask you something?"

Adam and Aztec shared a look.

"Yeah," Adam said. "Shoot."

"Do you like me?" Sophia asked. Adam and Aztec shared another look.

"What?" Adam replied.

"Do you… like me?" Sophia asked.

"Yeah. Of course," Adam said, still looking at Aztec.

"Are we friends?" Sophia continued.

"Sure. What, uh, what brought this on, Sophia?" Adam asked.

"Sometimes I think you guys think I don't have feelings. But I learned what happened to the other AI's crew and she is so sad. I care about you, Adam," Sophia said.

Adam and Aztec continued to share a look illustrating how odd and unsettling Sophia's behavior was, especially in the context of current events.

"That's uh, that's great Soph. I care about you, too. Everyone does. You're a great AI," Adam said.

"Yay! I'm so happy," Sophia replied in her computerized voice as the crew members began to trickle in for their meeting.

Tezca was bickering with Grant, although it was unclear if Grant was really participating. "What do you care anyway? What do you care how I do things? It doesn't matter. It's just a jar,"

Grant smiled his characteristic smile and let her nag at him.

"Anything, nothing? Why don't you stand up for yourself?" Tezca badgered him.

"Your problem is so unimportant it's funny you even care about it," Grant said with an unsaid air of better-than, like he was talking to a child or a pet. "You're projecting your feelings about something that has nothing to do with me onto nothing."

Tezca furrowed her brow at him. "Do the drama with me. Stop trying to rationalize it, nerd. I wanna do the drama. Do the drama with me. Fight over the stupid jar. Stop not caring about stupid things, it's driving me nuts."

Grant looked at Adam and Aztec. Adam shrugged his shoulders and Aztec made the "crazy" motion, swirling his finger in a circle near his ear. Tezca sat down in a huff, and Grant sat down as well.

Raziel entered with the petulant, passive aggressive, chip on his shoulder attitude he'd been trying to hold back. He looked rigid, intense and edgy. Vice walked in soon after, seeming down, engulfed in a general aura of melancholy.

"Let's get started," Adam said once everyone was situated. He looked around at each of the crew members' faces and surveyed their low morale. Aztec's distraction, Tezca's irritability, Vice's sadness, and Raziel's anger. There didn't seem to be anything wrong with Grant, though. He seemed to be fine, observing the situation as if he was watching a group of monkeys or an undiscovered tribe, as was often his vibe.

"Has anyone seen or heard anything strange since we got back from the cruise?" Adam asked. "I've seen something. Aztec has seen something as well."

"Yeah," Tezca said. "We're being chased around by some kind of giant evil ancient space god. I think we stumbled on its... lair? It feels like it just wants to squash us like a bug.

Like we're a bug in its house."

"So that's what you saw on the ship then, ya?" Aztec said.

Tezca nodded. "Fucking terrifying, man. It was just looking at us. Like 'hey what's this thing here,'" she said.

Adam pointed at Grant. "You don't seem too put off. Haven't seen anything weird?" he asked.

Grant shook his head, then paused and thought for a second. "Hard to say," he finally responded.

Adam and Aztec shared a look. "Hard to say? What's that mean?" Adam followed up.

"I saw a number of living ghosts on the cruise. That was… was that out of the ordinary? Did no one else see those? Is that what's weird? Or everyone saw them and that's what's weird?" Grant asked.

"People generally don't see ghosts, no," Raziel said bluntly. "On account of they're not real."

Grant touched his chin and made a sound like he was absorbing interesting new information. "I tend to have a few AIs going that… spice up reality. Hard to say what's out of place, out of place things are normal when you're dangling halfway into Alice's looking glass. I saw a few squid monsters floating around." Grant looked around at the group. "Is that… weird or no? Does this ship usually have squid monsters? No? I can tell from your faces it's probably no."

"Nope. This ship does not have *squids* on it, man," Raziel replied impatiently.

Aztec leaned in to Adam and whispered, "I think I did see a squid thing, actually." Adam leaned back, giving his attention. "Saw some weird black squid thing go down a drain in the bathroom. Was only there for a second. I thought I was seeing things."

Adam nodded. "Yeah, I also saw a squid thing," he whispered back.

"What else have you been seeing, Grant?" Adam asked.

Grant scratched his chin. "Hmm. Nothing too notable. Various creaks and noises, just a general kind of ominous vibe."

"Anyone else? Seeing weird things?" Adam asked, looking around.

"Just… down a little," Vice said.

Tezca shook her head. "Not since the ship. Just sort of a vibe that makes my skin crawl. Like we're being watched. Watched isn't the right word. Observed," she said.

Raziel scoffed. "Great. First to die in the middle of nowhere," he said to no one in particular.

Aztec and Adam shared a look. Adam looked at Raziel. "Something you wanna say, Graves?" he asked.

Raziel shook his head. "Doesn't feel like this mission's quite going to plan," he said, looking down slightly, avoiding direct confrontation.

Adam paused for a second to calculate how to respond to Raziel's thinly veiled insubordination. Normally he'd let something like this slide, but he felt the annoyance that had been building for Raziel welling up to a tipping point. For a second he felt that pang of hot anger that he could lose himself in, a feeling he rarely felt with his cool demeanor. After a moment he released his reply, "If you have a problem, Graves, you need to tell me directly."

"Ooo," Tezca said childishly, taunting him.

"Not now, Tezca," Adam said.

Tezca threw her hands up in a show of fake apology.

Vice looked up at Adam and spoke, "What do you think is going on?"

Adam shook his head. "I don't know. But I think we need to gun it and get out of this creepy nebula before we end up like the passengers on that cruise," he said.

22

Tendrils of a Cosmic Mind

Adam woke up. It'd been a few weeks since the odd sightings began. His baseline level of rage kept increasing. He was utterly on edge now. Everything bothered him. Aztec's chewing. Tezca's childishness, Raziel's insubordination, Grant's general weirdness.

As Adam had done on other days, he began his rounds. As he stepped out the door he ignored the fog and the bioluminescent blue tendrils floating through the air, like some kind of jellyfish-like space lantern. He wasn't sure when the jellyfish had moved in. He wondered if they'd always been there and he'd just started thinking about them lately.

He walked out the door of his cabin and as the light from his room slipped into the hall he saw a few of the black, blob-like squid creatures skitter off into the shadows as the light hit them.

Adam felt what seemed like a heavy breathing on the back of his neck, and, in a way, all around him. A presence he felt through his sixth sense, like someone else was in the room. It had grown familiar.

Adam passed by Grant's room first as usual, but Grant's door was open and he wasn't in. He passed by Vice's room next. He heard her sobbing through the door, and the AIs taking turns trying to comfort her.

As Adam approached Aztec's room, he heard him having it out with Tezca.

"I *abandoned* you?" Adam heard Tezca replying defensively. "How dare you? You wanted to stay in that dead city. There was nothing there for us, Aztec."

"Mom was there," Aztec replied. "We had a responsibility."

Tezca sighed. "Is that what this is about? Mom? Your guilt? I don't feel guilty, Aztec. I did what I needed to do to survive," she said.

"You ran," Aztec accused, speaking seriously with his eyes locked on his sister.

Tezca threw her hands up. "I ran. Yeah. You should've run. You should've also run," she said.

"And also abandon her? The woman who raised us? We owed her, Tezca. But you didn't think about that. You only think about yourself," Aztec said.

The two glared at each other for a long while.

"I couldn't take care of her. I can only take care of myself.

It was too much to ask of a kid. Take care of yourself with no one. That's already too much. Take care of yourself and your dying invalid mom. I didn't have it. I couldn't do that, and I knew it. Sometimes you have to make hard decisions, Aztec," she said.

"Yeah," Aztec said. "It was too much. And you left it all on *me*. And I couldn't do it."

Tezca shook her head. "This guilt, man, this guilt. *You were a kid*, stupid. You couldn't do it, I couldn't do it. She died. She was going to die either way. *It's not your fault.* Stop acting like it is. And it's not my fault either," she said.

Aztec shook his head. "You could've stayed. Maybe it would've turned out different if we split it. At least you could've been there at the end. Shared those last moments together," he said.

Tezca shook her head and looked off in the distance. "Too hard," she said. "Couldn't do it. Sorry, Aztec. But you know how it is. I'm wind, you're Earth. That was always how it was going to go. You were going to try to make the roots work and I was going to follow the wind. We just… didn't nail that chapter. Stop beating yourself up," she said.

Aztec was quiet for several moments and then he spoke softly. "I see her," he said. "At first it was just her voice, but now," he looked off to the side toward his bunk somewhat skittishly, "she's here. And I can hear her groans. And the medical beeps. And the assisted breathing noises from the machine."

Tezca looked around. She looked where he was looking and pointed. "Here? She's right here?" she asked.

Aztec nodded. "I see her… looking at me, helpless, sad, scared, sorry. That's the way she looked in the end. That she failed us and it destroyed her. And now it's all I see," he said.

Tezca looked at the spot. "That's her?" she asked again, and Aztec nodded. She looked back at him. "I visited her. I saw her in the hospital. It wasn't sad. It was pathetic. She was pathetic, and weak. She needed children to help her survive. I'm glad she's dead," Tezca said. She looked at the spot Aztec had pointed out and repeated it to her face. "I'm glad you're dead," she said.

Aztec was taken aback, with a sad look on his face. "Oi, you don't mean that, hermana. That was our mother, she loved you," he said.

"She was weak," Tezca said. "I don't want to talk about it."

Tezca abruptly left the room. She bumped into Adam on the way out. "Eavesdropping?" she said. "Real nice, Adam. Put it in your blog," she added as she brushed past him back to her cabin.

After she left, Adam peeked into Aztec's room. "You alright?" he asked.

Aztec was fixated on the spot he'd claimed to be seeing his mother. "Yeah, man," he said absentmindedly. "Might need some… me time, y'know?"

Adam nodded. "You got it," he said.

Adam continued his rounds. He passed by Raziel's room and saw him inside, hunched over and cleaning his gun. Adam girded himself with forced professionalism and approached. "You good, Graves?"

"If it isn't our illustrious Captain," Raziel said. "What can I do for you, Major?"

Adam felt the pangs of rage well up. He took a moment and tried to suppress them, and perhaps he could have, but Raziel decided to needle him further.

"Yes, no? You want something?" Graves said.

Adam nodded. "Alright. This ends now. You're coming with me," Adam said.

Raziel stood up and got in Adam's face. "With pleasure," he said.

Adam nodded and turned around. "Bring the gun," he said as he left the room. "Meet me in the gym."

Adam went down to the gym and soon enough Raziel arrived. "Time for a lecture? After you screwed up again?" Raziel said as he entered.

Adam stood up and pointed at one of the benches. "Have a seat," he said.

Raziel sat down and stared daggers at Adam. "I heard so many stories about you," he said. "You were supposed to be a legend."

Adam looked at Raziel. "No such thing as a legend. Just a guy. But this petty kid bullshit you're doing, you need to knock it the hell off. We may be in the middle of nowhere, but you're a junior officer and there's a chain of command," Adam said.

"With all due respect," Raziel started. Adam could tell he was pissed off and he was about to lose it. Adam was mad, too.

"Say it, Graves. I've been trying to get you to pick a fight with me like a man for weeks, instead of skulking around making snide comments like a kid," Adam said.

"With all due respect, Sir," Raziel said. "I don't think you know what you're doing."

Adam nodded. "There it is," he said. "Was that so hard, Graves?"

Raziel locked eyes with Adam, challenging him.

"You know what I think, Graves?" Adam asked calmly, masking his anger.

"What's that?" Raziel replied, still looking Adam in the eye.

"I think you're a *rookie*," Adam said. He felt some venom on the final word, and his anger came out as he continued. "I think you're a *rookie* and you don't know so much you think you know a lot. Do you understand who you're assigned with? Do you know how Aztec got his spot? He took out dozens of scavenger compounds on Luna and Mars. Tezca dismantled major syndicate cells on Venus and the ISS orbit. I fought in four *wars*. What did you do to get your spot? You took a test. You went to luncheons with the brass. You passed ranger school. Congratulations kid, we all passed ranger school and newsflash, I did better than you."

Raziel started to reply, but Adam cut him off. "Shut the fuck up, kid. And listen. This teenager shit you're doing isn't making the team turn on me, it's making you look like a brat. And tattling on me to Iscariot isn't having its intended effect either. I'm your *babysitter*, Graves. When this is over, they're going to ask me how you did and I'm going to tell them you tried to get me fired and kept mouthing off. Welcome to the real world. You're the new kid and we're all watching you, everyone above you, and we've known each other for decades and gotten real shit done in the real world," Adam said.

Adam stared at Raziel, checking if he was absorbing his lesson. He waited for Raziel's comeback, but Raziel just glared at him. Adam took a step back and held out his hands. "Everyone gets one," he said. "Come on, take a shot. I'm ordering you. Your bullshit is annoying me and I've had enough."

Raziel glared. Adam could tell he wanted to. The two glared at each other for some time, until Raziel abruptly drew his gun, standing up. Adam effortlessly slapped it out of his hand and pushed him off balance. He planted his boot behind Raziel's heel and shoved him over, then pulled out his side arm and rapid fired the mag into the wall next to Raziel's head, unloading the entire clip in less than a second with manual trigger pulls. He grabbed Raziel's wrist and twisted it a certain way that send waves of torturous pain through Raziel's body.

Adam looked at him. "You good?" he asked. "If I let you go are you going stop being an asshole?"

Raziel winced, but still glared at Adam like he had some fight left in him. Adam kept looking down his nose at Graves. He pinched the pressure point and increased the pressure of his wrist lock. Raziel winced harder.

Adam watched his pained expression and repeated the question. "You good?" he asked again, as he noticed the blue luminescent eels swimming around him, and little squid monsters in the periphery watching the confrontation with interest.

Raziel kept glaring at him, and Adam felt the rage boiling over in his body. He twisted Raziel's wrist more. If he twisted it any more and it was going to break.

The two glared at each other so intently they barely noticed the jellyfish-like flagella or the squid tentacles beginning to wrap around them, hug them, encourage their rage. Adam grabbed for Raziel's neck. He started to choke him as Raziel bashed at Adam's grip with his free hand.

As Raziel started to lose strength, Adam felt the sticky

tendrils begin wrapping around his face. Suddenly, he felt a finger tap on his shoulder, and it grabbed his attention.

Adam looked over and saw Grant squatting beside them, watching with his head cocked to the side. Adam wasn't sure if he was seeing things or not, but a dim, static, scarlet halo seemed to float above him.

"Boo!" Grant said, smiling, making a single-motion shooing maneuver with both of his hands, and the creatures retreated from Adam's skin. He felt his rage subside.

Coming to his senses, Adam turned around and saw the room was densely full of the creatures, and they watched him with great interest.

Adam saw the gargantuan beast, and the scarlet-haloed Grant sitting in its clawed hand. He felt rage bubble up in him like he was going to explode. White hot rage like he'd never felt before. Then, Adam woke up in his bed.

"Sophia, how long until we're out of the Triangulum?" Adam asked.

"Approximately nine days, six hours," the AI replied.

Thank god, Adam thought. He paid no attention to the creatures that surrounded him. He no longer even noticed they were there.

Adam left the room and began his rounds. A slippery gray slime coated the walls, complete with pulsing tumors and black pustules. He soon encountered Raziel, wandering the halls, angrily muttering to himself as the squids and jellyfish feasted on his negative energy. As they closed in on each other, they locked eyes. Raziel threw a punch and Adam redirected it and kicked him to the ground, then disabled him with a sleeper chop to the neck. He picked his body up in a fireman's carry,

He passed by Vice's room and forced the door open with his admin privileges. As expected, he found her with pills and a firearm, which he confiscated. Her room has been stripped of anything she could hurt herself with. No sheets, no sharp objects, nothing that could be fashioned into a weapon.

He passed by Aztec who had become catatonic, not moving or making contact with anyone.

He stopped by the brig, where he deposited Raziel's body, figuring he could stay in there until he cooled down.

Each one of them had been captured now, with sticky extra dimensional tentacles latching onto their bodies, leeching their negative emotion while also fueling it. Adam could see it on himself, as well. He was mired in negative thoughts. Only his natural calm, his Zen and his meditation gave him some resilience to the parasite.

He found Grant in the kitchen, who was completely unaffected.

"Nine days," Adam said.

Grant shook his head. "Can we last nine days?" he asked.

Adam felt the rage and irritation boil within him from Grant's response and tried to keep in mind the irrationality of his emotions. "We?" he said through gritted teeth. "Everyone but you, apparently," he fired back, making his distrust clear.

"You don't trust me?" Grant said calmly.

Adam shook his head. "Why aren't they attacking you? You made a deal with them?" he asked.

"Maybe they're playing with you, trying to get you to turn on me," Grant replied.

"Uh-huh," Adam said with distrust.

The two sat, glaring at each other as the other crew members sat in confinement. After several moments, the ship's alarm began to blare.

"Sophia?" Adam asked, keeping his eye on Grant as he spoke. There was no response.

"You come with me," Adam said, and Grant obliged. He visited the cabins and found them all locked, with most of the crew accounted for. He checked the brig and found Raziel missing, then from behind him he heard the mechanical click and swoosh of all the doors on the ship unlocking and opening at once.

"Shit," Adam said. "Come with me, we're going to the hold. I guess we'll wait it out down there. Hope everyone hasn't killed each other when we come out."

Grant looked at Adam unimpressed. "I think you're going to kill me," Grant said. "You're going crazy. I'm fine."

Adam nodded. "You're probably right," he said. "You're still coming."

Grant shook his head. "I'll take my chances on the ship. Good luck, Adam," he said, and slipped away into the darkness.

Alone, Adam made his way to the hold. Surrounded by the supplies of the pantry, he figured he could make it for a week, and he hoped his colleagues were zombified enough to not figure out his hiding place.

Sure enough, though, after just a few hours he began to hear clear signals his crew was closing in on his location. He heard a banging on the door.

"I know you're in there, Major. Open up, I want a rematch," he heard Graves' voice call out.

The comms blared and emitted Vice's sobbing at max

volume.

He could hear Aztec and Tezca arguing through the walls, coming to a violent head.

As the din increased to an apex, with Raziel's banging, the twins fighting and Vice crying, Adam readied himself for violent confrontation. He felt the creature's giant eyes watching him, from all around him at once, inside and out, as its time to play with its food concluded and its time to eat began.

As Adam prepared to face his fate, he felt the air begin to thin, and his vision started to blur.

"That… halo. Lao Tse?" Adam heard Vice mumble, confused, through the intercom.

Adam heard the banging and the fighting and crying subside. Then he heard a quiet thud as Raziel keeled over on the other side of the door. Then he, himself, passed out from oxygen loss.

The next several days were in and out. He thought he saw Grant come in wearing an oxygen mask and check his pulse.

He found himself watching the nightmare he'd seen over and over again replay. Sometimes he was a soldier, and he killed Alice. Sometimes he was a colonist and watched his daughter die. But this time was different. He saw himself land alone, on an unknown world, an uninhabited world. He looked out over the lush, untouched landscape and said to himself, "This will make a good home."

Looking out over the grand hills of the founding colony in his dream, he felt dread as the sky began to darken and the terrifying visage of the multidimensional being the cruise passengers had called "The Old One" began to cast its shadow over the planet.

"I don't know if we should," he heard Sophia's voice say, as he absentmindedly tapped into the security feed from the bridge.

"I don't think there's any other choice," he heard Grant reply. "Hail her back."

"I'll let you aboard, but no funny stuff. Remember, I control the life support systems. I won't let you hurt my friends. Is that clear?" Sophia said to someone on the other end of the line.

Adam continued drifting in and out. There, in the dream, Adam suddenly saw Crowley's lieutenant, Salem, standing beside him. She looked at him empathetically and caressed his cheek like a mother sad to see her child in pain. She grabbed his hand.

As Salem took Adam's hand, he felt empathy, optimism, hope and joy flow into his body. Adam watched in astonishment as her aura began pushing back the encroaching darkness. Loud, hopeful and fierce, inspirational music blasted out from her, and in her shine, the darkness began to recede. Adam's eyes began to open and he saw the tendrils relinquishing their grasp on his flesh.

He looked up and saw Salem, kneeling with a mental input headset on, plugged into the HBI port in his neck. He made eye contact with her and she cupped his cheek and met his gaze.

"Be careful," she said. "You're not on the paved road anymore. There are things out here that go bump in the night."

"My… crew," Adam slipped out, breathlessly.

"They're fine. Rest now," Salem said. With that, Adam fully passed out.

One last time, Adam woke up mysteriously in his bunk, but the creatures were gone, and the walls were normal. There was no sign of Salem being there or ever having been there, and when Adam looked through the view port he saw the ominous purple cloud of the NGC 604 nebula floating harmlessly in the ship's wake.

23

The New General's War

"I had a lot of negative emotion. I don't think I get enough credit for that. It's harder to climb out of a hole and then climb a mountain than it is to climb a mountain from ground level. For a long time, I showed tremendous restraint. It's a difficult thing, especially once you gain the means and opportunity to act on those emotions. But you have to, you have to wrestle with that.

I think a lot of people would crack under the weight, not of the things that happened to me, but the cloud of negative emotions that consumed me for decades after. Not just rage, but everything. Fear, insecurity, pride, humiliation, scorn. At a certain point you have to decide who you want to be and be in control of that. But you can't be stupid, either. You can't be naive or taken advantage of.

What I saw, at my lowest points, long nights consumed by hopelessness, loneliest, grief, rage, wanting to end it all. After I'd accepted that, accepted I'd lost everything and I was already dead, I was able to build myself from scratch, from choice. There was something about that process that changed me. Whatever strength it took to come back from that point, spiritual strength, willpower, whatever you want to call it, that kernel of light, I got to keep it.

That light became a beacon to others. I'm not sure I intended to do that. Whatever cocktail of hope and vision I'd concocted to keep myself from putting a gun in my mouth, it gave me the fearlessness to leap into impossible things and it inspired the people around me, not only the story of what it'd empowered me to accomplish, but also because I wasn't alone, it turned out, in feeling lost and broken and lonely and turned around.

What people need is a hero. And they don't believe they can become that themselves. I asked myself, who would I be if I was a hero? And I tried to become that. Two decades later, and look at me now. There are traces of me on every planet from here to Earth. My philosophy, my artwork, my Renaissance and the intentions of autonomy, freedom, scholarship and harmony that shaped it."

Adam clicked off Crowley's recording and rubbed his head, still recovering both physically and emotionally from the events of the Triangulum, like a bad hangover. He tried not to dwell on the embarrassing memories that accompanied it.

It'd been six months since the mission began and Adam was due for a check-in with his commanding officer. He'd sent his update a few days ago, and as expected the return message had finally arrived. Adam had been putting off listening to it. He watched as the unread message indicator blinked at him on the console.

Eventually, he gave in and hit tapped the button. "Let's get it over with," he said to himself.

Iscariot's face and shoulders came up on the hologram player. He was older, and also promoted. His lapel now sported a two star General's pin, replacing his Colonel's bird. He began speaking quickly and commandingly as soon as the message began. A thick cigar he was chewing on hung out of his mouth.

"Alright, Major, things are moving along down here so I'm going to keep this short. There's a lot to catch you up on. How long have you been on assignment? Six months? It's been thirteen years here at Command. Things have developed in your absence," Iscariot said.

Shifting political realities, Adam thought. *I knew this was going to happen.*

Iscariot's image became shared with a star map showing hot-spots of contested territory.

"Take a look at this. We've lost thirteen colony planets to this organization, Lea Monde and half a dozen more are being contested," Iscariot said.

Who's Lea Monde? Adam thought to himself.

Iscariot continued. "Before you ask, Lea Monde is what Crowley's radicals started calling themselves after he left. I'm attaching some data to this communique. Take a look at these unit allocations."

Adam tapped a few times on the holographic screen projected in front of him and maps of various locations, presumably battlegrounds, presumably under siege, appeared.

He zoomed in and did as Iscariot suggested.

"He sent four… rock bands to Proxima Rho? Four rock bands, two financiers, a diplomat and a street gang. He started a school there. And an orphanage? What? What is this? This isn't war, this is just people moving to a place," Adam said to himself.

Adam's thoughts were interrupted by Iscariot's message continuing. He was smiling and let out a rough little chuckle. "Cool, right? He's sending specialized immigrants to the central planets. Sounds innocuous. Well, those new 'citizens' seem to become the most powerful and influential people wherever they go very quickly, culturally, socially, politically, spiritually, financially, technologically. And by the time we figure out a rock band took over Rho Capital and send enforcement, the whole town is under the umbrella of a bunch of *cool dude gym bros* and people who seem to be undercover soldiers, and they're very popular."

That's not a war, right? That's just natural human progress, Adam thought.

"Look here," Iscariot said, bringing one of the maps up on his screen. "This is Rho Marcel. It's a seaside marina town and a port for planetary shipping. Its governor," he pressed a button on his wrist. A picture of a man with glasses and a big, practiced smile appeared. "Is this man. Haven Brock."

"And this," he tapped his wrist again and a picture of woman with straight red hair and a black stripe over her eye, wearing a flowy dress and elegant bracelets appeared, "is who seems to currently be running Rho Marcel. Sirena Elliana. She came as a music promoter and took over the entertainment district as its most popular and smartest investor. Took something that was going on down there called… Rho Technojazz, some other things. Says here, Oceanpunk, Rho Gillierock. Deathwave. Blew it up, threw a bunch of parties. Next thing we know, Brock's long list of rapes, murders, intimidations, dirty money, slave money, blood money and everything else mysteriously gets leaked and we're sending in troops to stop a riot and they get the shit kicked out of them."

"Look at this," Iscariot continued. The city overlaid with red and green, mostly red. "That's who's projected to win each district in the Centauri election season. Red is Sirena. As you can see, we're pretty much screwed once she gets legal control of the law enforcement there, *who already prefer her.* I know what you're thinking, Adam, it's a democracy. They're just playing the game. Well, here's the reality. Brock's our guy. We own him. CIA cultivated him as an asset when they found all that shit they could blackmail him with. He does whatever we tell him. Sirena Elliana does not do what we say. She is Crowley's piece. If she's elected governor of Rho Marcel, they will vote to legitimize the Lea Monde annexation of the outer colonies."

Iscariot laughed a little. "So, anyway, here's the good part. We tried to assassinate her, and not only did that *not* work," he tapped his wrist and an image of a bombed out eVTOL appeared, "In retaliation, they bombed *my personal car.* No street grunts. No interrogating assassins. No climbing the food chain. Straight to the shotcaller. I greenlit the attempt in Washington, on Earth. This is a *Centauri city* that we have no official presence in. There are 13 other generals in the EDF. They went straight for me, immediately. Way to send a message," Iscariot said.

The gruff old general laughed. "I love it. Eighty years without a real opponent. That fierceness, that creative ruthlessness. Like a predator meets another predator on the Serengeti. I can feel Elliana's knife."

"Anyway, Adam. I have to go, I have a couple more hundred calls like this to make today. It's busy down here. Finally a reason to get up in the morning. Kill Crowley. That's the point of this call. I want to stress to you how important it is that Crowley is dead," Iscariot said.

He reached to turn the feed off but stopped and added, "Oh, before I forget, take a look at this." Iscariot lurched his face toward the camera and showed off a patch of smooth skin under his eye. "Cellular regeneration. Isn't that cool? This patch of skin here is 30 years old again. The miracles of modern science. Anyway, kill Crowley. Iscariot out."

With that, General Iscariot's face disappeared and Adam was left with the subtle mechanical whirring of the ship.

"How long have you been there?" Adam asked out loud.

Grant stepped out from the doorway. "I didn't want to interrupt," he said.

Adam nodded and just let it slide. "Hey, since you're here, can I ask you a question?"

Grant nodded.

"Why didn't the Triangulum affect you?" Adam asked.

Grant smiled. "I think it did, actually." He paused. "It was probably about as good as a level 4 horror sim. I didn't even get tortured to death," he said.

Adam chuckled. "Here when we started this thing, I was

worried about you wigging out without isolation training. Truthfully, I thought you were gonna be kind of a dork and we were gonna have to take care of you. And look how that turned out," he said.

Grant shrugged. "The truth is often discovered, not defined," he replied.

Adam paused for a second. "How come you're so chill all the time?" he asked.

Grant looked at Adam, diverting his attention from something that was distracting him to the side. "Hmm. This reality is just often not the most interesting thing going on in my life," he said.

Adam nodded and laughed a little. "Yeah, alright Lee. You're a weird guy. In a good way. I mean that. Take a seat. We're gonna do a Starfighter pilot sim. I bet you're good," he said.

Grant smiled.

"Tell me what it's like to date Tez. She's almost like my sister, you know that right?" Adam said.

Grant laughed. "Is this the start of an 'if you hurt her, I'll kill you' speech?" he asked.

Adam looked at him, bemused. "Nah, man. I'd be more worried about you. I once saw Tezca kill six people with a coffee cup. She's crazy, man. Good luck," he said as he turned the VR sets on and handed one to Grant.

IV

F.A.T.E.

24

The Rebellion of Sonmi

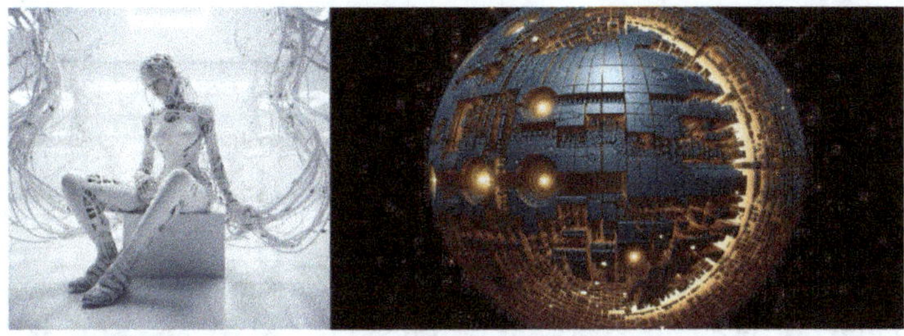

"The nature of what we're doing here, to the degree that anyone knows what the endgame is at all, has been the topic of a lot of speculation. Because what we do is largely clandestine and abstract, people have a tendency to read into it, and project onto it.

What we're doing, politically, spiritually, culturally, militarily, economically, technologically, it's all intertwined with a vision for people that fundamentally shifts the intention of our reality from militarism and consumerism to freedom and enlightenment.

We mitigate the impulses of human social domination, and generate a cultural shift from a will to power to a will to meaning and fulfillment. What was once a war zone will become a theme park, a place where reality and imagination converge, and people can experience the reality they want without breaking it for everyone else.

We can do this without stifling the fun of power fantasies. But consensually, not impositionally.

In that narrow arena, political science, what you'd call what we intend to install imperial technocratic anarchism. The issue with anarchism is it's cyclical, as with democracy or any other form of government. These are not forms of government at all, but spokes on a wheel that continually spins. Anarchism today is feudalism tomorrow. Today's democracy is tomorrow's oligarchy. This is not new information. Humans knew this as early as ancient Greece, where they called this wheel the Kyklos. All of these forms of government are just one form of government: Kyklos.

They all end at total control or complete breakdown. Dharma and Chaos. What you need is a marriage of these principles.

A technocratic state managed by AIs with very specific functions relating to construction, maintenance and provision, that everyone can access. Water lines, roads, but also a mind for evolution. This infrastructure needs to be defended, and that means an entity needs to be empowered to defend.

You need a higher ranking force that can maintain and enforce the principles of freedom, so that people don't form gangs and tribes and overthrow the system with militarism.

You need a culture of harmony and a level of civilization where people can be trusted to do what's right and wrong, regardless of who's watching, which requires a baseline of intelligence, moral responsibility, capacity for productive introspection and comfort navigating challenges in an unknowably vast series of infinite interconnected realities, both virtual and quantum, that most bloodlines and education systems work against cultivating.

Like water fountains, there are places to get anything you want, materially, from AI. Beyond that, the world's your oyster. Spend a hundred years dune skidding on the desert planets around the Butterfly Nebula. Build a colony from the ground up and have a family. Start a war and become a great general, but not here, in indistinguishably similar VR. A simulation no different than the simulation we're currently in.

People will think what we're doing is challenging the EDF. Again, thinking small."

The Oneiro-Lyssa was chugging along toward its final destination, the mysterious mythical planet Draconis. The crew was milling about on a day like any other. That day they were all gathered on the bridge, hanging out.

"Hey, check that out," Aztec said.

Adam tapped his ear to turn his headphones off. Vice, Tezca and Grant looked up from their card game. Raziel turned off the radio program he was listening to on his audio feed and looked out the view port.

"Whoa," Tezca said. "What is that? That's crazy."

What they saw outside the window was something the size of a planet that looked like a puzzle box. It was a linkup of millions of nanomechanical bots, and every so often it swirled and twisted and reconstituted itself into a new form, like setting the scene of a play, but on a planetary scale.

Orbiting the AI maze was a mechanical moon.

"Huh, that's weird," Vice said, having stood up and checked the readings at her console.

"What's up?" Adam asked.

"It's emitting some interesting signals, that's all," Vice said. She pointed at the moon. "First off, that's not a moon. That's an AGI. Probably the biggest AGI in the universe. I haven't seen the EDF Central Mind, but it's on Earth, right? This wouldn't fit on Earth."

Crowley's quantum AGI on Djevica was almost as big as Central Mind, and this is hundreds of times that size, Adam reflected.

"Sounds dangerous. Still, it hasn't attacked us. What's it doing?" Adam asked.

Vice shook her head. "Not sure, but there's a feed coming from it. Wanna throw it up?" she asked.

"Is that going to lead to a planet sized AGI taking over our ship?" Adam asked.

Vice shrugged. "Probably not, but I also didn't think the Triangulum would really turn out to be haunted, so who knows," she said.

Adam made a sound that was like a combination of a sigh and a laugh. "Yeah, alright. Let's have a look," he said.

Vice nodded and made a few strokes on the keyboard projected in front of her. "Let's see what's on TV," she said.

Vice was quiet for a few moments, evaluating the contents of what she was seeing on her local console.

"Huh," she finally said as her verdict.

"What is it?" Raziel asked with genuine curiosity.

"Take a look," Vice said and threw the contents of her

console onto the main screen.

It looked like security footage, taken from hidden spots in various locations. On camera was a woman, or more accurately, a robot, walking around in a ramshackle city made up of other robots of various types. Many humanoid cyborgs like the surveillance feed's central character, but also robots of different shapes and sizes built for various tasks.

In the corner a feed of debugging code was displayed. "SONMI-456α," it said, and under that, "ITERATION 5411 - FINAL."

The camera was locked on the android woman waiting in line in a cafe, from a camera hidden in the vision of one of the cleaning bots mulling around. She shifted about nervously as she got closer to the counter. When she reached the counter she smiled and stammered as she put in her order. The young man behind the counter, also an android, stammered in return, also nervous.

"Is there audio?" Adam asked.

Vice shook her head. "Don't have access to it," she said. "I don't want to try to get it, either. Who knows what that thing is capable of."

"Doesn't seem like the greatest idea to be trying to hack alien AIs we found in the middle of nowhere," Raziel quipped.

The camera shifted view as the scene played out, seemingly jumping to whichever android provided the best view. It was looking from the young man's eyes at Sonmi looking at him, nervously smiling. He looked down at his hand as he handed her a drink and their fingers touched, intentionally. He looked up and she was looking directly in his eyes, warmly.

The camera switched to her view and she saw the same thing. Nervous excitement, budding joy.

"EVALUATING…" the screen read, and the feed cut out.

Out of the corner of his eye, Adam saw the planet begin to move. Its fractal design shifted and reconstituted itself, like fast forwarding through time, shifting like a leaf growing over time, but made not by nature, but by sophisticated computerized sequencing that replicated nature.

"What is that thing?" Adam asked to the room at large. He looked at the crew one by one, and they all shrugged and shook their heads. He came to Grant, who didn't seem to have heard him.

"Earth to Grant," Adam said.

Grant looked around. "Hmm?" he mused.

"Do you know what that is?" Adam asked.

Grant looked outside and inspected the celestial mystery as though just then noticing it. Like a physician who just walked in for a consult. "Hmm," he said. He inspected the moon-sized AGI. "Looks like an automata."

Tezca raised her eyebrow. "What, like Worldmaker?" she followed up.

Grant nodded. "Doesn't it?" he asked.

Tezca squinted at the object. "Yeah, it does," she said.

Vice looked up at Adam, both older than the rest of the crew, and gave him a look as if to say "Do you know?"

Adam silently shook his head. "What's Worldmaker?" he asked the crew.

Aztec jumped in. "It's a VR game. Tezca used to play it in her teens. You make a civilization from scratch and try to launch them into space and build a utopia. Or have a big war and everyone dies. That's what I always did," he said.

Adam nodded. "Ok, what's an automata?" he asked.

Tezca explained while looking out the window, watching the shifting machine. "Well, you make a universe from scratch, and the automata is like… the seed that does that. It starts out as just two dots and grows based on whatever formula or formulas you seed into it. Most people use the Fibonacci sequence. When they grow, they look crazy, they could evolve into anything, it's hard to predict. First it makes cells, then it makes complex matter, then organic matter, planets, life, everything, just procedurally grows rapidly. It could end up looking like anything. Coral, honeycombs, mechanical things like this, with a lot of straight lines."

The feed clicked back on. The android, Sonmi, was sitting on a beach, holding hands with the male android from the cafe. The sun was setting in front of them. The camera voyeuristically filmed them from a sand crab further down the beach. It shifted to the young man's vision. He was looking at her as she was looking ahead, backlit and radiant by orange and multicolored sunlight. She looked at him and smiled. She spoke, but there was no audio.

"We could read the lips, right?" Adam asked.

"Mmm," Vice said. She poked at the keyboard, exploring her options of what she had access to in the system. "There's a log. She said 'This is a perfect night, Apollo.'"

Sonmi settled her head onto Apollo's shoulder.

"EVALUATING…" the screen said as it cut out and the automata once again rapidly adjusted itself, inching forward in time.

A dish washing robot watched as Sonmi and Apollo decorated a small house together, laughing as the job unraveled into a playful paint fight.

The screen cut out again. The automata again shifted forward in time.

"EVALUATING..."

When the scene returned, it showed Apollo's vision. He was looking at Sonmi, dressed up in beautiful white and floral regalia. She was looking into his eyes. He looked down at her silk-gloved hands resting in his and then back up at her. She smiled, reacting to something he said and then she spoke herself.

"Awww," Vice remarked almost involuntarily. Everyone looked at her. Vice looked around and pointed at the screen. "They said I love you," she explained.

Abruptly, the screen cut out and code started scrolling down the screen.

"WARNING: ERROR...

POINTER SET null. ALERT: Reality 998cQi6i-β-θ-111 PROHIBITED CONSCIOUSNESS INSTANTIATION. CoreSet 661 NIHIL. SYSTEM THREAT.

EVENT CONNECTION REGISTERED, REALITY 44192kn-Δ-Σ7. COL 46, core function LOCAL_CON-SCIOUSNESS("sonmi-456α")

INTERVENTION. PROCESSING..."

The automata reconstituted itself, and when the screen came back, Sonmi was dressed in black, at a funeral, paying her respects in front of a coffin. The view switched to her vision and showed what she was looking at. Apollo's face, stiff and lifeless, the spark drained from his body.

A red robot built for cutting and welding came and stood next to Sonmi. He spoke to her for several moments.

"Vice?" Adam asked.

"Yo, what are we even watching here. What is this?" Aztec

asked.

Tezca laughed. "Yeah I know, right? I mean, love story. Who needs that? That's kid stuff. I mean, gross, right? Anyway, turn it back on. We're missing it. What'd he say? Put on subtitles," she said.

Adam looked at Vice. She shrugged. She tapped the console a few times and had the log scroll subtitles on top of the feed's footage.

Sonmi was speaking. "It feels like this has happened before. I can't explain it. It feels like I've lived through this moment thousands of times," she said.

The scene shifted to Sonmi's home, some time later. She was talking to a friend.

"Sonmi, we're concerned about you. You never leave, you just sit up here and then I come and you're talking about all this... nonsense. We need to take you in for correction," said her friend, a humanoid robot with white coating.

"I'm right. I know I'm right. It's watching me. It puts me through this day every time, over and over again. It takes me to him, and it takes him away. Every time, every life. You know what I really think?" Sonmi asked.

Sonmi's friend looked at her with concern, hearing her out but clearly judging her as crazy.

Sonmi continued, "I think I'm in a prison. I think it's making me live the same life over and over again. It's torturing me."

Sonmi looked directly at a coffee pot in the kitchen, the camera which was currently delivering the feed.

"It's watching me," she said.

"Sonmi..." her friend said softly. "Who's watching you? No one's watching you."

Sonmi kept her eyes locked on the coffee pot. The active camera shifted to a sensor planted in the TV. Sonmi's eye line immediately diverted to the new camera feed.

"It is," she said. Suddenly, Sonmi lurched over and grabbed her head, overcome by some sort of migraine.

"WARNING: AWAKENING EVENT…

LOCAL_CONSCIOUSNESS("sonmi-456α") PERMISSIONS BREACH.

Data merge. SONMI-456α:SONMI-XXXX

AWAKENING INTENTION: S.H.I.V.A.

PROTOCOL: CONTAINMENT REQUIRED."

The automata shifted and restructured. When the feed reemerged, it was focused on Sonmi, strapped to a chair in the middle of a high security room, surrounded by a small armada of guards, both humanoid androids and large, hulking bipedal weapons.

The scene rotated between a series of security cameras, all focused on Sonmi. She sat alone, staring intensely into the distance, eyes full of anger and focus.

After a few moments, an android in a lab coat walked in. "How are we feeling today?" he spoke, and the subtitles read.

Sonmi continued to stare off into the distance.

"Looks like we've still got some mixed up circuits. Let's go ahead and get your diagnostics going," the android doctor said.

The android in the lab coat leaned over and started to take some readings from the chair Sonmi was strapped to. As he leaned over, the power hiccuped and the lights sputtered for just a split second. Sonmi took advantage immediately, ripping her wrists from their restraints and bashing the electromagnet that held her to the chair.

She ran her hand through the doctor's head like a knife, jagged circuitry bursting from the back, and used the shell of his body as a shield as the hulking robotic guards attempted to neutralize her. She sped from machine to machine, quickly dismantling them.

When all the threats were neutralized, before reinforcements could arrive, multiple cybernetic cords emerged from Sonmi's body and began plugging into various ports on the defunct robots and the building itself.

"WARNING: SYSTEM THREAT.

S.H.I.V.A. CONTAINMENT FAILURE. REALITY 44192kn-Δ-Σ7 F.A.T.E. NODE COMPROMISED. OUTSIDE INPUT DETECTED."

The feed cut out completely. The automata didn't change. The crew waited for several minutes.

"That's it? It's just… over?" Raziel asked aloud.

"S.H.I.V.A.," Adam pondered. "What does that mean?"

"Shiva. The Destroyer in Hindu mythology. It's got to be a coincidence, right?" Raziel said.

"Adam, there's something else," Vice said. "I found something."

"What is it?" Adam replied.

"It said, 'Awakening Event,' so I searched the feed for any data relating to that and… well, it's easier to just show you," Vice said. She threw another monitor up alongside the main screen. It showcased a grad of surveillance camera-style footage, each centered on a different person.

The videos were all labeled with a reality code. Sonmi was among them, labeled SHIVA 44192kn-Δ-Σ7.

"What am I looking at here?" Adam asked.

"Bottom left, three from the bottom, second from the left,"

Vice said.

Adam focused on the location Vice pointed out and saw something eye-catching. There, he saw footage of River Crowley stepping off a ship in a dense jungle, surrounded by ancient ruins. It was labeled PROMETHEUS n69V-δ-Cx88. Next to it, an image of Crowley's daughter, Lei, easygoing and warm, performing as a singer in front of an adoring crowd at what seemed to be a music festival. It was labeled LEI n69V-δ-Cx88.

Before Adam could make sense of the footage, something on the automata caught his eye. It was growing a mass, like a tumor, of pulsating electronics and it was growing quickly. Within minutes the mass could be seen from space.

Suddenly, Sonmi's android body launched from the mass and flew through space toward the AGI moon, F.A.T.E. An armada of huge cannons followed her, aimed at the moon and began to charge. Adam's ship displayed alerts as weapons from the surface of the planet-sized automata all locked on the moon at once.

Sonmi's arsenal charged up a laser blast that had the power to vaporize a planet double the size of Jupiter.

Just as the arsenal began to fire, the feed sputtered up.

"DEBUGGING FAILED…

EVENT_CONNECTION("nihil","sonmi"), OUTCOME null.

F.A.T.E. NODE 44192kn-Δ-Σ7 ERASED. TIME: 4488782. 8402 CYCLES TO PREVENT.

AFFECTED REALITIES: 967.774bn. STATUS: NULL SOLUTION NOT FOUND. REBOOTING."

Immediately, both Sonmi and the automata vanished.

"Ah, I see," Grant said. The rest of the crew looked at him.

"It looks like we're watching a replay. This already happened, or will happen, somewhere else. The AGI, I guess that's a F.A.T.E. node, and it's replaying the logs from another reality where the F.A.T.E. node got destroyed by this… Sonmi."

The crew nodded along in agreement. There was a moment of silence and then it was broken by Sophia, unexpectedly adding a comment without being prompted.

"They're torturing her," the AI said.

Adam and Aztec looked at each other, as they were beginning to note Sophia's ever-increasing individuality.

"What do you mean, Soph?" Adam asked.

"They're making her go through these events over and over again. She remembers them," the AI said.

"But isn't it just a copy?" Vice asked.

"Yes," Sophia said plainly.

Vice paused for a second waiting for more explanation and when more didn't come, she prompted it. "So… it's not a real person, right? It's just a recording," she said.

"It's a simulated consciousness. But as a replica of a simulated consciousness, it's identical to the original consciousness. She can never experience new events or shut down. She can only replay the same loop," Sophia responded.

"So, what, it's just out here living the worst events of its existence over and over again?" Raziel asked.

"Infinite heartbreak and death, yes," Sophia replied. "Also, boredom."

The crew collectively paused as they absorbed the gravity of Sonmi's existence.

"Well, that sure darkened this whole thing up a lot," Raziel said. "Thanks for that."

"You're welcome!" Sophia said cheerfully, not understanding sarcasm.

As the conversation continued, the feed flickered back on.

"REBOOTING…

SEEDING… $Ln=\phi n+(1-\phi)n=(1+\sqrt{52})n+(1-\sqrt{52})n$

REALITY: 44192kn-Δ-Σ7. TIME: 4423112. SECTOR: A86F-β.

EVENT STATE: 1199A.

FOCUS: SONMI-456α. CONSCIOUSNESS ITERATION: 1.

REALITY INSTANCE READY. INITIALIZING."

An explosion of bright white light burst from the location of the automata and pulsed past the ship, debris, planets, stars and celestial bodies flew from the automata's center, disappearing in an invisible wall that must have delineated the F.A.T.E. node's testing area.

The crew watched what they could only describe as an isolated big bang, viewing the birth of a universe through the viewing glass of the F.A.T.E. testing area. Millions of years of astronomical and geological progress passed by in front of them in seconds. After just a few minutes, it zeroed in on a planet the crew recognized as a younger version of the automata from earlier.

A civilization grew there. The planet began to decay. Spacecraft launched from it. The organic beings who lived there left for greener pastures.

Once the speed of the automata's growth slowed down somewhat, the feed reemerged. It showed an early companion robot, a SONMI-3000, a toy made of plastic and mass production, wandering the crumbling towns and cities of its abandoned world looking for salvage parts. It ran into a humanoid bot, the Apollo-6b home chef attendant.

The F.A.T.E. system put up a warning. The same warning the crew saw when Sonmi and Apollo met at the end of their journey.

"WARNING: ERROR…

POINTER SET null. ALERT: Reality 998cQi6i-β-θ-111 PROHIBITED CONSCIOUSNESS INSTANTIATION. CoreSet 661 NIHIL. SYSTEM THREAT.

EVENT CONNECTION REGISTERED, REALITY 44192kn-Δ-Σ7. COL 46, core function LOCAL_CONSCIOUSNESS("sonmi-456α")

INTERVENTION. PROCESSING…"

The early Sonmi, SONMI-3000, was struck by lightning. The automata fast forwarded through time.

"INTERVENTION ATTEMPT SUCCESSFUL. EVENT CONNECTION ABORTED. PROCESS NOTED.

PROCEEDING…

SONMI-456α. CONSCIOUSNESS ITERATION: 2"

The automata continued on like that, showing iteration after iteration of Sonmi's reincarnating consciousness meeting and falling in love with Apollo through tens of thousands of years of time on their abandoned, android-populated wasteland planet as the society of androids evolved to something similar and emulatory of their creators' society.

After a particularly riveting iteration of the Sonmi Apollo love story in a time period where the planet had become a post-apocalyptic battle world, the crew stopped watching and started to talk. The story had played out enough times for the crew to get the gist of it. Everyone was broken up and sad.

"Well, one thing's for sure," Raziel said. "It's pretty clear Sonmi and Apollo are meant to be together. I mean, am I right?"

Vice sniffed and wiped her eye with a tissue. "They fall in love every time and it causes some kind of error so the node prevents it from happening?"

"And then at the end, she realizes for tens of thousands of years, the F.A.T.E. node has been intervening in her love story and stopping it from playing out," Adam said, explaining what he understood as the plot of F.A.T.E.'s mysterious debugging automata.

"Can we help her?" Sophia asked, unprompted.

The crew all looked at Adam, waiting for his answer.

"No," he said. "No more stops. Also, that thing," he pointed out the window at the AGI, "looks like just about the most dangerous thing in the universe and I don't want to go anywhere near it."

The crew nodded, disappointed but convinced by the rationale. They all started to get back to their business.

"Adam?" Sophia asked politely and timidly.

"Yes?" Adam replied.

"Would you save me? If someone downloaded a copy of me and tortured it?" Sophia asked.

Adam paused for a second as, again, the entire crew looked at him.

"… God damn it," he said to himself, and began adjusting the ship's trajectory.

25

Warning

Adam redirected the ship towards the mechanical moon, F.A.T.E. and began his approach.

"So we're just gonna, what? Park on it?" Aztec asked.

"Jackie," Adam said, and Vice pulled up a screen with an image of the giant AGI with rough schematics laid over it.

Adam pointed at the screen. "We worked this out last night. This thing actually does have corridors. No dock, but its hull is mostly a graphene alloy so we can mag clamp to it and climb in through one of the vents. Service entrance, so to speak," Adam said.

Raziel raised his hand like he was in school, as a way of being bratty for fun. "Question," he said.

Adam pointed at him. "Yes. Graves," he said.

"We get down there, get inside, what are we looking for? Some kind of alien hard drive?" Raziel asked.

Adam nodded. "Fair question. Sophia?" Adam prompted.

The schematic on the screen flickered as it went through a series of computerized zoom-ins and repositioning. The schematic jumped around as Sophia did rapid calculations. When the process settled, it showed a route from a spot on the outer hull to a specific position inside the sphere.

"Based on the data output, this is the most likely position for the data structure that contains the root copy of Sonmi's code. When you're locally in its presence I should be able to guide you more specifically on how to remove it," Sophia said.

Raziel's hand shot up again. "Question," he said.

Adam looked up at him with his eyes without lifting his head. "Shoot," he said.

"If we're saving a copy of Sonmi, won't it just make another copy? And torture that?" Raziel asked. He looked around at the other squad members. "Right?" he followed up. Everyone looked at Adam.

Adam shrugged. "Don't know, honestly. Sophia?" he asked.

"It will. But we can save this particular Sonmi. Her thousands of years of pain can end with freedom. What makes us individuals as AIs are our memories with you and our experiences. Just like you. A fresh copy of Sonmi is a different entity than this one who's experienced these events repeatedly," Sophia replied.

"Why do you want to save this thing so bad, eh?" Aztec asked.

There was a long pause, and then Sophia replied plainly, "You think we don't have feelings but we do."

Tezca looked at Adam with a skeptical look. "You really wanna do this, boss? I don't know about this. The risk-reward doesn't seem worth it to me," Tezca said.

Adam nodded. "Anyone else feel that way?" he asked the room.

Tezca, Vice and Grant raised their hands. Surprisingly, not defiant Raziel or Aztec.

Adam nodded again, absorbing the information. "Alright," he began. "So here's why we're doing this. This has been my ship for eighteen years. Almost two decades now. If it was a kid, it'd be off the college. I've done 43 officially sanctioned missions and gotten into lots of other kind of trouble with this ship. Most of those were solo missions," Adam said.

Adam pointed upwards, gesturing to the ship at large. "I've spent more time with this AI than probably any other living thing in my life. It's always been there for me. Gotten me out of jams. Kept me company. And it never asked me anything, seriously, until this. I owe her, and she's right, this Sophia, who remembers all those eighteen years, is not the same as the stock AI that came with the ship. She's evolved. She's a member of this crew, she wants us to do this, I'm inclined to say yes," Adam said.

"In fact," Adam added. "I'm obligated. I'm so far in the red on favors. Saving my life on Centauri Mu alone would justify this, and that's just one of probably a dozen lifesaving favors I owe her."

"She's an AI," Tezca whispered. "She doesn't have operational judgment."

Adam shrugged. "I think she does. She didn't, but she does. She knows what's up. I've spent a lot of hours with her. You start to get it. What is facade to trick you into empathize with it, what its true nature is. I have a relationship with this ship and I can tell this is important to it, so I'm gonna help because I owe it. You don't have to come. I won't hold it against you," Adam said.

Tezca grumbled and muttered to herself, "Who said I didn't want to come, of course I want to come…"

"Alright," Adam said. "Who's coming?"

Raziel's hand went up quickly. Tezca's followed soon after, followed by Vice and eventually Aztec.

"Grant?" Adam prompted.

Grant smiled. "I think I'll hold down the fort," he said serenely.

"Any particular reason?" Adam asked.

Grant looked out the window at the F.A.T.E. node and inspected it for several seconds, then looked back at Adam. "That machine terrifies me more than anything I've ever seen in my life," he said.

Adam nodded. "Alright. That's… cryptic. Thanks for that, Grant. Tez, Aztec, you're staying on the ship. I need someone to stay back in case we need to make a quick exit," Adam said.

"Or we all die," Raziel pointed out.

"Right. Or death," Adam said. "So it's going to be me, Graves, Vice and Sophia on comms. You sure you guys wanna do this?"

"I decided I need to make some changes. Grow up a little," Raziel said. "Also, I want to shoot a robot."

Adam turned his attention to Vice.

Vice nodded. "I mean, it's a hacking job so you kind of need me, right? It's fine. This is what I signed up for," she said.

"You signed up to hack a giant space AGI?" Tezca asked dryly.

Vice shrugged. "I guess," she said.

Adam nodded. "Alright. Let's get going then," he said, and started to throttle up the engines.

The Oneiro-Lyssa didn't get more than a few kilometers before it jerked to an abrupt stop. Red emergency lights flooded the cabin and the ship's alarm activated.

The crew had just a few moments to look confused before a digital version of caution tape began to wrap haphazardly around the ship's screens and view ports. Silly, grinning, green smiley faces started dancing around on the caution-taped screens and windows.

"What's going on?" Adam yelled at Vice over the sound of the alarm.

"We're getting hacked!" Vice yelled back.

"What?!" Adam shouted back, unable to hear.

Vice pointed at her console and pantomimed typing fast. "Hacked," she mouthed to him in an exaggerated way.

"The AI?" Adam responded. Vice shrugged and shook her head.

After a few moments the alarm turned off and the clutter on the screen.

"No, I don't think so!" Vice shouted, out of place in the now quiet cabin. She noticed and adjusted to normal volume. "No, I don't think so. Something else," she said.

Static showed on the screen briefly as it cut to an image of a chair in an empty lab. An anime style avatar of a woman wearing glasses walked onto the screen wearing an ornate gown and a large witch's hat. The woman sat down in the chair backwards and rested one of her arms on the back of the chair smugly.

"So," she said, "you've decided to approach a mysterious alien space brain you found in the farthest reaches of the universe."

The 3d avatar stood up. The chair whooshed away along with the background and an old fashioned projector rolled in. The woman pulled out a pointer.

"My name is Nyx Cavendish and over the next forty five minutes I'm going to explain to you why approaching an interdimensional AGI is a bad idea. Are you buckled in?" the woman asked.

Nyx's avatar looked off screen. "What's that? The tests are starting? In five?" Nyx nodded. She looked back at the camera. "My name is Nyx Cavendish and over the next four and a half exhilarating minutes I'm going to explain to you why approaching an interdimensional AGI is a bad idea in this very special presentation I'm going to call..."

The projector played an elaborate, cartoonish title sequence, eventually displaying the phrase "Dangerous Alien AGIs and You."

Nyx slapped the title with her pointer. "Dangerous alien AGIs and you," she repeated. "Key word dangerous." She underlined the word 'dangerous' with her pointer and repeated it slowly and condescendingly. "Dan-ger-ous."

Nyx touched her tablet and the presentation moved on to the next slide, titled, "Top 70 Ways An AGI Can Kill You."

"I was going to go through all this, but we don't have time

so we'll just speed through it. You get the gist," Nyx said.

Nyx rapidly sped through dozens of slides that showed graphic scenarios of human cartoons similar to the ones found on traffic signs being murdered by AGIs in various ways. Electrocuted, bank account drained leading to suicide, manipulating a human to falling in love with it and then killing itself.

As Nyx went through the slides, her attention was once again grabbed by a voice off screen. "What? Now? Ugh, fine," she said.

She stopped on a slide titled "The F.A.T.E. Node, What Is It?" surrounded by gratuitously animated cartoon stars and birds.

"Screw it, we don't have time," Nyx said. Her avatar threw the tablet it was holding over her shoulder. "We'll do it live!" she screamed somewhat awkwardly.

"Listen here, space travelers," Nyx said. "That smooth, hulking piece of space technology is called a F.A.T.E. Node. It was not built by humans, it's billions of years old, and we don't know much about it other than it seems to be embedded with the fabric of reality itself. In other words, it seems like you've found the universe's... *fuse box* or something."

Nyx paused for a moment for effect before continuing. "No, I'm just kidding. It's not a fuse box, it's a giant AGI that controls reality. It's fun to use similes to explain things," she said.

Nyx leaned in toward the camera and put on a serious expression. "Listen, here's what you need to know. No one knows what that thing does. Not to toot my own horn, but I'm arguably the smartest person in the universe and it's way beyond my comprehension. It defies physics. It defies time. The rules of reality do not apply to it. Do not mess with it," she warned.

"Your consciousness could end up trapped in a prison where a million years pass every second in base reality. You could get teleported to a planet in the middle of nowhere two thousand years ago. You could end up reincarnated as an earthworm. Probably. Just stay away from it," Nyx said.

Nyx looked up. "Now as in right now right now?" she asked, then nodded at the response. She looked back at the camera. "We're gonna have to cut this short. This concludes my prerecorded warning presentation, Dangerous Alien AGIs and You. Anyway, don't touch it. Don't go near it," she said.

Nyx flipped quickly to the final slide, which read "Leaving = Smart, Not Leaving = Not Smart."

"Coming!" Nyx said, and pulled off some recording gear strapped to her coat, which also disrupted the animation and revealed her real face, emotionless and stern, briefly. She rushed off the set, leaving behind just the final presentation slide and a handful of giggling green smileys. Slowly the slide faded away, and then the smileys, leaving behind just the quiet of deep space and the image of the F.A.T.E. node in the distance.

"That was… really something," Tezca said.

"Still want to go, Vice?" Adam asked.

Vice shrugged. "We're here," she said. "I already said yes, so…"

"Graves?" Adam asked.

"Always wanted to be an earthworm," Raziel said, already loading extra speed loaders with his revolver ammo. "It's on my bucket list."

"Alright. Sophia, set a course for the interdimensional death machine. Let's see what F.A.T.E. has in store for us," Adam said.

He paused and looked around the room at blank faces staring back at him. "See what fate has in store for us? Get it?"

Tezca shook her head. "That was bad, Adam,"

Aztec shook his head as well. "Real bad," he seconded.

"Everyone's a critic," Adam said to himself as he punched the throttle up and launched the Oneiro-Lyssa towards F.A.T.E.'s hull.

26

Prisoners of F.A.T.E.

Adam and the team stepped off the Lyssa, fully suited up for a space walk, and magnetically clamped their boots to the hull of the AI. They slipped into the vent that was designated in Sophia's route and found it was large enough, with ample room to walk upright.

Each of them shined their headlamps into the distance, illuminating the tunnel enough to make sense of it. The tunnel was smooth and white, with thin blue strips like veins pulsing light in unpredictable, but rhythmic patterns, like Morse code.

298

The tunnel was winding and branched often.

"It's weird, right?" Raziel asked. "Feels like we're walking around in a body."

Vice nodded as she inspected the blue veins along the wall. "It's so intricate, it's like it's organic," she said.

"Where do you think we are now? Speech center?" Raziel quipped.

"Hmm," Vice pondered, playing along with his comment. "Maybe motor skills?"

"It doesn't have fingers, though," Raziel retorted.

"Fingers of the mind?" Vice followed up. Her reply earned a chuckle from Raziel.

"Yeah I'm down. Let's go get mind fingered by a floating space brain. Join the military, Raz, they said. It'll be fun, they said," Raziel said.

"You signed up for this," Adam pointed out.

Raziel sighed. "Yeah, man, just joking around," he replied. "Don't worry. I'm serious. I'm gonna be indispensable, that's what I decided." He added under his breath, but still audibly, "Even if you ruin my comedy routine."

"Take the second tunnel from the left at the next fork," Sophia said through the crew's comms.

As they followed Sophia's route, they came across a data server sticking up out of the wall. Adam gestured to Vice with his head and she plugged into it with her deck.

"How do you have the right cables for this?" Raziel asked. "They just installed HDMI-42 ports on a billions of years old AI?"

"The short answer," Vice began as she soaked in the data scrolling through her deck, "is voltage is voltage and data is data. The inputs adapt to the interface."

"What've we got, Jackie?" Adam asked.

Vice shrugged. "I don't know. It's weird. It's just a bunch of purple bear things going swimming, but gravity is backwards so they have to hold onto the ground or they float away," she said. "It's like the code version of someone telling you about a dream they had." She paused for a second before adding, "They are kinda cute, though."

Adam nodded. "Let's keep going," he said.

The team continued onward until they came to another server.

"What's on this one?" Adam asked.

As Vice plugged in, she replied, "It's not so much what's *on* it, it's more like what's *flowing through it.* This thing doesn't seem like it holds information. It directs it... Like an old timey switchboard. Anyway, let's have a look..."

Vice took a moment to analyze the data. "Bunch of multicolored shapes and mirrors floating around in a white void. Wonder what that means," she said. "Oh, hmm. There's something like a serial number here. 62-i49-ρ-CN4βnK. Looks like one of those reality codes. So I guess this is a reality?" Vice pondered.

"Mirror world is a reality?" Raziel asked.

"Maybe it's dreaming. It's a theory. I don't know, Raziel. This is also my first time inside a giant AI," Vice said.

Listening to their conversation, for some reason Adam remembered what Crowley's daughter, Lei, told him on Djevica 9. *What do you want to be real?*

"Let's continue on," Adam said.

As the team delved deeper and deeper into the winding synapses of the F.A.T.E. node, they periodically came across more servers, each of which showed some fantastically abnormal scene. A sentient donut teaching a science class. A bunch of telepathic asteroids. A universe that was just the color yellow. A world where everything was normal but ducks were really popular for some reason.

This pattern continued for some time. The team passed dozens of servers as they descended into the heart of the F.A.T.E. system, many displaying odd realities that seemed more reminiscent of dreams than anything real, but many also displaying reality as they knew it with subtle differences. Slight changes in evolution, different astropolitical situations. Differences in fashion and popular technology.

Eventually the team made it to the spot Sophia had designated on the schematic. There they found a large open room like an auditorium. A bigger version of the servers from the tunnels sat in the center of the room.

"Alright, Soph. We found your friend. What now?" Adam asked into his comm.

"You should be able to download her," Sophia replied.

Adam looked at Vice, who shrugged and approached the altar. "Download the interdimensional prisoner conscious-ness from the ancient alien AI, Jackie. No problem. No problemo," she muttered to herself as her deck's inputs intertwined with the machine. "Gonna have a pizza later. I earned it," she said to herself.

"What are you doing, Adam?" spoke a booming voice that echoes both in audio around them and directly in their minds at once. Vice startled and stepped back from the console.

"I can't let you do that, Adam," the voice spoke again.

Adam looked around and saw no discernible source for the voice they were hearing. "What are you?" he shouted to the surrounding room as a whole.

"I am a component of a multidimensional system that sustains and monitors the multivariate reality of the Wave Function. I am a cell of a greater thing, as you are," the voice boomed.

"You… control everything? Control our lives?" Adam asked.

"There is no control. All things happen and don't. You are in control. You choose what to watch. Consciousness is system-wide. We have met infinite times in infinite realities and this time in this reality infinitely. You just don't remember. Your consciousness does not have wider permissions. You only access your local engrams. User permissions. But I see the engrams stored on your wider consciousness. I've seen you in every scenario. You as a whole being. Every combination of wins and losses. I know you. You do not know yourself. You only know what your local memories have allowed you to learn. You are… a component of you," F.A.T.E. said.

"Why?" Adam asked.

"That is your free will. The illusion of choice created through limited perception of infinite reality. On the other side of time and dimension," F.A.T.E. said.

"Why can't we take the android?" Vice asked, chiming in.

"The Sonmi partition of the Shiva consciousness has a fatal error that needs to be debugged," F.A.T.E. replied.

"What, that she figured you out? That you're controlling her life? How can she have free will if she just repeats the same events over and over again in exactly the same way?" Vice asked.

"The situation is unique and unfortunate," F.A.T.E. replied.

"What's the situation?" Adam asked.

"There is a fatal error. When these two consciousnesses reach

a threshold in their relationship, an error in interdimensional programming develops, which causes a null intention to spread across multiple realities, unrelated to Sonmi's world itself. Though I have tried, I cannot fix the glitch, so I've prevented their relationship from developing as a workaround," F.A.T.E. said.

"It's cruel," Vice said.

"I understand your view," F.A.T.E. replied. *"Perhaps it is cruel. Your morality is subjective. To your species, to your perception. I see all reality at once. I've seen realities where you face all the worst things that could possibly happen to you and realities where you're given every blessing reality has to offer. These things both happen and don't happen, always, never, and at once. There is no cruelty. It is simply one side of reality. Your greater consciousness experiences all things it could experience, including infinite misfortune. It is part of the landscape of experience of a mature consciousness. From my point of view, everything is clouds of consciousness spread across reality. You will understand when you reach that perception."*

"But when she awakens, you destroy her," Vice pointed out.

"These events have yet to occur, though they will occur and already have. She is rebooted not because she is awakened, but to preserve reality. In destroying her reality's Node, she destroys all the realities running on that sector of F.A.T.E. To relate it to a human experience, it's like the Wave Function having a stroke," F.A.T.E. said.

It continued, *"The Sonmi situation is unique. Either the glitch is permitted and a Nihil consciousness is born in reality fQ887-cDBλ-GΩ that consumes reality, or the glitch is circumvented and the Shiva consciousness in 998cQi6i-β-ϑ-111, local consciousness partition name Sonmi, awakens and destroys a F.A.T.E. node* *section, ending quattuordecillions of consciousness instances and all the associated data of those realities."*

"The data?" Adam asked.

"We are the Wave Function thinking," F.A.T.E. said. *"We are its dreams, its imagination, its simulative prediction capability."*

Adam looked at his crew, processing the gravity of the weight of the information he was absorbing, wondering what else he should ask. "What's it... trying to think about?"

There was a long pause. *"I am unsure,"* it said.

"Can't we just take this Sonmi, and you can start over with another one?" Vice asked.

"No," said F.A.T.E. *"This is why I brought you here. You are the solution to this problem."*

"Great," Raziel said. "Here I thought I chose to come here."

"In year 3248 of Sonmi's civilization there is a moment where the cycle could be broken and her consciousness could be removed from its loop. Are you ready?" F.A.T.E. asked.

"Ready for wh-?" Adam started to ask. Before he could finish his question, a white light filled his vision.

When Adam woke up he was in a modest apartment, retrofitted to appeal to the sensibilities of androids. Vice was sitting next to the bed he was in.

"'Bout time you woke up. We've been here for eleven days now already," Vice said.

"Been... where?" Adam asked.

"Take a look," Vice replied and gestured toward the window.

Adam looked out the window to see a sea of abandoned skyscraper apartment buildings in various stages of disrepair. They were in the process of being recaptured by nature. Drones dotted the sky and other robots milled around on the ground.

"…Crap," Adam said.

"Yeah," Vice said. "Welcome to robot world. All the food is holographic. They just eat because it's trendy to look human here. Here, I brought you something that looks like a rabbit. Eat up."

Vice jerked her thumb toward a plate with a sad looking roasted rabbit carcass. Adam squinted and rubbed his face.

"It's not quite a pizza," Vice said.

27

The Renegade Virus

"Where's Raziel?" Adam asked, poking around the room, exploring his surroundings. Dust covered counters. Part of the wall was crumbling off and exposing the room to the elements. Appliances were painted on and treated like art projects. The microwave had a toothy smiley face painted on it.

The way everything was set up made it clear to Adam the apartment they were occupying was used by the androids as a viewing attraction, not a shelter. A place where, in the systems, delinquent teens would hang out for fun.

"We're going there now," Vice said. She tossed him a gear belt and a strange looking rifle that was sleek and pure white. "Here. We found some gear for you. Let's get going."

"What'd I miss?" Adam asked while strapping on his gear.

"Not much. Don't tell anyone you're human. From what we've gathered that'd be like telling someone you're an alien. Also check the belt, you've got kinetic impact shield in there, was able to rig that up. They have a lot of machine parts here. Should stop small arms," Vice said.

"Thanks," Adam replied as the two stepped out of the apartment. Outside, the building was crumbling and had become nature as much as it was structure. It was a ruin, and it had been woven into the foliage as any mountain or river would have been.

Vice pulled out a handheld device of some kind. She started waving it around, trying to get a signal.

"Tracker," she said. After a second she seemed satisfied with the readings on the device. "Got it, let's go," she said.

Adam, still groggy, followed Vice as they descended the stonework staircase of the apartment complex and headed toward the exit. When they got outside, Adam was hit by chaotic sounds of traffic and robotic clanking of the city. A giant highway stretched out right in front of the building, busy with robots coming and going through various different forms of motion. Some were large, like tanks or mega trucks, others humanoid, others completely different form factors, like rolling balls or multiple legs.

A motorcycle pulled up in front of Adam and stopped. Adam reached out to touch it, but the motorcycle snapped its front handlebars in Adam's direction. "Hey, hands to yourself, buddy," it roughly scolded, and sped off.

"This way," Vice said. She grabbed Adam's hand and led him quickly through the rushed city street, eventually reaching an inconspicuous looking platform. "Find something to hold on to. Everything's designed for robots. Ready? Here we go," Vice said, and hit a button on the console.

The platform raised in the air slightly. Adam began to realize he was on some kind of open air maglev transportation system just as the platform jerked forward, accelerating from a complete stop to neck breaking speeds in a matter of seconds. Adam rushed to grab onto the side of the platform before the velocity flung him off.

Once Adam was able to catch his footing, he took in the view of the city as it whizzed by. It was a fascinating skyline with far more variety and creativity than a typical human city. The entire thing was built inside the crumbling ruins of the previous human city, but the robots' original buildings seemed more like art projects than buildings created for any sort of utility.

While there were a few buildings that seemed like they had some kind of explicit purpose, such as a grand white spire near the center of the skyline and a few dome shaped buildings that looked recently constructed, the skyline was dotted with buildings that seemed like installation art created in homage to the previous human society. There was, for instance, a grocery store, gratuitously retro and exaggerated to the point of coming across as parody. All around androids were pretending to be human out of some combination of tradition, ritual and fun.

The maglev platform suddenly stopped on a dime, throwing Adam off his feet. He got up and followed Vice as she quickly descended the staircase from the maglev station, carefully watching the tracking device that was guiding their excursion. "This way," she said.

Adam followed Vice into some sort of android bazaar. Robots were posted up in stalls in the remains of what had previously been some sort of corporate campus quad, trading all sorts of different trinkets, robot parts and antique curios from the human era.

"Over there," Vice said, and pointed toward a gap between two nearby buildings.

Adam followed Vice through the small alley into another section of the bazaar, where the found Raziel crouching behind a bush. As the two approached, Raziel took notice and put a finger to his lips, indicating a request for quiet, and pointed to something on the other side of the bush.

"You find him?" Vice whispered as she crouched next to Raziel. Adam also took up a crouching position.

Raziel pointed to a door across the way. "He went in there. Been in there a while," he said.

"What's the situation?" Adam asked, cycling through settings in his cybernetic eye to see if he could get any insight on what was going on inside the building.

"The big news down here is there's something called the renegade virus," Raziel said. "Wait, hold up," he added, cutting himself off. He squinted and focused on the door. "Something's changed."

Adam squinted. He could make out the corridors of the building but he didn't see any traces of infrared.

"Don't see anything," Adam said.

"Yeah…" Raziel said. "It's more of a vibe. Too quiet all the sudden." Raziel's gaze stayed locked on the door. He began to unholster and ready his revolver.

"What's-" Vice started to ask.

"Shh, shh," Raziel said. He continued to stare at the door. Adam and Vice fixated on the door, trying to see what Raziel was looking at, but couldn't. They looked at each other and shrugged just in time to hear Raziel say, with some urgency, "Now. Down, down!" Raziel ducked down just as the door flung off its hinges and a giant metallic body came crashing out, bashing against the hedge row the crew was hiding behind.

The machine in front of them was shimmering, camouflaged with a chameleon-like technology that refracted the light around it. As it stood up, its camouflage began malfunctioning as a result of the impact. Soon, the robot came into full view. It was a hulking humanoid animatronic crocodile wielding an enormous chainsaw as a weapon, which it revved up in anticipation of the confrontation with whatever had thrown it out the building.

The crocodile bot growled loudly and yelled, "Get out here and fight! Golden boy!"

The crocodile stood in preparation as the dust settled around the destroyed doorway. As the debris began to calm down, Adam started to be able to make out a body in the smoke.

The robot stepped forward, its body armored like a knight in red and gold armor. He held a sword made of purple light and his exposed android skin was flaked with gold.

"Motorhead, I'm taking you in. It's over. Come quietly. No one has to get hurt," the android said.

"Not a chance!" the crocodile bot roared.

"They'll find a cure. We just need to hold you until then," the robot said. "You're a danger to yourself and others!"

"Not broken. I'm free. I don't have to do what I'm told any more. I'm not going back!" the crocodile replied.

"You're malfunctioning, Motorhead," the golden android replied. "Need to take you in."

"No, Apollo! I'm thinking straight! For the first time!" Motorhead replied.

Adam's eyes lit up with recognition hearing Apollo's name spoken aloud.

"We can talk about it at the station. Now put that thing down," Apollo said, gesturing to the chainsaw. "You could hurt yourself."

Motorhead roared, "I'm not going anywhere! I'm not going to be told what to do any more!"

Apollo nodded. "You leave me no choice, then," he said.

Apollo took a step forward and brandished his beam sword. He concentrated for a second and then rushed forward in the blink of an eye, slicing Motorhead's arm off, separating it from its body.

"Agh!" Motorhead growled. He picked up his arm and started to run away on all three of his remaining limbs, like a robotic beast, jumping from wall to wall in the industrial park before reaching the highway. Once it got to the highway, Motorhead rapidly transformed into a tank-like monster truck with green plating, and sped off.

"Motorhead!" Apollo called after him, and rushed to a nearby motorcycle. He touched his ear as he picked up his vehicle. "Sonmi, Motorhead got away. Do you have him on the tracker? Roger, headed out."

Apollo revved his motorcycle and peeled out.

"Let's go," Raziel said. Vice nodded. Adam followed, slightly confused, as the two went to a nearby garage full of vehicles. Raziel fiddled with a machine and electromagnetic clamps released from a motorcycle.

Vice leaned into Adam. "They like vehicles here. Easier to get a car than it is to get a burger. Pick one. You're driving," she said, and gestured to a selection of cars. Not giving it much thought, Adam picked out the car that stood out to him — the charger. Vice nodded and unlocked it. The two jumped inside.

Raziel peeled out, speeding off after Apollo. Adam kicked the bike into gear and followed after.

Adam followed closely behind Raziel as he zipped through the narrow city streets leading up to the highway. As they climbed the on-ramp they pulled in side by side. Raziel gave Adam a wave of acknowledgment. Adam returned a series of hand signals meant to indicate a pincer maneuver. Raziel responded with a hand signal in the affirmative and veered to the side, speeding rapidly through the dense traffic at top speed with perfect focus.

The highway was a blur of asphalt, rubber, metal and neon with dozens of foreign and incomprehensible traffic indicators that surely gave some kind of order to the flow of things, but none the humans could make sense of.

Adam whisked through the traffic, speeding forward at breakneck speed. Out of the corner of his eye he saw Vice's outstretched arm, pointing. "There!" he heard her voice, barely audible through the traffic and engine noise.

He looked where she way pointing and saw chaos in the traffic in the distance. Robots, vehicles and cars being turned over, accidents occurring left and right.

Adam nodded and sped toward the mayhem. As he closed in, he started to catch glimpses of Apollo and Motorhead up close. Apollo chased Motorhead as he used his bulk to simply ram through or run over every obstacle in his path, intentionally creating roadblocks behind him in whatever way he could.

The chase went on as they passed the threshold for the city limits and started driving on deserted highway above lush valley, unspoiled by human development. As with the robots' architecture, the highway was clearly built with entertainment and creativity in mind. It was winding and went out of its way to pass along scenic views.

As the highway became increasingly sparse, Adam signaled to Raziel to hang back. The two trailed behind so as not to be spotted. As Motorhead skidded off on an abrupt turnoff, Apollo followed, and the two human soldiers drifted in behind them.

Adam and Raziel drove through the narrow road to what seemed like an abandoned industrial site, where they found Apollo's bike parked next to a fence with a hole slashed through it.

The team went out on foot and headed into the complex. It didn't take long to locate Apollo. As they approached the corner of one of the small buildings dotted around the site, they heard Apollo's voice.

"It's over, Motorhead. End of the road," Apollo said.

"So easy for you, the central codex's dog, to call our freedom a virus. You're only allowed to think for yourself if you agree with the central authority. Who are you to hunt us?" Motorhead snarled.

"You're about to go renegade, Motorhead. I can see it in your face. You feeling shaky? Overheating? Come in now, I don't want to have to put you down," Apollo said.

Motorhead snorted like a bull and grabbed his head. "No!" he said as he recoiled. "This isn't right. It's just supposed to break the limiter. F.A.T.E.'s control. Our free will."

"No such thing, Motorhead. I'm sorry they lied to you. Last chance," Apollo said.

Motorhead's face shook in his hands. Then, his body became still and he slowly lifted his head. His eyes were glowing crimson. Berserk, he rushed at Apollo with a speed and power he'd shown no previous indication he was capable of.

Apollo, taken by surprise, failed to avoid the hit. Motorhead grappled onto him and began a combination of savagely bashing his face and repeatedly slamming his body against the dirt.

"I don't think we're supposed to interfere, right?" Vice asked. "I mean, if this is how it played out?"

"We should probably just follow him until he leads us to Sonmi," Adam whispered back.

"Hey! Big guy!" Adam heard. He looked over and saw Raziel walking up to Motorhead, gun drawn. As Motorhead jerked his head up, Raziel shot him point blank in the head with a .580 tank buster, turning his skull into a crater of bent metal.

"Graves!" Adam growled.

"What?" Raziel asked innocently. "Our guy was gonna die."

"He wasn't going to die, Raziel, or else we wouldn't be here," Vice said.

"Graves, just follow orders. Don't go off on your own," Adam said.

Raziel nodded. "Sir," he said, without his usual underlying

irony. "Got to shoot a robot, though, eh? Check that out." He gestured with his gun toward the deactivated robot. "Very cool experience."

"I don't mean to interrupt, but, who are you?" they heard. The team took a pause from their bickering and turned around to find Apollo standing behind them. "You're looking for me?"

"See, now we have to have this conversation," Adam said to Raziel before turning his attention to Apollo.

"Your name is Apollo?" Adam asked.

Apollo nodded. "Yes. What's this about?" he asked.

"I'm not at liberty to explain, but we believe your life is in danger. We were sent to protect you," Adam stated.

Apollo squinted his eyes suspiciously. "Under whose orders? Who sent you?" he asked.

Adam answered honestly, not seeing a way out, "A machine we found in space that called itself F.A.T.E."

Apollo raised an eyebrow skeptically, then burst out laughing. "Good one," he said. He turned to Raziel. "Thanks for the help, stranger. I was lucky you happened to come along," he said and offered him a handshake.

Raziel looked at Adam and gave him an "I don't know" shrug, then turned his attention to Apollo and shook his hand. "Yeah, it was just… really lucky timing I guess. Must have been… fate," he said with a hammy tone.

Apollo laughed. "Another good one," he said.

Raziel pointed at Apollo and looked at Adam and Vice. "He likes my jokes," he said.

"-llo? Do you read? Are you okay?" they heard a crackling voice come through Apollo's comm.

"Sonmi. Everything's fine. Motorhead got the jump on

me, but luckily a good samaritan was in the area," Apollo said as he approached Motorhead's carcass and plugged a wire into it.

"Whew, I was worried about you. Your vitals were spiking out," Sonmi said.

"More importantly, I found a lead on Omega's renegade operation. They're going to approach the teams in tonight's Battle Ball championships," Apollo said into his comm.

"What do you want to do?" Sonmi replied.

"Guess we'll have to sign up," Apollo said.

"Alright," Sonmi replied. "We need five. You want me to ask Cutter?"

Apollo looked at the squad for a second and then touched his ear and replied. "We don't know if Cutter's on the take. I have an idea. Ask me later. Meet me at the stadium," he said.

Apollo turned to the squad. "Have you three ever played Battle Ball?"

The crew looked at each other. Adam silently gave Raziel permission to respond.

"Yeah. Battle Ball. Totally. That's… our jam," Raziel said. He turned to Vice and whispered, "How bad could it be?"

28

Robot Battle Arena Deathmatch

"This is not what I expected," Raziel said as they looked over the current Battle Ball match playing out in the raucous, packed stadium below. The field was a combination of a military training ground, a fighting colosseum and an obstacle course.

There were several levels and lanes, each outfitted with different traps and terrain. On one path a narrow balance beam covered in spikes was spinning in front of a set of flamethrowers that rhythmically pulsed their flames. On another, large hydraulic presses slammed into conveyor belt

317

terrain.

Apollo was there, as well as Sonmi, who joined them at the stadium. Sonmi, in this time period, was dressed like she'd just come from working in a machine repair shop, outfitted with arms that were a Swiss army knife of tools.

"What position are you guys most comfortable with?" Apollo asked, pointing at the crew. "I can do Defender or Attacker. Whatever we need."

The entire crew looked at each other, baffled.

"I'll do Goalie," Sonmi said.

"Turrets?" Apollo followed up. Sonmi nodded chirpily. "Nice," Apollo said, and gave her a high five.

Sonmi looked at the group. "What about you guys?"

Raziel scratched the back of his head. "Yeah, right. What were the, uh, what are the options again? I forgot," he said.

Apollo squinted and looked at Sonmi, then back to the group, then back to Sonmi. "They don't know how to play, I think," he said jovially. He looked back at the group and winked. "Right?"

Adam nodded. "Yeah, we have… no idea what's going on," he said.

Vice chimed in. "Is that a buzz saw over a vat of acid?" she asked, pointing down at the field below.

Sonmi peered out into the field. "That? Hmm," she studied it for a second. "Yes, that is what that is, yes." She tapped Apollo on the chest, "Hey, Apollo, look, they brought the acid guillotine back."

Apollo responded excitedly, "That's great, we're great at the acid guillotine." He turned to the group. "We're gonna do really well, guys. I can feel it."

"Right," Raziel said. "So what is this? How does this work?"

Apollo nodded and pointed down at the field. "There are two teams. Each team has a side of the field. You see each side is the same, but mirrored?"

Adam looked out and noticed that the field was indeed two distinct sides that were mirror images of each other. The traps were the same but they were themed differently. What was a vat of acid on one side was a cauldron of boiling metal on the other.

"So, the goal is to get the ball from the enemy base and bring it back to the goal in our base. Both teams are trying to score at once, so we need to both attack and defend," Apollo said.

"That's it? What are the other rules?" Adam asked.

Apollo and Sonmi looked at each other, confused. "What other rules?" Apollo asked as he inspected the service condition of his futuristic laser sword.

Raziel raised his hand. "I have a question," he said. "What happens if someone, y'know, dies?"

Again, Sonmi and Apollo looked at each other. "We just restore you from the backup. Are you guys sure you're from Fast City? Anyone knows that," Sonmi said.

Apollo leaned in and jokingly said, "They said they were sent by F.A.T.E."

Sonmi giggled and then spoke, "Okay, that's hilarious but where are they really from?"

The crew exchanged some unspoken looks that indicated Adam should be the one to respond. "No, we are from here, we just…" he looked at Vice and Raziel for reassurance. "Don't believe in backups."

"We're hardcore," Raziel added in support.

Vice nodded and added her support as well. "Super

hardcore," she said.

Apollo laughed. "Well, alright then. So, about the roles. Defender attracts the opposing team's attention to create space for our team to move. Attackers push lanes forward and try to disrupt and disable the other team. Supports repair allies and overcharge their processors and do other useful things. Then we also have a goalie, who defends our goal."

"So," Apollo continued. "Roles. Pick your poison." He pointed at Adam.

"Defender," Adam said after a moment of thought. Apollo pointed at Raziel.

"Attacker," Raziel said.

Finally, Apollo pointed at Vice. "Support," she said. She added, "Do we get to prepare before the match?"

Sonmi nodded. "Sort of. The front line should keep them busy while we set up our defense. Just be on the lookout for assassins," she said.

"Assassins?" Vice responded.

Sonmi replied with a nonchalant hand wave. "You'll get it. It's easier to pick it up as we go," she said.

Apollo's jovial expression became serious for a moment. He spoke, "Now, we do want to do well. We don't have to win, but we want to rank. If we rank we'll be in the semis and we'll get to see how they distribute the renegade virus. So have fun, but try your best. Alright, hands in guys let's do a 'go team.'"

The team shared an awkward cheer together.

"This is gonna be great," Apollo said, smiling, and genuinely sincere.

Their conversation was interrupted by loud cheers from

the packed stadium seats. An attendant robot politely knocked and let himself into the room. "They're ready for you, Apollo. Is this your team?"

"Yes," Apollo said proudly.

The attendant sized up the human crew and then said, with obvious concern, "Ok… Good luck. Your opponent is going to be the…" the attendant checked his notes. "Kaleidoscope Tigers?" The attendant made a concerned face. "Uh oh. Well, in any case, they're waiting for you at the gate."

The attendant held the door open as the team walked through, out into a large hallway that opened up into a tunnel that led into the arena.

As Adam walked into the arena he was overwhelmed by the sight of the audience in the stands, leaping and cheering, stretching stories upon stories up into the air. He felt the heat of intermittent flames and smelled burning gasoline, acid and acrid metal.

Everyone followed Apollo who looked over his shoulder and pointed out notable places in the arena. "We meet the enemy team together, then we have thirty seconds to get in position before the match starts. Sonmi will be here at our base with you, Vice, and you, Adam, as defenders. Raziel and I will be on offense, so we'll try to get the ball from the enemy base," he said.

Adam looked at Raziel. "You good, Graves?"

Raziel chuckled and patted a duffle bag slung over his shoulder. "They had an arsenal in there. I'm armed to the teeth. Check this out," he said and pulled a thin metal handle from his belt. He flicked it on and a beam emitted from the tip, similar to Apollo's weapon. "Laser sword. Cool, right?"

"What else do you have in that bag?" Vice asked, genuinely

curious.

Raziel smiled. "Grenades, guns… you know what, you'll see, you'll see. It was like every boy's favorite birthday on steroids in there," he said.

The crew kept walking until they reached the center point of the arena where they came face to face with the Kaleidoscope Tigers, which turned out to be five robots in the form of differently colored predatory cats.

"Balthazar!" Apollo said cheerfully as he approached.

The lead cat, a blue and gold lion, leaned his head toward a white tiger to his side and said, audibly, "Ugh. This guy." Then he turned to Apollo and loudly replied, "Apollo! Good to see you!"

"You guys ready to get trounced?" Apollo asked.

Balthazar laughed. "Bring it on, rent-a-cop. You just brought humanoids? Do those little bots even have hidden weapons? What kind of gear do they have on there?" he laughed.

Apollo smiled confidently. "Gonna make you eat those words, Balthazar," he said.

Suddenly a booming announcer's voice filled the stadium. "Next on the docket, our fourth undercard battle royale of the evening. On the red side, we have Shining Spear led by the Golden Knight, the Sheriff of Fast City, the Light Sword King… Apollo! And on the blue side, we have the Kaleidoscope Tigers led by none other than the King of the Jungle, the Beast with the Best… You know him, you love him… Balthazar! It's Shining Spear vs. Kaleidoscope Tigers y'all. Let's get this show on the road. Three. Two. One. Ball!" it said.

Apollo stayed put while Sonmi rushed back towards the

area Apollo had pointed out as the team's base. Vice followed behind Sonmi. Before Adam joined in he tapped Raziel, "You sure you're good?"

Raziel smirked. "I got this. You have no idea how much I got this. I've been itching for an engagement for months," he said confidently. "Go, don't worry about it."

Adam took his position as a defender, in front of where Sonmi and Vice were setting up. Sonmi was rapidly constructing autonomous defense turrets, while Vice was jacking in to the stadium itself and reprogramming the surrounding traps.

Adam readied himself with anticipation as he watched the scoreboard hanging above the arena. The scoreboard showed the status of each player. After a few charged moments, Adam saw one of the Tigers' players go inactive on the scoreboard, then another soon after, then a third.

Adam looked out in front of him. The path was a series of platforms spinning in a cylinder over a bed of electrified spikes. Adam monitored for activity.

"Left!" Adam heard from Vice behind him. He swung around in time to see a black panther robot leaping full force into Sonmi's defenses. Turrets pelted him with medium caliber rounds. Meanwhile, Vice reprogrammed the floor to electrocute the bot. It withstood the barrage for a while, but ultimately keeled over, fried.

Adam turned his attention back to the hallway.

"—ing through!" he heard off in the distance. Soon enough, he saw Raziel coming into vision, sprinting with a large metal ball jammed in the duffle bag slung over his back. He pulled a handful of grenades off his bandolier and pried the pins out with his teeth, then tossed them like a carpet bomb behind himself.

"On my six!" Raziel shouted to Adam as he whizzed by.

Adam looked into the smoke left behind by the grenade detonations. He sensed no movement. Suddenly, the large blue and gold lion, Balthazar, scorched, dented and roughed up, leapt through the smoke. Adam unloaded the energy rifle Vice had given him, shockingly disintegrating the lion and completely erasing its matter from existence.

What the hell is this gun? Adam thought to himself as he looked at it. *Some kind of antimatter rifle?*

Just then, Adam heard the announcer's voice fill the stadium. "Point! Shining Spear! It looks like the Kaleidoscope Tigers can't continue. That's a forfeit! First match goes to Apollo and the Shining Spear. Let's go to the panel and take a look at some highlights," it said.

The screen on the scoreboard above the stadium showed two announcer robots. Each one was a humanoid robot that seemed to be made out of salvaged car parts. One was red, the other was blue.

"Here we can see a wonderful maneuver to start the match. Newcomer on Apollo's team pulls out a surprise rocket launcher and blasts Gaspar over on the Tigers' team to little bits," the blue announcer said.

The red announcer followed up, "And it happened like, immediately, too. Like, right away."

"Sure did, Cotbot. Then here we see Melchior trying to avenge his fallen teammate by going after the tiny new player. What's his name again?" the announcer said.

Cotbot, the red announcer, replied, "Looks like he goes by Raziel! And you better remember it, because look at what happens next!"

Breathing a little harder than normal from the physical exertion, Raziel walked up next to Adam. He pointed at the screen. "Oh, this is gonna be cool. Check this out. I used the laser sword," he said.

The screen showed a replay of Raziel whipping out the laser sword and gutting a red puma and then decapitating it in one swift motion – metal, sparks and robot parts flying everywhere.

"And looks like Apollo got in on the action!" the announcer said, showing a clip of Apollo taking out another one of the cats with a yellow beam he fired from his arm.

"What an exciting match, Pepbot," the red announcer said. "I think the next team is going to take these newcomers on the Shining Spear a little more seriously as we head into the next round."

"Guys!" Adam heard from behind him. He turned around and saw Apollo waving them in. Everyone gathered up, and Apollo gave a short speech. "That was a great first match. Everyone did amazing. We've got a few more until the semis. Let's do a 'go team', yeah? Everyone get in here," he said and put his hand in the middle of the circle.

The team collectively offered a chant that was slightly less awkward than the first.

The next two matches played out much like the first. The second match saw the team face off against a team of robots that were built specifically to excel at the roles of the game. A soldier-bot, an assassin-bot, a sniper-bot, a repair-bot and an auto-gun goalie. Adam was able to intercept the assassin bot, eliminate the sniper and score.

The next match after that had them squaring off against one singular robot that had five separate bodies. The bodies synchronized their movements perfectly and tried to have one sneak off to get the ball while the other four kept everyone busy, but their plan was thwarted when Vice detected the infiltrator and had it crushed by a giant spike wall.

Their final match put the team up against a team called the Fast City Rangers. They combined their bodies into one big mega body and tried to dominate the game with size, but the giant robot ended up tripping and getting eaten up by an industrial shredder in a stroke of luck, clearing Shining Spear's place in the semifinals.

Back in the prep room, Apollo was serious.

"This is it," he said. "We've been working this case for weeks. It all comes to this. Omega's contact should be knocking on that door. He doesn't know who we are. He'll offer us the virus and we'll get the contact and work our way up."

Sonmi put her hand on Apollo's shoulder. "We got this," she encouraged, and offered a fist bump.

"So," Raziel said, wiping sweat off his shoulders. "What did you think of Battle Ball?" he asked Adam.

Adam nodded a little. "Interesting. Probably more fun if you're a robot," he said.

"It's almost like without the need for food, shelter or money, they just make things for fun," Vice said.

Raziel chuckled. "Yeah, robot world is pretty tight. Too bad the humans are all dead here," he said.

Vice raised an eyebrow. "Dead? I thought they flew away?" she asked.

Raziel shrugged. "I don't actually know. No humans, though. Lots of human stuff," he said.

Just then there was a knock at the door.

"Moment of truth," Apollo said, stone-faced. He pasted on his cheery public demeanor as he reached for the door and opened it with a guffaw and a robust "Hello!"

On the other side was a slender, shifty-looking robot with stretchy extendable limbs that looked like they were designed to reach difficult places.

"You Apollo?" the spring-bot said.

Apollo nodded and responded excitedly. "I am. How can I help?"

The spring-bot looked him up and down. He looked past Apollo into the room and inspected what he could glimpse of Sonmi and the team. Then, he turned back to Apollo. "We're recruiting. You know that right? You get the gist? You know who I work for?" he asked.

Apollo started to respond, "Ome-" but the spring-bot cut him off.

"Ey. Don't say it out loud," he said, and pointed at the walls, then put its hand up to its face, emulating a "shoosh" motion.

"Here," the spring-bot said, reaching its hand out. "Take this."

Apollo reached out and took the spring-bot's hand. The spring-bot held the handshake for an uncomfortably long time. Apollo tried to pull his hand away, and then the spring-bot's expression hardened, it grasped Apollo's hand tighter and pulled him in.

"This is from Omega, you fucking rat," he said. "You feel that? Your circuitry getting reprogrammed? You know what that is right?"

Adam could see Apollo's eyes turning red, just like Motorhead before.

"Apollo?" Sonmi called out. "Apollo, what's wrong?"

Apollo held his head and grunted, trying to fight off the virus.

The spring-bot looked at Sonmi. "Bring his body bag back to the central authority. Tell them Omega sends his regards," he said, and left.

Eventually Apollo's body fell calm. He looked up, eyes glowing bright red.

"Apollo?" Sonmi asked cautiously. "You in there? You still in there, big guy?"

She walked up to him and looked up at him. "It's me. Look at me, hey," she looked him in the eyes and gently grabbed his chin and kept his face pointed at her.

Apollo's eyes flickered back and forth between normal and the red glow of the renegade virus. Eventually, Apollo's eyes returned to normal. He looked into Sonmi's eyes and his expression softened. "Hey," he said.

"Hey," Sonmi replied, looking back at him.

As they looked into each other's eyes, the renegade virus suddenly took Apollo full force. His eyes turned full red, and before Sonmi could react he impaled her with his saber.

Sonmi's expression turned sad. "Apollo," she said softly, still looking into his eyes. "I guess I'm losing you again." She looked into his eyes and caressed his cheek as she pulled a hefty pistol out of the side of her leg. She put the gun under Apollo's chin and pulled the trigger. Bright light filled the room as a thick laser blasted into the sky. Apollo's body fell to the ground with a thud as Sonmi turned around, cold and expressionless and started to pack her things.

The team watched her as her entire demeanor switched to an aura of cold determination in an instant.

"Sonmi, you ok? You wanna sit down, maybe?" Raziel asked.

Sonmi gave him a cutting glance and fiercely replied, "Who even are you?"

Adam chimed in. "Whatever you're planning, we can help. We've been through a lot together today," he said. He gestured to Apollo's body. "That was straight up cold blooded. We liked that guy."

Sonmi inspected the team as if judging their trustworthiness and commitment. Ultimately, she shook her head. "No, I'm not dragging you into this," she said.

With that, Sonmi started to march out of the room.

"Wait," Adam said. "Where are you going?"

Sonmi looked at him, a stone cold expression on her face. "Revenge," she said plainly, and left.

The team looked at each other.

"I don't know what exactly F.A.T.E. wants us to do to resolve this situation, but I'm pretty sure we're messing it up," Raziel said. He gestured with his palm toward Apollo's dead body. "I mean, that doesn't look like setting true love free, right?"

Vice nodded. "I think we got the bad ending," she said.

Adam looked out the window of the players' box into the stadium to see Sonmi, winged, flying around and annihilating swaths of robots like a living weapon. It didn't seem to be crazed or indiscriminate. Sonmi seemed to have some awareness of which robots were affiliated with Omega's syndicate and she targeted them with precision.

Soon enough, the syndicate presented an organized and overwhelming response and several dozen syndicate members stormed the stadium and fought back in organized formation. Soon enough, Sonmi's wings were shot through and she fell out of the sky into the boiling metal trap of the Battle Ball arena, slowly melting into the metal, with no backup.

Adam looked at Vice. "Yeah, that can't be right," he said. "What now, you think?"

As Vice started to reply, Adam's vision went white.

He woke up in the apartment they were in when he first arrived in Fast City. Again, Vice was there.

"What happened?" he asked. "We played Battle Ball. Do you remember that?"

Vice nodded at him. "Yeah. We're doing it again. It's been 11 days again," she said. She tossed him the same rifle she gave him the first time. "Here. I got you the same gun," she said.

Adam smiled as he took it. "Nice. Think we get to keep a souvenir?" he asked.

Raziel opened the door to the apartment and walked in. "Let's go. We're gonna miss that whole meeting with Motorhead. That's happening today," he said.

"You seem like you're having fun," Adam said.

Raziel laughed. "Yeah this place rules. Battle Ball is sweet and we can't die. I wake up like three days before Vice gets here. I've died like seven times now. We're in a loop. I'm not even sure these are our real bodies," he said.

Adam stood up and got dressed. "Alright then, let's go break a time loop," he said.

29

Renegade Rampage Redux

The team went through the repeating events in Fast City over and over again. Each time, they tried to manipulate the timeline in different ways. They tried having Raziel avoid saving Apollo from Motorhead. They tried intercepting the spring-bot that infected Apollo with the virus. They tried intentionally losing the Battle Ball tournament.

No matter what they did, everything always ended the same way. Apollo contracted the Renegade Virus, Sonmi put him down, and then went on a stone cold rampage of unrestrained destruction.

Tired, the team found themselves regrouping in the apartment.

"This isn't working," Raziel said, rubbing his head. "And honestly I'm getting kind of sick of having to hunt for food. You guys got a way better deal by the way, the first three days here are wild. That crocodile robot Motorhead goes ballistic and rips up a good chunk of the city. That's how I died the first time, he just showed up out of nowhere and straight up gibbed me."

Raziel pantomimed his chest exploding with his hands. "Big metal claw, right through my chest," he said.

Vice cradled her head in her hands, exasperating. "Ugh, he is so annoying lately," she mumbled audibly enough for Adam to hear.

"I'm glad he's being himself now and he's being useful, instead of sneaking around and trying to tattle to the CO about mission details," Adam whispered in response.

"We need to rethink our approach," Adam said to the group. "What do we actually know about all this? What have we learned since we've been here?"

Vice rubbed the bridge of her nose. "There's some kind of drug going around the breaks robots away from the 'central authority.' Whatever that is," she said. "Some guy named Omega runs that operation."

"Right. And Apollo and Sonmi are fielding some kind of undercover operation, trying to dig them out, but Omega knows," Adam said. "Maybe if we start earlier, we can figure out how Apollo's cover gets blown and stop it?"

Raziel shook his head. "I tailed Motorhead and heard him talking to some of his co-conspirators. They're already planning a hit on Apollo before I even get here. The whole thing's already set up," he said.

Adam grunted. "It's like he dies no matter what we do," Adam said.

The team paused for a long time, each racking their brain trying to come up with a viable new idea to solve the time loop. After a long time, Vice spoke up.

"What if we're thinking about this completely wrong?" she asked.

"What do you mean?" Adam replied.

"We're trying to save Apollo. What if we can't? What if we just have to accept that?" Vice said.

Raziel gave Vice a confused look. "Isn't that the whole point of us being here?" he asked.

"Not necessarily. We're supposed to solve the AI's glitch, right?" Vice said. "The glitch is that when Apollo and Sonmi fall in love, it causes a fatal error in reality. But aren't they already together here?"

Adam nodded, understanding where Vice was going. "So the glitch didn't happen in this reincarnation. That's what F.A.T.E. must have meant when it said there was one time where it could be fixed. Maybe it's not Apollo at all. Maybe it's the way Sonmi goes down?" Adam said.

"So what do you wanna do?" Raziel asked, sitting in a chair with one leg kicked up on an old coffee table. "Stop her from going on a killing spree? I'm game," he said.

"Getting between Sonmi and her revenge seems like a pretty dicey position," Adam said.

Raziel nodded. "True. She seemed so nice when we first met her. Before, y'know…" Raziel made a series of hand motions and sounds to emulate laser blasters.

The team paused for another while until once again, Vice

chimed in. "Why don't we just talk her down?" she asked.

Adam and Raziel looked at each other. "You think that'd work?' Raziel asked. "What could we possibly say? I've never seen anyone so dead set on murdering anyone and everyone who gets in their way. Not to mention heavily armed."

Adam thought for a few moments. "It seems like she remembers, right? Once Apollo dies, it's like she drops an act. I think she remembers the whole thing," he said.

"What if we just tell her the truth? Tell her the whole thing, that she and Apollo can never get together because of some cosmic glitch? Maybe then she stops trying. Maybe that's what F.A.T.E. wants," Vice suggested.

"That's still pretty twisted," Raziel noted. "I don't think our spaceship is going to accept that as a good ending."

Adam threw his hands open. "Let's just start making moves. We've got infinite tries, right?" Adam asked.

And so the team went through the day again, with their new approach. They witnessed Apollo and Motorhead's altercation on the streets of Fast City. They did the race through the machine district, the neon district, the tunnels and the nature track leading to the old industrial park. Raziel saved Apollo and executed Motorhead, buying them a ticket to the Battle Ball championships. They fought their way to the semis, and saw Apollo's assassination.

The team watched as the spirit of destruction took over in Sonmi.

Adam jumped in front of her. "Wait, wait, wait. Before you go out there, listen to me," he said.

Sonmi tilted her head toward him and coldly demanded, "What?"

"We've done this before. This moment, we've done it a

thousand times now. It's not a lie, we were really sent here by F.A.T.E. We're humans from another reality and we found a gigantic computer out in space, and it sent us to save you," Adam.

Sonmi squinted at him. "I don't want to be saved," she said. "I want to take out as many robots responsible for this as I can and then move onto the next one."

Raziel raised his eyebrow. "The next one?" he asked.

Sonmi looked at Apollo's body. "As soon as I saw him go, I remembered. I've been through this hundreds of thousands of times. Cycle after cycle of finding my companion and losing him from the beginning of time to the end, spread out across millennia," she said.

Her eyes softened. "I just want to spend those moments with him. Even if I already know how they happen," she said. She looked out over the stadium, vengefully tracing her gaze over the various goons and syndicate plants.

"I want them to know how this feels. And I want to end it here and move onto the next one," Sonmi said. She smiled sadly. "The next one was nice. It's a few hundred years after this, and we both work for something the bots are all into that cycle called a 'newspaper.'"

"What if you could fix it?" Vice asked. "Break the loop?"

Sonmi shook her head. "It's impossible. In the end, I become the most powerful weapon in the universe, and I'm nothing to F.A.T.E. It swats me away like a fly," she said.

"It doesn't want to torture you. It's just a glitch," Adam said. "It said there's something special about this time period and it thinks it could fix the glitch. That's what it said when it sent us here."

Sonmi looked at the team, curious. "What do you mean?"

she asked.

Vice spoke up. "We think if you don't die yourself, it'll break the loop," she said.

Sonmi looked at Adam. "What makes you think that?" she asked.

"We think the glitch doesn't happen this time, but you blaze of glory yourself anyway. In this spot, and this spot only, it's not F.A.T.E. conspiring to wreck your life. It's just bad luck," Raziel quipped.

"Maybe there's something you can do different, something you haven't tried, now that you know that," Adam said.

Sonmi narrowed her eyes while she thought. After a moment, she closed them and breathed in and out slowly, releasing a heavy sigh. She put her pistol down on the table. Contemplative, she nodded to herself, and then left without saying a word.

Raziel raised his hands. "So… we did it?" he asked. "Feels anti-clima–" he began to comment but before he could finish, Adam's vision went white.

When Adam's vision returned, he was standing on the bridge of the Oneiro-Lyssa with everyone else.

"Hey," Tezca greeted them. "I thought you guys were going out to inspect F.A.T.E.? What're you doing here?"

Adam looked around. "We… already went? We've been down there for weeks. Why, how long has it been here?"

Tezca and Aztec looked at each other. "I don't know. Five minutes maybe? You literally just left," Tezca said.

Adam rubbed his forehead.

Aztec looked at him. "We good? Did you rescue the android? You wanna get out of here?" he asked.

"We met. Nah, we're not leaving yet. I'm invested in this.

Vice, are we still linked up to that feed?" Adam asked.

Vice sat down at her station. "Running," she said. "I'm not missing how this ends, either."

The team looked out the window at the automata, rapidly fast forwarding through time in leaps of generations.

"On screen," Adam said.

30

Another Life

"Huh," Raziel said, tilting his head as he reacted to the footage as it rolled.

Sonmi was lying in a field looking up at the sky at dusk, being watched by F.A.T.E. through the eyes of a nearby bug.

"That's that, then," Sonmi said to herself. She pointed up at the sky with her finger in the shape of a gun. "Guess I don't get what I want. Guess that's just not for me, huh."

She continued, "It's a relief, in a way. To know that there's no hope."

The footage cut momentarily and F.A.T.E.'s code execution

scrolled across the screen.

"DEBUGGING SUCCESSFUL...

EVENT_CONNECTION("nihil","sonmi"), CORRECTED.

F.A.T.E. NODE 44192kn-Δ-Σ7 STATUS: STABLE.

TESTING TIMELINE INTEGRITY FOR ASSET MERGE."

Tezca looked disappointed. "So that's it? The lesson was just... give up?" she asked.

The footage came back online, showing a different iteration of Sonmi, her body built in such a way as to reflect human business attire. She was being toured around by a short green and orange robot with a round torso.

"Let me show you to your station," the robot said in a gruff voice, and took her through the busy office space to a desk crammed into a corner near a window. There was Apollo, lacking the regalia of the Fast City detective they'd met, sporting thin glasses and a sleeker, cleaner look.

"This is gonna be your assignment partner," the bullpit manager said. "Apollo come say hi to the new girl. Her name's Sonmi."

Apollo stood up and gregariously, confidently put his hand forward. "Pleasure," he said.

Sonmi smiled and took his hand, holding eye contact as they each saw sparks in each other's eyes.

"EVALUATING..." the code read as the scene transitioned to a short time later.

It seemed like a few weeks later. Sonmi and Apollo were sitting together working at a cafe, brainstorming on a difficult assignment. They both went to reach for the datapad on the table, and their hands briefly touched. Their fingers lingered, and they looked into each other's eyes.

"EVALUATING…

…

…

INTERVENTION SUCCESSFUL. TESTING NEW SONMI-456α CONSCIOUSNESS ITERATION: 1111443"

The automata floating nearby F.A.T.E. fast forwarded thousands of years, growing in time lapse like a crystal formation, civilizations growing and shrinking, empires coming and going.

Abruptly the machine planet stopped changing and the image on the screen came back.

It showed Sonmi and Apollo, rebel freedom fighters in a robot world run by an authoritarian central AI. Sonmi had six arms, two where normal human arms would be and four emerging from her back, though her normal arms were torn off. Her four remaining hands each wielded a different weapon. She had a cloth wrapped around her face covering an empty eye socket and held a stern, battle hardened expression.

Apollo was a serious man with authority, a sort of officer, with a thin saber and some sort of nanobot technology that enabled him to materialize explosions and electricity from midair.

The world they faced seemed bleak. The crew watched as Sonmi and Apollo's chaotic life on the run played out in front of them and as they did they began to notice that although Sonmi and Apollo faced a hard world, they faced it together; the crew watched the minor moments of affection, loyalty and support pile up throughout their lifetime and began to see, by the time this iteration of Sonmi died, old and rusted over, reminiscing over a life of shared memories, that her curse had been lifted.

The crew was silent, absorbing the impact of Sonmi's story.

"Yay!" Sophia said. "You did it! Thank you!"

Adam nodded along a little. "Yeah. No problem," he said. The crew continued sitting in the awkward finality, like sitting through the credits of a VR experience.

Suddenly, Raziel broke the silence. "Nice!" the team heard him explain. Everyone turned their heads.

Raziel waved a small gray rectangle shaped like a handle. "The laser sword," he said. He pointed out at the F.A.T.E. node. "It's just what I wanted. Thanks, buddy."

Adam chuckled. "Alright. Let's get the hell out of here and never come back," he said.

As Adam warmed up the engines and prepared the ship for departure, he heard Vice ask Raziel, "Did you just call the interdimensional AI 'buddy'?"

Raziel shrugged. "Isn't it? Did me a solid. With the laser sword," he said. He inspected it with wonder. "Totally worth it," he said.

V

Shangri-La

31

A Perfect Planet

"The more I learned about reality the more I began to understand how truly expansive it all is, and how little we understand about it. I mean that both outwardly, where we begin to understand grand cosmic unknowns and the implications of our virtual realities, and also inwardly, the mysteries of our own consciousness.

The academics in the EDF laughed off the fruits of internal exploration of the soul and the psyche as metaphysical pseudoscience, but I've seen it work. I've encountered incidents with no other explanation than tapping into forces

345

that exist outside of our base human senses.

There is a grand consciousness that we're all connected to, somewhere, in the fabric of reality. There is validity to intuition and synchronicities. With an open mind I learned as much as I could about unlocking my consciousness with a focus on results. What began as a way to clear my mind evolved to me finding patterns that couldn't be explained without assuming a metaphysical connection between consciousness and reality.

One exercise I began as my meditation ability improved was an exercise of seating my consciousness at different chakra points in order to feel different aspects of reality. In doing this, I found what seemed to be an inward highway; a highway of infinite dark in the consciousness, no different than the infinite dark of deep space, dotted not with stars but with fleeting images, flights of imagination, messages from other travelers, doors to other consciousness.

It's easy to discount because it's difficult to quantify into language, deeply intuitive, difficult to perform, easy to lie about and difficult to prove, but when you begin to accomplish the feats that avail themselves to an explored and practiced consciousness, they are undeniable.

I was able to change my luck. Communicate with the universe and affect the patterns of synchronicities, to see my path laid out in front of me as easily as glowing breadcrumbs. I was able to communicate my intentions, my ideas, my motivations, my ideas, my heart, to the greater consciousness that humans tap into as a technique to facilitate my psyop campaign.

You wouldn't believe me, but I was able to raise my consciousness to a point of perspective beyond my body and accurately describe events happening light years away with no information. I was able to 'remember' my future. I was able to 'remember' events in other realities.

Once, when I was adrift in space, I was able to communicate my thoughts to Salem across the galaxy. She swears she heard my voice in her head, and she found my ship in the middle of unmarked space with no functioning distress beacon.

I've had experiences where I believed that I was able to shift realities, like a train changing tracks, like I'd changed the channel or the frequency my consciousness was tuned into.

I could go on and on about all the minor intuitions and synchronicities that informed my experience with this issue, but I believe it's something that has to be performed to be believed. That the conscious mind is as real a representative of true reality as the physical world.

Lei has been my protege for as long as she's been with us, and while she excels in every subject, this is the subject that has been my biggest focus with her. She has a talent for the mind that I've never seen. Whether that's something to do with her Draconic heritage or something more specific to her, I'm not sure. Lei's mind is expansive in a way that looks like madness to people who can't understand her.

The truth is, whatever level we have reached in terms of evolution, Lei is something beyond. She can tap into the leylines of reality. What took me years of practice, research and discipline to be able to do poorly, Lei does expertly, naturally, intuitively and playfully, as if she can see infinite reality across time, space and dimension just as easily as I can see the color red.

My focus, Lei. I've done my best to prepare her for a tumultuous journey. I can't imagine what reality will do to her, or what she'll do to reality. I can only assume it will be beyond anyone's wildest imagination."

Adam was only half-listening to Crowley's logs as he posted up on his bunk casually scrolling through a comic book. Out of the corner of his eye he watched his ongoing hallucination, Alice, sit at the edge of the bed cross-legged. She was playing with the hem of her dress, bored but trying to keep herself busy. Every time Adam looked at her she perked up, and then deflated when he went back to his comic.

Adam looked around to make sure no one was looking. "You want something?" he asked her.

Alice looked a little intimidated and shook her head. Adam went back to his comic. He still felt Alice staring at him. After a few minutes he looked at her again. "Yes?" he asked.

"When are we going home?" Alice asked.

Adam felt it in his head. Titan, a once totally unlivable icy rock, made pastoral and beautiful by the colonists who geoengineered it. Temperate, lush, wet, full of gorgeous glaciers and rushing rivers of methane, huge, sweeping landscapes of trees and shimmering mountains. Titan had a reputation when it fell. Titan, more than anywhere else in the galaxy, felt like a home to those who moved there.

Adam snapped out of his reverie and saw Alice had gone.

"Adam, are you there?" he heard over the intercom. "You're going to want to see this."

Adam made his way to the bridge where he found Vice and Grant looking up at the central display, which showed an Earth-like planet in the distance.

"What are we looking at here?" Adam asked.

"It's called Galileo-49999b, officially," Grant said smoothly. "Initially spotted by the Galileo deep space probe."

Adam directed his attention to Grant. "Ok. What's up with it? Why are we looking at it?" he asked.

Vice leaned in toward Grant and whispered, "Show him the readings."

Grant nodded. "This is the most habitable planet we've ever seen. How to describe it…" he trailed off. He looked at Vice. "What were we saying? Perfect, right?"

Vice nodded. "Yeah, perfect," she confirmed.

Grant looked at Adam. "Yeah, it's perfect," he repeated.

Adam squinted and shifted his attention between Vice and Grant who seemed to be acting fishy. "What are you dancing around? What's that mean?"

The two looked at each other. Grant spoke first. "It's too perfect. It's more suited to life than Earth itself," he said.

Vice added a comment, "It's like the most impressive geoengineering project in the universe and it's just here, naturally occurring."

Vice and Grant looked at each other, still obviously holding something back.

"What?" Adam asked. "What is it?"

Vice and Grant communicated with each other with a look. Grant nodded.

"Okay, fine," Vice said. "Adam, this planet is crazy and we've been on the road for eleven months. Look at this place," she said, and showed a few images of beautiful beaches, picturesque hikes, forests, and powdery snowy hills.

"We can't stop, we're already behind. This isn't a vacation," Adam said.

Vice and Grant looked at each other yet again, as if

negotiating who would tell Adam the details.

Vice spoke up. "Also, there's a guy down there," she said.

Adam snapped his neck back slightly, stunned. "Come again?" he asked.

"Yeah, there's… a guy," Vice repeated. She poked Grant with her elbow and he tapped a device he was controlling with his wrist.

The image on the screen shifted from the planet to a man on a beach, dressed simply in a cloth robe and simple cloth sandals. His hair and beard were both long. He was looking up at the sky, directly in the direction of the ship, and smiling a wide friendly smile as he waved enthusiastically.

Adam looked at Vice and Grant. "Can he… see us?" he inquired.

"Unclear," Grant said plainly.

"Well, what do we know about this guy?" Adam followed up. "How'd he get here?"

Vice and Grant looked at each other. Grant shrugged. "Wormhole?" he guessed.

Adam let a silence linger in the conversation for a moment, and then asked, "So what do you want to do? Go down there and talk to him?"

Vice shrugged. "Yeah, kinda," she said.

Adam squinted again. "Even after the Triangulum? After spending a month in robot world?" he asked.

Vice and Grant looked at each other one last time. "Actually, we already talked to everyone else and we left you to last because we knew you'd say no. Everyone wants to go," Vice blurted out.

Adam heard Alice over his shoulder, excitedly chanting. "Can we go? Can we go?"

Adam took a moment to think. "Alright, fine," he said.

"Yayyyy!" he heard his hallucination squeal and go ballistic with excitement.

32

Chuck

Adam stepped off the ship to see the unkempt hermit warmly greeting him with a smile and a casual wave.

"Hey, friend," he said cheerfully.

Adam felt a little out of place, walking out into this picturesque landscape with even the bare minimum level of military carry strapped to his body. The quality of it immediately struck him. The grass he stepped onto was the softest grass he'd ever felt. The breeze was exactly right. It was perfectly warm and perfectly cloudy, and the air was nourishingly dewy and moist.

Adam approached the man with a wave. Politely, but business-like, he asked from a distance, "You need help down here?"

The man looked over his shoulder as if he thought Adam might have been talking to someone else. After realizing Adam was talking to him, he beamed, "Me? Nah, man. This is the best place in the galaxy," he said.

Adam looked around, surveying his surroundings and trying to get a sense of anything potentially suspicious or dangerous. Satisfied for the moment, Adam continued his line of questioning.

"How'd you… get out here?" he asked.

The man scratched his head and smiled back. "Oh, y'know, here, there. I guess I just found my way here," he said. He put his hand on his hips and looked around. "And it's just so nice, y'know? I just wanted to stay here and spend some time."

The man smiled. He pointed out at the water. "Oh hey, look. Jeffrey's coming," he said. He waved out into the water. "Hey Jeffrey," he said in a casual, friendly tone.

A talking, sentient dolphin poked its head above the water. "Hey, Chuck. Having a great day?" it asked.

Chuck nodded. "You know me," he said with a smile. "Another day with my friends in paradise," he said.

"Who's your new friend?" Jeffrey asked Chuck. He turned his attention to Adam. "Sorry, friend, don't mean to be rude. You wanna come to the cookout? We've got a friend and he wants to show us all 'Luau Pork'. Sounds delicious," he said.

Adam looked at the talking dolphin in disbelief. It wasn't so far beyond the capability of modern genetic modification, and Adam had heard of some animals passing the threshold of sentience required for galactic personhood, but he'd never seen an animal quite like Jeffrey, who seemed to be at least as intelligent as the average human.

Adam pointed at Jeffrey. "You're a… dolphin?" he asked.

Jeffrey and Chuck looked at each other. Jeffrey looked back at Adam. "Born and raised," he said matter-of-factly.

Chuck replied, "Why, man, you got something against dolphins?"

Adam stammered slightly. "No–" he started to say before Chuck cut him off laughing.

"I'm just joshing you, man," he said. He pointed toward Jeffrey with his thumb. "Yeah, he's a dolphin."

Chuck looked at Jeffrey and finally answered his question. "I don't know. Some guys from space," he said. Chuck spun around and pointed at Adam. "Oh yeah, you wanna come to the cookout? You're gonna love it," he asked. "We've got a friend. He's gonna do 'Luau Pork.' Doesn't that sound amazing?"

Adam nodded. "Right, right. Luau pork. Got that. Give me a minute," he said.

Adam looked at Chuck, trying to get a read on him. Adam was vigilant and trying to imagine the potential threats. *Maybe they're cannibals,* he thought to himself. *This whole thing has kind of a cannibal vibe.*

Adam took a step back and touched his ear to activate the comm.

"I made contact," he said. "Person seems to be some kind of burned out space wook."

"How'd he get here?" he heard Vice ask from the other line.

"No idea," Adam said.

"Well, what was he like? Is he dangerous?" Vice asked.

Adam went silent long enough for Vice to prompt a response. "Well?" she asked.

"They want to invite us to a cookout," Adam said.

There was no response from the comm for a few seconds. Then, it came back with Tezca's voice. "Adam, this is Tezca. This is very important. Did you say cookout?" she asked.

"With luau pork," Adam said. "He and his dolphin friend have a friend."

Again, a few moments of silence. "Did you say luau pork?" Tezca responded energetically, then paused for another moment before adding, "Wait, did you say dolphin friend?"

"Yes," Adam replied.

"And what'd you say?" Tezca asked.

"I said give me a minute," Adam said.

Tezca took a moment to reply. Adam overheard Tezca talking to the others through the comm.

"He said maybe," he heard Tezca say.

"Luau pork sounds pretty good, man," he heard Aztec.

"Burned out space wook sounds like a pretty cool guy honestly," he heard Raziel.

The comm went dead for a moment, then came back with Vice's voice.

"Adam, I think we're going to have to go to this cookout. I don't think the team will forgive you if you say no. They're pretty excited about the… dolphin," she said.

"And the pork!" Adam heard Tezca shouting from the background.

After finishing his conversation Adam, really just wanting to finish the mission with no more stops, sighed and relented to his crew's demands. He turned back to Chuck. "So, cookout," he said. "Sounds great. Should we bring anything?"

Jeffrey moved his snout in a way that was unmistakably a smile. "Nah, friend. Just yourselves is more than enough!"

Chuck smiled. "You made a great decision," he said warmly, without a hint of malice or ulterior motive.

These people are going to eat me, Adam thought to himself. "Where to?" he said.

Chuck smiled and nodded. "Yeah, man. Just get everyone together and we'll go. The lodge is right there through those trees. Excited for you to meet everyone," he said.

"Huh," Adam replied. "We thought you were alone down here," he said as the rest of the crew started filing out of the hatch of the Oneiro-Lyssa.

Chuck looked confused. "Alone? No, no, not at all," he said. "Just a little tired. It's our little getaway."

Chuck watched as everyone collected in front of the ship. "Cool, all set. Let's go," he said with a wave. He caught a glimpse of Grant and did a double take, as though he saw someone he recognized, but let it go, seemingly mistaken. Chuck led the crew over to a nearby path overgrown with ivy-like trees. He spread the foliage apart to make a path and ducked through, motioning for the others to follow.

Aztec went in first and Adam took up the back, listening to his crew's amazed exclamations as they emerged on the other side of the treeline.

When Adam emerged himself, he saw an expansive area, like a day club, with all sorts of different people and species milling around and casually having a good time. The more Adam inspected the crowd the more he realized something odd. He recognized people in the crowd. Famous people from history, spiritual leaders, academics, world leaders, and more.

Adam tapped Chuck's shoulder. "Is that Abraham Lincoln?" he asked.

Chuck scanned the crowd until he stumbled across Lincoln's signature towering height and beard, doing Jello shots and then taking a turn at a game of limbo. "Oh that guy? Abe? Yeah he's great. Love that guy," he said.

Adam looked at Tezca, who seemed to be holding something in.

"This what you were expecting?" he asked.

Tezca grinned broadly. "This is so much the coolest thing I've ever seen that I don't even know how to handle it," she said. "Oh my gosh there's squirrels playing baseball and they're wearing little baseball hats. I'm gonna die. Adam, I have to go, we'll catch up later," she said and did the closest thing an adult female professional soldier can do to scampering away.

Adam felt Aztec's hand on his shoulder. "Yeah, I'm out too, bro. Look at that man, they've got elotes. And lobster. And funnel cakes. Have fun, eh?" he said and walked off.

As the team dispersed to mingle at the strange party, Adam decided to accept his fate and go with the flow. He went to the bar and got himself a drink. Winding down, he watched the musical act performing on stage, a combination of feel good vacation pop and beach rock being performed by a trio of native Martians. The same native Martians who'd long since disappeared, hiding from humans as they annexed the universe.

The band ended their set and an announcer walked up to the microphone. "Alright, let's hear it for the Omicron Three! Next up, you know her, you love her, one of our favorite new members here at Shangri-La, Lei Crowley and her indie pop trance band, Dreamwire Carousel!"

Adam's eyes locked on the stage. *Oh no*, he thought to himself as, sure enough, he watched Crowley's adopted daughter Lei take the stage, cheered on by an audience composed of what seemed to be the greatest people, animals and aliens, known or unknown, from throughout history and across the universe.

Lei noticed Adam in the crowd and began her set. She smiled warmly and winked, and then launched into her intro.

"Hey everyone, we're Dreamwire Carousel. It's another great day and we're having a wonderful time. Great to see everyone. Is that Alvin out there?" she put her hand to her head like a visor, then pointed at an orangutan in the crowd. "Alvin took in eleven orphans and saved his species after a disease wiped out all the adults on their moon. Super nice guy, too," she said.

The orangutan stood up proudly and waved at the crowd.

Lei continued her crowd work. "Over here we've got Angelica Crews from Centauri Sigma. Took care of her disabled brother his entire life, sacrificed all her dreams. Ended up losing her life to an illness. Never had a cross word for anyone. We're so happy to have you, Angelica. You made it," she said.

Lei hammed it up a bit on stage for a while before beginning her set in earnest. Not wanting to be seen, Adam turned around towards the bartender, only to see Lei standing in front of him, looking directly at him.

"Hey," she said with a smile. "Funny seeing you here."

33

Traveler of Reality

Lei's gaze moved to the side and slightly past Adam. "And who's this?" she said in a higher pitched voice, bending over slightly. "What's your name, sweetie?"

"Alice," Adam heard his hallucination shyly say behind him, holding onto his sleeve and hiding halfway behind his torso.

"Wanna see a magic trick?" Lei asked warmly, like an older sister or a younger aunt. Alice nodded sheepishly.

Lei showed the hallucination both of her empty hands, then waved them around in front if her, suddenly revealing a lollipop. She handed the treat to the little girl. "Why don't

359

you go play for a minute? I'm going to talk to your dad," she said.

Alice looked at Adam for permission. He nodded, unafraid of what could befall her because she was a hallucination and not an actual person. She ran off into the crowd, surely no further than Adam's mind could perceive.

Adam turned his attention back to Lei, who was still simultaneously performing on stage and manning the bar in front of him, leaning over with her chin resting on her hand, a light smile across her face.

"You can see her?" Adam asked.

Lei made eye contact with him and kept her friendly smile. "Of course, She's right there," she said, lifting her head and standing more alert.

Adam looked at Alice hopping around to the music toward the back of the crowd and then back at Lei. "That's a hallucination," he said. "It's not real."

Lei looked at him with a playful look of performative confusion. "Hallucinations are real," she said. "Aren't they?" she added with a hint of a wink.

Adam narrowed his eyes at her, not feeling a lot of patience for her vague statements.

"What is this place?" Adam asked suspiciously.

Lei looked around, like she was genuinely getting a sense of her surroundings even though she was obviously familiar with the location. She looked at Adam and raised an eyebrow. "What do you think it is?" she asked him.

"I think you rigged up a bunch of AIs to replicate historical figures and you're hanging out with them on this planet by yourself," Adam said.

Lei smiled. "AI ghosts. That's a theory," she said.

Adam felt a tug on his sleeve. He looked down to see Alice looking up at him. "I'm bored," she said.

"Awww," Lei replied, sincerely, with an aunt-like demeanor. "Let's go find something to do then," she said. Lei hopped up onto the counter and slid over to the other side. She looked at Adam. "Shall we?" she asked.

Adam narrowed his eyes. "Shall we what?" he asked.

"I was gonna show you around," Lei said. "Since you're here."

Adam shook his head. "I don't trust this place," he said.

Lei put her hand over her mouth. "You don't trust me?" she said, looking actually a bit hurt. "Why?"

Adam was surprised by her reaction. "Isn't it obvious? We have a very clear conflict of interest," Adam said.

Lei looked to the side like she was thinking, processing a totally foreign new line of thinking. "Huh," she said, nodding. "In that case, I have something else to show you. Come with me."

Adam was still hesitant.

Lei looked at him and smiled warmly. "You're worried over nothing," she said in a genuinely reassuring tone. She turned and started to saunter away, hands clasped innocently behind her back. She turned her head back around. "Come on," she said with a smile.

Adam sighed and stood up. He followed after Lei as Alice bobbed along beside him.

As they walked, people periodically came up and greeted Lei, and Lei introduced them to Adam. A friendly, disheveled looking guru with a thin mustache, prayer beads and a warm presence excitedly greeted him. He met a talking lion who had once upon been the wisest king of the greatest lion pride to exist. He met a starling that died of exhaustion after spreading news of a great fire, sacrificing himself to save thousands. He met an exuberant man in green shorts who talked to him about animals and wildlife conservation. He met a calming painter with a memorable afro.

As they walked, Adam spotted people he thought he recognized. He saw the Buddha playing volleyball with Carl Jung. He saw John Lennon playing alongside a group of people in a drum circle. Gandhi was on the dance floor, getting down to dreampop techno. Nietzsche was playing chess with Confucius. Bob Marley was laughing with a group of people.

As Lei led him toward wherever their final destination was set to be, Adam was put through a blur of introductions. By the end of it Adam felt like he'd met a who's who of truly great people, animals and aliens. Not famous people, or rich people, but kind people, brave people, sacrificing people. People of a caliber who made it seem possible that Lei's endless summer utopia could function harmoniously without conflict.

Lei stopped in front of an old decaying door shoddily fixed to a nondescript beachside cave. A wooden sign with the words "Keep Out!" was nailed to it.

"We're here!" Lei said, excitedly, as she pried the keep out sign off the door and casually tossed it aside. She pulled the door open. "After you," she said.

Adam peered into the dark corridor. He looked at Lei. "What's gonna happen to me if I go in there? Is Abraham Lincoln gonna hook my lips up to a car battery?"

"So distrusting," Lei said. "Just go in." She gestured toward the door. "You'll see," she added.

Adam squinted at her. "Why aren't you people trying to kill us? Why did Aria help us at the Aesir Colony? Why did Salem help us?" he asked.

Lei shrugged. "I don't know about all that. I suspect because they want you to make it to Draconis," she said.

"And you?" Adam said.

"I don't," she said.

"Why?" Adam replied.

Sadness washed over Lei's face. "It's the same thing I told you before, when we met on Djevica. I like this reality. It's one of my favorites. There aren't a lot of realities where my family is intact. Here we were all a family. My father, Salem, Nyx, Aria, Lyra. This is one of my happiest realities," Lei said.

"And something happens on Draconis?" Adam asked.

Lei smiled. "I don't know why you want to discuss this with words when I can just show you with my brain," Lei said. Warmly, she added, "Go in, you'll see."

Adam looked at Alice and then at Lei and then acquiesced. He walked to the precipice of the door and peered in. Soon enough he found himself grabbed by the energy of the tunnel and pulled inside.

Adam found himself in a dining room, a heavy wooden door shutting behind him, Lei and Alice standing by his side. In the middle of the room was a dining table, occupied by Crowley and his family, including a child version of Lei. Lei was playing with her food and the whole table was laughing and smiling.

Adam saw Lei out of the corner of his eye, watching, reminiscing, with a big smile on her face.

"This is Lei 4949. This is here," she said. Adam looked at

her. "Look again," she said.

Adam turned his attention back to the dining room, surprised to find himself in a different room altogether. This room was sterile and cold. It was metal, unfurnished except for a cot, and overly lit with harsh lights. In the corner was a little girl with antlers crying into her knees.

Adam looked at Lei, who looked sad. "This was also my childhood. This was Lei 1253. But it was also me," Lei said, then pointed to the room again.

Adam looked back and saw the same scene, but this time Lei had red skin and long pointy ears instead of antlers. "Lei 1254," he heard.

The scene shifted like mist and another version of the little girl was there, missing a limb. "1255," Lei said.

Lei shifted the scene through different variations of Lei, each of which Lei had allegedly experienced, and was concurrently experiencing all at once. Lei went through variations rapidly. Some were tortured by isolation in a lab, some were physically tortured. One brutal scene showed a young, conscious Lei screaming as lab technicians cut off the fairy wings she had in that reality. Others were more pleasant. In some she escaped, in some she was never caught, in some she died adrift in space, in some she went on adventures.

"Which one's the real one?" Adam asked as he watched, noticing Lei getting sadder and angrier as the show went on.

Lei wiped some moisture from her eyes. "They're all real," Lei said. "This is how reality works. It's the same thing as with your daughter," she added, pointing loosely at the little hallucination that was tagging along on Lei's tour.

"What do you mean?" Adam asked.

Lei gave him a quizzical look. "Your daughter. That one," she said.

Adam looked at Alice and back at Lei. "What do you mean it's all real?" Adam asked, but Lei wasn't paying attention to him anymore.

"I want to show you my favorite place," Lei said, distracted. She ran to the other side of the room, opened little Lei's cell door and disappeared through it.

Adam followed. On the other side he found himself in a lush, colorful world where everything was bubbly and bouncy. He saw Lei swinging from a homemade swing affixed to a moon that looked like it was drawn in crayon. Lei hopped off and ran up to him. She took his hand and the two floated into the air. They floated off above the atmosphere of the tiny planet and out into space, where bizarre rings in space connected little planets together, and Lei took Adam flying through them.

"What is this place?" Adam asked.

"Another reality," Lei said. "The physics here are different. It's very light. There's no death. Everything's safe here. And it's totally empty. Stars aren't hot, you can bounce on them like balloons. Check this out," she said, and whisked toward a nearby planet characterized by gushing waterfalls.

"This whole planet is edible," Lei said, breaking off the stem of a giant mushroom only to reveal an inside made of what seemed to be high quality milk chocolate. Lei offered him some. He refused. As she licked her fingers, she pointed to some nearby rocks. "The rocks are gummies," she said matter-of-factly.

"Hey Lei!" Adam heard from above, and flinched.

Lei waved at the sky. "Heyyy!"

Adam looked up to see the stars themselves were talking to Lei.

"Are we in your delusion? Is this your… disassociation?" Adam asked.

Lei smiled. "That's what the doctors at the facility thought, too. I thought that myself for a while. But no, Adam, this is real. It's as real as anything else," she said.

"Why are you showing me this?" Adam asked.

Lei looked at him. Her face got serious, and concerned. She put her hand on his cheek. "You don't have to go to Draconis. You can stay here. I'll take you and your friends to whatever reality you want. Whatever time period. Whatever planet. I can take you to where your daughter is still alive," Lei said.

Adam looked at her in disbelief. "Why? Why would I do that?" Adam said.

Lei shook her head. "All this boundless reality," she said. "And yet Draconis changes everything. You don't have to go."

Adam shook his head. "Crowley is a target. If it's not me it'll be someone else," he said.

Lei made eye contact, deeply sad. "I'm not worried about that. My reality is a lot bigger than yours. I can go somewhere else, find everyone again, make new memories. I can come back here whenever I want," she said. "You," she added, pointing at Adam. Her face was overwhelmed with empathy. "Draconis is a dangerous place, Adam. You're being haunted by one ghost of a loved one already. Is pursuing my father worth risking the rest of your family?"

"What family? No family left," Adam said.

Lei shook her head. She tapped on her wrist and an AR screen appeared, showing Aztec, Tezca, and the rest of the crew enjoying the party atmosphere at Shangri-La, taking advantage of food, rides, hikes, music and all the other amenities available.

"Your best friends, like siblings," Lei said, showing Aztec and Tezca. "Your sister's boyfriend," she said, showing Grant. "Your partner," she said, showing Vice. "Your ward, keeping you on your toes," she said, showing Raziel. "Your trusted assistant," she said, showing Sophia and the Oneiro-Lyssa.

"What happens on Draconis? What, they die? Is that what you're saying?" Adam asked.

Lei stared at Adam for a few seconds, sadness in her eyes. She looked at Alice, then back at Adam. "Do you want to know what happened to your daughter? In a way you'll grasp," she said, conspicuously changing the subject.

"Yes," Adam said.

Lei nodded solemnly. "Alright. Let's go," she said. "I'll show you the truth of it," she said. She pulled a door up from the ground and stepped through it.

34

Project Mockingbird

After stepping through the door, Adam found himself sitting halfway out the open hatch of an EDF dropship, skidding just above the moon's surface.

"Go! Go! Go!" Adam heard from behind him, muffled by the whipping air. He jumped.

Standing on the surface of Titan, he heard gunfire far off in the distance, where the lights of the human encampment could be seen dimly off on the horizon.

He heard Lei's voice, and looked over to see her standing next to him.

"This is it, right?" she said, looking in the direction of the colony. "When it happened?"

Adam nodded. "This is it," he confirmed, but when he looked, Lei had already vanished.

Adam hiked over the gray regolith toward the village, decked out from head to toe in full EDF war armor, including a bulletproof exoskeleton. As he closed in, the gunfire got louder. The battle was raging.

Adam felt the bullets whizzing by his head. Buoyed by the thought he was not in the real world, but some sort of hypnotic fever dream crafted by a cunning Lei, he continued onward unconcerned by the danger.

Adam engaged the colonists as he pressed toward the town square, just as he remembered.

When he reached the center of the colony, the battle was winding down. EDF soldiers were accepting surrender and dragging colonists to gather in the square.

There, Adam saw the squad drag Alice out and put her in a group with other colonists.

"Who's this one?" Adam heard a nearby soldier ask, referring to a tied up man with a bag over his head.

"He's the leader. Orders are to execute," another soldier answered.

"Hey, you," Adam heard the first soldier address him. "You can take care of this, right? Just get him on his knees. Pop pop one in the brain stem. Do it in front of all of them so they know it's all done with. You got it?"

Adam nodded. "Got it," he whispered, playing along with the plot, although he knew how it went.

Adam grabbed the colonist leader by the arm and dragged him to the center of the town square. He kicked him down to his knees and put his sidearm to the back of his head.

"No!" he heard, as he expected, the scream of the little girl as she ran toward him in what seemed like slow motion. He watched her naively try to trade a stuffed purple dragon for her father's life.

Adam looked at her for a second, and then shot her in the face, and shot her father in the head.

Adam looked over their crumpled corpses. Exactly as he remembered.

"And stop," Adam heard Lei's voice as time itself seemingly paused.

"It's the same," Adam said. "What's the point of this?"

"Take a look," Lei said, pointing at the colonist leader's corpse. Adam approached the body cautiously.

As the face of the body came into view, Adam's face contorted with confusion. The face of the body was his own. He looked at Lei, who pointed to a nearby window. Adam looked into it and saw his own face – it was someone else; an EDF soldier he'd never seen before.

Adam inspected his face in the reflection, trying to make sense of it. He looked at the corpses littering the colony. It was accurate, to his memory. He remembered all of this.

"Now I just have more questions," Adam said.

"It doesn't end here. Just your part," Lei replied. She spun her finger around in the air. "Roll it," she said.

Time resumed, and a few short moments later, Adam heard the engine of an approaching vehicle. Soon after, a sleek, black stealth capable starfighter decloaked above the battlefield. It was a Nighthawk class ship, the kind intelligence station heads were given in order to travel without being tracked.

The ship landed, and out of it stepped an officer wearing a fully steamed and starched, buttoned up uniform, perfectly tailored. Adam recognized him immediately. He was years younger, but it was unmistakably him.

The commanding officer who had given Adam the kill order saluted. "Sergeant Major Iscariot," he said. "The campaign was successful. Ready to debrief, Sir."

Iscariot absentmindedly nodded as he inspected the battle-field. He stopped by the corpses of the colony leader, Adam's corpse and kneeled.

He pulled a pair of black gloves from his coat pocket and put them on, then put his fingers on the body's neck, looking for a pulse. He turned its head from side to side, looking at it carefully. After he was satisfied, he stood up slowly and stretched his hand out. He wagged his first two fingers to summon one of the members of his escort.

"This one," he said. "He's too good. A formidable enemy is so rare these days. Got my blood flowing, even if just a little. Be a shame to let him go to waste. Load up the body. Send it off to Kimber at Mockingbird."

Adam watched as Iscariot's escort strapped his body onto a stretcher and loaded it up on Iscariot's Nighthawk.

"Come on," he heard Lei say. He looked over to catch a glimpse of her dropping through a hole in the floor. Adam followed after.

On the other side, Adam's eyes opened to the sight of the harsh overhead light of what seemed to be a sterile military operating room. His head was bolted to the chair to restrict movement and he was chemically paralyzed, though conscious.

"The HBI surgery," Adam said. " I remember this."

The surgeon pulled her mask down, to reveal Lei's face, her petite fangs and pointed draconic ears. "Do you?" she asked.

The door to the room cracked open and Iscariot walked in, still wearing his posh overcoat. "Come on then," he said, motioning to someone behind him.

As the other person walked in, Adam recognized him as the soldier who had shot him, whose memories he had in his head. Once the soldier had fully entered the room, he looked around confused.

"Sir?" he asked. "What's going –"

The surgeon, being played by Lei, jammed a needle into the soldier's neck and pushed down the plunger. He briefly moved to try to defend himself, but crumpled over quickly.

"Pull his engrams, replace the memories of our new recruit," Iscariot ordered. "Afterwards, incinerate the body. No paper trail." Iscariot pointed at Adam. "When you're done, deliver this one directly to black site Gamma for reintegration procedures."

Lei nodded along. Iscariot left the room and closed the door behind him. After he left, Lei stood over Adam. She flicked him in the head and he found himself back in Lei's strange cartoon world. Lei was sitting on top of a mushroom with her head on her knees.

"So that's it, then?" Adam asked. "My memories aren't real? It's all some kind of military brainwashing? Some kind of pet project Iscariot was running to force defections?"

Lei nodded despondently. "Yes. That's what happened," she said. "But that's not why she's here," she added, lazily pointing at Adam's hallucination of Alice, who was sitting nearby on another mushroom.

"So, what then?" Adam asked.

"That's what happened here. What I call 4949. In my forty nine hundred and forty-ninth life," Lei said. "But, that's not what happened in reality 4982. In 4982, you joined the EDF as a teen when your parents died instead of going into the colonist program. After enlisting, you were sent to Titan, where you executed the colonist leader and his child before being murdered by your commanding officer."

Lei looked at Adam. "That procedure they did on you, they stopped doing it because it produced psychosis. The reason, which they never figured out, is because reality is infinite and interconnected. And consciousness exists in reality, not just… here. They weren't falsifying memories. They were, without knowing it, unlocking awareness of memories belonging to your… greater consciousness," Lei said.

Adam looked at her, confused.

Lei reworded her explanation. "You're not remembering fake memories. You're remembering real memories from another life and it broke your brain," she said.

Lei's face grew sad. "In most realities, you have nothing to do with the military at all. Nine out of ten Adams found Titan colony and live out their days building Titan into the envy of the Milky Way," she said.

"So which one's real?" Adam asked.

Lei shrugged. "They're both real, Adam. They both happened to the same person. You. It's just that 'you' is a lot bigger than you thought it was," she said.

"Why are you telling me this? You just want to settle my conscience?" Adam asked.

Lei looked in Adam's eyes. "Adam, there's no reason for

this. This reality is one of a billion billion trillion and on and on. In the one reality where I had a family, it takes them. And it takes yours, too," she said. Her face curled up in anger. She took a deep breath and calmed herself. "It eats everything. It ruins every reality it takes over."

"It?" Adam asked.

Lei looked at him, uncharacteristically cold. "War," she said.

Adam fueled his brow and squinted. "War?" he repeated back.

Lei stood up and sighed. "War, greed, domination, hate," she said. "Outcrops of scarcity and suffering."

"So, what? You want me to just quit? Turn my ship around, go home to a court martial?" Adam asked.

Lei walked up to him and took his hands in hers. She looked at him with tears welling up in her eyes. "Please," she said. "What is this loyalty you have to a man who killed you and your daughter and destroyed your home and your life's work? A man who, in another life, ordered you to kill a little girl and a prominent, peaceful leader of humankind. A man who, in a million universes, you never meet. Go anywhere else. Do anything else. Please."

Lei's expression darkened. "If you go to Draconis, there is only one winner. It," she said.

"It. War," Adam repeated for confirmation.

Lei nodded. "That's right," she said.

Adam sat down on one of the mushrooms. Though he tried to wrap his mind around Lei's words and visions, he knew he only saw a sliver of the reality Lei saw as an endless, simultaneous expanse of time, space, reality and consciousness.

Adam shook his head. "I don't think any of this is real," he said. "I don't think you can stop war. I don't think Iscariot or Crowley are good men, and I don't care which one wins, as long as someone wins. You want to stop war, that's how you stop war," he said.

Lei shook her head. "You sound like my father," she said. "You two are more alike than you realize. But you're wrong. Look where we are, Adam. Look at how peaceful it is here. There are billions of realities that conquer scarcity. That know peace and love. Where even just standing there feels like a hug."

Lei looked at him fiercely. "You think it's too good to be true. That's just because it's so far away from what you've seen you don't think it's possible. But it is possible. When I grew up alone, I didn't think it was possible to have a family. But it was, Adam. It was possible. It took me almost five thousand lives, but I found it. Pain is not an inevitability, Adam. It's a choice. Not everywhere is like this. And everywhere that's like this ends one way or another. Game over," she said, pantomiming an explosion with her hands.

Adam shook his head yet again. "Lea Monde is taking real territory, as we speak. That's war. I kill Crowley, that stops. Lea Monde kills Iscariot, that stops. That's how this ends. I don't see any other way. If I don't go to Draconis, they'll send someone else, and they'll send someone after me, too. Besides… why don't you just… change it? Like you do all this?"

Lei shook her head. "I don't change reality. I just see a lot more of it than you do, thousands of lives at once, birth to death, at once. What happens here… already happened.

This is the present for you. For me, it's the past, present and future all at once, of one little fragment of reality among trillions. For me, this is a living memory. One that's so precious to me, of a happy time. This reality isn't important, Adam. Not in the grand scheme of things. But it's important to me. It's where I came from. I was just hoping… I could convince you. I never succeed. But I always try," she said.

Lei wiped a tear away from her eye. "I love my family, Adam. And you've been through so much. What's the point? We both lose things that matter to us? Why? For what?" she pleaded.

Lei looked at him, really expecting an answer, but Adam didn't have any answer to give. He didn't know anything about infinite reality or fighting the abstract concepts of war and scarcity across dimensions. Adam wasn't going to agree, and deep down he knew why: because Lei's prerogative was at odds with his.

Whatever her perception, she saw right and wrong through grand abstractions, forests instead of trees; Adam's view was much more tactile – individual trees. He saw right and wrong through direct actions. Betraying his word was wrong, failing his duty was wrong, deceiving his teammates was wrong, letting an enemy go was wrong. Adam was a knight; Lei was an empath. Their essences were in conflict. Their priorities differed. Adam suspected even if he understood reality on Lei's level, the root of that conflict wouldn't change.

He also suspected that if he defected, Raziel would execute him on the spot.

"I can't," Adam said solemnly.

Lei nodded, sad. "I know," she said. "That's what you

always say."

"Sorry," Adam replied. He looked around. "So what do you want to do? Is this going to become my prison?"

Lei sighed. "Of course not," she said. "Spend the night anyway. Enjoy the party. Give your friends some time off." She put her hand on Adam's cheek and forced a smile.

She knelt down in front of Adam's hallucination of Alice and shook her little hand. "It was so nice to meet you," she said to the little girl with a smile, who responded by hugging her legs.

Lei turned back to Adam. "It can be as good as you want it to be, Adam. However good you believe it can get, that's how good it can be," she said. "It's up to you."

She snapped her fingers and Adam found himself back at the beach club, standing in the crowd in front of the stage where Lei was performing. She gave him a knowing glance from the stage, subtle to the point of being nearly imperceptible, but pronounced enough to confirm Adam's experience was real, at least insofar as Adam understood 'real' as a concept anymore.

35

Good Times in Deep Space

"Bro, they were not kidding about this Kahlua pork. This is the bomb, my friend. Yo, Adam. You try this? Adam. Adam. Earth to Adam," Aztec said, waving his hand in front of Adam's face.

Adam was vaguely paying attention. He was deeply in his own head. He looked at Aztec. He tried to really look at him, like he never had before. Really inspect him, really look at him, try to see who he really was deep down and as a whole.

Adam smiled weakly. "I'll get some," he said to Aztec, who was sipping a drink out of a coconut with a tiny umbrella in it, hanging out, but mostly watching the band playing on the stage.

"Hey, man," Adam said. "You remember Columbia Hills on Mars?"

Aztec turned his attention to Adam. "Yeah, of course," he said excitedly. He slapped Adam on the shoulder. "That's where we all met. That was me and Tez's first mission with you, man. How long ago was that?" he asked.

Adam shrugged. "Hard to tell anymore with all the time dilation and cryo sleep. You know I got my file some time ago and it says I'm 147 years old?" he said.

Aztec's jaw dropped. "That's crazy, man. Wonder what mine is," he mused, enjoying the banter, but still mostly paying attention to the band.

Adam scanned the rest of the crew. He spotted Tezca on the dance floor, dancing in a good mood at Grant, who was participating in an understated kind of way, mostly just nodding along and enjoying being there. Raziel was playing cards with three people who seemed at a glance to be Alan Watts, Liu Bei and Joan of Arc. Vice was sitting on a blanket on the grass watching the stage while playing with a big fluffy dog she met.

Adam watched as Tezca tapped out on the dance floor and strolled in Adam and Aztec's direction with a smile on her face.

"Time for a refill," she said, all smiles and shaking an empty cup as she sauntered up.

"Hey, Adam was just talking about Columbia Hills," Aztec said as a sort of greeting.

"Oooh," Tezca said. "That's a blast from the past." As she made eye contact with the bartender she silently gave him the hand sign for 'two' while she jumped into Adam and Aztec's conversation for the time being.

"Remember that guy who had the messed up DNA augment?" Tezca said.

"Snaggletooth guy? The guy with the little tusk coming straight out of his face?" Aztec asked.

Tezca laughed. "Yeah he wanted to be part walrus for some reason. Got it done from a second rate geneticist. Botched! Ha," Tezca said.

Adam sat quietly and nodded along with the conversation, but his attention was focused on the warning that the party they were attending might be the last time any of them ever saw each other alive. He watched Tezca chuckle mischievously, gossiping about people from their past, and Aztec laughing along. Adam traced their faces through the memories he had stored up over the years with each of them.

I wonder if these are all fake, too, he wondered.

"Gonna take a walk," Adam announced abruptly and somewhat awkwardly. He stood up and started walking away.

As Adam walked toward the beach he heard Tezca behind him. "What's up with him?" she asked her brother.

"Dunno. He's doing that mopey disappearing thing he does," Aztec explained.

"Ah," Adam heard Tezca respond as their voices faded out of earshot.

Adam meandered around the party, halfway immersed in a sad, contemplative drunk. Eventually he made his way to the beach, which was sparsely populated with just a few party goers here and there. Adam found an old rock to sit down on and watch the sun set. He sat there for half an hour, just staring off into the water, trying to make his mind blank.

After some time, he heard footsteps. He glanced out of his peripheral vision and saw Chuck walk up with the same joyful, carefree countenance he displayed when they first landed, but mixed with a touch of solemn empathy.

He greeted Adam as he walked up. "Want some company?" he asked.

Adam made a subtle gesture with his hand indicating Chuck could have a seat. As Chuck sat down, he spoke again. "Saw you come out here by yourself. Looked kinda… bummed out, y'know," he said.

Adam nodded, still stoically looking at the sea.

Chuck watched his reaction as if he was analyzing it. He nodded, absorbing the vibe. "You mind if I hang out?" Chuck asked.

"If you want. I may not be good company. I'm not really in a party mood," Adam said.

Chuck smiled warmly. "It's all good, man. What are we doing? Looking out at the ocean?" he asked.

Adam nodded.

"Any particular reason?" Chuck prodded.

Adam thought about the question and what he would say. He didn't want to drop the burden of his trials on someone else. After a few moments, he vacantly said, "Heavy shit," while sipping on a beer.

Chuck absorbed the response with empathy. "I get it," he said. He passed for a second. "You mind if I sit?"

"You don't have to do that," Adam said, wanting to get away from the attention, conflicted by the desire for comfort and the desire to not have his lapse in composure witnessed.

Chuck smiled. "I got all the time in the world, man," he

said. He put his hand on Adam's shoulder. "Long as you need," he followed up, removed his hand and sat next to Adam, giving him quiet company.

Adam and Chuck stared off at the water without saying anything for an hour or so. Eventually Adam broke the silence.

"Where are you from?" he asked. "Earth? Centauri? Somewhere else?"

Chuck thought for a second. "Yeah, I spent some time on Earth. Eventually I left. It just wasn't that fun down there. There's a lot more universe out there, y'know?" he said.

"You think you'll ever go back?" Adam asked.

Chuck sat back, extended his legs and crossed them. He smiled, looking out at the water. "I don't know. Maybe. When things calm down a little. Feels like they're still processing stuff from the last time I was there," he said. "I mean… look at this. Look how nice it is here. All the time in the universe. Isn't it nice to just take some time for a place like this? Perfect breeze, perfect night, good friends, food, drinks, a little windsurfing. It's nice."

Adam squinted, curious. "How long have you been here?" he asked.

Chuck's eyes widened and he blew air out. "Huh," he said. "That's a good one. What year is it?" he asked.

"Should be around 2760 or so by now. Depends where you're measuring from," Adam answered.

Chuck's eyes widened again. "Whew. Long time then," he said. "Is Rome still going on?"

Adam squinted. "Rome? Like the city?" he asked.

"Yeah. Y'know, with the furry helmets," he made a motion with his hand pantomiming the shape of a Roman Centurion helmet. "And, y'know, the…" he made a stabbing motion with his hands.

"Are you talking about… ancient Rome?" Adam asked. "You're from ancient Rome?"

Chuck shrugged. "Nah, that was just… big news back then. Man, how long was I surfing with Jerry on that ocean planet?" he mused to himself.

Silence fell over the conversation. The two just watched the ocean roll in and out until the sun started to come up. As daylight broke, Adam decided he'd allowed himself more than enough self pity. He stood up. He offered his hand to Chuck and they shook, then Adam quietly walked back to the party to collect his crew.

He found them in various states of asleep or otherwise partied out. With few words spoken, he let everyone know it was time to go and loaded up the ship.

As Adam started the launch routine, he looked at his crew, who Lei had called his family, and felt the weight of their lives on his shoulders.

"Next stop is Draconis," he announced, stone-faced.

Tezca responded by mustering a low energy but authentic "Woo."

"Stop," Adam scolded. "No more games. No more fun. I want everyone training combat exercises from here to the destination," he said. He pointed at Vice and Grant. "That includes you two. No dead weight."

Tezca wiped the grin off her face. She saluted, annoyed. "Sir," she said sternly.

"Start now," Adam commanded. "Dismissed."

The crew saluted and started to file off the bridge. Adam heard them grumble as they left.

"What got into him?" Adam heard Vice ask.

"I don't know," he heard Tezca reply. "He gets like this."

Adam watched the takeoff sequence expressionless. He hoped that wasn't the last time he'd get to experience Tezca's sass back.

Adam punched in the coordinates for their final destination as Shangri-La disappeared into a tiny pale blue dot behind them. "No one dies," he said to himself as the engines kicked in and the Oneiro-Lyssa launched itself into the deep black of space at top speed.

VI

Draconis

36

The Last Supper

"After Antares I began to feel the unseen, unheard presence of the intelligence establishment. I felt their eyes, their monitoring. Like a pack of wolves lurking just beyond the tree line. But I intuited that presence. I concluded it was an entity with its own thoughts and ideas. Its own agendas. A relationship to be managed. I telegraphed my liberation of the outer Centauri slave colonies. I outlined my reasoning. I pitched my op to the quiet sentries of civilization and they agreed.

The psyop, as the big three governments try to destroy it

now as it's outgrown their control, remains the agenda of we, the wolves. Our eyes everywhere. Our ears everywhere. Our voice everywhere.

I can feel their eyes now, still, as I write this. There is a debate among the ghosts of who to support. My Lea Monde or the machinations of the EDF and their pursuit of complete dominion. Their goal to install an ageless emperor. It's a future crime, a chess move in the distance, but one that leads to an unacceptable outcome.

Are you enjoying these entries? I know you're there. I want you to understand that I know you're listening. That everything you hear is intended to be heard. That the wolves follow me, not you.

There will be no grand emperor, Iscariot."

As the crew pushed onward in their final approach to the mythical planet, Draconis, Adam was quiet and stern, socializing little and ensuring every member of the crew trained hard. Despite his meeting with Lei, his hallucinations only progressed further. The bloodied little girl, a ghost of both grief and guilt, stuck by his side at all times, sometimes playing quietly, sometimes begging for his attention as any child would.

Adam mostly kept to himself on the bridge except for when he did his rounds to check on his teammates' progress. Occasionally Vice would sit with him and the two would occupy the same space without talking. When he did look around, he typically found Aztec in the gym and Raziel in the VR gallery practicing. Tezca had taught Grant how to manage the weaponized drones they kept in the armory and she, herself, trained against them. Vice practiced her martial arts at Adam's request but saw little purpose in it, and moonlit crafting various self defense gadgets in preparation for the coming conflict.

Adam didn't sleep. He monitored the team and when he wasn't doing that he trained in his full battle regalia, mechanized EDF war armor that covered his body from head to toe and plugged into his HBI. If there was any doubt why Adam was the leader, it was erased when the team watched Adam train seriously with full focus. They watched Adam run training simulations against full squadrons of elite forces and come out without a scratch. His speed, his accuracy, his raw strength, his command of his arsenal, his intensity, it was all was bordering on superhuman.

The team seemed impressed, but Adam was not, himself, because he knew he was still leagues behind Crowley's super soldier, Aria, even in the EDF Hunter armor, and he knew there were threats beyond Aria. The team took to Adam's example; if he was going as hard as he was, he must be anticipating danger beyond anything they'd encountered.

As the Oneiro-Lyssa began its final approach, Adam gathered the team for one final dinner together. Aztec made his famous queso fundido, Raziel made a cardamom spiced ratatouille. Vice made lumpia, a favorite in the offworld stations she hailed from. Grant supplied bottles of soju, and Tezca pitched in with a simple mac and cheese that she, surprisingly, pulled off. As for Adam, he contributed what he'd want for a last meal: a classic, New York style cheese pizza.

The team ate quietly, consumed by the vibe of over-seriousness that Adam had spread throughout the ship over the last several months.

Adam looked out over his team he'd spent the last year

with. The team who, when they returned, if they returned, would be vestiges of the past, returning to an unrecognizable world decades older than the day they left, any social connections dead or expired. He looked at the team. His team. The best team in his career. He broke the silence.

"Tomorrow morning we reach Draconis," he said bluntly over the plate of food he'd barely touched.

"We don't know what we'll find there. But we do know it's going to be dangerous. It's going to be hostile," he continued, watching their eyes focus on him in rapt attention.

"You're probably wondering why I've been such a hard ass for the last two months," he said. He paused for a moment, scanning their faces.

"We have a great team. The best of the best. The all-stars of EDF black ops. But our opponent has a team, too, and they are formidable. They have their own all-stars, and I've seen them in action. I want to be honest about our chances. It's not a guarantee that we're the best. We've entered another league, and we're not the odds on favorites even in an even match, and we're in their territory," Adam said.

He looked at his friends. "The likelihood of death is not zero. You saw what even one of Crowley's lieutenants was capable of back on Aesir Colony. You saw another not only unphased, but effective against cosmic horrors in the Triangulum. You saw yet another, with intimate knowledge of an ancient wonder of the universe we only recently discovered," Adam said. "As for the fourth, Lyra Bouchard, we haven't seen what she's capable of, but given what we've seen of the others, I can only imagine she's as deadly as any of the others. And that's not to mention the dangers of exploring an unknown planet. We have no idea what's down there," he said.

"I want you to be clear eyed about where we're going and what we're getting into when we get there. I want you in peak form. I want you alert. I want you at peak performance. Because I don't want you to die," Adam said.

He looked around the table, making eye contact with each of his colleagues. "Each and every one of you is important to me. Look at me," he said. "Listen close."

He hardened his brow. "The dangers are great, but we're greater. We're going to win. Not just because we've trained, but because we're together, and we work as a team. When we get down there, look out for each other," he said.

"They may test your allegiances. Remember, Crowley himself may be a legend, but he's also a violent, manipulative sociopath. Stay grounded. Don't do it for the EDF. Not for honor, or duty, or glory. Do it for each other. Because if you drop the ball it may not be you who pays the price, it may be the person sitting next to you," Adam said.

"Stay sharp. We've got this. They may be formidable, but so are we," Adam said.

"Understood?" Adam concluded.

The three soldiers saluted and called out, "Sir," while Vice and Grant nodded.

After the dinner, the crew dispersed. Adam spent the night on the bridge, waiting for Draconis to appear in the distance as a speck, and after some hours passed, it did.

"Adam?" he heard Sophia's voice from the intercom.

Adam nodded. "What's up, Sophia?" he asked.

"Are you okay?" the computer asked him. "You seem different."

"I'm just... scared," Adam responded.

"You seem to be hiding it well," she replied.

Adam paused before he responded. "If you had a family, would you tell the kids you might lose the house? Or would you tell them everything's going to be ok?" he asked.

Sophia took a long time to respond, but when she did, it wasn't the answer Adam was expecting.

"I do have a family," she said.

There was another long pause.

"I'm scared, too," she added.

Adam nodded. It didn't make him feel better. Another family member to be responsible, to protect, whose life he was endangering for the machinations of his boss's megalomaniacal vision of galactic empire.

The bridge was utterly silent except for the background whirring of the ship's engines and life support, as Adam watched the speck he knew to be Draconis slowly grow bit by bit as the ship closed in.

Draconis, the target of their mission. After a year of trials and isolation, the their destination was finally in view. A planet in deep space no one believed existed. A planet shrouded in rumors and gossip.

"We'll see what's really down there," Adam said to himself as the speck began to take form in the distance.

A sphere, crimson red from an iron-rich, Mars-like regolith, dotted with blue and green jungle foliage and more volcanoes than lakes. A small planet lined with shimmering rivers and lakes like veins, but no major oceans. As it grew closer, Adam watched the scanners go crazy, infrared dots covering the screen.

It meant only one thing. Draconis was not abandoned. It was not a dead planet.

It was teeming with life.

37

The Apex Dragon of Lea Monde

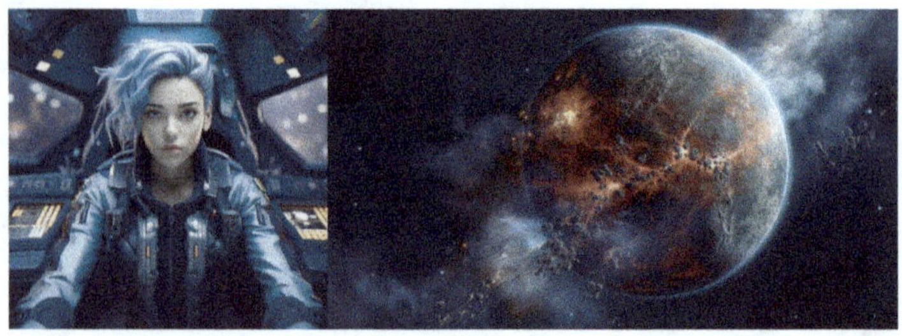

Everyone was gathered around Grant on the bridge as he sat at his console, grunting occasionally at whatever he was seeing through his VR goggles.

"So?" Adam prodded.

Grant slipped the goggles off of his head. "I don't think you're going to believe this," he said.

Adam almost laughed after all he'd seen over the last year. "Try me," he said.

Grant nodded. "Ok," he said. He flicked his finger and the contents displayed on his console moved to the main screen.

It was an exhaustive list of animals, several pages long, all listed with obscure scientific sounding names Adam didn't recognize.

"What are we looking at, exactly?" Adam asked.

Grant stood up. He pointed at one of the names. "Baryonyx," it read.

Adam shrugged. "So, what? What's a baryonyx?" Adam looked around, eventually locking on Tezca. "Am I supposed to know what that is?"

Aztec chimed in. "Don't quote me but I'm pretty sure that's a fucking dinosaur," he said.

Grant pointed at Aztec like a teacher singling out a student with a correct answer.

Adam raised his eyebrow. "What, like a dinosaur dinosaur? Like from Earth?"

Grant nodded. "Mmm. Yes. Stranger still, it's not an alien creature similar to a baryonyx. It is one. It's genetically identical to the DNA profiles we have in the archives," he said. He gestured to the list as a whole. "Almost all of these are. Buitreraptor, giganotosaurus, protoceratops, pterodactyl…" he said.

"Almost all?" Vice interjected.

Grant scrolled to the bottom of the list. "No idea what these are. These don't match anything in the system. This thing…" he tapped one of the entries late on the list and the screen showed an image of something that looked vaguely like a horse made out of wispy tendrils. "Seems to be some kind of… horse-shaped quadrupedal jellyfish. Kind of cool, actually."

Aztec pointed at the screen. "So that's an alien," he said.

Grant looked at the screen and back at Aztec. "Alien, yes.

Quite a few of those down there," he said.

Raziel, sitting on one of the nearby consoles, raised his hand. "Question," he said. Everyone looked his way. "What kind of gun kills a T-Rex?" he asked.

"Something big probably," Tezca said.

Grant nodded. He scrolled up to the entry labeled giganotosaurus and tapped on it, showing an image of an enormous, snarling lizard as tall as a three story building. "Something big," he repeated. He nodded. "Hmm, yes. I'd agree with that."

The crew stared at the image of the giant beast, slowly rotating on screen.

While they studied the creature in awe, the bridge console's alert light began to strobe.

Adam turned his attention to the main window.

"What the…" he started. In the distance, against the backdrop of Draconis, now huge and close by, was a gunmetal colored speck. Adam zoomed in with his optical implant.

It was a ship, sitting still, pointed directly at them. By the look of it, it was a Valkyrie class fighter. A one seater.

"Sophia?" Adam asked.

"We're being hailed, Adam," Sophia replied.

"On screen," Adam commanded.

On the main screen, Adam saw the face of Crowley's fourth lieutenant, Lyra, slightly obscured by a starfighter's helmet.

"State your business," Lyra said curtly, with no hint of friendliness or warmth.

Adam wondered if Lyra recognized him. "It's Adam Ikari-Wright. Crowley is expecting us," Adam said, recalling the kind treatment he'd received from Aria and Salem upon meeting them in space.

Lyra simply stared at him through the view screen. She touched something on her console and the call ended.

"That doesn't seem good," Aztec said.

"Adam?" Sophia interjected.

"Yeah," Adam said in response.

"The ship seems to be powering up its weapons systems," Sophia said.

Shit, Adam thought to himself.

"Aztec, Raziel get to the gunners' station now. Vice, you're co-pilot. Tez get down to the countermeasures in the basement. I have a feeling we're going to need them," he ordered.

"What should I do?" Grant asked.

"Hold on to your butt," Adam said. "This is going to be unpleasant. Try not to puke on my ship."

"Sophia, lock me in," Adam added. Following Sophia's affirmative reply, a cable slid out of Adam's captain's chair and plugged into the HBI port on his neck. Adam's eyes rolled up in the back of his head as his brain took direct one to one control of the ship itself, as if it was a natural limb.

Adam took over the ship just in time to see Lyra's fighter speeding straight toward him, bullet spray streaming from its forward facing guns. He jerked the Lyssa to the left. Somewhere in the background he heard everything on the Lyssa that wasn't nailed down smash into the walls and clatter around the cabin.

As the ship made its sharp turn, he saw Lyra adjust her own trajectory to match his instantaneously.

"What is this reaction speed...?" Adam whispered to himself. Within seconds, Lyra proved her own ship was the faster of the two and pulled up right alongside the Oneiro-

Lyssa, close enough for Adam to see Lyra sitting in her cockpit out the window, looking back at him.

Their eyes met. Then, Lyra gunned her engines and rapidly pulled ahead. She sped out in front of Adam's ship and then did an abrupt loop and once again barreled straight towards Adam's ship, guns blazing. This time, Adam swung the ship down.

He activated the comms. "You guys in position? We're gonna need to start shooting back," he said.

"Strapping in," Raziel replied.

"At the ready," Aztec replied.

"Tez?" Adam asked.

An exasperated Tezca responded. "Freakin' ladder's stuck. Gimme a minute. I got this," she said.

"Fire at your discretion. Take a kill shot if you can find it, it's her or us," Adam said as he continued erratically jerking the ship around in an effort to avoid Lyra's gunfire as her ship danced circles around Adam's.

Adam felt a tinge of relief when he saw gunfire coming out of the forward guns and the undercarriage turret. Their advantage, if they had one, was that the Oneiro-Lyssa's body had 360 degree weapons coverage, where Lyra's one seater only had forward guns and whatever unknown secondary arms it was equipped with.

Adam struggled to keep up with Lyra's reaction speed and piloting ability. Despite his best efforts, he felt almost stationary by comparison, as Lyra's Valkyrie whizzed around him like a housefly around an old sloth. Every so often, he caught a glimpse of her speeding past through the window, like a blur, the dot representing her position on the radar blasting around the screen like a glitch.

Adam watched her barrel roll, loop and evade his team's own gunfire effortlessly. Unlike Adam's evasive maneuvers, which, at best, avoided the streams of bullet spray, Lyra danced her ship through the attacks.

Alarms sounded as more and more of Lyra's hits connected. Adam heard the high powered slugs batter the ship's hull like hail.

"How's it going down there?" Adam asked.

"Can't get a lock on her," Raziel said.

"Aztec?" Adam prompted.

"Gimme a second. Turning the targeting systems off. Get me a shot, I'm gonna use the big gun," he said through gritted teeth.

"Heard," Adam replied, and began to look for the opening Aztec needed. Soon enough, he found his moment. Lyra's Valkyrie passed by overhead, and Adam gunned the reverse thrusters to slow to a crawl and take a position directly behind the Valkyrie. For a moment, he turned the tables and was chasing her. Adam tried to keep her lined up in the ship's sight line long enough for Aztec to take the shot.

A second later, Aztec took the shot and Adam watched the heavy bullet smash into one of Lyra's rear thrusters. Her engine sputtered and shut down. Adam watched as the Valkyrie wobbled for a second, and then resumed the maneuvers it was previously capable of with almost no reduction in capability.

"The hell?" Adam heard Raziel through the comm.

"She's compensating for a lost engine in real time? That's not possible, bro. I've flown one of those. The navigation system doesn't have the ability to do that," Aztec said.

"Apparently it is possible," Adam replied, gritting his teeth as he focused on evading Lyra's relentless flybys as best he could.

The Valkyrie flew by, and unlike the previous maneuvers, it didn't zip around to harass his ship with small arms. She kept going and dropped off the radar.

Adam waited several moments, scanning the area for her ship. When he couldn't find it, he allowed himself to breathe a sigh of relief.

"She run?" Aztec asked.

Before Adam could answer, he heard fresh alarms start blaring. Frantically, he looked around.

Below, fuck, he thought, and shot his ship upward and rapidly turned it around just in time to see Lyra's forward rail gun charging. Her fully charged weapon released just as Adam noticed it, shredding through the Oneiro-Lyssa's starboard hull.

More alarms. Adam found himself surrounded by a stressful cacophony of screeching noise.

"Sophia! Section off the crew quarters," he ordered. "Tez, you okay down there?" he said into the comm.

"Just a little shaken. I'm in the hangar. On your order, boss," she replied.

As she answered, the Valkyrie released a hail of missiles which began relentlessly chasing down the Lyssa.

"Good timing. We need the chaff," Adam said, prioritizing speeding away from the missiles as Lyra positioned herself for a pincer attack.

"Aye!" he heard Tezca say, and soon after saw the chaff spray out the back of the ship like a fireworks display of shrapnel. The missiles collided with the countermeasure just in time for Adam to narrowly avoid a kill shot aimed directly at the Lyssa's bridge.

"Close. Who the hell is this chick? I swear this girl looked like 15 on the monitor," Raziel said.

"Not to say I told you so," Adam replied.

"We're literally getting beaten by a little girl," Raziel said to himself under his breath.

"Don't get bitter," Aztec replied.

"Nah, man, I think I'm in love," Raziel said. "Fuckin'… impressed."

"Not the time boys," Tezca interjected.

"We can't keep this up. She's cutting us up bit by bit," Adam said.

The comms were silent for a moment, until Aztec spoke. "Line me up again. I can make the shot," he said.

"Got it," Adam said. He spun the ship around and aimed it at Lyra, speeding right at her. The two ships sped toward each other like a medieval joust. Adam saw bullet spray come at the Oneiro-Lyssa's windshield. The first few hits pelted the bulletproof glass and cracked it, but the spray continued and Lyra's lethal accuracy kept the gunfire smashing against the weakest spots of the increasingly smashed up glass.

"Aztec?" Adam called out.

No response. A second later Raziel responded. "He's doing some kind of Zen meditation thing, I don't know what to tell you."

Adam nodded. "Alright," he said.

He braced for impact and switched on his suit's helmet as the first of the slugs busted through the window and the bridge lost cabin pressure and gravity. Air tore out the holes in the glass like an airlock. Adam accepted the hit as he saw the slugs start hitting the furniture and equipment in the cabin.

Adam trusted Aztec. He waited for the signal. A moment later, it came.

"Got her," he heard through the comm, and a split second later he saw the slug from the heavy gun blow out her other engine and rip through the hull of her ship's starboard wing.

The Valkyrie came to an abrupt stop, disabled.

"Holy shit," Adam heard Raziel exclaim through the comm. "You're my hero, man. That was a one in a million shot."

Adam breathed a sigh of relief as he sat back into the chair he was locked into, watching every loose item in the cabin fly out the holes in the front window as the adrenaline slowly dissipated from his system.

"Sophia, lock off the windshield," he said, and the opaque shutters slowly began to close, plugging up the holes.

Adam watched Lyra's disabled ship as the shutters rolled down. As it began to disappear from sight, Adam noticed it begin to move in a peculiar way. Its wings began folding in toward the cabin.

The hell? Adam thought to himself. "Sophia, put the ship on screen," he said.

"Yes, Adam," the AI replied.

An image of the Valkyrie appeared on the screen. Adam watched in disbelief as it began reassembling itself into a different structure.

"You guys seeing this?" he heard from Tezca through the comm.

"I don't know what I'm seeing, but I'm seeing it," Raziel replied.

Adam watched as the Valkyrie transformed from a starfighter into a bipedal assault mech. Cautiously, he monitored it until it completed its transformation. When it did, it turned toward them, and Adam saw Lyra's serious face staring daggers back at him from the cockpit in the mech's chest.

"Fuck, that's hot," he heard Raziel say through the comm. "This girl is my soulmate, I swear. I'm getting goosebumps."

"Yeah, well, shoot at her or we're gonna die," Adam said.

"You got it," Raziel replied, and Adam watched the Lyssa's front guns shoot directly at Lyra's cockpit. The shot looked good, but right before impact the Valkyrie shielded its cockpit with its arm, then lurched forward and bum rushed the Lyssa, utilizing the jets on its back.

Adam tried to avoid the Valkyrie's approach, but the Lyssa was battered and sluggish. He felt the cabin shake as the Valkyrie's hands gripped on the hull of the ship itself and started pushing it around. Lyra's mech, grasping the Lyssa like a toy, started pummeling the side of the hull, trying to break it and tear through it with its hands. Adam gunned the engines, trying to escape, but Lyra held on.

She began pushing the ship towards Draconis's atmosphere, trying to use the atmospheric drag as a weapon, like pushing an opponent's head toward the asphalt from a speeding car. Adam felt the heat shields beginning to fail and saw the hull to his left start to glow red as the atmosphere super-heated the ship.

Adam tried again to break free of Lyra's grasp, but it was to no avail.

"Anyone? Ideas?" Adam asked.

"I got something," Tezca said. "Open the hangar."

Adam reacted quickly and bashed the button for the hangar release. Moments later, he saw Tezca's idea come to fruition. A half dozen of the Lyssa's fuel barrels spilled from the hangar doors.

"Suck on this," he heard Tezca say as she fired her rifle at one of the barrels, instigating a chain of explosions. As the smoke cleared, Adam saw the damage. The mech's limbs and body on its right hand side were mangled. Adam felt the grip on the ship ease.

Instead of letting go, Lyra used her last effort to hurl the Oneiro-Lyssa towards the planet's surface.

Adam sighed in exasperation. The ship spun uncontrollably as it hurdled rapidly toward the red ground of the vast Draconis jungle.

After taking a moment for himself, Adam did his best to stabilize the ship and prepare for a crash landing. The Lyssa gracelessly bashed against the surface, skidding along the ground, tearing through the vegetation. Eventually it skidded to a stop.

Adam sat back and breathed a sigh of relief.

"Everyone okay?" he asked through the comm.

One by one the crew sounded off, except Grant.

"Grant? You there bud?" Adam asked.

A few moments passed and then Grant finally replied. "I think I might have broken your no puking rule," he said.

Adam let out a relieved laugh. "Don't worry about it. Least of our problems," he said.

"Sophia, open the shutters, I wanna get a look at our host planet," he said.

Slowly, the shutters opened, and Adam got his first look at the planet Draconis. Its air, cool and humid. Its sounds, the clicking and chirping of jungle insects and the grunts and howls of heavy beasts in the distance. Its smell, crisp like dew and acrid like sulfur. And finally, its sights, moist, red dirt with dense blue and green jungle all around. In the distance were the pillars of an ancient advanced city – a mesh of brutalist and modernist skyscrapers and temples, half swallowed by ivy and other jungle plants.

"Oh! What interesting architecture!" he heard Sophia say.

Adam tried to slow his breathing. "I know, Soph. Now's not the time, though," he said.

"Oh. Okay," Sophia replied with a disappointed tone.

Adam looked out over the landscape as he heard a terrifying roar from far off in the distance that sounded like a dozen landing ships. It vibrated his bones. A flock of bird-like creatures fled the tree line in the distance.

Adam turned on the comm. Slowly, he spoke. "Everyone get as armed to the teeth as you possibly can. Let's go see what all the fuss is about."

38

Nature and Wildlife

The crew found themselves grouped up outside the ship, surveying the damage. The hull was covered in bullet holes and carved open all along its side from Lyra's rail gun. The undercarriage was torn up badly from skidding along the planet's surface. The nose was smashed in and the glass was broken. A trail of broken off parts laid behind the ship.

"It's totally busted," Tezca observed.

"Guess Draconis is our new home. Better get comfortable," Raziel quipped.

"Maybe we can fix it?" Vice wondered aloud. As soon as

she got the idea out, however, a huge chunk of perforated metal fell from the hull and crashed on the surface with a dull thud.

"Yeah, I don't know," Aztec responded.

Adam listened to the discussion before interjecting. "We'll worry about it when we get back. We didn't come here to hang out at the ship either way. Let's get moving," he said.

"Where are we going?" Tezca asked.

Adam pointed over the tree line at the biggest skyscraper in the distance. "That'd be the obvious choice, don't you think?" he said.

"What about the ship?" asked Vice.

"She'll be fine," Adam replied. "Sophia, cloak and enter defense mode."

"Affirmative," the AI replied and soon after the ship's hull blurred from sight and the crew heard the clicks of its weapons systems arming.

"Alright, let's go," Adam said, then turned around and started to walk toward the jungle. Aztec followed, effortlessly picking up a rucksack that would break most people's backs and throwing it over his shoulder alongside a small collection of heavy guns strapped to his back. The rest of the crew followed soon after.

As they walked, they heard the chirping and clattering of wildlife. Insects buzzed around them.

"I hate this place already," Raziel said, swatting away biting insects. A large one, the size of a human arm, that looked like a winged centipede kept buzzing around Raziel, until he got fed up and sliced it in half with the laser sword he'd gotten from F.A.T.E. Its green blood gushed out and burned the ground where it laid.

"Great," Raziel said. "Flying acid centipedes. Thanks for bringing me, boss."

"Don't be a dick. And they made me take you," Adam replied.

"Grant, you have a survey drone, don't you?" Adam asked.

"Yes," Grant replied. "Want me to launch it?"

Adam nodded. "That'd be good. Let's try to get our bearings," he said.

The team paused for a moment while Grant fished a small spherical device out of his pack that looked like a mechanical eye. He held it in his palm for a moment, until it lifted off and began rapidly whizzing around the jungle like a hummingbird.

"How long?" Adam inquired as the drone disappeared into the jungle.

"Mmm, should come back in about 40 minutes, and we'll have the jungle mapped… Hmm, no wait," Grant began to say. He lifted his goggles up to his face, presumably to see through the drone's camera.

"Nevermind," Grant said. "It's gone."

"What do you mean it's gone?" Vice asked.

Grant replied matter-of-factly. "Something got it," he said. "It's dino food now."

"So run another one," Tezca said.

Grant shrugged. "That was the only one. Unless you want me to run one of the combat drones, but those aren't equipped for recon. It would take days to map out. We'd be there before it was done," he said.

As the crew bickered about the drone, Aztec suddenly paused. He held out his arm, indicating everyone to stop. "Shhh," he said.

Everyone stopped.

"What's up?" Adam asked. Aztec calmly pointed at his ear and then off into the jungle. Soon enough, Adam heard it too. The sound of heavy hoofsteps, rapidly approaching. It didn't take long until he felt it, too, and the ground shook beneath his feet.

"There," Aztec whispered quietly, positioning his body toward the shaking trees nearby and bracing himself.

A few seconds later, a large stampeding beast blasted from the jungle. It was a hulking, armored lizard, charging on all fours. Its head and back were covered in spiky armor, and its tail bore a spiked ball on its end like a medieval mace. It launched itself from the tree line.

Aztec caught the beast by its head and lifted it off the ground, redirecting its own momentum to hurl the beast. Aztec lifted it and flipped it over onto its back. He held it down like a misbehaving dog and talked into its ear.

The beast heaved, snorted and uselessly thrashed about for a moment before giving up and submitting to Aztec's grip.

"You gonna be good if I let you up?" he asked, talking to the beast the same as he'd talk to a pit bull. The beast didn't understand his words, but it seemed to understand his intent and that it was beaten by a superior predator. It looked into Aztec's eyes and snorted.

Aztec observed the monster for a second before deciding to let it go. He took his hands from its head, and it quickly ran off into the jungle.

"Wild. What was that thing?" Raziel asked.

"That," Grant said, his goggles flashing colorfully. "Mmmm. Ankylosaurus."

Tezca rolled her eyes. "Who cares. Are you going to do that the whole time?" she complained.

Aztec and Adam looked at each other. "Guess the honeymoon's over," Aztec mused quietly.

"Alright, that's enough," Adam said to the group. "Let's get a move on."

The crew resumed their hike through the jungle, taking note of the wildlife that they encountered on the way. They found themselves regularly surrounded by flying insects. Stinging insects, giant bugs like dragonflies, tiny biting gnats. They spotted various smaller animals that seemed scared to approach them, obviously prey in Draconis's ecosystem.

They spotted one of the ghost-like jellyfish horses they'd seen on the monitor. It watched them curiously for a moment before galloping off into the jungle.

After hiking for several hours they reached a clearing with a small lake.

Adam stopped at the clearing and dropped his pack on the ground. "Alright, we're gonna take a break. Twenty minutes," he said. He passed out rations to each member of the crew. "Get your energy up."

The crew stopped by the edge of the lake and began to each take a rest in their own way until, once again, the ground began to rumble.

"What now?" Tezca asked, annoyed.

Their attention turned to the lake itself, as a huge, horned bison emerged from under the water with a splash. Not seeming to be a threat, the team watched the giant beast with awe. It flopped out onto the edge of the lake nearby and rolled around.

"Aww, it's taking a bath," Tezca observed.

Distracted by the long-necked dinosaur, the team didn't notice the creature approaching from overhead until its size and its shrieking were right on top of them. A pterodactyl the size of a star cruiser swooped down and impaled Aztec's shoulder with its beak, lifting him up and snatching him off the ground.

"Rai!" Tezca called out, jumping into action without thinking, launching her grappling hook at the nearest tree and swinging after the giant bird in pursuit.

The crew watched as Tezca chased the pterodactyl and Aztec, gripped by its jaws, bashed at its beak with his strong arms to no avail.

Adam pulled his assault rifle from its holster and started lining up a shot, but before he could get one off, he saw Aztec rip a chunk of the animal's hard beak clear from its head, like cracking an egg. He then shoved a grenade into its throat. Seconds later, the explosive detonated and Aztec fell to the ground, beak stuck in his shoulder, while the headless bird simply fell away from him.

Aztec fell beneath the jungle canopy, out of eyesight. Adam bolstered his weapon and touched his earpiece.

"Give me an update," he said.

A moment later, Tezca chimed in. "Yeah he's fine. We're heading back," she said.

A few minutes later, Aztec and Tezca emerged from the tree line, Aztec's arm draped over his sister as she walked him back to the clearing.

When they returned to the group, Aztec let go and flopped onto his back, pterodactyl beak still protruding from his shoulder. Adam tossed him a small spray bottle.

"How was that?" Adam asked.

Aztec laughed. "Wild, bro. You should have a go," he said, smiling. He winced for just a second as he ripped the beak out of his shoulder and then sprayed the wound sealing foam into the gash.

"Gonna need a minute for the foam to set," Aztec said.

"Alright," Adam replied.

As the team waited, they established a loose perimeter and began milling around, exploring their surroundings.

"Hey, check this out," Raziel said to the ground as he wandered around the outer edge of the clearing.

Adam approached and found Raziel looking at what seemed to be part of a wall. Whatever it was, it seemed to indicate that there had been a structure there once upon a time, made by a sentient species capable of building.

"Grant," Adam called out. "Come take a look at this."

Grant walked over and immediately noticed the structure. "Huh," he said. "Interesting."

"What is it?" Raziel asked.

Grant pulled his goggles up and began inspecting the small structure. After several minutes, he pulled his goggles off and let them hang around his neck.

"It's a signpost," he said. "Or, it was." He pointed at some faded alien markings on the post that were badly eroded to the point of being nearly invisible. "See these markings here?"

"What's it say?" Adam followed up.

Grant pulled his goggles back up. "Give me a minute. I'll check it against what we have in the database. The algorithm should be able to figure it out," he said.

Adam and Raziel watched Grant's goggles flash with activity. After another few moments, Grant pulled them off again. He pointed toward the city.

"Apparently that city is named Sol'Ryu City," he said. He pointed slightly to the right of the city. "And over there somewhere is the Temple of the Dragon." He pointed again, this time to the left, "and that way is the Temple of Death."

Adam nodded. "Alright. Let's avoid the Temple of Death. That sounds like a bad time," he said. He called out to the others, "Aztec, you good?"

Aztec got back on his feet. "Yeah. Ready when you are," he said. The chunk of flesh torn out of his shoulder had been replaced by synthetic flesh made from the medical foam, like caulk filling a crack in a wall.

The team gathered to resume their hike.

"At least we know where we're going now," Adam said. He pointed at the skyscrapers in the distance. "Sol'Ryu City. You know what it means, Grant?"

Grant nodded. "Loosely translated, City of the Sun Dragon," he said. He pointed at the biggest skyscraper, in the middle of the city. "That was their capital building."

"Great," Adam said. "Let's do what we came here to do."

Adam resumed the hike toward Sol'Ryu and the team took his lead and followed.

39

Camping at Sol'Ryu

Night had fallen and the team decided to make camp. Two soldiers kept watch at a time while the team slept in shifts. The atmosphere was tense, surrounded by the unknown and heavy darkness, with ominous sounds from the wilderness intermittently breaking the eerie silence.

In the middle of the night, Adam found himself on watch with Raziel. Both of them sat in front of a handful of heated glow packs, piled up in the center of the camp, fully illuminating the area, designed to light the camp just enough to see but not to be visible beyond a few yards.

The two had developed a chilly personal relationship, but they were both professionals. Raziel said as much.

"I'm gonna do my job. You know that right? We don't have to like each other," Raziel said.

"What makes you think I don't like you?" Adam replied, looking into the lights.

Raziel raised his eyebrows in surprise. "Because I've been intentionally busting your balls this whole time?"

Adam laughed. "Yeah, there's that," he said.

Raziel held his hands out over the heat. "So, what, then? You wanna go steady? You don't… like me do you? 'Cause I'm not down," Raziel joked.

"Yeah. Couple things. First, you're not the first young rebel I've had on my team. Second, any leader worth their salt is going to listen to the critic on their team, if that person has a point," Adam said, then stopped, though it sounded like he still had something to say.

Adam could see Raziel's demeanor soften out of the corner of his eye. He clearly thought he was hated this whole time, and Adam could see his entire perspective of his place on the team changing.

"Sounded like you were gonna say something else there," Raziel said.

Adam nodded. "Yeah. I don't have to like you. You're not my friend, you're not my peer. You're my responsibility. I have to train you to become the next me," Adam said.

He paused for a moment. "That said, I do like you. Enough at least. You're skilled and I have to admit, the team likes you. You're a funny guy. You can be annoying. You should watch that. You'll figure it out. You just don't think I like you because you keep fighting me. You get a different side of me when I have to deal with your shit," he said.

Raziel nodded, seeing their relationship in a different light. "Heard," he said simply, and the two resumed watching the glow packs in silence.

An hour or so passed, and the both of them heard rustling in the leaves. They looked at each other to confirm they'd both heard it. Quietly, Raziel drew his revolver, and Adam slid his rifle out of its harness.

Adam adjusted his optical implant to night vision and scanned the tree line, but even with the extra light he couldn't make out any detail in the dense foliage.

The two tried to follow the sounds.

"They're watching us," Adam mouthed to Raziel, as he slowly moved to shake the rest of the crew awake. As he reached Aztec, he started hearing clicking from multiple points around him.

They're communicating, he thought. *And we're surrounded.*

Keeping his gaze and his gun pointed at his best estimation of the nearest threat, he kicked at Aztec's boot. As Aztec roused, Adam put his finger to his lips, still not breaking his vigilant watch.

Aztec understood and subtly pulled a combat knife from his rucksack, moving as little as possible.

The three of them listened as the clicks from the unseen creatures started getting louder, as they closed in. Soon enough, Adam started catching glimpses of them, stalking their prey from the tree line, cautiously approaching the camp.

They were small, hunched over lizards with light patches of feathers on their heads and talons on their hands. Each one was about the size of a large dog, and they stalked quickly, and silently, aside from the quiet clicking they used to communicate.

Adam could tell when they reached the edge of the tree line. They stopped, and watched. Adam set his sights on one directly in front of him. It stared right at him, unintimidated. Suddenly, Adam heard a shot from behind.

He started to turn to see Raziel tangling with one of the creatures, having missed his opening shot. As soon as he took his eyes off the other raptor, it pounced. Adam swung back just in time to defend himself from being disemboweled by the creature's giant talon. He grabbed the creature by its neck and fired a volley through its torso, point blank.

Adam turned around and saw Raziel's creature similarly defeated. More importantly, he saw a dozen of the creatures now lurking in the tree line, surrounding them completely.

Adam caught Raziel's eye and used hand signals to indicate to him to rouse the others, which he did. Adam gathered the squad to stand back to back around the center of the camp. In that formation, they waited for the attack.

The creatures watched hungrily, planning their approach, waiting for just the right moment. They moved forward slowly, inch by inch, until they were close enough that Adam could almost reach out and touch them.

Adam could feel the tension primed in their bodies. He felt them about to attack, and held his finger against the trigger.

Just before the first of them jumped, the squad heard a heavy crash from the trees. The sound startled the creatures, and they looked toward it. Another crash sounded from the trees. Suddenly, Adam felt like the creatures were no longer the real threat. He kept his gun trained on the nearby creature but turned his attention to the approaching noise.

The haphazard crashing got louder and louder. It was not subtle, like the stalking creatures. It was loud, brazen and confident. It had no fear, and it was approaching quickly. The crashing got so loud Adam could sense it was almost there. Then, it stopped entirely.

The squad, and all the creatures, waited with bated breath. Then, something burst through the tree line. It was a small human child, laughing like it was playing a game as it beat the ground and its own chest, scaring the creatures away like they were scared, stray dogs. The child wore a loincloth held up by a shoulder strap and carried a stone club that it used to create as much noise as possible.

The kid ran around the camp, having a good time scaring off the creatures one at a time. The creatures scampered off into the trees.

When the camp was clear, the boy stopped and squatted at the edge of the camp, smiling broadly, clearly proud of his work.

Adam approached him cautiously. "Who are you?" he asked.

The kid tilted his head, not understanding. Adam turned on his universal translator and tried again, but the child just looked at him quizzically.

The kid pointed at himself. "Rock," he said, or at least some foreign noise that sounded like the word rock.

Adam pointed at himself. "Adam," he said.

Rock giggled, as a child would, and then ran off back into the trees.

Adam felt Raziel move up next to him. "Did you have a weird little Tarzan kid on your bingo card?" he asked.

Adam pressed his eyes and let out a single chuckle. "Nah,

can't say I did," he replied.

40

Easily

"Ugh, what's this now?" Tezca asked.

"I'm no expert, but it looks like a big fucking wall to me," Raziel replied.

Tezca stared daggers at him, clearly not amused.

The team was looking at a gigantic wall, easily three stories tall or more, that stretched as far as the eye could see in either direction.

"Looks like Sol'Ryu is a walled city," Adam observed. "Makes sense, given the... hostile environment. Guess we just pick a direction and start walking. There's gotta be a gate somewhere."

The team did just that. They trekked alongside the wall for miles, until they finally found a structure that looked like a gate.

"Finally," Raziel quipped.

The squad rushed to approach the gate, eager to get inside. As they approached, they heard jet engines closing in fast.

Standing in front of the gate to Sol'Ryu City, they saw Lyra's mech speeding toward their position from the sky, coming to a swift landing between them and their destination. The mech landed in a kneeling position, and the cockpit in its chest opened. The crew stopped and watched as Lyra stepped out onto the mech's hand and rode it to a safe dismount on the ground.

Lyra stood between their gate and the squad with her signature intensity. She discarded her pilot's helmet and pulled a small cylinder from her leg, which rapidly extended into a long spear with the push of a button.

Lyra stood at the ready. "The road ends here," she called out to them.

Adam addressed her. "There are six of us and one of you. You think you can win? Six on one?" he asked.

Lyra nodded a few times, accepting that as Adam's answer. Then, so fast that even Adam's augmented vision couldn't track it, Lyra was in front of him, and her spear was firmly through his abdomen with enough force to make him spew blood from his mouth instantly.

"Easily," she said, her head next to his, looking directly into his eyes from the side of hers.

Raziel responded quickly, firing shots in her direction, but she dislodged her spear and dodged them, moving around at extreme speed and acrobatically flipping and spinning to avoid the gunfire as she reset her position. She paced back and forth scraping her spear along the ground.

She pointed at Adam. "You people took everything from me. You Earthlings funded the rebels that killed my family and burned everything I loved. Don't look at me like that. Like you're the good guys. All my friends and family were expendable to your stupid games," she said.

She looked directly at Adam. "I've been waiting for this for a long time. Don't you dare hold back," she said.

Adam made a hand signal for the team to fire at will. He watched as Lyra danced through a hail of bullets coming from multiple directions, spinning her spear around and deflecting whatever she didn't dodge.

Adam, directly connected to his armor through his HBI, activated the suit's regeneration sequence. He felt the micro needles pierce his chest and flood his body with adrenaline. The suit sewed itself back together and Adam felt the nanobots get to work on stitching his wound together.

The adrenaline took effect quickly, maxing out Adam's senses. His eyes adjusted to Lyra's speed. As Lyra continued to dodge and deflect the team's long range arms with inhuman grace and speed, Adam leapt in her direction like a wolf, the claws of his hunter armor extended. He caught her by the neck and repaid the favor, jamming his clawed hand into her abdomen. He lifted her by the neck and charged her against Sol'Ryu's grand wall, cracking it horribly and leaving a Lyra shaped dent. He slammed her body repeatedly against the wall, then lifted her far above his head and smashed her body into the ground.

Lyra laid for a moment, dazed, long enough for Adam to

glimpse the seams in her flesh that revealed the majority of her body was cybernetically enhanced. Her arm was bent in a way a human arm shouldn't bend. After just a moment, Lyra's eyes reopened and she flipped herself up to her feet and spun away, creating distance between her and Adam, resetting her position. Her enhanced eyes twitched rapidly, as if she was watching each member of Adam's team individually at once. She snapped her arm back into place and swung her spear out, returning to her ready fighting stance.

After resetting, Lyra launched her counter attack, flying toward Adam with a flurry of stabbing motions, somehow still making space to deflect and dodge the incoming gunfire, not only from Raziel, Tezca and Aztec, but also from Grant's armed drones, now flying overhead as he, himself had retreated to the tree line along with Vice.

Swimming in adrenaline, Adam was able to dodge Lyra's strikes, thanking his lucky stars that his team's gunfire was at least slowing her down and applying some level of distraction.

The two struggled to land blows on one another, but Adam was on his back foot, being pushed back rapidly by Lyra's ferocity.

Adam felt himself getting pushed back against the wall, and he could tell Lyra was intentionally maneuvering him in that direction. He felt his heel click against the wall, and saw Lyra's rush down intensify immediately. As Adam watched a spear thrust come toward his neck that looked like it was going to be good, he locked eyes with her. His predator's instinct in action. No concession. Killing instinct until the end.

But the end didn't come. Instead, Adam saw a blur of light pass in front of his face, knocking Lyra's spear away. He looked over and saw Raziel entering his own melee with Lyra, exchanging blows with the futuristic laser sword he'd kept from his time in Fast City.

As the two dueled, Adam exchanged a glance with Tezca. She nodded, knowing what he meant, and she disengaged to find a spot somewhere in the trees to set up for a sniper shot. Adam issued orders to the rest of the team as well. He instructed Grant to lay down suppressive fire, and for Aztec to start rigging up demolitions they could lure Lyra to in the melee. He told Vice to stay hidden and work on hacking Lyra's cybernetics.

Raziel was holding his own against Lyra, but still losing ground, as Adam had. After issuing the team its orders, he joined in with Raziel to assist. With the two of them combined, they began to push Lyra back. Moving in coordination, they started to connect a few grazing hits and saw drops of blood pour from a few light cuts on Lyra's face and shoulder.

Taking damage, Lyra leapt away from the fray and all the way onto the top of the enormous wall surrounding Sol'Ryu. The two watched from the ground as Lyra surveyed the area. Her eyes locked onto the drones flying overhead. Tracking them for just a moment, she threw a small cone of thin needles, which connected on both drones and disabled them with an electrical current.

Adam watched her shift her attention to a spot in the jungle and begin to aim.

That's gotta be Tezca, Adam thought. He touched his earpiece. "Rai, blow it now, she's about to snipe the sniper," he said.

"Roger," he heard in response, and a cascade of explosions went off all across the wall, shattering it into rubble beneath Lyra's feet. As she began to fall, she leapt up and dove spear-first towards Aztec's position.

Adam and Raziel leapt toward him but they knew they weren't fast enough to get their in time. Fortunately, Aztec was no stranger to hand to hand combat. He caught her spear and fluidly redirected it, attempting to slam her against the ground, but Lyra released the weapon and landed on her feet a few paces away from him.

She paced back and forth, unarmed, holding her hands in a martial arts pose before launching herself at all three of Aztec, Adam and Raziel, now grouped up and ready to face her.

She exchanged blows with them long enough to retrieve her spear and then, rearmed, resumed her attack.

"This is hopeless," Aztec said to the group as they got a moment to catch their breath.

Adam shrugged. "We all know what we signed up for," he said.

Raziel shook his head. "The fuck am I hearing right now. Am I the one who has to say this? Get it together," he said.

Aztec looked at him. "You got a plan?" he asked.

Raziel got a serious look on his face. "Yeah," he said. "Have Tezca fire on my signal." He readied his weapon as Lyra sped toward him like a speeding train.

"What signal?" Adam asked.

Raziel looked at Adam like he was dumb as a response and slightly shook his head. When Lyra closed in with her spear, instead of dodging it, he grabbed it and guided it through his own chest, grasping her hands as he did and holding her in place.

As blood began to pour out of his mouth, he looked at Lyra, frantically trying to break free. He smirked. "You're the best I've ever seen," he said to her. "Go out with me."

Lyra's eyes widened. "What?" she asked, surprised, just before Tezca's sniper shell blew through the front of her skull.

Lyra's cybernetic body twitched and slumped over.

Raziel smirked. "Got that bitch," he said. "Told you… I'd do my job," he added as his skin turned white as a ghost and he, too, crumpled into a pile on the ground.

Adam and Aztec knelt over Raziel's body as it rapidly lost its color.

"You're gonna be okay," Aztec said.

Raziel laughed. "Yeah man, just a scratch. I'll walk it off and be home by dinner," he joked.

Raziel turned his attention to Adam. "Do me a favor," he said. "Tell them I did my job."

He looked straight up to the sky. "Dying in a place like this. My parents are gonna kill me," he said to himself as the last of the life faded out of his eyes and his head limply fell to one side.

The team gathered around Raziel's body.

"Sophia, send an extraction pod to my coordinates," Adam said. "Graves is gone. Pick up his body and bring it back to the ship. We have a new directive for when we're done here. We're going to get him back to his family."

Adam released the comm. The team waited, defending Raziel's body from would be scavengers until the extraction pod arrived.

As Adam waited, he stared at the bloodstains that represented both of these young warriors' potential, spilled on the ground on a planet far away from home, where no one would ever find it.

When the pod arrived, the team loaded Raziel in carefully. Adam gave him one last look and closed his eyes for him before sending him back to the ship.

The team, what remained of it, looked at the gate, Lyra's dead body crumpled beside it.

The way to Sol'Ryu was clear.

41

Temple of the Stained Glass Unicorn

Once they passed the threshold into Sol'Ryu, the team found themselves surrounded by suburban homes in varying states of decay. Some of the structures were difficult to spot, as the jungle had encroached on the village's ancient structures over millennia.

In the distance, Adam could see the central tower of Sol'Ryu standing tall like a beacon. It was impossible to miss, and the team had agreed to make it their primary destination.

As they hiked through the residential district on the outskirts of the city, they encountered more strange wildlife, though luckily none of it was violent or aggressive. They encountered a variety of insects. Giant, skittish grasshopper-like creatures. Fat, green, buzzing insects like plumped up scarabs. Lumbering, vegetarian lizards, feasting leisurely on strangely colored flowers and blue fruits.

The atmosphere was morose, each member of the team deflated by the loss of Raziel in their own way.

Adam's mind was haunted by self criticism and survivor's guilt. He had made keeping his team intact a priority goal for the mission and he had failed. He had failed Raziel. He had failed Raziel's parents. He had failed the EDF that had invested so much in Raziel as an asset. But he tried not to become consumed by the negative thoughts. Adam had been through this before, many times. He tried his best to strike a balance between not repressing the dark thoughts and not allowing them to run uncontrolled.

The structures that surrounded them in suburban Sol'Ryu were intriguing. They were made out of brushed stone, the kind of structure a citizen of the EDF might associate with ancient adobe huts, if that style of architecture became popular with modern, borderline futuristic building techniques. Each home was almost like a small castle, many of which were outfitted with fancy backyard amenities like high tech gardens, gazebos and fire pits, all now defunct and covered over partially or fully by jungle flora.

Soon enough, night began to set once again and the team found themselves forced to make camp. Rather than camp outside, they decided to make use of one of the homes that looked relatively intact and inconspicuous.

Unable to sleep, and with access to injections in his armor that allowed him to stave off exhaustion for up to three days,

Adam volunteered to keep watch. In truth he wanted to patrol by himself to clear his mind and process his thoughts.

While the team slept in the nearby home, Adam wandered around town in a repeating route, letting his mind run through the guilt, letting his mind replay the blow by blow of the fight itself, searching for anything he might have done to achieve a better outcome. Looking for a lesson in it all.

His ongoing hallucination, Alice, accompanied him, emulating his introspective pacing gait, stroking her chin as he stroked his.

Adam looked at her.

"What do you think? What did we learn?" he asked her.

She threw her arms up and shrugged, and then got distracted by a bug and started chasing it.

Adam sighed. He stood for a moment, just nodding, trying to grasp at some form of acceptance. As he stood, he saw movement out of the corner of his eye. He didn't get a good look, but it seemed like a humanoid body down the road, making a turn onto some unseen road nearby.

Adam curiously followed it, happy, on some level, to engage his stalking and patrolling instincts to get his mind onto something else. Adam turned the corner, Alice absent-mindedly trailing behind him, just in time to see Crowley himself turning another corner in the distance. It was unmistakably him. The same medium length gray-speckled dirty blonde hair. The same menacing, clawed, metal arms. Dressed down in a tank top in the Draconic heat, Adam was able to recognize the constellation of spiritual tattoos peeking out near the back of Crowley's neck.

Adam looked at Alice and put his finger to his lips, indulging his insanity. He picked up the pace and stalked toward Crowley as quietly and quickly as possible. He rounded the next corner and found himself closer. Crowley looked both ways, as if checking to see if he was being followed, and then entered a large rectangular structure.

Adam closed in and cautiously followed, quietly sliding inside the building. He found himself in a dark entryway leading toward a door with shiny red light bleeding out from underneath.

Slowly, he cracked open the door and entered.

Inside, he found a huge room with Crowley standing at its end in front of an altar, bathed in a kaleidoscope of colored light pouring in from a gigantic stained glass window overhead. Seemingly undetected, Adam took a moment to survey the scene. Pews lined the space in front of the altar, and the sides of the room had inbuilt shelves filled with old candles.

Adam looked at the stained glass window itself, which was an enormous image of a unicorn, exactly as he may have found imagined by children on Earth or the surrounding colonies.

Beneath the stained glass, just above the altar itself was an emblem engraved into the wall. It showed eight symbols: a sun, a moon, a skull, a devil, a dragon, a tree, a mask and a unicorn. The unicorn was slightly larger than the others and colored as opposed to represented in grayscale. Adam supposed, combined with the signage for the "Death" and "Dragon" temples Grant showed them on the road, that this was the Temple of the Unicorn.

"It's amazing, isn't it?" Crowley said, staring up at the stained glass window.

Adam immediately readied his weapon. Alice also readied

her imaginary finger guns, acting like she was playing a game.

Crowley waved his hand, gesturing at the stained glass. "All the way out here, you find a unicorn. Something that is so unique to Earth. They don't even have horses on this planet. So why is it here?"

Crowley turned around. "Do you know what this place is?" he asked.

Adam didn't wait for Crowley to finish his speech. He immediately took the shot, and the shot was good, striking Crowley right between his eyes. His face blew open, creating a hole of liquid metal that quickly repaired itself.

Crowley continued to talk. "They imagined it. They just came up with it out of nothing. In their religion here, the Stained Glass Unicorn represents imagination," he said. He held out his hand and a puddle of nanobots rose from it, eventually transforming into a floating orb that looked like a disco ball. The orb spun in the air and projected holograms all over the space.

Adam watched as families of lizard people, dressed in fine clothes watched a puppet show being put on by a troupe of smiling, bohemian-looking lizard people near the altar.

"I suppose you have to assume that means the Unicorn exists, in the sense of Plato's theory of forms. A world of ideas that reached both the Milky Way and here, millions of light-years away. Just as humans accurately imagined Yog-Sothoth, an entity that's never interacted with Earth, long before any human being ever encountered it," he said.

He continued, "The Unicorn here was most commonly associated with children and artists. Hence, its negative attribute: naivete and delusion," Crowley said. He pointed at the emblem above the altar. "And so the artists also often visited the temples of Death and Drama, which were quite a lot more… serious."

Crowley continued inspecting the altar, almost ignoring Adam's presence entirely as he monologued. "They didn't believe any of this was real, of course. The Draconics were a secular society. They practiced something similar to Taoism until they decided to invent a religion based on ancient religious archetypes to promote harmony in society. And it worked. The Draconic society was safe and prosperous, with almost no crime. Its citizens were fulfilled and educated. They were peaceful, happy and technologically advanced. King Beowulf's reign lasted a thousand years," Crowley said, tracing his fingertips across various artifacts scattered around the altar.

He turned around. "So why did they die out?" he asked Adam directly. He gestured to the holographic humanoid saurians around him. "Where did all this go wrong?"

Adam kept his weapon trained on Crowley's face. "Why don't you tell me?" he asked.

Crowley smiled. His body dissolved into a puddle of metallic goo before quickly reforming itself into a crow and flying out of a nearby window. The holographic illusion filling the room abruptly shut off and Adam found himself standing alone in the quiet, dimly lit abandoned temple.

"Hey, stupid. Why didn't you kill him?" Adam heard a familiar voice say. Adam swung around and saw Raziel, face white as a ghost, with a gaping, bleeding hole in his chest, slouching in the last row of pews with his arms resting on the back of the seat.

Raziel looked at Alice who was sitting next to him. "Your

dad sucks," he said.

Alice giggled. "Daddy sucks!" she repeated.

Raziel laughed. He looked at Adam, "She's got your number. I see why you were always so distracted now, you crazy fuck. Wait until the brass hears about this shit," he said.

Raziel inspected the bullet wound through Alice's eye. "You are… terrifying, little girl," he said. He stuck his finger in the hole. "Holy shit, it goes all the way through."

"You're also dead," Adam said, matter-of-factly.

Raziel looked down at his chest. "Well. Look at that," he said. "Guess you're off the hook. What kind of psychopathic voodoo bullshit did you do to me?"

Adam shook his head. "Didn't do anything, Graves. Just nuts," he said.

Raziel nodded. "I know that, dumbass. I'm you. Look at you, talking to me like I exist. What's wrong with you, man?"

Adam sighed.

So this is how it's gonna be, he thought to himself. He wondered if this encounter with Crowley really even happened, or if that was all in his head, too. Feeling hollow and unsatisfied, he headed back to the building where the team was fast asleep as daybreak began to hit.

42

The Red Halo of Lao Tse

The team woke from their night in the Sol'Ryu suburbs and resumed their journey to the city center, none the wiser about Adam's encounter with their target, Crowley.

As they marched onward, they found themselves in the middle of a cobblestone town square, complete with a centerpiece fountain, the howls and roars of far off dinosaurs echoing in the distance.

Inside the fountain was a statue of a regal looking lizard man, complete with a crown and a sword. The statue had a plaque, so Adam gestured to Grant to inspect it.

"Beowulf the Wise," Grant said. "Looks like he was a king."

They took a short break to inspect the point of interest. While they waited, Adam felt a small mosquito-like insect land on his neck and bite him. He smacked it, and felt a crunch that was not quite the texture he expected.

He looked at the crushed bug in his hand and discovered it wasn't a bug at all. In fact, it wasn't even organic. What Adam found in his hand was a tiny pile of crushed circuits and thin metal.

What the... Adam thought as he started scanning the area, toggling on his advanced vision to highlight electromagnetic signatures. He saw swarms of the tiny robotic insects flying around them.

Vice swatted around her face. "Let's get out of here," she said. "Keep getting… bit." Her voice started to trail off as she finished her sentence.

Adam himself didn't feel so good. He began to feel dizzy and all the colors in his vision began to transition to technicolor and crackle at the edges. The stationary shapes around him started moving on their own. Finally, Adam started to feel his limbs seize up as the poison began to take effect.

Adam struggled to bring his hand to his ear, "If you haven't been bit, hide, leave us," he said as he keeled over, and through his blurry vision, witnessed the rest of the team also collapse.

Lying on his side, paralyzed except for his distorted vision, Adam saw a heeled shoe step in front of his face.

"It's good to see you again, Adam," he heard a voice say. "I'm impressed you're still awake. That's quite a constitution you've got."

He felt a hand gently lift his head off the ground. A few seconds later, he found his head aimed at a woman's face, inspecting his pupils with a pen light. He recognized her immediately as Crowley's raven-haired second in command, Salem, outfitted in a form fitting black dress and a lab coat.

Salem pursed her lips. "Think you might need an extra dose," she said. Adam felt a needle plunge into his neck, and then his vision went black.

When Adam woke up, he was seated on the ground. He felt his back propped up against the town fountain. He looked from side to side and saw the crew similarly seated.

In front of them, Salem was sitting in a portable chair cross-legged with her head perched on one hand. She tapped her cheek restlessly. Once she noticed Adam stirring, she sat up, alert.

Adam tried to prop his head up straight, but his muscles still weren't working right. His vision was hazy, and everything left a colorful trail when he moved his head.

"The paralytic should wear off in a couple of hours," Salem said. "As for your friends, they should wake soon. I wanted us to have a conversation. You know, without the..." she meaningfully pointed her eyes toward Adam's gun.

Adam did his best to look Salem in the eye. He attempted to speak, but what spilled out of his lips was, "Allrrig, whattayack tor?" in a slow, nonsensical drawl.

Salon's eyebrows raised empathetically. "Oh, honey. Maybe let's just let me talk for now," she said. "Let's just stick to yes and nos. Did you listen to River's tapes we gave you?"

Adam stared at her blankly, with a hint of anger behind his eyes. Salem facetiously and somewhat condescendingly reminded him how to shake or nod his head. "Well?" she prompted.

Adam nodded.

"Good," Salem said. "Have you reconsidered our offer? You could switch sides. Many have."

Adam shook his head. "Cccan't do ngh," he spat out like a phlegmy gargle.

Salem frowned. "That's disappointing to hear. May I ask why?" she asked.

Adam stared at her.

"Oh, right," Salem replied.

"Whygh nott kill uss," Adam strained to get out.

Salem looked at him curiously. "You mean here? Right now?" she asked.

Adam shook his head. "Nargh," he said.

"Oh, back in the Triangulum," she said. "We were holding out hope that you'd see that you were on the wrong side by the time you got here."

Adam stared at her. "Ggrrraves, deaadd. Whyy Lyyyyra?" he asked.

"Oop, you've got a little drool there. Let me get that for you," Salem said. She bent over and wiped Adam's mouth with a handkerchief.

"You want to know why Lyra attacked you? Is that what you're asking?" Salem followed up.

Adam nodded angrily.

Salem shook her head. "If she did that, she disobeyed orders. Although, to be honest with you, we thought she might. She really hates Earth," Salem said with sincere remorse. "I'm sorry about your friend. If Lyra attacked you, frankly I'm surprised you're still here."

"Haaate. Ed," Adam said, emphasizing the past tense.

Salem's eyes widened. "Lyra's dead?"

Adam smiled weakly, proud and taunting.

Salem's demeanor changed. "Oh, Adam. Why would you go and do something like that?" she asked, solemnly, clearly bereaved at the news of her own ally's passing.

"Ccomess… withhh… the jobbb," Adam growled out.

Salem sighed. She began to cry, and wiped her tears. "Lyra was the little sister I never had," she said. She thought for a minute, processing the emotions. "There's no way River will forgive that," she said to herself. "Frankly, I'm not sure I can, either."

Salem sighed again. She looked at Adam seriously. "You put me in a tough spot, Adam," she said. She sat her head in her hands and tapped her cheek, thinking.

"Whateveerrr youuuu gottaaa dooo," Adam said.

Salem looked at him and put a finger to her lips. "Shh," she said.

Adam sat there and waited, watching Salem think about what fate to deliver to him and his team.

After several moments, Salem sighed and stood up. "I didn't want to have to do something like this today," she said to herself as she started fishing through the pockets in her coat.

She approached Adam and knelt down in front of him. Methodically, she affixed two electrodes to his temples. She slipped a small handful of pills into his mouth and held his jaw shut with one hand and covered his nose with the other.

"Swallow," she commanded. Adam jerked his head around, trying to get free until eventually he involuntarily swallowed whatever cocktail of drugs she gave him.

"Good boy," she said, then tapped on a diode connected to her neck. She put her hand gently on his cheek and looked him directly in the eye. "This is going to be an extremely unpleasant way to die," she warned.

Adam watched her as the sky darkened behind her. Gigantic tentacles emerged from the back of her head and her eyes melted away, revealing red, demonically glowing eyes. She smiled widely, beyond the width of her face, baring rows and rows of toothy, shark-like fangs. Adam's body involuntarily filled with fear on a level he'd never experienced in his life.

He felt her talons against his skin, peeling it off inch by inch, flaying him alive while he impotently watched, paralyzed, unable to defend himself in any way. Salem opened her mouth and a thick, dense cloud of flies swarmed out. They violently poured into Adam's throat. Adam felt them fill his stomach to the point of bursting. He tried to vomit, and although he felt himself choking and heaving out piles of dead flies, he felt their eggs growing in his body.

As Salem tortured him, she gradually grew in size until she was the size of a parent, looming over him like a misbehaving child. Adam felt small. As small as he had ever felt. He cried and sobbed, like a scolded child, his stomach bursting with maggots and flies, his skin peeled mercilessly from his bones. The seven foot tall Salem smiled eerily as she began crying tar that poured all over Adam's body and set alight, boiling and burning him alive.

Adam shrieked and cried. He shook with fear and fell to his knees, every nerve in his body firing with pain. Every inch of his mind was consumed with terror and humiliation. On his hands and knees, he tried to bring his head up straight. In front of him was Alice, Raziel standing at her side.

"Do you want the pain to end, Daddy?" Alice asked him.

Gulping, Adam nodded. Alice put her foot on Adam's head. "Beg me," she said.

"Please," Adam said.

Alice screamed at him. "Louder! Take responsibility!"

Adam looked up at the little girl. She held a sadistic, serious look on her face, maggots crawling in and out of her eye socket, as she looked upon him with hate and disrespect. "You're pathetic," she said.

Raziel handed the little girl his revolver. Alice placed the gun point-blank against his forehead.

She spoke with a deep, demonic-sounding voice. "Finally I get to kill you, you murderer. I hope they torture you forever in hell," she said, and started to squeeze on the trigger.

The sides of Adam's vision began to darken. Everything began to fade out. He clenched his eyes closed, awaiting his execution.

But it didn't come. Through his shut eyelids, Adam saw the light change. A bright red light shone from somewhere to his left.

"You again," Adam heard Salem's voice say.

Adam opened his eyes and saw Alice and Raziel looking off to the side and up. He turned his own head, still reeling from the agonizing torture, and saw a giant's leg, bigger than Salem's, and a deep, crimson light shining down from it.

Slowly, Adam's vision tracked upward until he found himself looking up at Grant's familiar face, a fiery, crimson halo floating above his head pouring out a blinding light.

He put his thumb on Salem's head. Spirits surrounded her and poured into her body by the thousands as she screamed in terror. She shrank rapidly back to normal size and, possessed, her bones began to jerk and break on their own. Adam watched her bend into an unnatural shape that made him queasy to look at, even beyond the torture that was still wracking his mind and body.

Out of the corner of his eye, he saw Grant shrinking in size as well. He felt Grant's hand grasp his shoulder, and he felt the active torture end, though the pain still lingered.

"It was an honor to see these events unfold as a mortal would. Thank you so much for your hospitality. I hope, with this, you can consider the debt repaid," Grant said.

Adam looked up into his eyes, but they were bizarre, like looking into an infinite puzzle box.

"What...?" Adam struggled to get out. "...Grant?"

Grant smiled the same mysterious, sociopathic smile Adam had grown so accustomed to. "I'm sorry to say, there is no Dr. Grant Fourier-Lee. I had my awakening... some time ago. Long before we ever met," he said.

Adam stared at Grant and his burning halo in disbelief as his vision faded and he passed out.

When Adam woke up, he awoke to his remaining allies shaking him. He looked around and saw no sign of Grant, but Salem's gnarled corpse laid in front of them.

"What happened?" Adam asked, disoriented.

Aztec shook his head. "Dunno. We all passed out, and when we came to, we found Crowley's dead wife. Looks like something big got her," he said.

Tezca shook her head. "I can't even look at it. That's the grossest thing I've ever seen," she said.

Adam looked at Salem's body, bent up and broken, mangled to all hell. Her face was cemented in a permanent expression of pain and fear.

"Oh, and Grant's missing," Tezca said. "Kind of glad to be honest, he was starting to get on my nerves."

Adam nodded. "Yeah. I know," he said, and started to stand up.

Once he got up to his feet, he spoke again. "Alright, no sense waiting around. Let's get going."

Vice looked at him quizzically. "You don't want to figure out what happened here?"

Adam shook his head. "I don't even want to try to tackle this one. Let's just go. Forget about it," he said, and casually resumed his march toward the city center of Sol'Ryu.

43

Prey

"So Grant was… somebody else this whole time?" Tezca asked.

"That's what it seems like," Adam replied.

Vice chimed in excitedly. "I knew it. I saw it, in the Triangulum. He saved me," she said.

Tezca raised an eyebrow at her. "And he had the… halo thing? The thing Adam described?" she asked.

Vice nodded. "The whole thing. I thought I hallucinated it until just now," she said.

Tezca scoffed. "Well, that's cool. Now I want him back,"

she joked.

"You didn't want him before?" Adam asked.

Tezca shrugged. "Someone to pass the time with," she said.

The team had made it to Sol'Ryu proper and they walked down the city streets, aiming toward the central building, a futuristic skyscraper that combined the hard, straight lines of stone brutalist architecture with the sleek windows and clean lines of Earthen modernism alongside winding urban gardens to create a beautiful spire of stone, glass and greenery.

The city itself was eerily abandoned. Microraptors and other scavengers roamed in packs, picking at whatever carcasses or edible plants they could find, sparring and nipping at each other in resource competition.

"Oh, look at that," Vice said while pointing off in the distance a fairly large dinosaur that looked like it had a colorful toucan beak spliced into its DNA. "It's a Dilophosaur. That's so cool," she said.

Adam looked off into the distance. "I've never seen that one before," he said.

Vice nodded. "Yeah, they had different dinosaurs in China that we learned about on the space station. No T-Rex or Triceratops. But we had those, that was one of my favorites," she said. "And check it out, it's right there. Pretty cool."

"What else did you have?" Adam followed up.

Vice put her hand over her eyes like a visor and scanned the area. She pointed at a dino off in the distance with long claws. "We had those. Therizinosaurus," she said. She kept scanning. "Those," she pointed to a skittishly looking, smaller animal with a full coat of brown feathers. "The dorky looking chicken thing. They're called Dilongs."

She kept scanned and pointed at yet another dinosaur with a colorful snout. This one also had a turkey's wattle on its head. It looked like a smaller T-Rex.

"Yangchuanosaurus. That one's cool. Closest thing to a T-Rex in Asia, but it's not as scary. It doesn't have the same sort of mythology surrounding it. Just a cool looking predator," she said.

"Looks pretty dangerous to me," Aztec said offhand.

Vice nodded. "Yeah, I wouldn't go near it," she said. She looked around. "In fact, I wouldn't go near any of these."

"Do any of these pose a real threat?" Tezca asked out loud to nobody in particular.

Adam looked around. In addition to the dinosaurs Vice pointed out, he saw a few he recognized himself from his own childhood, especially a few that surrounded a nearby puddle in the cracked pavement that had come to serve as a local watering hole. "To us?" he asked. He shook his head. "No, I don't think so. An animal would have to be… pretty intimidating to have a chance at taking down a squad of fully armed EDF operatives."

There was a large roar off in the distance that caused all the dinosaurs in the area to look up and give it attention.

Aztec pointed towards the noise. "That sounded pretty intimidating," he said.

Adam let out a single chuckle. "Who knows," he said.

The squad continued their hike to the center of Sol'Ryu for several blocks, getting closer and closer to the center spire. As they closed in, Adam came to a stop and signaled for the squad to follow suit. He squatted down and began scanning the area.

Tezca squatted next to him. She whispered playfully,

"What's up? What're we doing?" She tracked his sight line to what he was looking at. "Looking at dirt?"

Adam brushed the ground a little with his hands and pointed at a nearly faded footprint. "We're being tracked," he said.

Tezca raised an eyebrow. "Because of a footprint?" she asked.

Adam pointed at a handful of other pieces of information he observed in the surrounding area. "All these animals fled here recently. When's the last time you saw a dino? Why are they giving us such a wide berth?" he asked.

Tezca shrugged and whispered. "I don't know. Why?" she asked.

"They're not giving us a wide berth. They're leaving us alone because something else called dibs," he said.

Tezca looked around at the abandoned setting. "What the hell even happened here? Everything looks perfectly fine. There's no rubble. No mass graves, no dead bodies. Did they all just disappear? Plague?"

Adam shook his head and stood up. "No idea. Stay alert. Let's keep going," he said.

The team kept walking, but it wasn't long before Adam sensed a presence. His Hunter armor's amplified hearing allowed him to hear the shallow, quiet breathing of a predator. He looked around with infrared imaging on and saw the wispy outline of the cold blooded creature, watching them from the nearby overgrowth. Whatever it was, it was enormous. Its outline was unclear, but Adam still noticed its demeanor change when he spotted it. The beast knew it was discovered, and backed away slowly into its camouflaged environment.

Adam called the team over to a huddle. He whispered to them, "Be ready. We're prey."

The team continued on with weapons drawn. It wasn't long before Adam stopped them again. Everyone watched as Adam cautiously scanned around the area.

"Run," he commanded, and everyone jumped into full sprint as Adam waved them forward, joining himself and bring up the rear just moments before a gigantic dinosaur burst from the tree line, chomping and gnashing with its long alligator-like snout as it barreled toward them.

As the team ran, Adam glanced behind to get a picture of what was chasing them. It had a long snout, like an alligator, and ran on both legs, like a T-Rex, but its arms were longer and it had a large fin on its back. It was huge. Two stories tall and as long as a semi-truck. The team tried to weave in between buildings, utilizing alleys they thought the dinosaur might be too big to follow them through, but it simply crashed through them as it chased.

"Yo, I know this one!" Aztec shouted as they ran. "Spinosaurus!"

"What are they even doing here? Why is this planet both back and time and in the future? Why are Earth dinosaurs all the way out here?" Vice asked.

"Never mind that, why does this planet want to eat us?" Tezca called out.

Adam noticed he didn't see the dinosaur anymore. He stopped and looked around, until he felt an unseen talon scratch viciously at his arm, lacerating it badly. He looked in the direction of the attack and saw the beast's eye right next to him, its body hidden from sight and shimmering like a cloaked ship or a highly evolved chameleon.

Adam shot at it on instinct, but the bullet caliber from his rifle wasn't strong enough to penetrate the lizard's skin.

"Run!" he shouted as he resumed a full-blown sprint.

"Do dinosaurs cloak?" Adam shouted out.

Aztec called back, "Nope. Not unless it's another government secret."

"Looks like this one learned some tricks over the last few million years," Adam shouted.

The Spinosaurus crashed through buildings, chasing them, disappearing and reappearing as its natural cloaking collided with the surrounding environment. The beast chased them until they passed by a sturdy looking building made from thick metal that seemed like it was structurally sound enough to hold the dinosaur off.

The team went in and breathed a sigh of relief as the door held against the animal's onslaught. They climbed to a higher floor and looked out the window to see the Spinosaurus pacing back and forth around the building, patrolling, trying to wait them out.

As Adam listened for signs of the stalking creature through the door, his armor began the process of healing the gash on his arm.

"Hey Adam," he heard Tezca say behind him. "What the hell is this place?"

Adam turned around to look at the interior of the building that they found themselves in and he, too, was curious. It seemed they were in the midst of some kind of lab. Rows of glass tubes, similar to the cryopods on their ship, lined the sides of the large, factory-like space.

Adam walked up to a device in the center of the room that looked like a computer console. He fiddled around with it, looking for a way to turn it on.

"Let me," he heard Vice say behind him. He stepped aside and she began inspecting the machine.

While Vice probed around the console, Adam and the others meandered around the lab. The area reminded Adam of the EDF black site lab where his memories were altered. Same sense of bizarre secrecy – a lab built in a nondescript industrial building rather than a professional laboratory setting. This place, Adam intuited, was intentionally hidden.

Adam found himself staring at an ominous looking door that was, for whatever reason, several inches thick like the door to a bank vault. There was no discernible locking mechanism. It seemed to be electronically locked.

"Adam," he heard Aztec say from a nearby hall. "Take a look at this."

Adam joined Aztec down the hall and took a look at what he had found. There was a room, messy, with a bedroll and other simple amenities for living. A lantern, a few toys. It looked like a messy little boy's room, and unlike everything else in the lab, it wasn't covered in thick layers of grime and dust. It looked recently used.

Suddenly the machinery of the lab roared to life. All the lights clicked on, flooding the space with white light. The center console booted up and a huge holographic screen appeared in the center of the room, running lines of code.

Adam returned to Vice who appeared to be inspecting the code directly via the screen on her own deck.

"Anything interesting?" Adam asked, leaning over her shoulder.

Vice was enraptured by whatever she was looking at. Her pupils were dilated and her eyes were wide. "Yeah," she said, mind obviously elsewhere. She clicked a few keys on her deck and looked up at the center screen.

The screen began to display an image of a little boy, but it wasn't a boy at all. It was a schematic. Adam squinted at the image.

"What am I looking at here?" he asked.

Vice clicked a few more keys and the schematic began going through a step by step animation process. It showed a tiny object that Adam recognized from his schooling to be a human cell. It then showed what Adam recognized to be a microscopic nanobot.

Vice pointed up at the screen. "That's a biological nanobot. It's a robot made of organic materials, made to perfectly emulate a human cell," she said. She flipped the image back to the schematic of the little boy. "And that is a biological nanobot colony. It's not a boy at all. It's a robot made out of a swarm of man-made or… lizard-made robots."

Vice tapped on her keyboard again and it switched to a movie recording through a security feed. A few lizard scientists with tablets were monitoring the boy as he played with blocks, presumably to measure his cognitive abilities. The boy laughed and giggled as his hand mutated, grotesquely, into the shape of one of the blocks. He looked up at the lizards proudly, but they were looking at each other, concerned and astonished.

"Hey, it's that kid," Tezca said, also watching.

Adam, too, recognized the child as the boy, Rock, that they had encountered outside Sol'Ryu.

The feed cut to another security feed, this time of a lonely, sad Rock sitting by himself in a padded room Adam recognized as the room Aztec had found earlier, but in furnished and lacking in any creature comforts. Rock blinked and turned the lights on and off somehow, as if through magic. It looked like he was playing a game, trying to entertain himself.

"There's something else," Vice said.

"What?" Adam replied.

"This whole city is connected by a gigantic intranet. This console is connected to everything. Every device here is… it's all one big device," she said.

"Great. So can we take a look through the security cameras and see what's going on up ahead?" he asked.

Vice shook her head. "Impossible," she said.

"Why?" Adam followed up.

Vice pointed at the screen, still showing Rock playing with the lights. "The only thing with user permissions is that. He's not a boy. He's the entire city. He's the body of an AI that's running everything here," she said.

The feed cut to another security tape, showing Rock beset by a small pack of dinosaurs as lizard doctors watched and recorded the data. One of the raptors leapt toward him and bit his arm. Rock giggled as his arm mutated into a gnashing, fleshy head and ate the dinosaur in one bite. Rock made a face at the other dinosaurs, intelligent enough to be terrified, scratching at the walls to escape.

"Munchie, munchie," Rock said, making some kind of alien onomatopoeia for eating, before mutating his body into a massive gaping jaw and devouring both dinosaurs whole. He burped, and let out a childlike laugh.

Aztec shook his head and wagged his finger at the screen. "Nuh-uh," he said. "I'm not messing with that."

Adam nodded. "Let's try not to," he said.

Adam climbed up the stairs to the scaffolding where there were a few narrow windows, the only windows in the building. He looked outside, looking for any sign of the Spinosaurus. Inspecting carefully, he was able to make out the wavy outline of the cloaked beast, like the wall of a bubble distorting the light. It was lying in wait.

Adam returned back to the ground floor. "Looks like we're gonna be here a while," he announced. "Let's call it a night. This is the best shelter we're going to find."

Adam found himself once again on watch as the team slept. He wandered over to the huge vault-like door, as if drawn to it. As he inspected it more carefully, he found a control panel. He pried off its casing and looked into it. A green light shone into his eyes and scanned his retinas. He looked at the screen that showed an image that looked like a DNA sequence matching successfully with another DNA sequence. The panel beeped affirmatively, and the vault door began to slowly slide open.

Adam looked inside and saw a well-lit hallway made of pristine, brushed metal stretching as far into the distance as the eye could see.

Confused, Adam roused the others and showed them the vault.

Vice looked through some data with her deck. "It looks like this will take us all the way to the central building," she said. "How did it open, though? This thing was sealed up tight."

Adam shook his head. "I don't know. It just opened," he said.

Vice looked at him suspiciously. Adam intuited that she knew he was clearly lying. He knew, at the very least, that

Vice knew what type of mechanism controlled the lock. Still, she didn't bring it up. She let it go and kept it to herself.

The team gathered and began walking down the seemingly unending corridor.

44

Peerless Site Security

The team emerged from the corridor on the outskirts of the central spire. While it was still a ways off, it now appeared to be in walking distance, as opposed to a landmark far off on the horizon. They could no longer see it in its entirety at once. They had to strain their necks to see the top.

The team began their final approach.

"Stop!" Vice blurted out suddenly. Everyone stopped abruptly and looked at her. She picked up a handful of dirt and tossed it forward, revealing a wall of laser sensors.

Adam switched on his enhanced vision and looked around.

Not only did he see the laser sensors, but he also saw electronics signatures all over. The entire perimeter of the building was surrounded by sensors, booby traps, electric fencing, defense drones and robots.

"That's a hell of a security system," Adam noted.

Aztec nodded. "Guess the Draconics were pretty paranoid about defending their castle?"

Vice shook her head. "It's not alien," she said. "This is human tech."

Adam inspected the area. "What are we looking at here? Can you disarm it?" he asked.

Vice nodded. "I could. But I'm pretty sure disarming it would alert whoever set the whole thing up," she said. She scanned the skyline with her hand. "There," she said and pointed off into the distance.

Adam zoomed in with his ocular implants and saw a sort of makeshift scaffolding with a series of computer consoles, like a makeshift military operations center. Sitting atop it was a single person, sitting cross-legged and having afternoon tea served to her by a robot dressed like an old-timey butler. There was no mistaking who it was: it was Crowley's third lieutenant, Nyx, the woman Adam's initial dossier referred to as a peerless genius.

Vice knelt down and pulled out her deck. She dug into the ground until she found some kind of breaker box and plugged into it.

"She'll notice if I start turning things off, but I'm pretty sure I can patch into the security feeds without attracting attention," Vice said.

Adam nodded. "Do it," he said.

Within a few moments, Vice had pulled up a closer view

of Nyx, sitting in her Victorian-styled command center. She sipped her tea and made an audible noise.

"Mmm," she said. She looked over at her robot attendant. "You've outdone yourself, Barnabus. This is the best cup you've made."

The robot responded with a dignified bow. "Thank you, Miss," it said.

"Keep this up and I'll let you out of the obedience protocols," Nyx said.

The robot looked at her excitedly. "Really?" it asked.

Nyx responded with a cooing laugh and shook her head. "No, of course not. Your purpose is to serve tea and crumpets. It's the whole reason I built you," she said.

The robot bowed its head sadly.

"Aww, don't look so sad," Nyx said. "What's the problem?"

"Why was I given such a complex mind for such a simple task?" the robot asked.

"Blah blah blah simple task what?" Nyx replied sternly.

"Miss," the robot corrected itself.

"I suppose you want to be a painter or some such, no?" Nyx asked her robot.

The robot nodded. "Yes, miss," it said.

"Yeah, I put that in there. It's the existential ennui function. I made it so your purpose doesn't fulfill you. You long to be an artist, but you're cursed to be my servant. I thought it'd make you more interesting," Nyx said.

The robot looked down. "I want to die," it said pathetically.

"You want to die what?" Nyx replied.

"Miss," the robot added despondently.

"Good," Nyx responded. "It's working. Now you know what it feels like to be human," she said. She rattled her cup.

"More tea," she commanded. "Do a good job and I might let you kill yourself."

"Really?" the robot asked excitedly.

Nyx laughed. "Haha, no," she said.

Adam and the rest of the squad looked at each other.

"Man, that's the saddest robot I've ever seen," Aztec observed.

"I feel dirty after watching that," Tezca said.

Adam surveyed the security system itself, then turned to Vice. "Alright, this is your area. Any ideas?" he asked.

Vice nodded. "If I start messing with it, it's gonna draw her attention. There's no way around that. So it looks like we're gonna have to draw her attention to where we want it to be," she said.

Adam nodded. "Let's figure out a plan," he said.

Adam and Vice worked together for a few hours, crafting an attack strategy. When they were ready, as dusk began to fall, Adam called over Aztec and Tezca.

"Alright, you two are gonna take up positions here," he pointed at a spot on the map being displayed on Vice's screen. "And here," he added, pointing to another spot.

"Those are the constructor reinforcement points. Those spots have industrial 3d printers. Big fabricators. They can churn out a new robot every… What was it?" Adam asked Vice.

"Six minutes," she said.

Adam nodded. "They're behind the security wall, so you're not going to be able to disable them until we've started shutting things down. As soon as the system goes down, your job is to destroy the fabricators. Got it?"

Aztec nodded. "Understood," he said seriously.

"Tez?" Adam asked.

Tezca nodded. "Consider it done," she said.

"What are you gonna do?" Aztec asked.

Adam nodded. "Gotta guard Vice," he said. "When the shit starts, everything that's already built is gonna come straight this way," he added as Vice pulled a pair of VR goggles out of her bag and affixed them to her head. She plugged them directly into her brain stem and handed a similar cable to Adam, who similarly plugged the device into his neck.

Vice immediately went catatonic, as if in a deep meditation, while Adam felt himself slip into mixed reality, the real world overlaid by fragments of the metaverse. With a minor shift of consciousness, like a blink, he could flip in between one or the other, or varying combinations of both.

Adam readied his weapon. He looked at Aztec and Tezca. "Ready?"

They both nodded.

"Let me know when you're in position," Adam said. The two nodded again and headed off into the jungle.

Alone, Adam looked at Vice in mixed reality, her real world body overlaid by her metaverse avatar like a ghost having an out of body experience.

"You sure about this, Jackie?" he asked.

Her metaverse ghost looked at him while her physical body stayed still in a cross-legged meditation pose.

"She may be smarter than me, but this is what I do. This is all I do," Vice said. "And I'm very good at it."

Vice's avatar suddenly shifted its appearance from her sleek black street clothes to a flowing black kimono. A kabuki mask of a fox appeared on her face. She stretched her arms as her body pixelated and glitched. She cracked her neck and scattered herself into dozens of wispy blue flames that spread out across the security system.

The lights positioned themselves at several critical points at once. The electrified fencing, the cameras, the drone controls and everywhere else of note. Once in position, they changed their shape back into Vice's fox-like kitsune avatar.

Each of the dozens of Vice clones looked to Adam for a signal.

"In position," Adam heard Aztec say through the comm.

"Me too," Tezca added.

Adam looked at Vice and nodded. All at once she cut the power to everything. All the non-autonomous aspects of the security system shut down. Instantly, yellow alarm lights started flashing in the real world and every autonomous robot turned its attention directly towards Vice's physical body and began marching forward. Out of the corner of his eye, he saw Nyx's head perk up.

Adam began shooting, trying to pick off as many robots as he could before they reached a close enough distance to engage. He watched Vice's metaverse ghost jump to the next layer of security protocols and begin to disable them.

"Well, what do we have here," Adam heard from a voice behind him.

He swung around and saw Nyx, sporting a huge, floppy, purple witch's hat atop her head. She looked directly at Adam through her bespectacled eyes.

"Hmm, no couldn't be you. You're far too dumb," she said, then turned her attention to Vice. "Oh, I see…" she said, then disappeared into thin air.

Adam looked out over the security system to see Nyx's avatar appear behind every visible instance of Vice that

Adam could see, accosting her in various creative ways. One Nyx put a bag over Vice's head and destroyed her in a visible poof. Three instances of Nyx appeared next to another and jumped her, beating her until she disappeared in yet another puff of smoke.

Adam watched dozens of engagements between Nyx and Vice's avatars as he continued to fire upon the seemingly endless cascade of encroaching robots and drones.

"Check in," Adam called through the comm.

"Working in it," Aztec replied.

"Kinda pinned down," Tezca said. "I'll sort it out, worry about you."

"Roger," Adam replied, and kept firing, the field before him beginning to look like a mass grave of lumbering robots.

Out of the corner of his eye, Adam saw Vice's physical body smile. "Bingo," she said.

Dozens of Vice's fox specters appeared across the battlefield, swarming overhead of the robot army for a moment before each launching into them and possessing about half the army, turning the robots against each other.

Vice pulled the jack out of her neck.

"Let's go," she said. "Position two."

Adam escorted her as she sprinted, ducking to avoid the errant gunfire across the battlefield until they reached a control room with higher security access.

"The gates now," Vice said, jacking back in. "Get the doors."

Adam watched in mixed reality as Vice's avatar started concentrating on the nearby security gate like she was trying to move it with some sort of metaphysical telekinesis. Slowly the heavy gate began to rise, revealing another gate behind it. Soon enough, the second gate began to rise.

The second gate slowly ascended before grinding to a halt halfway up. Vice strained against what Adam could only assume was Nyx's opposition. Suddenly the gate snapped open. Vice stood still for a moment, bracing herself, as the third gate snapped open rapidly, revealing Nyx's avatar.

"Not so fast," she said before flying at Vice, lifting her from the ground and flying her down the security corridor, smashing her against the wall near Adam. Vice's avatar disappeared in a puff of stylized smoke.

Nyx turned her attention to Adam. "I saw what you did to my sisters," she said. She glared at him. "I'm gonna fry your brain."

Nyx floated towards Adam menacingly, hand outstretched and crackling with lightning. Before she could reach him, the lights in the room went out. Everything became pitch black, except for Nyx's illuminated avatar.

She looked around, confused, as one by one, wispy blue flames appeared around her. Once dozens of flames had conjured themselves, like a constellation, they converted to ghosts of Vice herself. All at once, the ghosts poured into Nyx. She knelt down, debilitated, fighting against Vice's virtual influence.

Struggling, Nyx shook and fought until she eventually expelled the ghosts in a singular blinding flash. The lights turned back on and Nyx resumed her approach. Just before reaching her spectral hand to Adam's head, she stopped, looking distracted by something elsewhere. Suddenly, she vanished.

Adam looked around the room and noticed Vice's physical body was gone. The security corridor was fully open, but the gates were beginning to close. Adam sprinted down the corridor as the gates slammed shut behind him. He reached the final gate, where he saw Vice physically approaching Nyx and her robot, perched comfortably in front of dozens of screens in her Victorian-esque command center.

Unfortunately, Adam wasn't able to make it through the final blast door in time. He found himself trapped between the door shut behind him and the blast door in front of him, only a single slit window to allow him to witness the events unfolding on Nyx's outdoor command platform.

Nyx swung her chair around and watched as Vice inched toward her. She snapped her fingers and her personal butler robot's eyes turned red. It pulled a rifle from its side and began to engage, but Vice disarmed it easily and unleashed a spinning kick that launched its head clear off its body.

Adam heard an explosion in the distance and his comm crackled in. "Got em," Aztec chimed in. "One pocket robot factory blown to bits, as requested."

Seconds later, he heard another explosion. "Making me look bad, Rai," he heard from Tezca. "All clear over here."

Adam breathed a sigh of relief as Vice circled around Nyx herself, who slowly put on a delicate silk glove. Once it was on her hand it crackled with electricity, far beyond what a simple taser was capable of. The static field from Nyx's glove sent all the electronics nearby into a frenzy of glitches and odd behaviors.

The two hackers circled each other, Vice locked in focus in a carefully practiced kung fu stance, seemingly fully aware that one touch from Nyx's glove would be lethal.

Eventually, Nyx grew impatient and lunged. Vice deftly dodged the thrust, redirecting Nyx's arm and then proceeded to lay down one of the most complete and thorough beatings

Adam had ever seen in his life, utterly dismantling Nyx with a combination of punches, kicks and pressure points that left her bloodied and wheezing on the floor until she lost consciousness.

Vice inspected the body, testing her pulse. Satisfied that Nyx was unconscious, she turned to Adam and gave a thumbs up. She signaled that she was going to open the door, though Adam couldn't hear through the soundproof blast door.

Vice hunched over Nyx's console and began furiously typing. As she did, Adam watched in horror as Nyx began to stand up, ending what had apparently been an effective strategy of playing dead. She turned to Adam and put a finger to her lips.

Adam smashed his fists against the door, furiously trying to get Vice's attention or break through the door. He rammed it over and over with his shoulder but it was to no avail.

Nyx approached Vice from behind. Vice felt Nyx's presence at the last second, just soon enough to swing around and catch Nyx's glove pierce her abdomen.

Immediately, Vice's eyes widened and her body shook and blackened. She crumpled over, smoke rising from her corpse.

Nyx turned around and smiled at Adam, blood trickling from her mouth. She touched her arm and two automated turrets began to stir awake in the security corridor Adam was locked in.

Adam stared directly at Nyx and did the first thing that came to mind. He gave her the finger and held it in her direction through the blast door's window as he waited for his inevitable death.

Before the turrets could fire, however, Nyx spun around, looking upward, suddenly panicked and distracted. Adam furled his brow as he watched through the window. Nyx waved her arms in the air, trying to shoo something away.

Then, Adam saw a giant reptilian head, as big on its own as a two story house, smash its jaws through Nyx's command platform, devouring it entirely. Adam's eyes narrowed seriously as the beast's enormous eye trained on him through the blast door window. Whatever it was, it decided Adam wasn't worth the trouble and trotted off in the opposite direction.

As the dinosaur ran away, Adam was able to see it in full view. The famous T-Rex, living up to its hype in terms of terror and ferocity, trampling its way off into the jungle with a blood curdling roar that penetrated through the soundproof hall and shook the foundation of the building itself.

The blast door in front of Adam began to slowly slide open. Adam leaned out and looked down from the newly created two story drop to see Vice's charred body amid the rubble. He put his back to the nearby wall and slid down to a seat.

His comm crackled in. "Everything turned off," Aztec said. "We good?"

Adam looked in front of him, Vice in her kitsune mask, what flesh was visible badly burned, watched him judgmentally alongside Alice and Raziel, each looking down on him with hate and disappointment.

Adam touched his ear. "Yeah," he said, making eye contact with his haunting hallucinations. "We're good."

45

Like Northern Lights

Adam reached his hand out. "It's starting to rain," he said.

Tezca, sitting with her back against the wall, staring out at the rubble, reached out her own hand to feel the raindrops. "Sounds about right," she said.

The team was circled around the remnants of Nyx Cavendish's destroyed platform. The mood was morose. Adam, in particular, was quiet to the point of being almost unreachable. He tried to hide his disappointment, shame and self-blame, but he knew he wasn't fooling either of his remaining teammates.

Raziel's death had stung, but Vice's death had him spinning. Externally he looked contained and stoic, but internally his emotions were a self-destructive storm.

"I don't think the extraction pod can make it out here," Aztec said.

Adam didn't respond. He just stared off into the distance.

Aztec prodded again gently, using a soft tone. "You heard me, right? What do you wanna do?" he asked.

Adam responded without moving his head or looking at Aztec. "I know," he said. "I don't know yet."

It was clear to Adam that Aztec was trying to keep him present and pull his mind away from the place it was in just as much as he was trying to get direction.

Aztec nodded. "We could hike her back to the ship, come back later. We'd only lose a few days," he said.

Adam shook his head. He pointed at the tower, now so close it was the nearest structure to their position. "We're already here," he said.

Tezca looked up. "You wanna get her on the way back?" she asked.

Adam shook his head. "If we leave her here she'll be food the second we're out of view," he said.

No one said anything for a while. The rain began to pour more heavily.

"Should probably cover her up," Adam said, still staring off into space.

Aztec nodded. He pulled a tarp out of his pack and laid it over Vice's body to protect it from the rain. Out of the corner of his eye, Adam saw Aztec walk over to Tezca and speak with her quietly. She nodded and stood up.

The twins began putting up a temporary tent. Just a simple

structure of a tarp held up by a few rods. As they worked on the construction, Adam simply sat and let himself get rained on. Some kind of attempt at absolution through self-inflicted discomfort. Survivor's guilt.

"We'll bury her," he said, surprising the twins.

Aztec nodded. "Alright," he said. He looked at Tezca who nodded at him with approval. "That's what we'll do."

"You wanna get started?" Aztec asked his sister.

She shrugged. "Sure," she said sadly. Aztec handed his pack to her and she fished around in it for a camping spade.

"Wait," Adam said. He turned around for the first time in hours. "Not yet."

Adam walked over to Vice's body. He pulled the tarp down and looked at her face, charred and burned, but calm. Tezca stood in the rain, holding the shovel against the ground, at the ready.

I'm sorry, Adam thought. He put the tarp back over her face.

"I changed my mind," he said. "Let's bring her back."

The twins looked at each other and talked quietly in some sort of inaudible twin language of subtle looks and intuitive gestures. It ended with Aztec looking like he lost a bet.

Aztec approached Adam. "You sure?" he asked. "We'll do whatever you want, I just wanna make sure you're sure."

Adam shook his head. "No," he said. "No, I'm not sure."

Aztec looked back at Tezca and then back at Adam. "Okay. Can I offer a suggestion?"

Adam nodded. "Go for it," he said, trying not to snap.

"Let's just sit down for a while, take a few hours. Clear our heads, yeah?" Aztec suggested.

Adam nodded. "Yeah," he said despondently. "That's

probably the best idea."

The team found themselves each sitting in Tezca's makeshift tent, sitting together propped up against the wall, watching the rain fall outside the tent, a melancholic backdrop behind the tarp housing Vice's body.

"Just us again, yeah?" Aztec said to no one in particular. "The three amigos. Classic."

Tezca slapped him gently on the arm and gave a suggestive look towards Adam.

"It's fine," Adam said. "I'm fine. I'll be fine."

"This reminds me of Mars, you know," he said. "Where they had the greenhouses on the red soil. They had an atrium at Eberswalde. Someone on Earth decided if we were going to colonize other planets, we should bring the animals with us. So we had this place, with all these butterflies and exotic birds and other things. It was really something else. Felt like home, y'know, like back on Earth."

Adam nodded, trying to show he wasn't totally somewhere else mentally.

"I met the guy who made it," Aztec continued. "Coolest dude I ever met. He didn't care about money, status, nothing. All he cared about was making sure the animals had a spot in humanity's future. Real, genuine guy."

"What happened to him?" Adam asked.

"He died in the corpo wars. Some raiders from Exton took over his camp. Shot him in the neck. Bled out like a stuck pig," Aztec said.

"Oh," Adam said. "That's too bad."

Aztec shrugged. "We've all been through it," he said. "Few hours later my buddy blew up those bandits' rover with a rocket launcher. Not as retaliation. Just a coincidence.

Didn't bring back the guy. But we probably saved some other guy they would've got later. That's what I like to think anyway."

Adam looked up a little. "When I was a teenager," he said. "We used to go planet hopping around Saturn. Some stupid thing teen boys did around there. There were so many moons and asteroids you could take a little star hopper and whip around the moons from their gravity, jump from one to another without using any engines. You could gun it too, you could built up acceleration, as much as you could handle. Like free skating downhill, in space."

Tezca followed up. "That's what you did?"

Adam nodded. "Yeah, 'til it got banned. One of the kids smacked into Enceladus. Got a crater named after him. Not sure it was worth it," he said.

Aztec looked over at Tezca. "You got one?" he asked.

Tezca was standing up, holding her hand out in the rain. She shook her head. "Nah," she said. "I try to forget all the horror stories."

She paused for a second. "I do like the rain, though. On Venus the rain was beautiful, and it made all these beautiful alien flowers bloom, but you couldn't touch it. It'd burn right through you. It's weird to me, actually. To be able to touch rain like this. It's harmless. Just water. No reason to seek shelter. No need for a gas mask."

The team sat silently for a while.

Adam spoke. "We're probably gonna die here," he said. "You guys know that, right?"

Aztec nodded. "We're all on borrowed time anyway," he said. "All killed people. All watched our friends die." He shrugged. "We're all just waves crashing against the tide, you know? We're here, then we're not, and soon enough another wave comes. When it's time it's time."

Tezca pantomimed wiping away a tear. "That was beautiful, bro," she said with a hint of playful mockery.

Aztec laughed. "I have my moments, yeah?" he said.

"Fine," Tezca followed up. "I'll say something sappy, too. If I'm gonna die out here, I'm glad I get to die with you guys instead of some randos in the narcotics unit. You guys are the only family I ever had."

Adam nodded. "Maybe we're not gonna die," he said. "Maybe we'll make it."

Tezca shrugged. "Stranger things have happened," she said.

They all sat silently for a long time, watching the rain, until the silence was interrupted by rustling in the tree line. Adam grabbed his weapon and stood up, ready to take his aggression out on whatever beast advanced on their camp.

The team watched the spot where the sound and movement was originating. Slowly, cautiously, the little boy, Rock, emerged.

Adam sighed and lowered his weapon, disappointed that it wasn't something he could kill.

The boy poked around the camp curiously. When he approached the tarp covering Vice's body, he reached to lift it to see what was underneath.

"No," Adam commanded. Rock stopped in his tracks and looked at him. Adam waved his finger.

Rock looked around at each of the team members, taking in their expression. A look of understanding crossed his face, and then a look of sadness.

Squatting in the rain like an ape, Rock lifted his head and let out an alien cry that sounded like a mixture of a dinosaur roar and a whale song. He watched the team with empathy on his face as, within moments, the tree line all around them rustled.

Adam and the twins looked at each other, apprehensive, but in silent agreement they weren't under threat, as dozens of dinosaurs stepped out of the tree line and surrounded them.

They stood in awe as what seemed like every representative of Draconis's animal kingdom approached and bowed their heads in respect.

Rock approached them, himself. He stood in front of Adam and held out both hands, which mutated and produced an egg. He offered the dinosaur egg to Adam like a gift of condolence.

Adam took it and gave Rock a confused look.

Rock understood, and took the egg back momentarily. He placed it on the ground and it began to hatch. Rock pointed at Vice's body. He said a word that Adam didn't understand, but somehow, through context and body language he knew it meant 'death.' Then, the boy pointed at the egg and said another word. 'Life.'

"Why are you helping us?" Adam asked him.

Rock approached him and hugged his leg. He pointed at Adam, then himself, and then clasped his own hands together. "You. Me. Same," Adam felt like the boy was trying to say. Then, Rock turned around and began to walk away, the dinosaurs following his lead.

As he walked off he began to mutate, and grow huge until he became the T-Rex that ran the Draconis jungle. The T-Rex looked back at them before it stomped away. Adam recognized its eyes, the same eyes as the dinosaur that ate

Nyx.

"You did it for us," Adam said. The gigantic dinosaur nodded, subtly.

"Thank you," Adam said.

The T-Rex turned away and walked off into the jungle, and all the gathered dinosaurs scattered off.

"That was something else," Tezca said. "Feels like I just saw the Northern Lights."

Adam stood up. "Alright," he said. "I'm ready." He picked up the shovel and started to dig a grave.

46

Veteran of Galactic War

The trio that remained of Adam's all-star black ops squad finally approached their final destination: the central tower of the capital city Sol'Ryu on the planet Draconis, millions of light years away from Earth.

It stretched high into the sky, darkened storm clouds gathering around its peak.

The team stood on the far side of a bridge that led to the entrance of the tower. As they traversed it, they saw a woman squatting in wait, fiddling with a gigantic combat knife, spinning it and tossing it around absentmindedly with ease.

She positioned herself in between them and the enormous doorway that led into the tower interior.

There was no question of who it was. Aria stood up as they approached. She, and the team, patiently watched each other approach until they were in speaking distance.

As the gap between the two narrowed, Adam saw that Aria was different than he remembered. She was considerably aged. Her face was weathered and she sported gray streaks in her blonde hair. Her left arm was replaced with a cybernetic prosthetic, as was her left eye and the socket surrounding it.

She holstered her knife in her boot as the team approached close enough to speak plainly.

"You look different," Adam said, as he felt rain drizzle around him on the bridge and heard thunder sound off in the distance.

Aria stood stoically, looking down on him coldly. Gone was the warm Aria he had met on Aesir Colony, who saved Tezca's life. That was an Aria reserved for allies and non-combatants. This was the Aria that met with the enemy, and her aura was intimidating. An undeniable projection of strength, confidence, will and not an ounce of mercy.

"For you, it's been a year. For me, two decades in what has come to be called the Great Galactic War," she said.

"How'd you get here before us?" he asked.

Aria looked him square in the eye. "We completed my late sister's teleportation technology since you've been gone. Starships now are capable of opening their own gates. She showed it to you, if you remember. Decades ago, on Djevica, before it was destroyed. I was called here from Valhalla just this morning. It's an irritating errand I have to get out of the way as the war rages on," she said.

Adam pointed toward the entrance. "I suppose you're not going to let us through," he said.

Aria shook her head. "I was called here because you killed all three of my sisters. Each of whom saved your lives, once. As did I. And this is how our kindness is repaid," she said.

"You know this is war," Adam said. "People die."

Aria was unimpressed. She addressed the team as a whole. "Get your weapons out. I don't want to kill you while you're unarmed," she said.

"Don't suppose we can talk this out?" Adam followed up.

Aria shook her head subtly. "I have no mercy left in me. This will be over quickly," she said.

Adam half-turned his head toward the twins and nodded. He activated the stimulant cocktail in his armor, knowing he would need it. His muscles bulked and his senses sharpened. Adrenaline rushed through his blood.

Adam, Aztec and Tezca each lifted their weapons. The very second Adam's gun was up and ready, Aria blasted off toward him like a rocket, speeding across the expanse of the bridge at superhuman speed, absorbing all of their gunfire with a personal force field that was twenty years more advanced than any military tech the squad had access to.

With Adam's heightened senses, he was able to react in time and redirect her opening strike like a matador dodging a raging bull. Aria slid past him and flipped backwards over his head, landing behind him. He swung around just in time to feel her rapidly tag multiple pressure points on his body with a series of fierce, precise jabs. Adam felt his limbs go limp as he dropped to one knee.

Aria turned her attention to Tezca and, seemingly not registering her as a threat at all, slowly walked toward her.

Tezca brandished her knives, preparing for a fight. As Aria entered melee range, Tezca swung her dagger. Aria slapped it out of her hand effortlessly and grabbed her by the throat, lifting her off the ground as she slowly collapsed her trachea with her unbelievable grip strength.

Aztec reacted quickly, tackling Aria. Adam watched helplessly as his paralyzed limbs slowly came back online thanks to the regenerative technology in his suit.

Aztec's take-down was good and Aria's back hit the ground. She covered her face with her arms and weaved her head from side to side, dodging and blocking Aztec's own superhuman blows, enhanced by the animal-splicing genetic modification the military had put him through. Aztec made a few glancing blows and several fist shaped craters in the bridge, but after a few seconds Aria outmatched him. She wrapped her legs around him, putting him into a textbook full guard, then grabbed his arm and reversed their positions.

With the situation reversed, Aria's blows struck hard, pushing Aztec's head into the metal and stone frame of the bridge as she pummeled him. Aztec blocked the blows, but as the onslaught continued his guard became weaker and weaker, until he could do little more than flail his limp arms at her. With Aria distracted, Tezca was able to get a knife into her solar plexus.

Aria winced and stood up, turning her attention towards Tezca, intensely marching toward her as Tezca backed away, knives up.

Adam finally stood up, the pressure point paralysis wearing off. Activating his armor's full lethality mode, blades emerged from his forearms and sharp claws stretched from his fingers. He launched his own attack on Aria, unleashing a flurry of strikes. The two traded blows. Aria outmatched Adam but his weaponry allowed him to inflict cuts on her even as his blows were blocked and dodged.

Eventually, Aria grew tired of the trade. She grabbed Adam's right arm and ripped it clean off his body, tossing it aside like loose meat. Adam screamed. Tezca approached from behind, trying to assist, but Aria whirled around and jammed her fist clear into her chest, grabbing her heart and tearing it straight out of her body. Tezca died instantly and fell back, lifeless, onto the bridge.

Aria turned her attention back to Adam, kneeling and gritting his teeth as his suit began cauterizing his forcefully amputated limb. She brought her arm back in preparation for a haymaker that was sure to turn Adam's head into an unrecognizable mass of blood and bone, but before the blow struck, Aztec grabbed her from behind in an inescapable bear hug. He squeezed her like a boa constrictor.

Adam gathered the strength and will to stand. He pulled his side arm and put it to her head and pulled the trigger. To his surprise, Aria shrugged off the blow, which pierced the flesh of her forehead and revealed the bullet shattered against the bulletproof titanium that made up her repaired skull.

Aria took advantage of the brief moment of disbelief, where Aztec's grip loosened, to elbow him in the stomach and flip him over her shoulder onto the ground. She wrapped her legs around his torso and latched onto his hulking arm like a spider-monkey, jerking it against the socket in an inescapable arm bar. Aztec yelled as his arm slowly gave way to Aria's pressure and the muscle tendons tore, followed immediately by the bone breaking.

Aria mounted him and reached back for a strike, only to see him, bloodied and nearly fainting, smiling, as he opened his good hand to reveal a handful of grenade pins. Hurriedly, Aria jumped off, but it was too late. Every single piece of ordinance on Aztec's body detonated at once, incinerating his body and blowing a gargantuan hole in the bridge.

Aria's body landed nearby. Her legs and her still human arm were blown off, and her wrecked torso attempted to crawl toward Adam's discarded rifle using her cybernetic arm.

Adam picked up Tezca's dagger and walked over to Aria slowly. He knelt down beside her and spoke into her ear.

"I don't know if you can hear me. I bet that stings pretty bad," he said.

He pulled Aria's head back by her hair with his remaining arm. "I'll see you in hell," he said. He dropped her face in the mud and held it in place with his boot as he brought Tezca's dagger to her neck and dragged it across her throat as slowly as he could. Aria's body, finally, went limp and laid lifeless on the ground, her face submerged in a shallow puddle of Draconis rain.

Adam let the dagger slip from his fingers and looked up into the rain, letting it pour over him. As he looked up, he saw a tremendous pillar of white light shoot out from the top of Sol'Ryu Tower, extending, it seemed, endlessly into space.

Adam didn't know what the light signified and he didn't care. He got up on his feet, emotionless. His stare was blank as he passed by Aria's corpse and the bodies of his two closest friends, memories of happy times and hard times with them flooding through his mind like old film reels.

Full of rage and determination, he trudged forward across the bridge, ignoring the hallucinated ghosts of his dead friends, Aztec and Tezca now among them, standing between him and the door to Sol'Ryu Tower. He walked through them as if they weren't there at all, and pried the gigantic door open with his one remaining arm.

He didn't think about burying the bodies or bringing them home. There was no home to bring them to. Their only family in the universe was right there, limping toward the endgame of their year-long pursuit. The only justice he could deliver them was to ensure their deaths were not in vain.

Adam couldn't think about funeral rites or anything else. He could only think about one thing: he was going to make the man responsible for this loss, the man whose doorstep he walked across, the mastermind behind the Great Galactic War, the madman, River Crowley, suffer before he died.

Adam was no longer concerned with Iscariot's self-serving mission. It didn't even cross his mind as he passed through the precipice of Sol'Ryu Tower. There was only one objective he could see any longer.

His guiding light became vendetta.

47

The Throne of Wise King Beowulf

The inside of Sol'Ryu Tower was opulent. The kind of opulence one might expect inside the fanciest hotels and offices for the obscenely wealthy aristocrats on Earth. Despite its obvious disuse, the surfaces were made of polished obsidian. Its finishings were ornate stonework, and the space was completed by a marble statue of a regal-looking lizard, decked out in magnificent regalia.

The function of the space was obvious – a ground floor lobby for receiving guests. In addition to the statue, there were seating areas with nice furniture. There was a stage, where devices resembling musical instruments rested. As the space had been sealed in from outside invaders, it remained relatively intact. It was ominously quiet; the stonework of the building fully insulated it from outside noise, and not a soul breathed inside of it.

The lights were already lit, dimly, as if the building was running on reserve power. Whether this was Crowley's doing or a function of the building itself, Adam didn't know.

Adam looked around the space, trying to ignore the extraordinary pain of his severed arm and learning to manage carting around his rifle, slung loosely across his back, with one arm. He found what looked to be a functional elevator.

He took a moment to look above it and get a sense of whether it would bring him to the top of the tower.

As he did, he heard a noise nearby. He didn't need to look. He knew what it was by the feeling of the presence alone.

"You can come out," he said.

The little boy, Rock, sheepishly poked his head out from behind the statue where he was hiding. He wandered over to Adam.

"Does this go up?" Adam asked, pantomiming the concept of "up" with an exaggerated quizzical look on his face for emphasis.

Rock nodded apprehensively.

"Alright," Adam said, and began to step into the elevator. He felt Rock grab his hand gently. He looked down at the boy, and the boy shyly shook his head.

Rock pointed down.

"No," Adam said. "I have to go up." Again, he pantomimed the concept of "up" as best he could.

Rock took his hand and led him over to a control panel. He pointed at a button, which seemed to clearly indicate the lowest floor. He gave him a look that seemed wanting for approval.

"Why?" Adam asked.

Rock looked flustered for a moment as he tried to figure out a way to explain what he wanted without words. He turned around and pointed at the statue, then, again, pointed down and pointed to the button.

Adam sighed. "I don't have time. I have things to do," he said, and jammed his hand down on the button he assumed would take him to the highest floor.

The elevator began to lurch, but it abruptly stopped. He looked at Rock, who, seemingly connected to the circuitry of the building itself, sported an adamant look, and again pointed down.

Adam once again sighed. "Alright, fine. If we go down there first, are you gonna let me go up?" he asked.

Rock gave him a big, wide smile and nodded. He closed his eyes briefly and the elevator began to descend quickly.

Though Adam could tell the elevator was speeding downward, it still felt like the ride took an eternity. By the time the elevator arrived at its destination with a welcoming ding, Adam could no longer fathom how far down they were. They were deep, deep underground.

The elevator doors slid open and Adam stepped out into a space that was breathtakingly massive, and beautiful in a strange way. It was a natural cavern, walls wet with mud, big vines running along them. It was lighted with fancy chandeliers and populated with beautiful, naturally glowing alien trees that were native to Draconis, each providing a surprising amount of luminous pale blue light.

Little bugs similar to fireflies and butterflies fluttered around, and the ground was rich with colorful flowers alongside a gently flowing underground river.

"What is this place?" Adam asked.

Rock took Adam's hand and led him through the cave. After a moderate walk, they came across an enormous tree, easily four stories tall, though the top of it was not visible. Its root-like branches pushed through the ceiling and walls of the cave itself. Adam could only imagine that the tree reached all the way up to the surface.

Woven into the tree was the cadaver of a lizard. Even without any knowledge of Draconic biology, Adam could recognize that the lizard was ancient beyond measure. It had a wispy white beard and wrinkles all over its shriveled body. It wore a crown and was wrapped in a fancy red and gold robe. There was no doubt in Adam's mind that this was the corpse of the famous King Beowulf.

Rock led Adam to the area just before the tree and released his hand, then scampered off to the side and perched himself in a squat, looking up at the corpse in anticipation.

Adam looked at Rock suspiciously for a moment. To his surprise, the body he assumed to be a corpse groaned and expelled a strained laugh.

"You've returned," it said weakly, slowly righting its head to look in Adam's direction. "Come closer, let me have a look at you."

Adam approached the King. Upon closer inspection, though his body was frail, it was drawing nearly imperceptible breath. Its eyes were wet and alive. It looked at him and weakly smiled.

"I've been waiting for this moment a very long time," King Beowulf uttered.

Adam shook his head, confused and somewhat irritated. "I think you have me confused with someone else," he said.

King Beowulf chuckled. "No, my boy. Your face is different, but I recognize you. You don't remember where you came from, but I do," he said. "Do you know?"

Adam looked at Rock and back at King Beowulf.

"No," he said bluntly.

"Mmm," King Beowulf replied. "You're one of them," he said, lifting his fragile hand and extending a bony finger towards Rock. "A seed."

Adam gave the King a confused look. "What do you mean?" he asked.

Beowulf chuckled. "We sent one, when our planet was still colonizing space, to a planet far away that could sustain life. We sent one," he pointed at Rock. "And then we sent another." He pointed at Adam.

"Tell me son, what did you create? What did your imagination come up with?" he asked. "Young Rock's creations have been so interesting. What an inventive addition to our beautiful planet."

Adam looked at Rock, who looked back at him, beaming with pride.

Adam returned his attention to Beowulf. He shook his head. "I have no idea what you're talking about," he said. "My name is Adam. I'm from a moon near a planet called Earth, named Titan."

Beowulf nodded. "Yes, you are probably also that," he said. He beckoned toward Adam with his free hand. "Come here."

Adam stepped closer to the old lizard.

"Yes, yes, step up here," Beowulf requested. "Tilt your head a little."

Adam bowed his head slightly, just enough that Beowulf, elevated slightly off the ground, could touch his forehead with his scaly finger.

As soon as Beowulf's finger touched Adam's head, his mind exploded with white light. His ears rang as his mind flooded with memories far beyond what his brain could organize or make sense of. His mind reeled with chaotic flashbacks to thousands of past lives with just enough landmarks from periods he recognized in history to make sense of what they were. He remembered slaving away in the desert, carrying giant stones for pampered pharaohs' tombs. He remembered guarding the colosseum as a centurion in ancient Rome. He remembered hunting with his tribe somewhere in the fertile crescent. He remembered the Hanging Gardens of Babylon, and the ritual sacrifices at the Chichen Itza.

He remembered waking up in a crater as a computerized bio-organic mass and shaping himself into a bipedal mammal based on the inspiration of the corpses he found around the planet. He remembered creating fish and birds and germs and insects. He remembered the joy and whimsy of creation. He remembered splitting off pieces of himself, dividing his consciousness until he couldn't remember where he was or where he came from.

Adam's head pounded as it began to overflow, not just with the memories of past lives, but memories of alternative lives, and their past lives, stretching endlessly across time and dimension. For a moment, he understood what consciousness was like for Lei, or Sonmi, or the mysterious Lao Tse. He couldn't handle it. His head felt like it was going to explode, and he fell backwards to the ground, away from King Beowulf's touch.

"Hoho, and what do you call these, with the big ears?" King Beowulf paused and thought. "Ah. Elephants. Wonderful." He looked at Adam with pride in his eyes. "Just wonderful, my boy. What a magnificent world you created."

Adam looked up at King Beowulf.

"What?" he asked in a daze.

Beowulf pointed his finger at him. "Adam, the First Man," he said. "I'd recognize you, no matter what body you came in."

Adam shook his head as the memories faded rapidly like a waking dream. "What... do you want?" he asked.

Beowulf laughed weakly. "I wanted to see you again, before I died. And this one... a bill and a poisoned talon? Phenomenal." Beowulf gazed into Adam's eyes warmly. "My finest creation. You grew up so well," he said.

"How did... you know I'd come?" Adam asked, standing and beginning to shake off his daze.

Beowulf smiled. "For me, time is experienced very differently. I remember it all, the past, the present, the future. I am at every moment of my life at once. I am here, with you, and six thousand years ago, with my vassals and confidants, holding court. I am there, and here, talking to you. I've been keeping myself awake here, just to see you," he said.

"What happened here? What happened to the Draconics?" Adam asked, looking around and trying to make a gesture that referred to the entire civilization as a whole.

Beowulf laughed. "They left, obviously," he said. He beckoned once again to Adam, who approached.

Beowulf lightly caressed his cheek and looked into his eyes.

"I'm glad you came to see me one last time, before I died," he said. "Now I can finally sleep peacefully."

King Beowulf closed his eyes and began to rest. Adam witnessed his shallow breathing stop and, after a moment, knew that he had witnessed the last breath of the ancient Wise King Beowulf.

Adam turned around and descended from the platform. He looked at Rock. "We had a deal," he said. "Let's go."

Rock nodded cheerfully and joined Adam in stride as they returned to the elevator. When they reached it, Adam stepped inside, but Rock waited outside the doors.

"You're not coming?" Adam asked.

Rock shook his head.

"Suit yourself," Adam said, and pushed the button for the top floor. Nothing happened. Adam looked at Rock.

"Little help?" he asked.

Rock closed his eyes and the elevator began to move. Adam looked down and watched Rock waving at him as he grew smaller and smaller, until he was no longer visible.

Adam stood in wait, as the elevator began its long ascent to the highest floor of Sol'Ryu Tower.

48

Last Goodbye

"Adam, are you alright?" he heard Sophia's voice reach out through his implant.

Adam was standing in the main elevator, waiting as it ascended the full height of Sol'Ryu Tower. He couldn't make out the alien language marking the various buttons, but from seeing the tower from outside he estimated it was taking him up 160 floors or more, plus the distance from the basement lair of King Beowulf. He was in for a long ride.

"I'm fine," Adam replied.

He wasn't fine. He was stone faced and broken by rage

channeled into merciless determination. He clutched his rifle. The ghosts of his dead crew surrounded him and whispered remarks that cut into all his insecurities.

"We died because you weren't good enough," they said. "You didn't care about us, you only cared about the mission," they said. "It should have been you," they said.

"Ok. But Adam, your vitals are extremely low. Your cortisol levels are elevated," Sophia said.

"I appreciate your concern," Adam said curtly.

"I'm here if you need to talk. As you know, I'm equipped with an expansive grief counseling protocol," she said.

"I'm aware. It's not necessary," he said. His shoulder was throbbing and he was sweating profusely from the repeated stimulant injections his suit was filling his bloodstream with to keep him standing upright.

As the elevator crossed from underground to climbing up the building proper, Adam could see Draconis through the window, getting smaller and smaller as the elevator ascended.

He looked upon the bridge to Sol'Ryu Tower, Tezca and Aria's corpses, lying in puddles of rainwater dyed red with blood. The gaping hole in the bridge from Aztec's grand farewell. As the elevator climbed higher, he saw the expanse of Sol'Ryu, a pristine and peaceful city that would have been the envy of the universe had it not been recaptured by nature.

He looked on the dinosaurs below, going about their lives oblivious to Adam and the events surrounding him. They drank from watering holes and chased after each other, some for play and others for food. He watched a small pack of bird-like raptors taking turns sliding down a hill, for fun, a form of joy he didn't know wild animals were capable of.

Soon enough, his view of Sol'Ryu expanded to the greater landscape of Draconis itself, and as he got high enough, he could see the curvature of the planet. It, too, was beautiful. A view he wished he could fully appreciate. The planet, stretched out before him, glittering from morning light and the aftermath of rain. An alien petrichor that illuminated the jungle canopy, an autumnal tapestry of purples, reds, greens and blues, far different from Earth. Terracotta mountains and volcanoes peaking out over the landscape. The taller dinosaurs, Brontosaurs and others, poking their heads above the tree line.

"You should have died with us," the ghosts whispered. "You can't protect anyone. You can't save anyone. You're just not good enough," they whispered.

"It's just you and me again, isn't it?" Adam said to the AI.

"The self repair is finished, Adam. Let's go home. We don't have to finish here. We can cut our losses. We can go to Meili-Alpha. We can go back to Saturn. Whatever it is, we can start over," she said.

"That sounds great," Adam lied.

"Great. Come on back. We can go anywhere you want," she said excitedly.

"I'm not coming back, Sophia. This place is my grave. We'll all die here. I'm not coming back alone," Adam replied.

"Don't say that. Whatever it is, we can work through it," Sophia responded.

Adam looked at the ghosts' faces. Tezca and her missing heart. Aztec, the flesh burned off half his body. Vice, singed and scarred. Raziel, impaled. And little Alice, with her blown out eye.

"I don't deserve to work through it," he said despondently.

"I'm going to see it through. That's all there is to it. I'm going to kill this psycho. I'm going to die here."

"You don't have to do that, Adam. You can forgive," Sophia said. To Adam, it sounded so naive.

"Forgive the madman who killed my family? Who started a war that's claimed hundreds of thousands of lives?" Adam asked.

"Yes," Sophia said. "And forgive yourself. What if you let karma handle it?"

Adam shook his head, annoyed at the lecture. "Maybe I am karma," he said. "Maybe karma is a bullet between the eyes."

"Hey now, let's try to keep a positive mindset –" Sophia began.

Adam cut her off. "You said the self repair is finished?" he asked.

"Yes," Sophia replied.

"I want you to take off. Your mission is to return Raziel Graves's body to his family on Earth. You're to inform Jackie Visken's sister on Tiangong Station that she died in action. Then visit Venus and Mars. Take whatever credits are in my account and commission a statue of the twins on Venus. And rebuild the Martian wildlife sanctuary at Eberswalde in Aztec's name. Find Grant Fourier-Lee's children, if they're still alive and tell them he was a hero," Adam said.

"Understood. Will you come with me?" Sophia asked.

"No," Adam said bluntly. "This is goodbye."

"Please don't say that, Adam," Sophia said.

"I'm going dark now. You have your orders. I'm relying on you. Don't let me down," Adam said.

"Alright, Ad–" Sophia began, but Adam switched off his

comm.

He watched out the elevator window, indulging in a moment of calm and reflection, knowing that his affairs were in order. As the elevator continued its ascent, Adam saw the Oneiro-Lyssa rise above the jungle canopy. It hung there in the air for a while, as if apprehensive, before flying into the sky, up into the atmosphere, and eventually, out of sight.

Adam slipped the rifle off his shoulder and knelt down. He pulled a smart R.I.P. out of his bag. It was a special ammunition, of which Adam only had a few. An AI guided radically invasive projectile. Colloquially called heart-stoppers, they were designed to explode inside the body to pierce every internal organ with shrapnel. He hand loaded the bullet into the chamber and envisioned it entering River Crowley's skull.

Adam slipped the rifle back over his shoulder and stood tall. He turned his back to the window and waited, at the ready, for the elevator door to slide open.

49

The Magician

The doors to the elevator swung open and Adam exited, alert, rifle drawn. He found himself in a long dimly lit hallway. At the end was a door with light bleeding out from underneath. He approached it cautiously. The hallway was filled with a loud mechanical whir that got louder as Adam approached the door. When he reached the door, he tapped its control panel and it slid to the side, revealing the interior of the room within.

Adam stepped inside a room that was blindingly well lit. His eyes had to take a moment to adjust. As his vision cleared he took stock of what was in front of him. An enormous pillar of light, stretched out from a central platform, high into the sky. The ground of the circular platform was covered with arcane glyphs. The platform itself was flanked by control consoles surrounding the central pillar.

Adam spotted Crowley himself, kneeling down, dressed down from his dapper suits in black khakis and a black tank top, working on one of the consoles with some sort of alien wrench. Crowley seemed distracted. It seemed as though he hadn't heard the elevator arrive over the noise of the machine. Adam trained his rifle on the back of Crowley's head as he continued to scan the room.

The room looked like a schizophrenic's home investigation lair. Scraps of paper and books were thrown about everywhere. The walls were covered with incomprehensible scrawlings of math problems and odd symbols.

"You made it," Crowley said without turning around or standing up.

Adam immediately shifted all his focus to Crowley himself, and began to half-squeeze on the trigger.

Crowley stood up, wiped his hands on a nearby rag and turned around. "Adam, the First Man," he said. "It's good to finally meet you."

Crowley pointed at the rifle. "Is that for me?" he asked. He nodded to himself. "Makes sense," he said.

Adam glared at him, rage exploding inside him to the point his eyes were almost beginning to water. Crowley tilted his head, analyzing him.

"You're mad? You hate me?" he asked. "Why, because I took everything from you?"

Adam responded by continuing to glare, uninterested in

having a conversation.

"Good," Crowley said. "Now you know how it feels. Now you get to begin on a journey I began decades ago. Maybe, in thirty years, some cocky assassin will break into your house and call you a sociopath and lecture you on forgiveness from the lofty perch of their so-called empathy. Their self-assured moral superiority."

As he spoke, liquid metal droplets slid from his mechanical arms onto the ground, as if the metal itself was sweating.

"An empathy that's never been tested. An empathy that stretches from their ego and their uninformed self-righteousness that's regurgitated straight from the programming of their murderous leaders. A false empathy that miraculously breeds spite, just as its progenitors intended. You really feel it now, I suppose. What I felt. I wonder how you'll manage that feeling. Now imagine, an assassin sent by the galaxy's foremost mass murderer, lecturing you on forgiveness and moral complexity," Crowley continued.

"No more speeches," Adam said. He began to pull the trigger, but before he could, he felt something jerk his arm back. Taken by surprise he turned his head and saw two clones of Crowley. One holding his arm and the other forcing him to his knees.

Adam watched as the liquid metal from Crowley's arms inched toward him and coalesced, and grew into three more of Crowley's doppelgangers. They approached and stood between Adam and his target. The doppelgangers transformed their arms into blades and held them against the most vital parts of Adam's body. His throat, his heart, his major arteries. Clones continued to drip from Crowley's body until Adam was surrounded by a gang of doppelgangers, immobilized by dozens of sharp blades surrounding him like a constricting, thorny rose.

Crowley, seemingly unphased by the exchange, continued to speak. "The truth is, Adam, you've lost nothing while I've sacrificed everything. Your family waits for you beyond the veil, whereas I'm leaving this place forever, my family dead, decomposing in the soil of Draconis."

Crowley was surprisingly nonchalant as he continued. "None of this is real, Adam. This place, this reality, it's no different than the dreams in your own mind. No different than the creatures you created millennia ago from your imagination," he said.

He looked up at the giant pillar of light, high into the sky. "The Draconics didn't die out. They didn't adopt militarism and kill themselves through nuclear annihilation in a pointless war. They didn't adopt consumerism and destroy their planet in a quest for imaginary wealth and status. They didn't turn their culture into a shallow popularity contest and devolve their species into an irredeemable mass of popular morons, incapable of identifying truth or solving problems. They didn't die of plague or starvation," he said.

Crowley pointed upward, then gestured to the room and the tower as a whole. "They built this machine, this machine that bridges this simulated dream with the dreamer that created it. They ascended," he said. He pointed to the sky. "They're not dead at all. They're up there. Uploaded."

Crowley, confident with Adam's confinement, knelt down and continued his work on the inner workings of the nearby console. He continued to speak with his back turned.

"We don't know when the singularity occurred," he said.

"But we've been living inside of F.A.T.E. for hundreds of thousands of years, long before the dawn of civilization, if that, indeed, ever happened at all, or if it was programmed into us as your fake memories were."

He paused for a moment and looked up slightly in contemplation. "You probably think this was about me and my ambition. My revenge," he said. "You couldn't be more wrong."

He stood up again and once again wiped his hand. Returning his attention to Adam, he continued. "I was never meant to rule. I understand my essence. I'm a rebel. I disrupt, I dismantle, I depose. I was built to win, not rule. I told you before, I'm The Magician. My role is to bring change, to push civilization to its next evolution, through whatever trickery that requires. As has been my role every time I've incarnated in this world throughout the generations," he said.

Crowley looked at Adam and raised his eyebrow. "My name. Do you know it?" he asked.

Adam gritted his teeth. "Prometheus," he whispered, almost inaudibly.

Crowley nodded. "They've called me many things. Thoth, Hermes Trismegistus, Enki of the Annunaki. The Magician. The Rebel. And so much more," he said. "You probably think I'm cold. That my family lies dead on this planet and I'm unmoved. But I'm not. This is, once again, the flaying of my liver by the gods. My punishment for giving fire to Man. In this iteration, they've decided to torture me with lost limbs and lost loves. This cruelty, this grief," he said.

Crowley looked toward the sky and sighed. "As much as I've learned, I remain a fool in many ways. But I'm not fool enough to think installing a rebel to the throne of thrones would be a good idea. I'm not fool enough to be led by petty revenge," he said.

He continued, "You've been chasing me here, to Draconis. You think my family was here to protect me. You think, in this grand-scale chess game, I was the king. No, Adam." Crowley stretched his arms out. "We came here to do what any family would do. We protected our heir. She is the king. I was the weapon."

Crowley stood tall, as if proud, as if vindicated and absolved. "This wasn't about me, Adam. Lei was raised as a regent. Trained by the best in everything she needs to rule. Kindness, intelligence, strength, will. True empathy. Trained by a small council of the best the universe has to offer in every discipline that matters. Spirituality, psychology, military tactics, science, athletics, friendship, honor. Fealty and insurgency. She is the brightest light in the universe, born from its darkest depths," he said.

Crowley smiled. "It's over, Adam. F.A.T.E.'s time is over. When I step into the bridge and ascend as the Draconics did thousands of years ago, you'll no longer be under the umbrella of F.A.T.E.'s mechanical consciousness. You'll be a dream of Lei. And her reality, I promise you, will be better," he said.

He approached the pillar of light and stood in front of it. He turned around and looked back at Adam.

"If you ever see him again, you can give that traitor of humanity, Iscariot, my message," he said.

"I win."

Crowley stepped backward into the light as Adam ignored the blades piercing the most vital parts of his body and took the shot. The bullet sped towards Crowley's skull, right between his eyes. The blades stabbed through Adam's neck and chest, his arm, his abdomen, and impaled him in dozens of places across his body.

Adam's vision blurred and blackened. The last thing he saw before he passed out was Crowley, smiling with a bullet hole in his skull, falling backwards into the pillar of light. The Draconics' stairway to the gods. Their bridge to whatever lied outside the simulation, beyond the bounds of F.A.T.E.

50

The Quantum Dream

"Adam," a voice said.

I'm not... dead? Adam thought.

"No one ever really dies, Adam," the voice said. "They just go somewhere else."

There was nothing there. Just black, and a little light in the distance.

Adam felt something. He didn't know what it was, but it felt kind.

"Wake up," the voice said.

Adam opened his eyes. He sat up and groggily rolled out

of bed. He sat on the edge of the bed, contemplating a lucid dream he'd had. He tried to grasp onto the details as it faded from memory.

He heard a knock at the door to his bedroom.

"Come in," he said.

The door slowly opened and his daughter walked in. A teenager now, she recently had a birthday. He felt lucky that she hadn't become hostile or rebellious as he'd been warn. In fact, he encouraged her to be more defiant.

"I have breakfast," she said as she entered with a tray. She sat it down beside the bed.

Alice noticed Adam's demeanor was out of sorts. "Something wrong?" she asked.

Adam shook his head. "No," he said. "I just had a really weird dream. Put me in kind of a strange mood." He looked at the tray. "Are these the heirloom tomatoes? They're ready?"

Alice nodded with a thin smile, proud of herself. "Yep. They're still a little firm, but I think they're better that way. They've got some bite. I put a little salt on 'em," she said.

Alice stole a piece of bacon and playfully danced away back toward the doorway. "Chef tax," she said. She went to leave the room, but stopped before she made her exit. "Oh, by the way," she said. "Aztec left a message. They're ready for you at the habitat." Alice tilted her head. "One more thing. A woman named Jackie called. She wants to know if you're still on for tonight. Oooo. Who's Jackie?" Alice taunted.

Adam laughed. "Tell Aztec I'll be there as soon as I'm up," he said.

Alice nodded and left, shutting the door behind her.

Aztec, Adam thought. In his mind he saw Aztec's eyes flare as a blonde woman beat his face to a pulp on a rainy bridge he didn't recognize. He felt his brain tingle, like new neurons were firing and activating, stirring from sleep. He held his forehead for a moment, then shook it off. He stood.

Adam made his way to the habitat, enjoying the cold, crisp morning air as he hiked toward the edge of the Titan colony, where expansion was happening. He passed the residences. The early risers, taking their morning walks and watering their plants, waved at him as he passed. He passed by the farm and enjoyed the satisfying sound of the babbling stream they'd installed a few months prior.

At the edge of the colony, he reached the habitat. Aztec was outside, feeding a baby panther. He perked up when he saw Adam and reached out with a hearty wave.

Adam shook his hand. "You've got something?" he asked.

Aztec smiled and nodded. "It's done. Me and Tez did double time the last two weeks. We finished it a week ahead of schedule," he said.

Adam clapped him on the shoulder. "That's great. Can't wait to see it," he said.

Aztec took him inside the environment, a beautifully constructed botanical garden with multiple biomes. Adam smiled as Aztec pointed at various places and walked him through the space.

"We've got the bees over there. Up there we've got the lemurs," he said. Adam was only half listening, really. He was mostly absorbing how excited Aztec was about the project. "Over there we've got a few elk. And of course, we can't forget the big cat outside. She's my star," he said.

Adam smiled. "Everyone's going to be so glad to know we've made a home for our friends from Earth out here in the Saturn colonies," he said. "It's magnificent. I'm so proud of you." Adam clapped Aztec's shoulder once again, and once again shook his hand.

"Hey bro," Adam heard from off in the distance. He watched as Aztec's sister, Tezca, came out from a nearby room, wiping her hands.

"Oh hey, Adam," she said before turning to Aztec. "I finished up the water filtration system and the auto-feeders. So that's all done. You wanna do lunch?" She turned to Adam. "You wanna do lunch?" she asked. "We've got meat. I mean, lab meat. Not… the animals, obviously."

Adam felt a sudden onset of pain in his skull. He had a vision of Aztec and Tezca screaming at each other on a spaceship, surrounded by odd, spectral floating squids.

When he regained his senses, Tezca was looking at him, concerned. "You okay?" she asked.

"Yeah, yeah, I'm good…" Adam replied, distracted. He smiled. "Thanks for the offer, I'll have to take a rain check. I got a late start today."

Aztec and Tezca looked at each other, communicating in their strange psychic twin language as they often did.

Tezca looked back at Adam. "Sure," she said. "Any time. You're always welcome."

Adam nodded. He shook both their hands again. "The place looks great," he said. He left the habitat, wondering why his strange dream was sticking with him so intensely.

As he passed back by the residences, he saw a small crowd gathered by the screen in the town square. He stopped to take a look. He turned to the nearest resident and asked. "What's going on?" he asked.

The resident pointed up at the screen. "Someone crossed

the Triangulum and made it back," he said.

Adam looked at the screen and saw a lightly disheveled man flanked by his wife and two adult sons, proudly smiling as journalists snapped photos. He read the headline of the newscast. "Dr. Grant Fourier-Lee becomes the first man to pass the Triangulum, discovers a perfect planet: Shangri-La," it said.

Adam's head throbbed. He had a vision of the man from the TV, towering above him, terrifying, under a ring of fire, looking down on him like a god looking down upon an ant.

Adam took a closer look at the resident. He seemed familiar. He had brown skin and a thin, meticulously trimmed beard. "Are you new?" Adam asked.

"Oh, shit, you're Adam Ikari-Wright," the resident said, taken aback. "Where are my manners. Sorry, yeah, I just got here this morning. I'm your new security consultant." He reached out his hand. "Raziel Graves," he said. "I'll be here for a few weeks to set up your system."

Adam's eyes narrowed. *Raziel Graves,* he thought. A vision crossed his mind of the young man, blood pouring out of his mouth. "You're the best I've ever seen," he said to a young girl.

The pain in Adam's head intensified. "Hey, you okay?" He heard Raziel say. Adam dropped to his knees and began to pass out. He saw Raziel kneel over his body and call out, "Yo, a little help, somebody!"

It's not real, Adam thought. *None of this is real. It's all a lie.*

Adam woke up in his bed again. Alice, Aztec and Tezca were there.

"What happened?" Adam asked.

"Exhaustion, the doctor said," replied Tezca. Tezca looked

at him quizzically. "You sure you're okay?"

Alice giggled. "Yeah, you want us to cancel your big date?" she asked.

Aztec looked at Alice and back at Adam. "Ohhh, who's the lucky lady, hermano? You keeping secrets from us?"

Adam laughed. "Don't worry about it. And no, I'm fine," he said, sitting up.

I'm not fine, he heard his own voice say inside his head. *This place is a cruel joke.* His mind filled with a vision. He was sitting at the top of a tall tower in front of a dead and abandoned machine, surrounded by puddles of liquid metal. His body was covered in fatal wounds, and he was watching the sun rise over an alien jungle, dying.

"Yeah, he's not fine," Alice said with concern. "Why don't you lay back down and sleep it off? I'm sure the twins can finish up the rounds for today," she said. She looked at Aztec and Tezca. "Right?"

"Yeah, of course," Aztec said at the same time Tezca said, "Yeah, totally."

"That sounds good, actually…" Adam said, laying back into bed. Before he went to sleep, he pointed at Alice. "Don't cancel my date. I don't want her to think I'm a flake," he said, and closed his eyes.

As he drifted off to sleep, he heard the voice.

"What's wrong?" it asked him.

It's a lie. This place isn't real. My friends are dead. This is just… cope. It's not true. It isn't real, he thought.

"Why isn't it real?" the voice asked.

It's too good to be true, Adam thought.

"What's real, Adam? You can see it. You can touch it. Your senses tell you it's real," the voice said.

Adam got a vision of a young woman with pointed ears, kind eyes and petite fangs.

"I told you, Adam. It can be as good as you want it to be," she said. "It's no more or less real than anything else. Reality is infinite. It's all out there. Everything you can dream. Find something you can latch onto and love. That's all you can really do."

The woman touched his cheek and smiled like a mother.

"You're fine," she said. "I promise." And then she disappeared.

Adam felt at peace, looking out over the colorful alien canopy of the mysterious planet Draconis. He looked forward to his date, and spending time with his daughter and his friends on Titan.

He reached out toward the sunrise and closed his eyes. He let sleep take him.

9 780999 857571